Any Excuse
for a Party

Novels

Apology for a Hero
A Case Examined
The Middling
John Brown's Body
A Source of Embarrassment
A Heavy Feather
Relative Successes
The Gooseboy
The Woman Who Talked to Herself

Stories

Innocents
Novelette
The Joy Ride and After
Lost upon the Roundabout
Femina Real
Life Stories
No Word of Love

ANY EXCUSE FOR A PARTY

Collected Stories

A. L. Barker

HUTCHINSON

LONDON SYDNEY AUCKLAND JOHANNESBURG

This collection Copyright © A. L. Barker 1991

The right of A. L. Barker to be identified as Author of this work has been asserted by
A. L. Barker in accordance with the Copyright, Designs and Patents Act, 1988

This edition first published in 1991 by Hutchinson

Random Century Group Ltd
20 Vauxhall Bridge Road, London SW1V 2SA

Random Century Australia (Pty) Ltd
20 Alfred Street, Milsons Point, Sydney NSW 2061, Australia

Random Century (NZ) Ltd
9–11 Rothwell Avenue, Albany, Auckland 10, New Zealand

Random Century South Africa (Pty) Ltd
PO Box 337, Bergvlei 2012, South Africa

British Library Cataloguing in Publication Data
Barker, A. L. (Audrey Lilian) *1918–*
   Any excuse for a party.
   I. Title
   823.914 [F]

ISBN 0–09–174643–4

Photoset by Speedset Ltd, Ellesmere Port
Printed and bound by Biddles Ltd, Guildford, Surrey

Contents

Acknowledgements

The author would like to thank the following publishers for their kind permission to reproduce stories which first appeared in the following editions:

Any Excuse for a Party	*Penguin Modern Stories 8*, 1971
	Life Stories
The Iconoclasts	*Innocence*
	Penguin Anthology
	Bonneris Literary Magazine
	Rodney Philips Anthology
Submerged	*Innocence*
	Life Stories
	Pan Book of Horror, 1970
	Harper's Bazaar US
	Short Story Monthly
	Storytime, Radio 4
The Father	*Life Stories*
Watch It	*Penguin Modern Stories 8*
Dragons	*Woman*
A Considerable Speck	*Life Stories*
Almost an International Incident	*Penguin Modern Stories 8*
	Femina Real, 1971
Noon	*Femina Real*
A Love Affair	*Life Stories*
The Little People	*Country House Ghosts*, Kimber Anthology, 1981
A Picture from an Exhibition	*Life Stories*
Lunch with the Chairman	*S.E. Arts Review*, 1982
The Dream of Fair Women	Kimber Anthology, 1983
A Fairly Close Encounter	*Winter's Tales*, 1989
Happy Event	*Life Stories*
	Kimber Anthology

Introduction

Written over a lifetime, these stories constitute a kind of auto-
biography. Whilst writing them I uncovered sensibilities which I
have used as themes – as writers generally do.

In my first published collection I was occupied with the clash of
innocence and experience. 'The Iconoclasts' and 'Submerged'
illustrate my simple conviction that childhood was guileless and
adults perfidious. When I realised that innocence is neither wholly
pure nor wholly simple, I decided that, like freedom, it doesn't exist
and began to see the guile in the innocent heart. A later story was
about an old man's pleasure in watching children at play. Though
innocent he could not be at his age, harm there was in the lightly
smutched minds of wives and mothers who thought the worst, yet
were themselves virtual innocents.

It is not in my capacity to treat of the political and ideological
failures of communication which bring on wars, mayhem and global
disasters. Small domestic misunderstandings are my scope.
Marriage necessarily has a big corner. The wife who finds an excuse
for a party also needs her husband's adultery to indemnify them both
against apathy, lack of response, lack of love. The wife in 'A
Considerable Speck' is reduced to saving up the memory of her
wedded bliss, to use it not 'just for dreaming, but for really desperate
occasions', and an artist's widow believes that she has been able to
love two men at once and make them both happy. At a retrospective
exhibition of her husband's work, one of his paintings shows her how
little she knew about him.

I love stories of the supernatural, I love reading them and I love to
write them – if there aren't more things than are dreamed of in our
philosophies I think it's a poor lookout for us. But the necessary
suspension of disbelief is increasingly difficult to achieve. I tried to
bring the supernormal back to a sort of normality in 'Happy Event'
which implies a satanic pregnancy, and in 'The Dream of Fair
Women', when a confirmed womaniser tries to go to bed with a
ghost.

A short story is 'A Fairly Close Encounter': how much the reader
enjoys it is not altogether within the writer's power to arrange. A lot
will depend on time and place, whether it's read on a bus or train or
in an airport departure-lounge when departure is hours delayed. If
it's being leafed through in a dentist's waiting-room, the odds will be

stacked high against it. My ambition for this collection is that some of the stories will be enjoyed, whatever the reader may be waiting for.

Any Excuse for a Party

Leonie's first reaction was to wonder why she had been told.

'Because I thought you ought to know.'

'And you thought it was your duty to tell me?'

'Yes.'

'Did you really?' Leonie laughed. 'People always say that.'

'I haven't had previous experience.'

'I expect you thought Bernard hadn't told me.'

'Has he?'

'No.'

'I don't *enjoy* telling you.'

'Oh, I don't know,' Leonie said judiciously. 'There must be something rather delectable about it –'

'It's unfair and unkind of you to accuse me of gloating!'

'. . . and you are prey to conflicting emotions –'

'Who do you think is lying? Andrew, or me? Obviously one of us has to be.'

'I expect Andrew does see Bernard with a girl, probably it's his secretary. Is she small and sandy? You see, it isn't Andrew I don't believe, it's Bernard I can't believe it of.'

'That does you credit.'

Leonie opened the window, letting in a squall of rain. 'What a lovely day! We should all be out and about this lovely day.'

'Leonie, I'm sorry, I really am. If you knew how I've hated this! I'd have given anything not to be the one to tell you, but if I didn't someone else will – not necessarily a friend.'

'The truth is, not believing it of Bernard doesn't do me credit, it does him discredit.' Leonie sighed.

'I don't understand you.'

'Well, we don't understand each other. We'd have to be born again to do that. How green the grass is. Is there anything so deadly as all this for ever and evergreen, amen! Do you know I believe I could live to the top of my bent if there wasn't a blade of grass in sight. I could really live every moment in the desert or at the South Pole. Did Andrew say what she was like?'

'He said she wasn't his type. He was being cautious, but I've noticed that men are often seduced away by someone in direct contrast to their wives. Physically, I mean.'

'Then she –?'

1

'She's – well, fleshy, I gather, and not particularly pretty. She works for the Trust Company in the suite of offices above Bernard's. Andrew has spoken to her on the phone, he says she stutters. "Fee-fee-fee-Phoebe Robey speaking." '

'Miss or Mrs?'

'She calls herself "Miss".'

'Did Andrew think you should tell me?'

'Andrew? Andrew thinks men ought to stick together. I had to prise it out of him and if he knew I was telling you he'd probably go and apologise to Bernard. What will you do?'

'I have no plans. It will be something to think about.'

'Oh, Leonie,' said Monica sadly, and Leonie hid her smile. She felt she had been given a present of Bernard's infidelity. She was grateful to Monica and it would have been impolite to examine the gift in her presence and pinch it to see if it was real.

When Monica departed, subdued, into the green, Leonie watched her out of sight. So Bernard had a lover. At once the visible prospect right up to the paddock gate became full of significance; each leaf, each blade of grass, each pebble knew more than she did.

But when, she thought, pinching, and how? It was possible because although he came home at six-thirty each evening he was sometimes away for days, ostensibly on business. It was possible because he did not love her: on the other hand it was impossible because he did not love anyone. Could she amend that to did not appear to?

Yes, she thought, she could, because no one operating in human form could be totally inhuman, not even Bernard. He was bound to have some at least of the weaknesses of the breed as well as what passed for its strength. If 'love' was not admissible, lust would have to be and that passed, every time, as proof positive of strength. Inconsistent to think of Bernard in love or lusting. But apparently she had to.

She smiled, and when at last she looked and saw him coming home through the torrents of green she ran to greet him. In the porch he first collapsed his umbrella, then thrice aimed and shot it to shake off the rain. The clay soil, he was wont to say, was like pudding, and he worked at his shoes on the outside mat before stepping over the threshold of the house.

She lifted her cheek to his kiss. 'How dry your lips are.' That was fitting, she thought, if his passion had been spent elsewhere. Bernard, all the long wet afternoon, hanging on the lips of Miss Robey was a charming thought. 'You should touch them with cold cream at night.'

Bernard had drawn away, was already retreating to the other side of the room. She sometimes concluded that they had a mutual dread of contact with each other, she thought that Bernard had positively to steel himself to come near her.

He splashed whisky into a glass and turned with brows raised questioningly, sherry decanter in hand.

'No, I'll have the same as you.'

She could not resist teasing and put her fingers over his as he gave her the glass. He shuddered. So her touch was hateful after the hand of Miss Robey, he was all quick and another woman's touch pained him.

'How thin my fingers are.' She held them up. 'You must find them revolting.'

'I?'

He had a way of speaking, and looking, as if she had picked him out of a crowd – at the same time managing to imply that he was of course absolutely unique. Tonight, she understood, she had the key to the enigma of Bernard.

'Have you had a pleasant day?'

'Average.'

'What degree of pleasure are you used to?'

'What do you mean?'

'Your average could be another man's bliss. Have you a blissful average?'

'I'm sorry, I'm rather tired.'

'Of course!' Leonie said contritely. 'And you have a right to a little rest. Where else, if not here?'

Once upon a time she was irritated by the way he looked at her. Now she realised that he was contrasting her with Miss Robey who, according to Monica, was Leonie's direct opposite and must therefore be big, bosomy, and loving. Loving, that is, towards Bernard. What an unsatisfactory comparison he must be making!

'I think I'll have a bath before dinner.'

'We're having your favourite – grilled halibut.'

'Halibut?' He frowned. 'I don't especially enjoy it.'

'You mean it's not your favourite?' Leonie clapped both hands over her mouth. 'How awful! How thoroughly unsatisfactory of me not to get it right! I did so want to do something you'd like.'

'It doesn't matter.'

'Did you mean that remark to be hurtful? If I were emotionally unbalanced, as women who are left alone all day are said to be, it could prey on my mind. With tragic consequences. I assure you, some women weigh up feathers – hairs even! Oh, especially hairs!

3

But I'm not unbalanced. Being alone delights me and I know you didn't mean to be hurtful. You meant to be kind – which of course can amount to the same thing and be absolutely devastating.'

'Leonie –'

'Oh don't worry! I'm not devastated.'

Bernard stood up. She understood him to say 'Christ!' or perhaps it was 'Right!' or even 'OK' – except that he had never used the expression.

'Anyway, it's grilled halibut, which you're not actually nauseated by because that I should remember. Your extremes of feeling I have pigeonholed in my mind as a good wife should.'

'I have an extreme of feeling now.'

It was a long time since Leonie had looked at Bernard, perhaps she had never done so with the right attention. One so easily got into the habit of allowing people just to fill their bills and Bernard's bill had been modest from the start. No one had understood why she had married him and her mother still asked, out of the blue, which showed how baffled she was.

As Leonie remembered, love was a painful experience, shamefully so, and she had had no intention of contracting herself to a lifetime of pain. There had been no practical necessity to marry Bernard, or anyone, just on the asking. She was not poor, nor unhappy at home, nor pregnant, and she was only twenty-two years old. But a voice, her own – at least it came from her throat – had replied, 'Do you know, I think I will,' to his proposal of marriage. Leonie had been amused more than amazed and when she expressed surprise to herself it was 'Is that what I'm going to do!' – remarking something which was already as good as history.

Why had she married Bernard? Why not? The matter was as nicely poised as that. And there had been a marvellous reception afterwards, everyone said it was the best they had ever been to. Coming as it did at the beginning of the autumn and the end of the summer it had been the event of two seasons. Leonie's parents had organised everything, sparing neither expense nor effort. On hearing of Leonie's engagement the second thing her mother had said – the first was, 'Bernard Price! What on earth for?' – was 'Where shall we have the reception?'

They had held it at the White Tower. Defying tradition, Leonie had stayed until the end. She could not have borne to miss a minute of the most important social event of her life and when, in the early hours of morning she caught sight of Bernard, grey with fatigue, she was surprised that he should be remotely connected with it.

However, the marriage had been made for her somewhere, though not in heaven. In the economy of Nature, perhaps. Bernard had always been enough for her. Apparently, she now said to herself, she wasn't enough for him.

That should not surprise her. She must have somehow forgotten that Bernard was a man. Inexcusable of me, she thought, and chose from that moment to accept the story of Bernard and his mistress. It was a charming story, not to accept it would be looking a gift horse in the mouth.

'I shall be coming up to town tomorrow,' she said.

'Again? You were in town yesterday.'

'There isn't a total ban on town, is there?' Naturally he felt happier when she was tucked away in the country, but she had to see his Phoebe Robey. She had to get a look at her, just one look to fill in the background of the affair. 'You can give me lunch.'

'I shan't be able to. I have to go to the Leeds office in the morning.'

'Alone?'

'The area manager is going with me.'

'Ah, the area manager!' She sighed. 'Never mind, the time will soon pass and you'll be back again.'

'Who will mind if I don't?'

'What a thing to say!'

'It was hardly a thing for you to say.'

Under her breath, to his departing back, Leonie said, 'My poor, poor dear, I believe you're serious!'

Phoebe Robey was so important that not until she was speeding to Waterloo next morning did Leonie stop to think that there would be other people about. Comet though she was, Miss Robey would not blaze across an empty sky and, incredibly, Leonie might not know her when she saw her. Probably she would have to ask. Ideally she should see and talk to her face to face without Phoebe suspecting who she was talking to. Leonie decided to improvise. When the time came she would know what to do, she had such goodwill she couldn't possibly spoil anything.

But the time did not come. Miss Robey, it transpired, was away from her office. The Trust Company's receptionist said she was working at home.

'For some things it's safer.'

'No doubt.'

'Some of our work is highly confidential.'

'Of course!' cried Leonie. 'I wonder if you'd give me her home telephone number? I stupidly left my address and telephone book in my other handbag.'

'I have to have authority before giving private information about the staff.' The receptionist flicked up a key on her switchboard. 'Who shall I say is inquiring?'

'Oh don't. I mean, don't bother anyone. She'll be so vexed with me. My dear, you know what she's like!' Leonie smiled on the girl. 'I'm a very old friend of Fee-fee-fee-Phoebe's.'

The girl smiled too and wrote on a piece of paper. 'Call her from here if you like.'

'I haven't time now. I'll ring her after lunch.'

When Leonie picked up the receiver in a phone booth at Selfridge's all she had in mind was a resolution to hear Miss Robey's voice and a conviction that when she heard it she would know what to do. In fact she knew a second beforehand, it came to her as she pressed her coin into the slot.

'Hello. Fee-fee-Phoebe Robey speaking.'

Of course! It was a happy, beautiful, civilised thought. Materialised, it would give her a beautiful civilised picture of Bernard's love affair.

'Hoo-who's th-thatt?'

It might not be easy to materialise. Someone once said that between the thought and the deed fell the shadow. Leonie realised that she had the shadow to lift now, this very minute, without time for thought and with only instinct to guide her.

'Suss-suss-sssspeak up, please!'

'This is Mrs Bernard Price speaking.'

There was a blowy noise and a hush.

'You're surprised,' said Leonie. 'Do you like surprises? I do, I can never have too many.' She could hear Phoebe Robey's thoughts escaping, the sound was the same as the shrill soft sound in a seashell. 'Listen,' – but she well knew Phoebe was doing that – 'I'm giving a party on Saturday, just a few friends but it will be nice. Will you come?'

'No.'

'Oh, why not?'

'I don't think I sssshhhould – I mean I c-can't.'

'You mean what you said first, but you're wrong. You *should* come.'

'Why?'

'It will be better for you both. For you and Bernard. Do you understand?'

'Does he n-n-know?'

She did not beat about the bush, Leonie liked her for that. Perhaps Bernard did too, perhaps it was her directness which first captivated him.

'Naturally I consult my husband. Now, the party will begin at eight. You know where we live? Are there any more questions?'

'Why do you w-w-w-want me to c-come?'

'I strongly advise you to,' said Leonie, and hung up.

Next she rang Monica and told her about the party. 'You'll come, you and Andrew?'

'We'd love to. Is everything all right?'

'Monica, would you call me devious?'

'Devious? Oh no!'

'But I am rather,' Leonie said thoughtfully. 'By the way – and that's deviousness because really it's the whole point of the party – I've invited Phoebe Robey.'

'You've what?'

'She stutters very nicely, it sounds quite charming over the phone.'

'You haven't asked that woman to your house? Leonie, you can't!'

'Why can't I? It's my house and my husband.'

Monica's voice sharpened. 'What are you going to do? Are you planning a showdown? If you are, we don't want to be there. Andrew and I want no part of it and nor will anyone else. I'm surprised at you, Leonie, bringing your friends into it, I just don't understand you –'

'So you said before, but I'm not difficult to understand. I'm only planning a party. I shall ask everyone I can think of – especially Ted Lacey, he's such good company. Miss Robey will like Ted. It's absurd, I've not yet seen her you know, and I keep imagining she has bushy eyebrows and a bowler hat!'

'Leonie, stop fooling and think what you're doing. You're making a big mistake –'

'It's you who's making the mistake, Monica – about me. All I want is to have a wonderful party, for us all to be happy – *pour encourager les autres*. I do so want those two to be happy.' She said softly, her lips to the mouthpiece of the telephone, 'I want to see Bernard happy.'

'La Robey won't come.'

'Oh, she'll come.'

There would have to be flowers, before anything else, crimson and white roses were needed everywhere. Crimson for the colour of their passion, white for the virginity of Bernard's – he had never been a passionate man. Fortunately the garden was full of roses, especially old white American Beauties. If the rain didn't spoil them she would build a bower Saturday night.

He mustn't feel at home, familiarity was so hard on magic, though Phoebe Robey's might be strong enough to bewitch the whole world. Leonie realised that she could never know because she could not get under Bernard's skin where Miss Robey was and be in love with him as Miss Robey was. She could not know how Bernard felt, or be satisfied that he felt nothing, because he had undergone a metabolic change. Love destroyed and then re-formed as well she knew, and it was no simple shake-up. Who could say how the pieces of Bernard had fallen?

So she would have flowers, masses of them, because short of refurnishing the house there was no other way to make it strange and beautiful for him.

She telephoned the invitations, it was scant notice and some people already had engagements.

'Can't you put it off? This is special. No, I can't tell you why.' Of course she could have said, 'Because we shall see something special – my poor Bernard blossoming like the desert in the presence of his beloved' – but it would be a private manifestation, to appreciate it one had to be intimately in the know about Bernard and she was the only one with that kind of knowledge. 'Come because I specially want you to!'

She ordered champagne, it was the wine for the occasion. At their wedding Bernard had drunk more champagne than any one and become absolutely speechless. He might do that again, his emotions might be too strong for words and in the grip of them he would sit and stare at Phoebe Robey. Leonie smiled, all the time she was ringing the wine merchant she was smiling at the thought of Bernard eating Phoebe up with his eyes.

They would have a buffet supper, beautiful food, all tender elusive flavours, beautifully presented: she would compose a meal like a symphony, with dishes of everything that was out of season. An extravaganza. She was inspired. Well, she thought, it's certainly not ordinary, there can't be many other women doing what I'm going to do. There can't be any doing this for a soul as lost as Bernard's has always seemed to be.

She sat down to work out the details, marvelling how she had despaired of him, so *serviceable* he had seemed, so cut out, with nothing left over for foolishness, or vice, or for himself. She could have forgiven him so much if she had known of his secret passion, not least his inability to be a husband to her. Poor Bernard wasn't physically endowed to love two women at once.

But now she knew why he said 'I?' As the chosen of Miss Robey he spoke out of clouds of glory. How bewildering it must have been to be brought down from the heights. From Love's Olympus!

She wished it was a ball she was giving for Bernard and his Phoebe, a romantic setting with beautiful dresses and crystal chandeliers and music.

'I'll clear the floor in the dining-room and put on a stack of records, someone will start to dance – the Bannermans probably – and Bernard can take her in his arms and they can dance together.' She rose, smiling, gliding and turning between the furniture. 'Oh, Bernard, you're going to be happy for once!'

There was a lot to do in a short space of time but she loved doing it! She had two wonderful days concocting and preparing and arranging and when her mother telephoned she cried joyously, 'I'm giving a party for Bernard!'

'Is it his birthday? Oh God, have I forgotten it again?'

'No, silly, his birthday's – oh well it's not yet. This is just *for* him.'

'But Bernard doesn't like parties.'

'He'll like this one.' As she said that she found herself face to face with the Bernard of their wedding-day. She picked up the photograph. Bernard stood in his ceremonials – striped trousers, tail coat, and frilly gardenia – with his shoulders squared and his feet at five to one. The camera had caught what she called his not-waving-but-drowning look. 'This is another matter,' she laid the photograph down, 'another and another matter.' She would have to remember when next she saw him how much more to him there was. Perhaps she wouldn't have to make such an effort, it must all be there and surely she would see it now?

'What do you mean?' said her mother.

'You can be mistaken about people.'

'My dear, we warned you not to expect too much when you married him.'

'I know and I haven't been expecting enough.'

She was too busy actually to wait for him to come home but on Saturday she stopped to think now he will be on the train, he will be eating lunch, trying not to catch anyone's eye, he dislikes talking to strangers. Later she pictured him pumping his arm up and down outside Euston Station to summon a taxi. Her mother said that when he did that he reminded her of a schoolboy asking leave to go to the lavatory. Then she was entirely taken up with picking and arranging the roses and did not consciously think of him until it was time to picture him walking along the lane from the station. She looked out of the window and there he was coming through the gate.

So he would see the roses with the morning rain still on their petals and she was glad because later they wouldn't be quite so magical. He will always think of Phoebe when he sees roses with rain on them, she said to herself.

She went to greet him in the flower-decked hall. He carefully laid his hat beside a bowl of Gloire de Dijon.

'Did you have a good trip?'

'Average.' Touching her cheek with his lips he amended that. 'I mean, very fair.'

Bernard, you are like an onion, she thought, layer upon layer of passionate extremes and you have not lifted the top-most one for me.

'The train was hot and very noisy. From Waterloo, of course, it always is.'

'Come and sit down,' said Leonie. 'I'll get you a drink. We're having a party tonight but there's plenty of time.'

He stooped to the Gloire de Dijon. 'These are beautiful.'

'Aren't they! And do you notice how the rain brings out the scent?' She touched his arm. 'Let's go into the kitchen, I've set out a buffet supper in the dining-room.'

But first he must take off his coat and ease back his shoulders with a sigh.

'Bernard, we're going to have a party,' she said impatiently, she couldn't have him tired.

'Yes.'

'I believe you knew! Someone told you!'

'Yes.'

'Oh, it's too bad! I wanted it to be a surprise! People are unforgivable!'

He nodded. 'Yes, you find that.'

'Never mind, I still have the most wonderful surprise –'

'She isn't coming.'

'What? Who – isn't coming?'

'Phoebe Robey.'

He walked away into the kitchen. Leonie ran after him crying. 'What have you done? What have you *done*?'

'I've stopped her,' he said calmly. 'She told me what was afoot when I rang her this afternoon.'

'You had no right to interfere! No right! Everything is ruined!' She was incredulous with rage.

He went to the sink and concentratedly swilled and emptied, swilled and emptied a perfectly clean glass. He turned to her with it filled to the brim and she cried, 'You're not going to drink all that water?'

'Why did you ask her?'

'I asked her for you. I did everything for you – the party, the flowers – to give you an enchanted evening! Oh, you are like an onion, layer upon layer of awfulness!'

He sighed, 'Yes, I suppose it couldn't have been for anyone else. I've had Phoebe Robey on my back for years.'

'On your back? You love her!'

'I?' He said sombrely. 'Coming from anyone but you that would be funny.'

'Don't you understand? I know all about it and I'm' – that she was sorry for him was perhaps not the thing to say – 'I'm in sympathy. That shouldn't surprise you. I'm not like other wives, I never have been – and you're not like other husbands.'

They gazed at each other, taken aback, both of them. It was Bernard who elected not to go ahead – or at least not straight ahead.

'I don't want Phoebe here.' He said, quite roughly, 'I don't want her anywhere.'

'Since when? Have you quarrelled? How was I to know?'

'Since you said you would marry me.'

'But that was years ago!'

'She won't accept that it's over.'

'Then she's in love with you – hopelessly!'

'No. We were neither of us ever that. It was a matter of convenience.'

'And still is!'

'No. It's simply that Phoebe hates parting with anything – or anyone.'

'Oh, don't underestimate your charms!'

He smiled wryly. 'Do I have any?'

Leonie could have cried and would have done if he hadn't been there, he had a way of taking the heart even out of disappointment. But suddenly she stopped being angry.

'It strikes you as comic, does it?' said Bernard

If she was smiling, it was only reflex. In the mirror she saw that she did look faintly entertained.

'May I know what strikes you as funny, funny risible, funny peculiar, funny any way you like,' said Bernard, 'about me?'

'My dear, if you're special to me, everything you do will be special. Specially funny, specially clever.'

'I'm not anything to you. I never have been.'

'Specially happy. I wanted you to be that tonight.'

'With her?'

'With Phoebe, yes. You see, I would so like you to have been a man.'

'I'm a married man.'

From the kitchen window was a view across the fields and hedges to a plantation, thousands of young firs in stripes over the hillside.

'I hate green,' said Leonie. Picking so many roses had caused the garden to look greener. 'Prison green!'

'Not any more. We are tendering for a new borstal and the colour motif is to be teak and chrome yellow.'

11

When Leonie turned he was behind her. Their faces lost their identity, he was all peppered chin with grains of beard in every pore. She to him must have been all eye, all dark blue jelly, so close they stood.

For a full minute neither moved. They were stiff and tender as boards with each other. A bead of sweat gathered in the roots of his hair and slipped over his forehead, the one, full, clear bead wet their two cheeks.

'Why can't I touch you!'

It was the only outcry he had made or would ever make and Leonie would have liked a direct answer. But that could only come from him.

'Perhaps if you didn't shake so much?' she suggested.

The Iconoclasts

The top step was sacred. To tread on it was not only a crime but a deliberate thumbing at fate. Of course a lot of people did – his parents, the occasional gardener, and visitors who were being shown the paved walk under the lime trees. It worried Marcus to think what a lot of trouble they were storing up for themselves, until he decided that as they were adults, they had graduated out of the power of the step. One day, he too would be beyond it, he would be able to tread there without his footstep shaking loose some dreadful animus.

Just now it was necessary to stretch his legs from the penultimate step to the square of turf beyond the top, and Marcus, small for his five years, found the reach considerable. That was as it should be, he wouldn't want it to be easy, any more than one would wish the lion one had defeated to be tame.

With the pail of earth he was carrying, the step was doubly difficult to avoid, and he had to take the secondary route up the bank and under the flowering currants. Already there was quite a beaten track there. His father didn't like him to go in under the bushes, he said Marcus must have the proclivities of a cat and would probably take to the tiles in due course. Marcus had explained, he was always explaining, that it was a matter beyond his control – the detour was as much of a nuisance to him as it was to everyone else. But they never seemed to catch the gravity of the situation, and to Marcus's father it was just a source of humour.

On the paved part at the back of the toolshed was quite a pile of earth which Marcus had carried there. He was going to make a castle, like his seaside ones, and irrigate it. That was ambitious, especially as he had only inferior materials – earth and tap water instead of sand and sea.

Marcus thought he had enough earth now, but before he started work there was a routine job to be done. Puffing and severe, he climbed to the top of the rockery and stared between the garden trees to a sloping brown field, stitched all over with green. There was a scarecrow among the furrows, a poor trashy thing of sticks, sacking and a yellow trilby. At sight of the trilby, Marcus's frown relaxed and he nodded approvingly.

Some boys had once stolen the scarecrow's hat and the farmer said jokingly that in future perhaps Marcus would keep an eye on the new one. Marcus accepted the commission in all seriousness; twice a day he made sure that the turnip head was decently covered.

He went back to the toolshed. Boddy was propped against a flower-pot, and a big beetle which had crawled out of the loose earth was advancing on him. It looked too large to squash, no doubt it would crackle and spread out on the paving. But Boddy had to be saved, and not by retreat, either. Marcus shovelled up the beetle and threw it on to the flower-bed.

When the danger was past, he said sternly to Boddy, 'You'll have to be more careful. I haven't got time to turn around today.'

Marcus turned his back then, and Boddy, whose salient feature was his big lolling head, sat meekly by, grinning his golliwog's grin. His was the function of the subordinate, the apprentice. Marcus used him without mercy and it was only because he was made of good durable leather with a head full of straw shavings and thatched with nothing more sensitive than dusty wool, that he had survived.

Marcus was much attached to him because Boddy did what no one else did, he went in awe of Marcus. That made a full circle – Marcus's father looked up to his superior at the office, Marcus's mother looked up to Marcus's father, Marcus's grandmother looked up to them both, Marcus had to look up to everybody, and Boddy looked up to Marcus.

There was a worm in the pile of earth. Marcus showed it to Boddy. 'That's a snake. It's not safe just here, you'd better tuck your legs in.'

He thought he might keep the worm and let it swim in the moat of his castle, so he put it under a flower-pot.

'This is very important,' he said, making the earth into a tight pile and cutting it with his spade. 'It's a secret.'

The new venture was now on a par with treaties and plans, the movement of armies and the sinking of oilwells. For Marcus, frowning, absorbed, the world had very properly dwindled, it waited on his monumental mud just as it waits – for the single-minded – on diplomacy, the invention, the battle, the fortune in the making. Only Boddy, as the onlooker, could be expected to know that it never waited for anything.

As castles go, it was not a success. Marcus would not admit that it looked like a nasty chocolate pudding. He put the worm in the moat and told Boddy that it was better than any at the seaside. It was guarded by a sinister serpent and when the sun came out it would get hard as iron and no one would ever be able to knock it over. It would still be there by his next birthday – there could be no longer period of time than that. Secretly, Marcus was so disgusted with it that he couldn't stop saying what a wonderful castle it was, and pushed Boddy into the laurel bushes for not looking impressed.

After that, he gave way to baser instincts, flattened the castle, worm and all, and made some really excellent mud-pies. He chatted amiably, forgetting that Boddy was flat on his face under the ugly spotted laurels. That was the best of Boddy, whether he was there or not, he always listened.

Marcus was extremely busy when he heard his grandmother in the garden. She was calling him to lunch – that was the signal for him to double up like a jack-knife and creep through the shrubbery, away from the direction of her voice. Not because he was furtive or guilty, but simply because it was part of his policy to be elusive, not easily found – in fact, not to be found at all. He preferred to turn the tables and seek the seeker.

Coming into the shadow of the garden wall, he suddenly drew himself up, lifted one leg and began solemnly to hop. In one corner opposite him, was the husk of a summerhouse. Once it had stood on a pedestal and revolved so that anyone inside could always arrange to face the sun. That had been long before Marcus's time, and rain and frost had rotted the flimsy wood. It leaned against the wall, in the winter drenched black, in the summer whity-grey like an old bone. When Marcus looked inside, he saw the dark glint of water that had driven in through the roof, and something with fierce red eyes set it trembling.

Marcus had skipped off quickly. Whatever it was in the summerhouse, he believed it preferred him to hurry by and not stare too much. For dignity's sake he could not run past; he always, however sober his pace, began to skip and hop when he came in sight of the hut, thus placating its creature without loss of prestige. So the skipping and hopping became a ritual and after the manner of ritual, had a definite form. Two hops, three skips and a short jump took Marcus on a level with the summerhouse door. He was then entitled to assert himself and his command of the ritual by a deliberate stare. Two hops, three skips and a short jump took him well out of the creature's jurisdiction again.

Marcus had this belief in ceremony. It did not constrain him, rather was it a bone in his amorphous world. True, there existed a rigid routine, imposed on him from outside, and cutting the day which should have been elastic, into sections of food, play and sleep. Yet he felt the need of something immutable and his own, and ceremony had the sure reciprocal action of a slot-machine.

Marcus crept up behind his grandmother as she stood on the lawn. She looked as if she had forgotten all about him, so he hooted in a deep, frightening voice.

'Good heavens, Marcus, must you do that? Where on earth do you get to? I can never find you.' But she wasn't really interested. She was tapping her small rounded chin and looking at the grass. 'We ought to get the lawn re-laid before next summer,' she said to herself, and nodded with the same seriousness Marcus had shown towards his castle.

During lunch, Marcus learned that Neil Farncombe was coming to spend the afternoon. He was the son of a business friend of Marcus's father and he had come on a visit once before, some two years ago, when Marcus was still addicted to teddy bears and flop-eared rabbits. There had been a great deal of trouble, everyone except Marcus remembered it.

'But they'll get on better now,' said his grandmother. 'Marcus isn't such a baby.'

Neil was ten. He had a small angular face, high cheek-bones and eyes of a particular burning blue. Without waiting until they were out of hearing of the grown-ups, he said, 'What's that in aid of?' and nodded at Marcus's clothes.

Marcus looked down at his green boiler-suit with the tool pockets on the bib. 'Huh?' he said, frowning.

'Oh forget it.' Neil strolled off, casual and self-possessed in his zipped leather jacket and grey shorts. Marcus made to go in the opposite direction, but was called back by his grandmother.

'Go with Neil,' she said.

Reluctantly, Marcus trailed after the elder boy.

'No doubt,' said Marcus's grandmother, 'we shall have to buy the child a zipped leather jacket now.'

Neil mooched through the shrubbery and stopped at the bottom of the steps. He stared up at the sky from under his hand, they both heard a distant mumbling.

'Now what's that?' grunted Neil, squinting fearfully against the sunlight.

'It's an aeroplane,' said Marcus, pleased at being able to offer the information.

Neil's high cheek-bones burned scarlet. He glared at Marcus from under his shading hand. 'Don't try to be funny with me,' he said. 'Just don't try.'

Marcus was both offended and bewildered. To relieve his feelings he kicked viciously at the path.

'Blenheim,' said Neil laconically. 'It might be one of ours.'

'If it isn't, shall we go into the shelter?' Marcus was thrilled at the possibility.

Neil turned on him with the air of an officer about to rend a very raw recruit. 'What did I say that plane was?'

'Benim.'

'And a Blenheim's a British kite, isn't it? Don't you even know that? When I said it might be one of ours I meant it might have come from our field.'

'Your field?'

Neil turned away impatiently. 'Our aerodrome at Haydown.'

Marcus lost his temper. 'It's not yours! It's not your aerodrome!'

'It's as much mine as anybody else's.' Neil was still staring up from under his hand. 'I live right by it and I'm there nearly every day and I know all the men on it and all the planes. That's a Blenheim all right.'

'It's not!' shouted Marcus, red-faced and ridiculous. 'It's not! It's not!'

The visitor put his hands in his pocket, rocked to and fro on his heels and spoke with absolute authority. 'It's a twin-engined Blenheim bomber with "Mercury" engines and five machine-guns – one in the port wing, two in the turret and two in the blister under the nose. It can carry a thousand pounds of bombs, but I expect it's on a training trip now.'

Marcus looked sulky, yet he was impressed. Under his breath he muttered, 'It's not,' just once, without conviction.

As Neil watched the plane out of sight, he looked almost homesick. He glowered at Marcus. 'Don't you know anything about planes?'

'Course I do! I've got a plane of my own!'

'What – a toy?' Neil turned away.

Marcus danced earnestly beside him. 'It flies! It flies over the house!'

Neil said nothing. He was moodily climbing the steps. Marcus, in a passion to be first, wriggled past him and went on ahead. When he stretched over the final step he almost lost his balance. Neil put his foot squarely on the sacred stone.

'No!' shrieked Marcus.

'Eh?'

'No! No!'

Neil came on to the top of the steps. 'Are you crazy?'

'You shouldn't have trod on that step!'

Neil looked at it. 'Why not?'

'Something will happen to you!'

'Eh?'

Marcus backed away, wildly mysterious. 'The awfullest thing that could happen!'

'Guff,' declared Neil and deliberately went back and jumped about on the sacred step. 'How's that?'

They stood staring at each other in the sunshine, Marcus open-mouthed, horrified; Neil with eyebrows raised, hands in pockets, feet squarely on the forbidden stone.

'It'll get you – it'll be so angry!'

'What will? The bogey under the step? Pouf!' Neil gave it a final kick and strolled on. 'There's no such thing as bogeys. Of course,' he looked grave, 'there *are* gremlins. You have to watch out for them all right.'

'What's gremlins?'

'I say!' Neil stopped to look hard at Marcus. 'Your number's still pretty wet, isn't it? You don't know anything.'

'I do! I do! I know more than you! I know more than anyone!' But Marcus was not absolutely convinced. He catapulted fiercely to and fro across the path to hide his doubts.

'You don't either,' declared Neil crushingly. 'You don't even know what a gremlin is.'

'What is it?'

'It's a – well, it makes things go wrong.'

'Is it alive?'

'Of course it's alive. How could it upset things and get people into trouble if it was dead? It's something to be scared of, I can tell you. Not like an old step!'

'Has it got red eyes?'

'Some of them have. Some've got green eyes and horns. There's lots of them at our airfield.'

Marcus looked smug. 'I've got one!'

Neil sneered openly. 'Where? Under the step?'

' 'Course not! In the summrouse.'

'That's a load of guff! You only get them on airfields – anywhere where there're planes. What d'you think *you'd* have a gremlin for?'

'I got one. In the summrouse.'

'Guff.'

Marcus danced with fury. 'I'll show you! I'll show it you then!'

'All right, I'll take a look-see.'

'You be careful! It'll bite your head off – '

Neil frowned irritably. 'Oh get on with it! Beetle.'

'Ah?'

'Go on, show me – if you can.'

Fuming, but uneasy, Marcus led the way to the summerhouse. That dark corner of the garden was already in shadow, and to Marcus the chill in the air was sufficient warning. He hung back, pointing quite unnecessarily.

'Pouf! What a ropy old place!' Neil strolled towards it.

Marcus valiantly ran after the elder boy and dragged at his arm. 'You mustn't go in! It's inside.'

Neil looked down at him, his blue eyes were suddenly fierce. 'You're scared!'

18

'I'm not!'

'You are! Scared stiff of a dirty old hut! Well, I'm not!'

He shook off Marcus's hand and strode up to the summerhouse. At the doorway he stopped, one foot on the threshold, and muttered, 'There is something in here.'

Marcus's green boiler-suit swelled with pride. 'It's a gremlin!' he shouted. 'Jus' you come back –' He broke off, clapping one hand over his mouth in curiously feminine consternation.

Neil had disappeared inside. Next moment the boiler-suit wilted as there sounded a dreadful uproar from the summerhouse – a stamping and a shouting and a hollow clanging noise. Marcus was petrified, but when a long grey shape leapt from the hut and vanished into the shadows, he screamed at the top of his voice.

Neil, appearing at the summerhouse door, with a rusty spade in his hand, gave him one contemptuous glance. 'A gremlin says you – just a dirty old rat. I'd have flattened it if it hadn't been so dark in there.'

Marcus licked his lips and looked at Neil with new humility. He wouldn't have cared to face a rat any more than a gremlin.

Neil strolled off, looking moody and discontented. Marcus trotted at his heels. They came to the toolshed and Neil passed the mud-pies without a word. Marcus hoped he hadn't noticed them.

'What's this?'

Neil swooped into the bushes and dragged out poor forgotten Boddy. Dangling by one leg in mid-air, the limp arms flapped, the golliwog's grin and the white boot-button eyes looked frankly imbecile.

Marcus felt his cheeks burn, his eyes pricked with tears of shame as Neil swung the doll to and fro on a level with his face.

'This yours?'

'No!'

Neil's lips twisted. Tauntingly he swung the golliwog closer so that it brushed against Marcus's nose.

'Whose is it then?'

Marcus thought desperately. 'A little gurl's.'

'Yours, more likely. Got a teddy bear, too?'

'It's not! It's not! It's not!' Scarlet-faced, Marcus backed away, stamping and shouting. 'Not! Not! Not!'

Smiling thinly, Neil let the doll drop, his foot met it squarely as it fell, and poor, grinning Boddy went sailing over the shrubbery and out of sight.

'Pancaked,' said Neil obscurely, and Marcus was too deep in shame to ask what he meant.

They came out on to the lawn again. Neil threw himself down and tore up handfuls of grass. He spoke more to himself than to Marcus. 'Why shouldn't they let me go up to the airfield instead of coming here? I asked enough times!'

'There's an aeroplane coming!' Marcus stood over him, earnestly pointing in the wrong direction.

Neil rolled on his back, shaded his eyes and located the plane at once.

'It's a Benim,' declared Marcus, also squinting up from under his hand, but seeing nothing.

'It is not. It's a Bristol Beaufighter back from a recco. You don't know one kite from another.'

Marcus opened his mouth and shut it again. Even he had to admit that as an aircraft spotter he had his shortcomings.

Neil hugged his knees and chewed grass. Marcus plumped down close by, hugged his knees and chewed a gritty mouthful of grass which he had mistakenly grubbed up by the roots. The plane mumbled off into silence and the enormous province of the sun. After a while, Marcus grew bored and began to tumble laboriously about on the grass.

Neil took no notice until, in the middle of a somersault, Marcus felt a hand seize the slack of his boiler-suit and pull him upright. He swayed and blinked, Neil's fierce blue eyes, the sky and the green garden were see-sawing all together.

'The windmill –' Neil was saying, 'where is it?'

Dizzy with tumbling, Marcus could only open his mouth and say 'Ah?' very stupidly.

Neil shook him. 'The windmill! I saw it from the bus – which way is it?'

Marcus took a chance and pointed to one corner of the tipping world. Unfortunately it was in the direction of the house and Neil let go his hold on the green boiler-suit. Marcus sat down with a bump and stayed there waiting for things to sober up. Neil stood over him, scowling.

'You're the biggest dope I was ever stuck with. It's no matter, I'll find things out for myself.'

He stalked off. Marcus scrambled up and followed, conscious that once again he had cut rather a poor figure.

Neil must have had a knack of finding his way, for he went at once to the highest point in the garden – the top of the rockery – climbed it, and stared round like a sailor scanning the seas. 'There it is – about a mile away. Just right.'

He jumped from the rockery, landing lightly on all fours and springing upright almost in the same movement.

Marcus beamed. 'Are you going to the windmill?'

'Yes, I am. If anyone asks where I am, say we're playing hide-and-seek and I'm hiding. See?'

Marcus shook his head, still beaming. 'I'm coming too.'

'You're not.'

'I am!' His voice bellowed in the silence and seemed to echo against the dazzling windows of the house. Neil gripped him by the shoulder.

'Shut up! You're not coming.'

Marcus shut his mouth, but he looked mulish, and as soon as Neil moved off along the lime-walk, he trotted after, his lower lip jutting ominously. Neil knew he was being followed, but said nothing till they came to the arched door set in the garden wall. He pulled back the bolt, then turned.

'Go on back now. I'm doing this on my jack. Go on!'

'No! Won't. I'm coming too.'

Neil let the open door swing shut again. He advanced on Marcus, his long fingers twitching. 'You're asking for it! Will you go back or do I have to make you?'

Marcus was quite frightened. There was something of the pitiless stoop of a hawk in those bladed cheek-bones, the blue, burning eyes. But he could be obstinate, and even though he quailed, he planted his feet wide apart in desperation. 'If you don't let me come, I'll shout till they come and then I'll tell where you're going. I'll tell! I'll tell!'

So great was his awe of Neil that his voice grew louder and louder and he had to stamp to bolster up his courage.

Neil looked murderous, his face reddened with fury, he gathered himself as if to swoop on the yelling Marcus. And then all he did was to clap one hand over the younger boy's open mouth.

'All right! Come on – I'll settle with you later. Only shut up!'

Marcus obeyed at once and they went out into the lane. Some two or three fields and a paddock separated them from the windmill. Neil hauled Marcus bodily over the first stile and they began to tramp through long lush grass minted with buttercups. Marcus was soon dusted in yellow pollen up to his waist, and Neil's long brown legs with the socks draggling round his ankles, glinted with rich butter gold.

It was difficult to keep up with Neil because he didn't allow for anyone else having shorter legs or less wind. Marcus dared not complain, and anyway, he was husbanding his breath in order to ask two very important questions. He seized his chance when they were clambering over the gate into the second field.

'What are we going to the windmill for?'

'Wait and see,' was all the information he got.

The next field was full of dry, bristly grass that made little knocking noises against their legs. Marcus was so fascinated by it and by the faded blue flowers growing among it, that he forgot all about his other question until Neil turned and curtly told him to get a move on.

Then he said breathlessly and with just the right degree of deference and eagerness which even Neil could not resist, 'What you going to be when you grow up?'

Neil made a sound half-laugh, half-snort. 'That's a good one! What am I going to be when I grow up? I'll be a driver, of course.'

'An engine-driver?'

Neil hooted so loudly that there came a frightened scuttling in the undergrowth.

'Engine-driver! You must be the biggest swede in the world. Don't you even know what a driver is? It's the same as a peelo. Know what a peelo is?'

Marcus took the only course open to him. He stuck his hands in the patch pockets on the front of his boiler suit and sulked. Neil spat out the piece of grass he was chewing and strode on.

'All right – if you don't know, I'll tell you. A driver's a pilot – he takes the plane up and he's got to bring it down in one piece. Doesn't matter if it's a monoplane or a Halifax with nine machine-guns and five and a half tons of eggs – and that means bombs, not hen-fruit – the driver's the boss and what he says goes. But I'm going to be a fighter-pilot and make smoke-rings round every Messerschmitt they put up. As for Heinkels – I'll pop them off like paper bags.'

Neil was walking so fast that Marcus had to run to keep near. Suddenly he stopped and swung round.

'D'you say your prayers at night?'

Marcus nodded breathlessly.

'Then you pray for the war to go on for years – till I'm old enough to fly. If two people pray it might do more good than one.' He added threateningly: 'Will you do it?'

Marcus promised earnestly and Neil plunged on again. A blackberry trailer snaking out from the hedge caught him squarely across his bare leg and almost tripped him. He trampled it down but Marcus was petrified at sight of the blood streaming from the lacerations of the thorns. In the sunlight, against the pale grass, it looked bright and terrible.

Neil hardly glanced at it. 'Pah! Anyone that wanted to be a pilot wouldn't bother about that!'

As they were crossing the paddock, Marcus, who had been

dedicated to the trade of milkman for years, called out importantly, 'I'm going to be a pilot too!'

But Neil took no notice. He was intent on the windmill just ahead. Marcus looked at it too. Sometimes he was brought here by his mother – she would sit and try to paint. She was never pleased with what she did, she said the windmill was like an old bloated moth, it was all wrong.

Something in the grass caught Marcus's eye. He stepped aside to look, and Neil, turning to hurry him on, saw him stooping over a tiny rabbit caught in a trap. It was dead and its long ears were pressed back by the fear which had finally killed it. The small forepaws were daintily composed side by side, but the dark bubble eyes still stared – with death behind as well as before them. One hind leg, caught and smashed, had sprinkled the white scut with colour bold and incompatible among the fair grass and the faded blue flowers.

Marcus's eyes filled with tears. Gently he stroked the soft, cold fur. 'Poor rabbit, poor, poor rabbit!'

Neil's shadow fell across the grass. 'Are you coming or are you going to stay there all day?'

Marcus looked up, horrified. 'But the rabbit! The poor, poor rabbit – it's hurt!'

Neil frowned impatiently. 'Don't be daft – it's dead.'

'Dead?'

Marcus's smooth brows drew together as he pondered. He had encountered that word before. Roughly, he understood it to mean 'gone away'. When people were dead, they went away and you didn't see them any more.

'Can't you see it's dead?' Neil made as if to nudge the rabbit with his foot, but Marcus flung out his hands in protection.

'You're not to! You're not to hurt it!'

Neil's brown pointed face darkened, and as quickly cleared again. Shrugging, he looked down at Marcus with curling lip and chilly, remote scorn.

'You're soft,' he said, as one might to a worm. 'You're pappy. You'll never be a pilot. Go back and play with your dolls.'

He turned and strode off. Marcus looked down at the rabbit. It couldn't be dead because he could still see it, it hadn't disappeared as the kitten had last year, and old Mr Philpotts. He tried to pull the trap away and felt sick.

Neil had climbed over the gate and was out of sight. Marcus scrambled up, telling himself he would see to the rabbit on his way back. It was resting quietly, perhaps it would go to sleep until he returned.

He walked away carefully, so as not to disturb it. One or two black flies came and settled on the torn leg and crawled round the dark convex abyss of the staring eyes.

Neil was standing looking up at the windmill as Marcus came trundling across the field. It was built of wood, all bleached and bare like the walls of the summerhouse. Where the nails had given way, slats hung down so that you could see right through into the mill, and if you walked round, you caught twinkles of light where the holes linked up with other holes on the far side. The great sails had only their bones left, even these were snapped and shredded like the flimsiest cane – they lay back against the mill building with the exhaustion of broken mechanical things. Time had stripped off every vestige of use, rotted the last grain, blacked into cobwebs the honest crust of flour; the marks of labour were all lost in dissolution and decay.

Neil glanced at Marcus but hardly seemed to see him. He had eyes only for the windmill, he stared at it, and his queer blue eyes blazed above his high Slav cheek-bones. Marcus couldn't see what there was to be so excited about, but he was excited all the same. He trotted behind Neil, chattering and undismayed when the other boy never said a word.

Neil ignored Marcus until he wanted to go inside the mill. Then he said, 'Wait here,' and his tone was such that Marcus never thought of disobeying. Neil vanished silently into the blackness of the mill.

He was a long time gone; Marcus hopped first on one leg then on the other to occupy himself. He found a grasshopper and lost it immediately. He did somersaults until the mill took to dancing sombrely in the background. Marcus preferred it still, so he sat on the grass and listened.

There was no sound of Neil moving about inside. Marcus shouted, but no one answered. He decided that Neil was doing this on purpose to see how quickly he would get frightened. Then he would jump out and say that Marcus could never be a pilot.

That thought kept the green boiler-suit very still for a while. He sat bolt upright, chewing a stalk of grass as Neil had done. The slow, leathery flapping of a great black bird was the only sound in the afternoon quiet. If he had not been so excited, he might have gone to sleep.

And then Neil came suddenly out of the mill. Marcus ran up to him, chattering and effusive after his enforced silence. Neil took no notice of what Marcus said. He was whistling softly and looking at the mill-sails. His leather jacket was grey with dust, and the scummy fabric of a cobweb clung to his sleeve. Across the back of one hand was a long, important scratch. Marcus observed it with envy.

Neil flung himself down on the grass. 'See that sail – the top one on this side? I'm going to get out through a hole in the boards and hang on it and make it swing round. When it's pointing down at the ground, I'll let go and make a four-point landing.'

Marcus didn't understand just what Neil meant to do, but it sounded reckless and exciting beyond his dreams of adventure. He was completely carried away by the prospect of danger.

'Me too!' He stooped fervently over Neil. 'I'll make a point landing too!'

'You will not.' Neil stood up and calmly stripped off his jacket. 'You can stay here and mind this and watch what I do.'

'I'm going to do it too!'

Marcus was jumping up and down in a frenzy. Neil gripped and held him. 'You fool! You can't do what I do. It's a test, don't you understand – I have to test my nerve. I'm going to be a fighter-pilot, I've got to have nerve, I've got to be tough and take risks and keep cool. I might not be good enough. I've got to find out, I've got to keep testing myself!'

Marcus was too young to know what fanaticism was, or he might have seen in Neil's face the fatal unity, feral and precipitate, and no more amenable than flame. The clear, freckled brow, gathered and jutting over those oddly empty blue eyes, the firm, intolerant mouth, were dominated by an ardour so extreme, so pitiless that it chilled and almost repelled.

Marcus was sobered by it. He wriggled free of Neil's grasp and drew away, wary as an animal at another's oddity.

'All right.' Neil brushed aside Marcus and his change of heart like a bothersome gnat. He stood there rolling up the sleeves of his grey flannel shirt. Marcus watched, frowning. He felt unsure of himself. He did not properly understand what Neil meant to do, and the desire to emulate fought with his natural caution. It would be as well, perhaps, to see just what the feat might be before doing it himself. Besides, once Neil was busy with it, he wouldn't be so free to stop Marcus from doing as he wanted. So Marcus reasoned, scowling under the weight of his own cunning.

Neil nodded towards the windmill. 'It's not such a wonderful test at that. I guess anyone could do it.' All at once he looked quite miserable; driving his hands deep into his trouser pockets, he went off without another word.

Marcus waited until he had vanished inside the mill, then, carrying Neil's jacket, he found a point of vantage and settled himself with all the fuss of an audience in a theatre.

For a long while nothing happened. Marcus sat gravely attentive for a few moments, and then as there was nothing to attend to, began to swivel round and round on his seat – to the detriment of the boiler-suit. When that amusement palled, he wandered over to the hedge and pulled up armfuls of rank grass in a search for frogs. Soon his fingers were stained green. He smelt them curiously and in a spirit of strict empiricism, sucked his thumb. It tasted bitter and he began to feel irritable and thirsty and the corners of his mouth turned down in a sudden mood of discontent.

He would have gone on to the next stage of intoning wearily, over and over again, his need to go home, and from there proceeded to a restricted but persistent grizzle, had not a slight sound made him look towards the windmill.

In relation to the mill itself, the sails stood at the angle of an 'X'. Neil had emerged – miraculously as it seemed to Marcus, although in fact he had crept through a gap in the boarding which was hidden from below – and was now braced in the angle between the two right-hand sails. The lower sail looked fairly sound, but the upper one had been slashed by the winds until it was twisted and hung askew.

Marcus's mouth opened slowly. Weariness forgotten, he scrambled out of his ditch and ran back to the mill for a closer view of this performance. Neil had his back to Marcus, but he was manoeuvring to turn sideways, his left shoulder outward, and his right to the mill. Chips of dry, rotten wood flaked from under his feet and dropped softly to the grass. He glanced down once and called, 'It's a piece of cake!' and Marcus's mouth watered. He hoped Neil would save him some because he wasn't so sure, now, that he wanted to go and do what Neil was doing, even for a piece of cake.

The sails did not move, they hadn't changed their position since the boys came; but then there was no wind, so it was silly to expect them to turn. Neil moved out from the angle of the sails as far as he could, until the lower one sloped too much for him to reach it. Then he took a firm grip on the under edge of the upper sail; swinging up his feet, he caught and held with his hands so that he was strung along it, monkey-wise. In this position, he began to work his way up to the tilted tip of the sail. He was about ninety feet from the ground, Marcus could not have been more impressed if he had been a thousand feet up. From being merely a subject for imitation, with contagious habits and rare knowledge, Neil had become a hero. Blinking upwards, Marcus surrendered his own considerable ego to unquestioning devotion. He did not suppose now that he could do what Neil did. He would have to wait years before he was so tall and strong, before he would be able to test his nerve like this.

Marcus looked distastefully at his plump arm. It hadn't got any bronze hairs on it like Neil's had, and he hadn't any hairs on his legs, either. He pulled up one leg of the boiler suit and looked hopefully, but his knee was smooth as ivory, and the whole leg still had its generous baby curves. Frowning, Marcus blinked up again at the mill.

He forgot all about his unsatisfactory self at once; Neil had almost reached his objective. He was now over a hundred feet from the ground, at the highest point of the sail, still moving easily. Marcus almost forgot to breathe in his excitement.

The feat looked spectacular, yet it would have been straightforward enough for an agile boy with no fear of heights, had it not been for something which meant nothing to Marcus, but wherein lay the real unobtrusive danger.

The sails were rotten. They hardly supported their own weight; time and the winds had wilted them like sad feathers. The top right-hand sail juddered under Neil's weight, now and then chips of grey wood came away in his hands. Neil knew all about it, he regarded it as the saving danger which made this test of his nerve worth the while. When he reached the tip of the sail, he rested for a moment.

Marcus felt his heart beating so hard against his chest that he had to fold his arms to keep it quiet. He thought that Neil, with his pilot's magic, meant to jump from where he was and thus make the mysterious 'four-point' landing.

What Neil had planned was that his weight on the end of the sail would cause it to swing downwards and he would be taken within jumping distance of the ground. But he had reckoned without the axle being jammed and out of true, he had not thought of the years of binding rust. The sails would never turn again, they were splayed and fixed at the mercy of every gale. Neil thought only that they must be made to move, and he thought that he could do it. He did not care for the alternative of going back the way he had come. Besides, that would be an admission of defeat.

Marcus blinked as Neil let his feet drop and hung by his hands. He swung a little at first, then steadied himself. It was a sight Marcus could recall ever afterwards – the gaunt mill with the daylight in its broken sails, and that remote, impersonal figure dangling in the blue air.

Neil began to try to shift the sail. He could not bear that any obstacle should impede and change the course of his test. He believed that his weight would alter the balance, would drag his sail down according to plan. He had not understood the greater art of adapting plans to the speed of changing circumstance.

27

Again and again he tried to break down the rigidity of the sail and set it swinging. He drew himself up by his hands and then let himself drop, in the hope that the sudden jerk would disengage the cogs so that at least one half turn might be accomplished. That was all he needed – one half turn.

But the sails were fixed and the muscles of his arms already ached unbearably from his climb. He thought he might not be able to hold on much longer, he had strength enough for only one more effort. In a sort of bitter frenzy, his sight blurred by tears of pain and impotence, he drew himself up until his waist was on a level with his hands. His teeth bit deeply into his lip, the sweat shone on his pale forehead. The sail was an enemy which he must subdue or be subdued by it. When he could draw himself no higher, he hung there poised for a second to gather his strength and reinforce his grip. Then, savagely, he threw himself down from his hands.

Marcus was puzzled because Neil had not jumped and made his four-point landing. So, when after his last jerk, Neil parted company with the sail and came hurtling down, Marcus thought he was at last carrying out his plan, and in his opinion, the shrill cracking sounds which accompanied the fall greatly improved it as a spectacle.

And in fact, Neil seemed intent on making the performance as exciting as possible. He did not come straight to the ground. Instead, he fell on the lower right hand sail, lay across it for a second or so as if to prove his mastery, and then, almost languidly, tipped over and continued his journey to the ground.

He landed on his back. The ground shook him once, flinging up his arms and legs like a doll's, then he lay still. Marcus ran over to him shouting, 'I saw the point landing! I saw it! I saw it!'

Delightedly he capered round Neil, fulfilling the desire and purpose of the celebrant who marks a victory and honours a hero.

Neil did not move. He was so still that Marcus checked his dance with sudden misgivings. The performance might not be finished, or worse – he might have offended against the etiquette of the four-point landing. He had to admit that it was a far more impressive adventure than any of his own, it might well have a certain form which Neil would presently demonstrate.

So he waited patiently. It was quite silent now, the big black bird had flapped away; the sunlight, like a bright empty gas under a glass bowl, had dissolved all motion, even the crepitant motion of the beetles.

Neil said nothing. He did not even look at Marcus. His head was tilted back so that from where Marcus stood, only the under part of his chin and his brown throat were visible. Legs and arms were flung out just as Marcus had seen Boddy's arms and legs spread wide when he was thrown on the floor.

It was odd. On tiptoe, stretching his neck as if to peer over a fence, Marcus moved closer to Neil. He looked down at his face. The elder boy's eyes were closed and his skin, which had been brown and warm, was a cold creamy colour. A grey shadow seemed to be creeping over his jaw, changing his face. His lips were pale and dry like paper, his wide nostrils pinched.

Marcus stooped down, hands on his knees, deferential.

'Neil.'

No movement, no sign that he had even heard.

'Neil!' Marcus stooped lower, frowning. 'Neil – what you doing?'

Only one of the grasses by Neil's ear moved under Marcus's breath. Disapprovingly, he sat back on his heels, noting fragments of dry wood still gripped between the pale fingers. It was obvious then what had happened. Neil had gone to sleep, forgetting about everything, even forgetting to put down the bits of wood he had brought back.

Marcus roared in his ear. 'Wake up!'

Neil's head rolled a little to one side, his eyelids moved, lifted unwillingly; he looked out from under them like someone in a blessedly dark room looking out at the blaring daylight.

'You mustn't go to sleep,' said Marcus reprovingly. 'It's not night.'

Neil's eyes opened wider. It seemed as if he had to force himself to see Marcus, although he was only such a little way away. Marcus obligingly bent closer and touched his hand.

The touch troubled the elder boy. His whole body shuddered. He drew his arms slowly in to his sides and tried to raise himself. His head lifted slightly from the ground, then fell back. He did not move again, only the grey shadow deepened across his mouth.

'Aren't you going to get up?'

Neil licked his lips, looking at Marcus almost furtively. 'No, I – think I'll stay here a bit.'

'I saw you do the point landing!'

Neil closed his eyes and began to mutter. 'I came a crumper. The sail was stuck. I couldn't get it to turn like I wanted – I wanted it to turn –'

He moved his head restlessly from side to side. Marcus couldn't think why he didn't get up.

'Let's go home now.'

'I don't want to go home.' Neil felt around with his hand, picked a stalk of grass and stuck it in the side of his mouth. His lips closed on it, pressed together so tightly that his chin wrinkled. He did not chew the grass, he made it a gesture of defiance, and once it was made, seemed unable to carry it to any conclusion. The stalk just stayed there, straight and still, in the corner of his mouth.

Marcus wandered about, moodily kicking the ground with his heels. He could not understand this turn of events, it made him irritable that there was neither point nor pleasure in it.

'I want to go home now!' He shouted from a little way off and stamped.

Neil looked at him with hatred. But he spat out the grass, put his arms flat against the ground and pressed on them. His head lifted, his lower lip drew in under his teeth and even the grey shadow was dredged from his face. It was as if he had no flesh, only bone.

A sound came from deep in his throat, and with it, his rigidity collapsed. He fell back, gasping. Suddenly his eyes were dark and fierce with terror, they shone like the rabbit's eyes, rounded and brittle as a bubble. His fingers unclenched and let fall the chips of dry wood from the mill sail.

Marcus was deeply puzzled. He picked up the wood and examined it politely. It wasn't at all unusual – only out of deference to Neil he stowed two pieces away in the pocket of his boiler-suit. After that, he sat down and waited patiently for orders.

But Neil gave no orders. He lay there staring at Marcus, and now the shadow had come back. He had a grey cloth face. He never looked away, and the terror in his eyes was so violent and so inexplicable that Marcus was frightened too. He glanced round about; there was only the bland empty sunshine and the stooping mill. There was nothing to be afraid of – that made Marcus more frightened than ever. He began to whimper.

'I want to go home.'

The other boy moved his lips and Marcus stopped grizzling to listen hopefully. A rustle, as of some slight insect slipping through the dry grasses, was the only sound Neil made.

At that Marcus lost patience.

'I want to go home!' He seized Neil's arm to try to pull him up.

Neil seemed to flatten himself to the ground, his lips drew back, baring his teeth in another extreme of fear, both savage and agonized.

Marcus stepped back. Quite obviously Neil didn't want to get up. He had no intention of going home, he meant to stay here and sleep. Marcus's lower lip jutted. Never had home and tea seemed so important. Neil was trying to stop him, just because he wanted to go to sleep in the daytime.

He glared at the still figure on the ground – then caught sight of the wilting sails of the mill and remembered the four-point landing, how Neil had even paused in his descent to balance casually on the lower sail. Humility and deference returned immediately.

Pondering, he decided that this wish to sleep at a time so inappropriate, might be the habit of heroes. Perhaps it was a ritual to lie down on the ground and shut your eyes after an adventure. Marcus wondered if he ought to do the same. He thought not. He was too hungry and besides, it hadn't been his adventure. Instead, he would prove to Neil that he wasn't so soft and go home by himself, leaving Neil to follow when he was ready.

'I am going home now,' he said and beamed with self-sufficiency. He would have turned and marched off, had not Neil reached out to hold him by the ankle. Marcus skipped back, frowning. An odd qualm chilled him as he looked into Neil's face.

There was something wrong with his eyes. They had been blue before, Marcus could remember just how blue and fierce they had been. Now they were dark and they shone into the full glare of the sun without blinking or once looking away from Marcus. Yet he had a cold feeling that the darkness in the eyes was also outside them, so that Neil couldn't see properly. He kept moving his lips, they moved all the time as if he were speaking, but he didn't say anything. He didn't even whisper.

Marcus backed away. Neil's hand, flung out on the ground towards him, opened and shut like a crab. It puzzled Marcus that the look on Neil's face was of fear, and the dark, unblinking eyes were never turned away from him as if Neil dreaded being left alone.

But that could not be, Neil was never frightened, and there was nothing to be frightened of here. Besides – Marcus turned stoutly on his heel – Neil hadn't asked him to stay. He could have said if that was what he wanted.

At the gate into the paddock he stopped to look back. Neil had not moved. His body was spilled negligently on the grass, one arm still stretched towards Marcus, his face blurred by distance but turned the way Marcus had gone. The mill drooped behind him, the shadow would soon lie across him and he would be out of the sun.

There was something else on the grass near the mill. It was Neil's leather jacket. Marcus wrinkled his nose. He still thought it a funny time and place to go to sleep. Perhaps Neil would like his jacket as a pillow. He hesitated, on the verge of going back. But then he had a vision of Neil's scorn, his 'You're soft! You'll never be a pilot!' Neil would be contemptuous, and rightly so, if he went back for such a womanish gesture. Fighter pilots probably never used pillows but

31

just stretched out on the hard ground. Marcus was impressed by this Spartan routine, he knew he would find it very difficult to keep as still as Neil had for such a long time.

He waved to Neil and scrambled under the gate. Very soon he came to the place where the rabbit lay. He stalked past, head averted. Neil had said it was soft to worry about the rabbit, Neil had shown how to be tough and daring. He was going to be like Neil and some day test his nerve by doing a four-point landing.

It was the first time he had been out for a walk by himself, he felt grown-up and independent. He walked through the field of knocking grasses and his legs struck them stoutly aside.

In the last field he stopped, lifting his pink damp face to the sky. A far-off bumbling, filling the air, filling every nook and cranny, every mouse-hole, every fold in every shrivelled leaf – and there were three shapes, tiny, against the blue – oriental, precise.

'Benims,' said Marcus, and stood looking from under his hand, paying them due reverence until they were out of sight.

Submerged

Diving into the river, Peter Hume always felt he was entering something of his own. The brown water never rebuffed him, even the first chill on his skin had a curious softness, like snow; everything crisp and taut in his mind relaxed and was drenched.

It was a mild river, dropped into a steep slot between its banks and thatched over with trees. Some instinct for secrecy kept it at work, quietly shifting the soil, settling with the persistence of a hermit into a deeper, browner bed. The colours here were not the bright mirror colours of a river. Loosestrife, with its carnival purple, strong yellow ragwort and red campion, all had a diffidence; softened, almost brumous, they enriched without decking the river bank. Round the occasional eddies, bright beans of sunlight jumped and jazzed until late evening, and then all that was left of their energy was a thin, milky mist.

Peter couldn't often stay so long, he had to go home to supper, or there would be questions. He wasn't supposed to swim in the river anyway, there was some talk about its being dangerous because of the submerged roots of trees. Peter knew all about those, they added the essential risk which made the river perfect. He had been careful never to give any promise, for his conscience was lively and would have kept him to it. His mother supposed he swam in the quarry, and Peter's code, which was rigid enough within the letter of its law, did not require him to disillusion her.

The other boys rarely came to the river. They preferred the quarry which was twenty feet deep in places and ideal for diving. Peter sometimes went with them, but there was nothing to see under water, whereas here, once you had the knack of diving between the roots, it was like being in a bony world of dim arches and aqueducts, caverns and slanting forests. Peter did not try to persuade anyone else to his way of thinking, he preferred to keep the river to himself.

For his first dive, he always went to the left of the willow, where there was nothing more exacting than a couple of stumps which could knock every breath from his body at the slightest miscalculation. That first plunge, with the water roaring in his ears and the mud smoking up from his outflung hands, was the moment of relaxation. The world was at once bounded by a bank, the sky was a fragmentary blue between the leaves, and until it was time to put on his clothes again, he felt no distinction between himself and the

33

river-dwellers – the otters, water-rats, minnows and frogs. He was as contented as they, plundering the mud, or floating on his back and beating up a white spray which looked, on that sober water, surprising as a glimpse of petticoats under brown homespun.

This was a Saturday afternoon. From early morning the distance had never been still, the heat quenched all movement save a small, tireless jig of solid and motionless things. Peter's skin was thirsty for the river even while he went, meekly, to have his hair cut and, fuming, for his music-lesson. But the afternoon was his own, and that first plunge, to the left of the willow, past the stumps and up through ribbons of cool weed, absolved him of the morning's sufferance.

He came up breathless, shaking the wet hair out of his eyes. Ripples were widening round him, already they had reached the bank and were moving the grasses. It was nice to make himself felt like that, he wished he could see it happening in the air as he moved about, although he wouldn't care to have other people's ripples getting mixed up with his own.

He lay on his back, and the noise of the water in his ears was like the intermittent singing in a shell. When he thought about the river he could always remember that sound, and the way his hair was gently lifted from his scalp and floated.

Looking up, he saw that the blue sky was trying to burn through the leaves and get at the river. Had it ever been dry? How much hotter would it have to be before the sun could suck all this water up and bake the mud? It was supposed to have happened once, to the earth, and there were cracks so big that you would need a bridge to cross them, and looking down, you'd see the fires burning at the middle of the earth. That must have been some heat-wave. Peter let himself sink like a stone.

Of course, there could be two opinions as to the delights of the river-bed. Peter was not squeamish about the soft fleshy mud creeping round his ankles, or about the things which slid from under his feet. He trod firmly, feeling the weight of the water on his eyeballs, seeing only a little way through the greenish gloom. There was one thing he needed now, and that was a knife, carried between his teeth like a sponge-diver. He had almost saved enough to buy one.

Under water was no solidity except in touch. Banks and tree-roots had no more substance than the reeds, they moved together as in a tiny draught. Peter could see what appeared to be the ribs of a huge skeleton, greening and forgotten on the river-bed. They formed a narrow black tunnel with an arched opening which reminded him of a church door.

Peter shot up to the surface, drank in air and blinked in the violence of the sunlight. He stayed where he was – treading water – his wet head shining like glass. It was as well not to move away because he was positioned exactly for his performance. As usual, he was dubious about it, his heart began to knock. A certain excitement was permissible, due to the occasion as a whisper to a church. Any other, lesser emotion belonged to some girlish self which he would gladly have detached and drowned.

This performance was partly a pleasure, partly an endurance test. Until it was accomplished, Peter felt he had no more rights over the river than any of the myriad gadding gnats. Afterwards, by the law of possession of the tamed by the tamer, he considered himself established beyond deeds or bonds.

The ribs under water were tree-roots left arched and empty by the river's delving. They were big roots, thicker than Peter's wrist, and there were enough of them hooped over to form a short, tortuous tunnel. Peter had explored it and found he was just able to squeeze through before his breath gave out. It was a foolhardy trick, that was its great attraction. Peter knew that if he ever got wedged in that bony tunnel, he would drown as miserably as a cat in a sack.

But danger was a saving grace. Without it, Peter would not have been able – nor would he have needed – to establish his suzerainty over the river. He was convinced that if he ever swam here without going through the submerged tunnel, the river would be estranged from him, his sense of property and kinship would be lost.

He looked down at his hands, pawing the water like a dog to keep himself afloat. If he came often enough he might get webs across his fingers and his blood might cool. Then he could live here without any trouble and explore the river from beginning to end. He could follow it down to the sea and when he was tired of swimming he could make a boat with a cabin and a couple of guns in the poop. A boat was always useful – if he stayed in the water all the time his skin would probably go green and pimply like a frog's. That thought troubled, not his vanity, but his dread of the conspicuous.

A bird flashed past him and vanished in the shadows. For a moment the brown homely river was fired by something tropical – a flicker of cobalt, bronze and scarlet. The improbable kingfisher.

Sight of that pure violent motion inspired Peter. He dived fiercely. The tunnel rushed to meet him, the dark entrance quenching the image of the kingfisher. Then his head and shoulders were under the first root. Twisting, levelling, held fast in a green skeletal gullet, with mud clouding round him, shins and elbows scraped, he yet found some sizeable satisfaction in the ordeal. He was proving himself and the more desperate the struggle, the more splendid and impeccable the proof. All scars were honourable, his lungs withheld not only the river, but the force of a mighty and malignant enemy.

The tunnel ended in a last twisted hoop with a clump of shadowy weed beyond. Peter squeezed his head and one arm and shoulder through first. His hand slipped, then grasped the weed. Some of it came away, mud boiling up with it, but the main clump was firm and he hauled himself free by it. Then he was moving upwards and a dim, gnomish world dropped away under his feet.

It was like coming in out of the dark when the sun beat down on his head and shoulders. He swam grunting to the bank, pulling the water aside familiarly as one who casts off his tangled bed-sheets.

For a few moments he lay stretched out on the bank until his skin felt sticky and partly dry. Then he sat up, looked behind him at the empty blond fields, still juddering with heat, and back again at the river. There was wild angelica growing on the far bank, green umbrella ribs blown inside-out and ending in a frivolous froth of white. The water did not reflect it, there were too many bright beans just here, but Peter thought it looked cool and eatable. He wished now that he had brought something to eat, he began to tease himself with visions of ice-cream – enough to fill a decent-sized bowl, and a spoon in the middle, leaning a little sideways as the ice-cream came to the rich liquefying stage which he loved best.

But he was not inclined to hanker after hypothetical pleasures with real ones to hand. As he slipped back into the river there was no splash, only the slow ripples moving out. His mood was now leisurely and relaxed. He followed the ripples, letting himself sink slightly in his laziness before he would lift an arm to make a stroke. Pursing his lips, he blew fleets of bubbles along the top of the water, snuffled it, floated and enjoyed it with the intensity of a very young animal. Ice-cream was forgotten, even when he saw the angelica again it did not remind him of something to eat.

There was a faint lilac tinge on the flowers and the stalk was flushed a rich purple. It was prettier than any of the flowers his father grew in the garden, but then, he conceded as he floated idly into midstream, it was only right that his own river should have the best flowers.

The sun, the stillness, the drowsy boom of water in his ears, lulled him into a half-doze which the river's slight chill would not allow to become complete. Drifting from shadow to sunlight and back to shadow again, he watched the burnt-out blue of the sky, thickly figured with fiery leaves. Thoughts that were partly dreams slipped through his mind. Imperial, childish dreams. The mild river fostered them as school and home never did. Brittle, boy's bones stretched in a flash to the shape and substance of a man; his child's mind – bigoted and unsteady – was great with the sum of wisdom; fame, honour, wealth, were all got as glibly as prizes at a fair.

Peter was strictly practical. This mood being past, he would drop his fantasies and go back to the business of life as he found it. Day-dreaming was part of the river, and that was so much his province, he had every right to fill it with himself, life-size – and beyond.

A sudden noise, a thrusting among the undergrowth, jerked him wide-awake. Someone coming. Still on his back, he stared from under his hand. The bushes were snatched aside, an odd, ridiculous figure burst through and almost overbalanced into the river.

It was a woman in a red mackintosh. No longer very young, and so plump that the mackintosh sleeves stretched over her arms like the skin of scarlet saveloys. A green crescent-shaped hat with a spotted veil had tipped over one eye, leaving the other glaring round the polka-dots. She would have been funny, but there was something chilling about her, about the steep expanse of speckled red chest, heaving under her torn blouse, about the brassy hair tumbling down on her neck, and the skin of her face dreadfully, darkly suffused.

She stood there, too breathless to speak, turning her hands towards Peter with an awful beckoning motion. He stared in horror, and her one visible eye glared back at him. He was frightened by her, by the contagion of her own deadly fear. He thought she was mad; his skin prickled and he backed away through the water.

She cried, thickly, 'Come out! Come out of there for God's sake!'

As he gazed, open-mouthed, she looked over her shoulder back the way she had come, and her hands were moving towards him as if they could draw him ashore bodily.

Peter did not move. Those hands, that huge, speckled bosom bursting from the flimsy mackintosh, revolted his maidishness. He tried to avert his eyes, but he was almost mesmerized by her physical power – not of muscle and sinew, but the power of animal, abundant flesh.

'Come out! Come out, you idiot!' She stood on the very edge of the bank, leaning towards him.

'You've got to help! Do you hear? I've got to have help!'

Slowly Peter moved in to the bank, but when she reached out and tried to snatch at him, he drew away.

'Please turn your back while I get to my clothes.'

His voice sounded thin and ridiculous; the woman's one eye narrowed. 'So's you can make a bolt for it? Think I want to look at a tadpole like you? Get out!'

Peter stayed where he was, treading water, his face scarlet but stony. She swore at him, using words and threats which heightened the colour in his cheeks. He would not move, he stared past her at a disc of sunlight trembling on a tree-trunk.

'Oh, for God's sake!' She turned her back. 'Get out and get your trousers on. Unless you're so modest you want to dress in the water!'

Peter said nothing. He was scrambling up the slippery bank towards his clothes, draped over a branch. She swung round as he stepped into his trousers; with flaming cheeks and a horrible sickness in his stomach, he hauled them up over his wet skin.

She stared at him from between the leaves, and he had a feeling that she was staring right through his body and seeing something beyond.

'There's a man coming to kill me,' she said, and put a leaf aside with terrifying gentleness. 'I can't run any more, I've got to stay here. So have you. He won't lay a finger on me if there's a witness and a chance he'd swing for it. . . .'

He heard, before she did, the thudding of feet on the baked earth. She saw his look and turned to face the opening in the bushes through which she had come.

Instinctively, Peter crouched out of sight, screwing his shirt into a ball and pressing it against his chest. The man, when he came, was almost as bad as the woman. Almost, but not quite, because he was a man and although he was frightening, there was not that strange undertow of fascination. He was huge – to Peter it seemed both the man and the woman were mountainous while he had dwindled to something tiny and bloodless like a gnat, and the river was just a brown ditch.

The man stood on the top of the bank staring down at the woman. He had hardly any neck, and he must have weighed about fifteen stone. His little flat head was stuck between his shoulders, there was something of the tortoise about him, the same ponderous air of trouble and defeat, just now opposed by his mood.

People often got angry, and Peter found it amusing to watch, especially if they danced about, like his father. This man was angry, but it wasn't funny. His rage was quite outside him, as the woman's fear had been. It moved his hands for him, as her fear had moved hers. Over and over again they rehearsed an action inspired not by the brain, but by the blood. The fingers were drawn in, the fists thickened until they were bunched solid, and the grip expended on itself.

Peter shivered, he longed to run, but the impotence of nightmare kept him still. Very slowly, the man came down the bank. As he passed through a patch of sunlight, his face showed glistening wet, his bushy brows were loaded with the sweat streaming from his forehead.

The woman waited calmly. She had one hand on her hip and she did not seem to be so frightened now.

'Well,' she said scoldingly, 'you've got yourself into a fine old paddy, haven't you?'

The man came on, his expression unchanging, his hands rehearsing their action. Then, just before he reached her, she sprang forward, flung her arms round him and put her mouth on his. His hands came up, and the thumbs spread wide, and fastened round her neck.

And now, at sight of those two figures, locked together, the dread of the unspeakable was added to Peter's fear. Trembling, he waited for the man's hands to perform what they had practised, to close and crush as they crushed the air. They stayed where they were, round the woman's neck, almost hidden by the coil of brassy hair. After one convulsive grip, they fell away and just rested there, heavily.

Peter did not relax. He had been staring too hard, the figures of the man and woman dodged in front of his eyes, coloured solid blue and sometimes red. He knew that the worst was yet to come. There was no peace between them, only something violent which this embrace was muffling for a moment.

The woman drew away gently; put up her hands and took the man's loose fingers from her neck.

'Well, then,' she said smiling, 'what did you do with the knife?'

The man's size was of no account now, his rage had been snuffed out, and all that was left him was an odd, tortoise-like defeat. He looked at his empty hands and touched his pockets.

'You dropped it somewhere, didn't you?' She laughed at him. 'You would! You lose your savings, so you think you'll knife me in case I took them. But then you lose the knife – does it sound sense?' She eyed him, head on one side, like someone considering an awkward child. As he only stood there, looking dazed, she sighed and began to pin up her hair under the green hat. 'I've taken it very well, considering – accusing me of pinching your money and chasing me with a knife! Why, I've never touched a farthing – is it likely when you carry it round with you all the while? You've lost it somewhere. That's you all over.'

She stood there, her plump arms held up, fastening the last strands of hair in place, and she didn't seem to be looking at the man. But Peter could see that she was watching him with sideways glances which didn't go at all with what she was saying. Peter wondered when she would call to him to step out and be a witness. She seemed to have forgotten all about him, and although he was terribly cramped, he dared not move in case he made a sound and reminded her that he was there.

'Yes,' she went on, briskly tightening the belt of her mackintosh, 'that's what's funny about you – the way you lose everything. Though I must say, you did yourself a real good turn when you lost that knife. Others aren't so careless as you – they don't lose the rope they keep for hanging, you know!'

She thought that was a good parting shot, and with hands thrust into her pockets, turned her back on the man and started to clamber along the bank.

'Where are you going?' He asked a question, but there was no question in his tone. Rather was it as if he could not believe even in his defeat until she stated it.

She looked back over her shoulder at him, still standing bewildered by her kiss, almost searching for the fury which had driven him here and then dwindled like vapour. Perhaps she saw something of the troubled tortoise in him, because she laughed.

'Just one more thing you're losing – little me! So long!'

Still laughing, still looking back, she pushed her way through some clumps of purple loosestrife. Her scarlet mackintosh was overlaid with purple flowers, her face, all screwed up with laughter, looked back over the blossoms and then, just as Peter was thinking of making a dash for the open fields, the face seemed to drop out of sight, the red was suddenly blotted out, leaving only purple loosestrife, violently shaken. At the same moment, a scream and a great thudding splash froze Peter's first tentative stirring. The woman had fallen in.

In that moment, the river won back all Peter's esteem and affection. From his hiding-place, only part of the water was visible, and he dearly wanted to see what was happening. But he was naturally wary, he stayed still, contenting himself with the huge brown ripples brimming on the surface and lapping high up the bank.

After the splash it was very quiet. The man stood there, gaping at the loosestrife expectantly, like someone watching a conjuror's hat. The tall flowers settled back into stillness, there was only the stealthy chink of water as the eddies spread wide.

Peter wondered what the woman was doing. He held his bunched shirt against his mouth to stop himself from shouting. Why didn't the man move? He must be an idiot.

Peter was scornful of him now. If he had only a tiny brain like a pea, then his huge body was all the more ridiculous. It was nasty, too, as the woman's big speckled chest had been nasty – because there was too much of it.

The man trampled slowly into the loosestrife, parting it uncertainly with his hands. Peter followed him, dodging low out of sight.

It was easy to see where the woman had fallen in. Earth on the edge of the bank had powdered under her foot, leaving a scooped hollow. It was just here, by a great clubbed root, half-submerged, that Peter took his bearings for his 'performance'. The tunnel lay almost immediately below, it was even possible to dive to it from here because the bank dropped away into deep mud.

Mud was still clouding up from the river-bed, colouring the water like strong coffee, and the surface was not yet quiet. But there was no sign of the woman except that among the loosestrife lay the odious green hat with its spotted veil. The man picked it up gingerly, as if he expected her to be underneath. He turned it over in his hands, looked wonderingly at the river and then called out 'Eh?'

The sound of his voice startled him, he swung round, staring, and Peter only just had time to crouch out of sight. The woman was having a fine old game. Either she was under the water, waiting to bob up and startle the man, or she had swum downstream and climbed out further along.

When next Peter stretched his neck and looked over the loosestrife, the man had gone to the water's edge and was leaning down, hands on his knees, peering in. Peter would have gone and given him a brisk shove from behind, so wiping out the memory of his first ignoble fear, but the rustling loosestrife would have betrayed him before he got near enough.

The creature went down on his knees, rolled up one sleeve and plunged his arm into the water. It was so unexpectedly deep that he nearly overbalanced and he muttered in alarm. But he kept on, groping about under water, first with one arm, then the other. Obviously he was searching for the woman, and just as obviously, he wasn't able to swim. That completed his ignominy in Peter's eyes.

After a while the man had an idea. He searched about and found a long stick. With this he was able to prod the steeply-shelving earth immediately below the bank. Farther out the water went deeper than the length of the stick. He stood up, and with the dripping stick in his hand, called out 'Eh?'

Once again he was shocked by the loudness of his own voice. He called 'Eh?' twice more, the third time desperately. There was no answer. His face darkened, his lips grew loose and trembling – if he hadn't been a grown man, Peter would have sworn he was on the verge of tears.

He looked at the river for several minutes, then with a sudden movement, flung the stick away and charged up the bank, breaking and trampling everything in his way. All at once he was in this violent hurry, and when Peter climbed to the top of the bank and looked after him, he was thudding across the field in the white sunlight.

He had only just realised that the woman must have stolen a march on him, climbed ashore farther downstream and run home. How could a man be so stupid? There was a boy at school, Girlie Thomas, who was a famous dunce, but he wasn't as slow as that.

Peter watched the man out of sight. He was waiting in case the woman had hidden instead of leaving the river. He was ready to run if she appeared. Standing in the sunlight, he pulled on his shirt, scraping indifferently with his finger-nail at the patches of dry mud. He left the tails hanging outside his trousers for coolness and wandered round like a Russian boy in a smock.

The heat was changing. It was heavier now, oppressing the lungs instead of burning the skin. And the hills which had been blue all day were a thick vegetable yellow. There was a storm coming.

Peter concluded that the woman must have gone. There were one or two places where she could have climbed out while the man was fishing for her with his stick. The banks were pretty steep – you had to know where to get out, or you'd have no more luck than a frog trying to climb up a glass jar.

Peter walked along the bank looking, out of curiosity, for the spot where the woman had left the river. It would be easy enough to see, the grass would be flattened and the dry brown earth wet from her drenched clothes. He did not care what became of the woman, he hated and feared her, but his was a precise mind and here was an event which was not finished. Until it was complete, he did not know how he would confront it, how he would remember it, or whether it would be an advantage not to remember it at all. Those two had done something to his river, he knew he would need to make so many adjustments in his own mind that finally it could not be the same river. It was not such a hermit, perhaps; in some obscure way it had allied itself with them and he was mildly surprised, as one who discovers an old and sober friend in some cheap vulgarity.

But it was still better than anybody else's river, the underwater tunnel was still particularly his, and the bony aqueducts and the forests of tenuous weed. He would still want to come, even if he had to treat the river differently.

He frowned with his proprietor's frown, glancing along the bank. There were no signs of anyone having climbed out recently, no wet patches, no draggled grass. Had she gone to the other side? If she had, she must have been easily visible to the man, and besides, the river was narrow enough for Peter to see that the opposite bank was just as dry and untrampled.

Funny. He climbed on to a willow branch overhanging the water and from this vantage-point, stared up and down the river. A rat pottered by in the shadows, refusing to quicken its pace when Peter hissed. The water and the gnats were the only other things that moved; leaves and grasses were pinned under the heavy air.

Unwillingly, he went back to the spot where the woman had fallen in. The broken loosestrife was already limp and dark and there were some flies crawling on the green hat. The water was very deep here, so deep that looking up from the bottom you could only see a pale blur of light far above . . .

Suddenly he ran and seized up the stick which the man had thrown away. He flung himself down on his knees and poked about in the water. He could never touch bottom with the stick, but he might find if there was anything floating under the surface.

The thought was admitted, his skin grew greenish, a weight dropped and rolled in his stomach. He let the stick fall, knowing that either he would run away now, leaving this horror entrenched for ever in his river, or he would prove for himself that it was non-existent. There was only one way to prove it.

He came up, fighting, from the first wave of dread. Sight of the slow familiar waters made it so ridiculous that he stripped off his shirt and trousers with a fierce grin at his mawkishness.

All the same, he had never felt less like swimming, so he gave himself no chance to baulk at the water's edge. Even as his shirt – flung out behind him – settled on the grass, he dived deep.

When the water closed over him he was immediately reassured, and didn't believe any of it. Deep down nothing was changed, it was green and gnomish, the mud fumed up from his feet and his outstretched hands, the coolness braced his whole body.

The real river, the dim miniature landscape beneath the surface was still the same. There could be no invasion of his province here, he was a fool to think people on the bank above could make any difference. As for the man and woman, he decided as he stroked through the reeds, that he cared nothing about them, except that they should never come again; the unfinished event he could finish – when he was sufficiently interested – in his own way.

It was time he went home, but he felt the need of some act which would express his happiness at finding the river his own again. He had not forgotten the purpose of this dive, and now that his dread was groundless, he had every reason to be pleased with himself. As a formal conclusion, and to set the seal to his prowess, he decided to go through the underwater tunnel once more.

At the surface he breathed the heavy air and kicked a lacing of foam on the broad waters. Murmurous and still distant he heard the thunder and wondered how he would feel if that were artillery and a battle on the other side of the hills. He decided to pretend it on the way home, and dived just as the lightning stripped the sky like a blade.

At first Peter thought it had affected his eyes, because he could not see the tunnel until he was nearly on it. The dark church-like entrance appeared and then was inexplicably blotted out. Not until the moment of collision did he understand that there was something between himself and the tunnel.

Under water was no solidity except in touch, but he knew before his outflung hands confirmed, what it was hovering in front of him. His fingers slid on something soft; his dive carried him violently against a heavy mass. The impact swung it a little away, but then, as he crumpled on the bottom, it bore down on him from above with a dreadful, leisurely motion.

Peter had never fainted, he had never been under sufficient strain. Now, on the river-bed, he came so near it that even the green underwater gloom was blacked out. He saw nothing, he scarcely knew what he did. His mind ceased to calculate, it was his body, reacting to physical nausea, swamped and drowning, which made him strike out blindly, seeking to batter and break the web of water. His fist hit something yielding, he turned and hammered it with hands and feet and it gave like pulp. But it swung aside and he was free. Still fighting, still blind, he shot up to the surface.

Above water he heard, as if from some other person, the harsh see-sawing of his own breath. Without respite he struggled to the bank and dragged himself out. Never had the earth felt so brisk and salutary or the daylight so clean. His skin still crawled with the touch of soft and slimy things, he lay panting and shuddering.

It was the thunder which roused him, and the glare of lightning. He rubbed himself down with his hands and began to huddle into his clothes. The very daily-ness of dressing reassured him more than anything else and by the time he had tied his shoe-laces he was engaged – squeamishly but logically – with the method, instead of being obsessed by the result.

The mystery of how the woman left the river without trace, was solved. She had never left it, she was down at the bottom, out of sight. But drowned people usually floated on the surface. She must be caught up, perhaps by one of the roots, probably – Peter coldly conceded it – a foot or an arm was wedged in the vaulting of his tunnel. If that were so, why hadn't she struggled and freed herself? She could have, easily. Once he had wedged his foot under a root – only a sharp twist was needed to loosen it.

He went cautiously to the loosestrife and peered over. There was the clubbed root jutting from the bank. She might have hit her head on that as she fell, and been unconscious. Or she might have got her foot or arm so tightly fixed that she couldn't get away and so she just drowned down there while they watched for her on the bank above.

Peter found that deduction could have a purely cerebral excitement stronger than squeamishness. He so far forgot his diffidence as to push through the loosestrife and stand on the very spot where the woman had last stood. He examined the clubbed root for marks which might bear out his theory. To his disappointment, the dry, horny wood showed no signs of having been struck by anything recently. He went down on his hands and knees to look more closely, and was wishing he had a magnifying glass when he caught sight of the woman's green hat. It still lay there, and flies still crawled on it as if it were something that had been alive and was now dead.

All at once Peter realised what had happened. He scrambled up and stared at the river with loathing. It was knocking away a little earth from the bank, carrying it off, delving deeper into its quiet hermit bed. It had always looked secretive; it still did, only now it had a secret to keep. There would be something else, something strange, to move under water with the reeds and the solid roots, turning, dipping with a slow, waltz-like motion.

Peter ran all the way home, but the storm broke before he was indoors.

At first, Peter thought intermittently about what had happened. He never spoke of it to anyone. There was something shameful about it and anyway, it was none of his business.

He had the weapon of youth, the power to bury deep that which was more profitably forgotten. In a few days, not only the event, but the place of the event – the river – dropped out of his mind for long periods. And the river had been important to him. When he was unable to go and swim there, he had kept it as a retreat, a place of his own, and at rare moments – rare because he was not given to daydreaming – he would summon the memory and use it as a panacea for some grievance, or a vehicle for indolence.

He hardly noticed the loss. It was as if he had closed a lid on the river. If by chance it was lifted, he did not remember the brown soft water, the quiet colour, the jumping beans of sunlight. There came only a pang of alarm, a warning not to invite memory. This he

45

prudently heeded, the lid was replaced on the river and all its associations.

When the woman's body was found, weeks later, local gossip boiled over, and some of Peter's schoolfellows went to look at the place by the loosestrife. Peter usually fidgeted when they discussed it and turned the subject by some violent horseplay. As he had considerable authority among his friends and set for them the fashion of their interests, they soon followed his lead and talked no more about the drowned woman.

It was his parents who really irritated him by their transparent tact. They treated the subject as too extreme to fall within his knowledge or understanding. It confirmed his suspicion that there was nothing but a great deal of wilful mystery in adult affairs.

If the boys had dropped the matter, there were others who had not. Peter was cleaning his bicycle one morning when Girlie Thomas ran up and hung over the garden gate.

'Say, Hume! Heard about the murder?'

Peter looked up with interest. 'What murder?'

'That woman they got out of the river – she was murdered.'

Peter straightened, oily rag in hand. 'Who says?'

'Who?' Girlie Thomas hooted indignantly. 'Everyone knows she was. Anyone could tell that. She was hit on the head and thrown in the river, besides – they've got the man that did it!'

Peter resented hearing news from Girlie Thomas, especially this news. With his thumbnail he began to prise a flint from his tyre and refused to look impressed.

'It was a blacksmith from Mulheath way,' Girlie Thomas went on, his boots scraping the gate-panels. 'My pop says he'll swing for it, unless it's manslaughter. How many years do they get for manslaughter?'

'Don't know,' said Peter shortly.

Girlie Thomas looked over his glasses. 'You used to go swimming in the river, didn't you, Hume?'

'So what?'

'Well, you might have been there when it happened.'

Peter grunted. 'I never go to the river now. I don't like it. And stop kicking that gate, Thomas. My father doesn't like that gate being kicked.'

'Who'd tell him?'

'I would.'

'Yes, you would, squealer,' agreed Girlie Thomas, and when Peter made a dive at him, ran off, whistling amicably enough.

Peter went back to his bicycle. He stood frowning and spinning the cranks. It was quite true about not liking the river. He didn't. He hadn't been there since the day, and he wouldn't be going again. He preferred to swim in the quarry with the others.

Those two had done something to the river. He couldn't swim there any more, his skin crept at the thought of the brown water, the soft, pulpy mud. And the underwater tunnel – it belonged to the fat woman now.

They thought the man had killed her. That wasn't right, he should have thought anyone would know it wasn't. For a moment he was shocked at adult fallibility. Came again the pang of alarm, the warning not to remember, not to resurrect that pitiful self, shrinking in the lee of a nightmare. It had been ugly and stupid, most of all it had been shameful in a way he could not understand. There was in it the very substance of those whispers, innuendoes and stories which he heard often at school, which he did not disbelieve, but did not care to verify. It was not his affair, and there was no part which he would wish to claim as his.

The lid was replaced and it was almost as if there had never been any river. Whistling, he wheeled his bicycle into the road. He was going to swim in the quarry.

The Father

A father is a strange thing, he will leap
Across a generation and will peep
Out of a grandson's eyes when unexpected
With all the secrets of him resurrected.
                    (R.P.T. COFFIN)

Rowena Styles and Pearl Schenck met over a sand-tray on their first day at school. They had entered by a door marked 'Infants' but Pearl declared that she was not, and never had been, an infant. She maintained that she had been presented to her parents prettily dressed and boxed under a paper frill. Rowena was not absolutely clear what an infant was. Infants were bald and bare, Pearl told her, and cited a picture in her illustrated Bible of the judgement of Solomon, showing a man about to chop one in half. Rowena worried that it might have escaped notice that she had passed the bald bare phase. Pearl was deeply affronted at the arbitrary classification. They both feared they might not be in the infallibly good hands they had been led to expect. It was their first intimation of mortality.

Rowena was considered the more attractive child. She was fair-skinned and chubby. Her yellow curls, wound over her mother's finger every morning, unwound towards afternoon into charming tendrils. At first Pearl attracted less. Her hair was brown, her skin dark, her face condensed like a monkey's. But as they advanced into their teens the imbalance was adjusted. Rowena became plump and spotty. Pearl, more like lignite than nacre as her science teacher said, shone with an adventuring intelligence.

Rowena did not recover her looks. Pubescence set in permanently. She retained the damp but not the dewiness of youth. And in middle age there was something unformed, even poignant, about her lumpiness. She wore floral prints and knitted suits which clothed her with bad grace. Pearl tried to alert her to her possibilities but she said she couldn't live up to Pearl's ideas.

Pearl, who had been careful never to draw attention to her adolescence even in her conversation – if she could not think of the right thing to say she remained silent – became a slim, distracting girl and a shapely, devastating woman. She still had her monkey face but it sparkled. The adventuring intelligence took her everywhere and the monkey sadness scarcely ever showed.

They remained friends, even when Pearl went to college and Rowena did not, Pearl married and Rowena did not, when Rowena stayed on in SE20 and Pearl went to Italy. It mattered not at all how long they were apart. They could always take up where they had left off. Some part of their association never left off, it continued, steadily and prosaically, throughout the period when they did not actually communicate.

Not that they had any David and Jonathan affinity. When Pearl came to examine what she felt about Rowena, as she was eventually obliged to do, she realised that she could not have lived without her. At least, not the way she did live – it would have to have been some other way. It might have been better but there wasn't a hope in hell of knowing, and she was quite satisfied with the way things turned out. She owed a lot of her satisfaction to Rowena for being a fairly unmitigated mess. Of course she was fond of Rowena, otherwise they would never have gone beyond the sand-tray, but even that was a matter of some convenience because Pearl was lazy about personal relationships and wouldn't take trouble to check that she had chosen well. She frequently didn't choose, she just let people happen to her. It was a serious flaw in her character that she wasn't the calculating kind. She came to this conclusion at a time when she was having cause to regret it.

Her marriage broke up and Pearl went back to Penge to her parents. She had no deep sense of failure, nor was she taking her wounds home. There was simply nowhere else she could live free whilst fixing herself up with a flat and a job.

She and Rowena were then twenty-five years old. Rowena was working in the local library and Pearl did not need to be put in the picture. She saw it all, as soon as she set eyes on Rowena. Rowena was wearing a Hungarian peasant blouse and dirndl skirt and Pearl could have told, give or take a name or two, of her sporadic dates with locals and environmentals such as book-borrowers, shop-assistants, bus-boys – none of whom sought a second opportunity. She knew about the Amami nights at the Poly.

'Roo, you look terrible!'

Rowena nodded. 'It's that time of month with me.'

'It's those clothes!'

'You look lovely, Pearl.' If she had shown a touch of envy there might have been hope for her. 'I can't wear stripes.'

'Of course you can't! You're twice my size.'

For their different reasons they sought each other's company. Pearl felt as always what a good thing it was that she was Pearl Schenck and not Rowena Styles, and Rowena, when she was with

Pearl, felt she was being taken out of herself. She acquiesced in thinking it was no bad thing, but Pearl believed that she was not as dissatisfied with herself as she ought to be. Sometimes, Pearl suspected that, in her mulish way, Rowena was even quite pleased with herself.

Naturally, she wanted to hear about Pearl's marriage. Pearl was flippant about it although, she frankly admitted, there was nothing to laugh at. 'It's really quite tragic.' Fleetingly, her monkey face had a monkey sadness.

'Pearl, isn't there any hope?'

'Of a reconciliation? He'd have to be the last man on earth.' Pearl giggled. 'And if he were, there'd be small hope of replenishing it. He's absolutely incompetent in bed.'

'Incompetent? Oh.' Rowena blenched. 'I see.'

'Don't let anyone who wants to marry you pretend that that sort of thing doesn't matter. It's absolutely vital. With it, you can hang on together, whatever else you lack. But if you don't have the feeling – never mind about true minds – the marriage is a mockery.' She wondered how useful the information would be. Poor Roo was so wholesome, so *whole*. Whereas I, thought Pearl without regret, am a woman of parts, not all nice and some actually prurient.

She found herself a job and took a room in Earls Court. The months passed, and the year. They continued to know each other and from time to time they met. Pearl would tell Rowena about her experiences, amatory and other. None of them was wholly one or the other. Pearl had settled on a career as a designer of fabrics and wall papers. Although she had no outstanding talent for design, she did have a considerable instinct for deploying her resources, physical and mental. She found that it was possible to succeed, up to a quite satisfactory point, with that instinct alone. Rowena continued absorbed and fascinated by Pearl's adventures. She had none of her own, seemed merely to be getting through life, as if only time, and little else, had been allowed her.

Pearl tried. She introduced her to people whose opinions she did not have to value too much and whom she thought should be able to take Rowena in their stride. Rowena was either desperately eager or torpid with shyness, and having met her, people prepared at once to forget her. The ruthless ones did not need any preparation, they forgot her to her face. It was, Pearl said warmly, an awful shame and absolutely amoral: Roo was a much more worthwhile person than any of them. Whereupon certain people whose opinions Pearl *did* value, revised them in her favour. It seemed she was vulnerable after all, and could be hurt by hurt and saddened by sadness.

Pearl was abroad on business with pleasure, studying ancient frescos as inspiration for new designs and rattling along the Italian coast in an old Cadillac with a restless American when she was not altogether agreeably surprised by the news in a letter from Rowena. It had followed her from Ancona to Brindisi and from Brindisi to Syracuse and caught up with her in Naples. Recognising the hand and the postmark and being about to drive out to Vesuvius, she put it aside unopened. When she was unpacking in Rome a week later she found it again.

Rowena wrote that she was going to be married, 'quietly', to 'the most wonderful man in the world'. 'Please, please try to come. I know it's short notice, but everything has happened so quickly. It's like a dream. He doesn't want us to wait. He says every day is a gift and our days together are the most precious gift of all. He has been married before, he had to divorce his wife because she wasn't true to him' – What the hell does she mean? raged Pearl – 'so we are being married in a registry office. He is a wonderful person, I can't think what I've done to deserve him. Pearl, you have had so much sorrow in your life, I do so want you to share our joy on our wedding-day –'

The letter was dated over a month ago. 'She was married yesterday!' cried Pearl, and her restless American said, 'Shame you didn't open it before. We could have caught Bastille Day in Paris and gone right on over. I'd like to have seen the registration rites.'

From Italy Pearl went to the States, and thence to Canada, and months passed before she actually saw Rowena in her wedded bliss. She got letters full of references to 'my adored husband', 'our little nest, our home', 'our oneness'. Pearl could have screamed.

She did scream in Manitoba, to the home-loving Canadian who had usurped the restless American. A letter reached her with the news that 'the most wonderful thing in the world' had happened, 'our union is to be blessed – Pearl, I am to become a mother.'

'I don't believe it!' cried Pearl in a frenzy. 'She's not real!'

'Why not?' said the Canadian. 'Why shouldn't she have a baby?'

'That's what I mean, what's wonderful about it? Anyone can get pregnant!'

Rowena Styles had become Mrs Porteous Clay. She called him 'Porty' and surely Pearl could be forgiven the image she put together of a rotund, heavy-natured person, damp to the eye and touch. There was, in the husky air of Manitoba, an obsolescence about the whole thing. Rowena was as old-fashioned as the hills. That sort of innocence belonged to the past. It was ignorance really, and doomed to enlightenment, and Rowena was lucky – or unlucky, whichever way you looked at it – to find someone with whom she could hold on to hers a little longer.

At last Pearl went on the long-projected visit to the Clays' maisonette in Uxbridge. She wasn't bitchy, she always maintained that she had learned what true bitchiness was from the young men who did nursery frescos, but she needed to be right about Rowena. Otherwise it made big nonsense.

'Porty's dying to meet you,' said Rowena. Clay shook Pearl's hand to and fro as if it was a ratchet. 'We've been friends all our lives,' Rowena said to him. 'I can't think why. I mean, why Pearl ever bothered with me. She's so much cleverer than me.' She sounded thankful, but the thankfulness was all to Porteous Clay, for taking her on.

Having finished shaking Pearl's hand, he shoved it back at her. He was uncouth rather than rude. He had the bones of a labouring man and the chalky flesh of a clown. His nose was like a trumpet. He had exophthalmic eyes of woolly grey. Looking into them, Pearl thought she saw an area of unbroken dark between his eyeballs. She hoped – after all, she was fond of Rowena – that it was only an absence of light.

At their first encounter he hardly spoke. Rowena talked for him: it was 'Porty says', 'Porty thinks', 'Porty wants', without his saying or seeming to think, or expressing a preference. The gospel proclaimed, thought Pearl, only half amused. But she could not fail to notice the looks that passed between them. If Rowena referred to him for inspiration she certainly got it, somehow. And he, sitting stacked in his chair, gazed at her and was totally absorbed by the prospect. Held by it, thought Pearl, you could say it *sustained* him.

He was a bad mover, due largely to bad timing. He tended to be too late or too soon. At table he attempted to pass dishes to Pearl as she was in the act of helping herself and things were spilt. Later, out of the same misjudged politeness, he left her struggling into her coat while he went to open the front door and she must either prolong the entry of the wind and rain or go out half-dressed.

There was a vase of marguerites in the middle of the supper-table. Pearl, who thought them smelly, asked nicely if they could be removed. There was a stricken hush, Rowena turned to Clay and he put his hand over hers and said no.

'No?'

'They cannot be removed.' It was the first time he had spoken directly to Pearl.

'I'm sorry, but daisies upset me.'

'Oh Pearl!' wailed Rowena.

'They're not daisies, they're marguerites,' said Clay.

'The smell makes me feel sick.'

'Pearl – they're for our daughter!'

'Your what?'

Rowena, blushing, gathered the flowers to her breast. 'We're going to call her Marguerite.'

'So that's it! Mamma mia, aren't you afraid they'll be dead before she gets here?'

'They are in memory of her,' said Clay.

'You're sure she'll come? I mean, suppose someone else does.'

'Someone else?'

'Porty Junior.'

'Porty wants a girl,' said Rowena.

White, daily, and ox-eyed, thought Pearl: himself in a tender new Rowena package. Happy families. Well, he couldn't lose, not with Rowena. She was glad, for Rowena's sake. 'I don't see how you can remember someone who hasn't yet been.'

'We can remember her as she will be,' said Clay.

Pearl did not see Rowena again until just before the baby was born. She refused several invitations to Uxbridge, on each occasion having something better to do. Almost anything was better to do than listening to Rowena spreading the gospel according to St Clay.

Towards the end of her pregnancy, Rowena went into hospital. There were some complications, and when Pearl visited her she heard about them in detail. Rowena's eyes were dark, but her lips shone. She savoured every whispered word.

'What a pretty paper I could do for the labour-ward,' said Pearl. 'A pattern of fallopian tubes and speculums and sweet pink placentas.'

Rowena flushed, and because of weakness or over-excitement, little tendrils of steam actually curled up from her neck and bosom. Then she laughed, they laughed together, hands over their mouths, spilling and catching the laughter from each other, more than was reasonable or necessary, more than the joke warranted. Rowena was soon exhausted. She fell back on her pillows and closed her eyes.

'Oh Pearl, I do so want you and Porty to love each other.'

Pearl stopped laughing. It seemed to her that she hadn't actually been amused, but that now she was. Privately she was tickled pink. '*Love*, Roo?'

'You are the two people in the world who matter most to me.'

Pearl gazed at Rowena's blank eyelids. The things that happen, she thought, raging, not marvelling, the absurdities and crudities that pass for real. 'He's got you and he'll have Marguerite. He doesn't want me.'

'I'm not clever like you, Pearl –'

Pearl said sharply, 'You're tired. I'd better go.'

'Not yet.' Rowena sat up. 'I want to tell you about Porty.'

He was the last person Pearl wanted to hear about. Almost anyone else – Khrushchev or old Nokomis or the ward-sister – any sister, any ward – would have interested her more.

'He's not like other people,' said Rowena.

Pearl wondered how long it had taken her to be pleased about that. Because she was – gravely, respectfully pleased. She was even grateful. How absurd! When all her life other people had been her criterion and she had sought, faithfully, to be the same. And the joke, of course, the real joke, was that Clay was as ordinary as they came.

'He had such an unhappy childhood,' said Rowena.

'Didn't we all?'

Rowena blinked. 'I didn't. Nor did you.'

'I suffered agonies!'

'Agonies?'

'I used to cry myself to sleep!'

'But you were always so gay –' It was like her to use that word – as if nothing had happened to it. 'Why, Pearl? What was the matter?'

'I was sensitive – raw.'

'I always thought – I didn't know–' Her face had a way of spreading, from singleness to doubt to confusion to broad dismay.

'I grew out of it. Didn't we all?'

'With some things it's the other way round.'

'What things?'

Rowena took a dangerously deep breath. She had big obstructive breasts and now, enriched by motherhood, they brimmed out of her Marks and Spencer's negligé. 'Some things grow into you. He can never forget.'

'He will. Emotionally, men are late developers.'

'He won't talk about it. He says such things are not for my ears. But he dreams about it.'

'Dreams?'

'Nightmares. Oh Pearl, Pearl, I ask myself what did they do to him?'

'His father belted him.'

'His father died before he was born. He was brought up by his uncle.'

Pearl shrugged. 'Well, so he got a few beatings. He probably deserved it. Boys do.'

'His mother was terrified – of her own brother. She couldn't lift a finger. Porty says she was a penitent.'

'A what?'

'She deliberately humiliated herself. She tried to wipe the coalman's boots with her hair and he refused to bring any more coal to the house.'

Pearl sat back and laughed and laughed. She couldn't help it.

'Porty never knew what happiness was until he met me.' Rowena's face glistened, her lips quivered. 'Pearl, that's what he said –'

'Then believe him.' Pearl touched a finger to her lips and transferred the kiss to Rowena's cheek. 'I wasn't laughing at you or at him or his mother. It was the way you said it. Everything's going to be fine, just fine, for both of you.'

Rowena sat up, held on to Pearl's hand. 'Suppose I'm not enough? Suppose he needs more than I can give him to make him forget? After all he's been through –' Rowena's voice rose to a wail. 'Love isn't everything!'

'You're getting morbid.'

'I need you Pearl, and he needs you –'

'If your endearing young charms can't help, how can I?'

'You're clever, and strong. You could get him to talk.'

'About the things that are not for your ears? Don't worry. The baby will take his mind off himself. Walking the floor with Marguerite in the small hours won't leave him so much time for nightmares.'

Clay did not get his ox-eyed daughter. The child was a boy. The day after the birth, Pearl went to the hospital with chocolates for Rowena and a matinée coat for the baby. 'If he hurries he'll catch the tea-interval at the Aldwych,' she said. The Dutch Portuguese who was sharing her flat did not understand the reference.

She found Clay sitting in the corridor outside the ward. He held a bunch of green carnations between his knees and the same sickly colour was in his unshaven cheeks. He looked as if he had slept in his clothes and taken a bath and dried in them.

'You can't go in,' he said. 'They're doing something to her.'

Pearl thought what a disaster he was: physically, mentally, socially, financially. Even the baby was a mistake, for they couldn't afford it. With Porteous Clay sex would not be an experience or a rapture or a purpose or even a sin. Just a mistake, in all senses of the word.

'Congratulations on the birth of your son and heir.'

'She couldn't – they had to –' He flinched. 'They cut her.'

'A Caesarian section? Oh well,' Pearl said cheerfully, 'that would save her a lot of trouble. Caesar wasn't really born that way, you know.'

'Caesar?'

'He couldn't have been. Mrs Caesar lived for years after, and in those days it was only done if a woman died before she could give birth.' Those woolly eyes: Pearl wondered who had pulled the stuff over them in the first place. He couldn't see out and no one could see in. 'That was then. It's different now, it's a technique, used all the time. It's a simple extraction, like having a tooth out. Some women never have their babies any other way.'

'She's going to die.'

'Probably not even so traumatic as having a tooth out. Of course she's not going to die – not yet.'

'I'm going to lose her. Oh my God –' He stared at Pearl as if he saw some old wooden god of his in her face.

'Don't be ridiculous.'

'I can't live without her.'

'You already did,' said Pearl tartly. The complete egotist, she was thinking. It was the only way in which any man was complete. That same morning the Dutch Portuguese had left his underpants soaking in her bath.

A nurse whisked out of the ward. 'You may go in for a few moments.'

Clay stood up and the carnations fell round his feet. He trod on them as he went into the ward.

'She's going to be all right, isn't she?' Pearl said to the nurse.

'Mrs Clay is as strong as a trivet. I hope you aren't going to leave those flowers on the floor.'

The nurse whisked back into the ward, Pearl gathered up the carnations and followed her.

Actually Rowena looked blooming. Like a blown rose, blown in some pure and wholesome way from within. Of course she was entitled to a sense of achievement. Let's admit it, thought Pearl, giving it a passing wave: she's provided the world with another human being which is something it may well become short of at any moment.

'Congratulations, Roo dear.'

'Oh Pearl!' Rowena flung her arms round Pearl's neck.

'Now, now,' said the nurse, 'no tears. We have to think of our milk.'

'What?'

'Pearl, don't laugh,' Rowena said faintly. 'I'd rather cry, it would be less painful.'

'Why do either? You've produced a handsome son, what's sad or comic about that?'

'Daddy's tickled pink. Of course he is,' said the nurse. Clay was standing pressed against Rowena's bed rather as if he had been hit in the back of the knees and couldn't help himself. 'She got it into her head she was going to have a girl and she put it into his head and now they act as if they've been passed the salt and not the sugar.'

'That's absurd,' said Pearl.

'Look, dear, your husband brought these.' The nurse, as she took the carnations out of Pearl's hand, hissed in Pearl's ear, 'Let her think he did. It will give her something to hang on to.'

'He did bring them –'

'Porty wanted a girl.' Rowena smiled shyly at him. Far from being ashamed, she had an air of having produced something a great deal better than he had asked for, and of being ready to justify herself for getting the best.

'You're pleased, of course you are,' Pearl said to Clay. He was gazing at Rowena, his trumpet nose drooping. There'd be no voluntary, thought Pearl, only a feeble toot.

Rowena picked up the green carnations and tried to bury her face in them. 'How lovely!'

'So much nicer than marguerites,' said Pearl. Clay was plucking at Rowena's sheet and it occurred to Pearl that he was the sick and needy one.

'Oh Pearl, you haven't seen him yet. He's beautiful, so perfect, so tiny – yet so grand.'

'Grand?'

'I know it's a funny thing to say about a baby, but he is. Like mountains or monuments – so terribly grand.'

Pearl smiled. 'I'm longing to see him.'

'Babies are not taken up between feeds,' said the nurse. 'Not in this hospital.'

'I don't want to take him up, I just want to look –'

'Try the viewing room.'

'Television?'

'Pearl, there's a glass panel in the wall of the nursery for relatives and friends to look through at the babies.'

'How will I know which is yours?'

'He has the loveliest pink eyelashes –'

'I must ask you to leave,' said the nurse.

'But we've only just come.'

'I'm sorry, the doctor will be here in a moment to examine the patient.'

Clay fell to his knees beside the bed and hid his face. He had said not one word and now he was either going to cry or pray. Rowena tenderly stroked his hair. Pearl watched with interest and the nurse, shocked at the sight of a man on his knees, put out an unprofessional hand and gave him a shove.

'Mr Clay, please get up at once!'

'Poor darling,' Rowena murmured, 'he's worn out with worry.'

At the same moment the doctor appeared in the doorway. The nurse uttered a squawk of alarm and beat round Clay like a clockwork bird. There was a scuffle, Pearl thought she saw the nurse kick his bottom. Clay got to his feet, the nurse scooped up the carnations and the next thing Pearl knew she and Clay and the carnations were out in the corridor.

'They can't allow genuine emotion in here,' said Pearl. 'They'd go under in the flood.' She hoped he wouldn't take it as carte blanche to let himself go when they got outside. 'You needn't worry, you know Roo's going to be absolutely fine. The nurse says she's as strong as a trivet and she's in the very best hands.' Actually Pearl would have felt more confident if the nurse hadn't mixed her metaphor. 'Do you mind if we go and see Porty Junior? Why should you mind? I bet you're dying to go and gloat over him.' In his awful overcoat and the way he had of poking his neck out – she felt she was walking with a giant tortoise.

When they reached the nursery corridor and she looked through the glass panel at the rows of identical cribs she thought Heavens, how clinical! After all that cosy mess in the womb! She asked a passing nurse, 'Which is the Clay baby?'

'What?' The nurse paused, affronted.

'Mr Clay wants to see his baby.'

The nurse tutted impatiently and whirled into the nursery. After a glance along the cribs she pointed to the end one.

Pearl pressed her face to the glass. 'Is that him?' After all, Roo had said the child had pink eyelashes. She would tell the Dutch Portuguese, 'My dear, she's blonde and he's brown and their infant's as red as a fox.'

Turning, she found that Clay wasn't looking through the panel. He was looking at her and it gave her something of a shock. Now he was like a bear more than a tortoise. She could see that violence had been building up in him since they left Rowena's bedside. He was a bear stopped in his tracks. He stood there swaying a little and she began to feel at risk – not as herself, Pearl Schenck, but as an object in his path. She managed to smile, she asked, even while she was asking herself if it was a potentially dangerous question, 'Has your son really got red hair?'

Oddly, it seemed to take the spirit quite out of him. He dropped the carnations in a laundry basket. 'Anything is possible.'

  The boy was to be named Harold. 'Harold Clay?' said Pearl when Rowena told her.

  'After my father. Daddy would have been so proud.'

  'What about Porty's father?'

  'You must never, never mention him.'

  'Why not?'

  'Porty can't bear to talk about him, or about any of his family.'

  'So you said. I believe if I knew why, I'd remember to keep off the subject.'

  'They did something terrible. When I first told him we were going to have a baby he wasn't a bit pleased.' Rowena's eyes rounded. 'He was terrified!'

  'Of being a father?'

  'He won't ever say what happened. He still suffers from the memory of it.'

  'The unhappy childhood syndrome.'

  'Oh Pearl, if you had seen him! I begged him to tell me what was the matter. He wouldn't. He said it would add to my burden and couldn't lessen his. He seemed afraid it might – something might – be communicated.'

  'Perhaps it was.' Pearl needed a cigarette but was stopped in the act of lighting up by a frown and a shake of the head from the nurse. 'Did Porty's father have red hair?'

  'Red hair?'

  'Anyway he died, didn't you say, and an uncle brought Porty up. Was he a ginger uncle, by any chance?'

  'Pearl, I don't know. Why?'

  'It might account for the thing Porty's got about the baby.'

  'Thing?' Rowena's face spread alarmingly from wholesomeness to doubt to confusion and wide open dismay. 'Oh Pearl! You mean he –'

  'Of course I don't. But obviously it's come as a surprise that his son's got red hair.'

  'Red hair?'

  'The nurse pointed him out – a mop like Basil Brush.'

  'But Pearl, he hasn't any hair at all yet.'

  'Then I must have been shown the wrong one. Such inefficiency!' Pearl glared at the nurse's back. 'Does Porty know the baby's bald?'

  'Of course. He saw him right after he was born. We were all three together. Oh Pearl, do you think he minds terribly not having a girl?'

'Of course not,' Pearl said stoutly. 'He's tickled –' she found she had had enough of the word 'pink' – 'he's proud and pleased as Punch. What man wouldn't be? They all want sons.'

'He didn't actually *say* he wanted a girl.' Rowena's eyes were big with honesty. Pearl saw that she believed herself safe. 'He only said it would be different.'

'Different from what?'

'From whatever he –' Too late she saw the pitfall. Promptly she dissolved into tears. 'Oh Pearl! Oh Pearl!'

Pearl had no time to open her mouth. The nurse swooped. 'How often must I tell you not to distress my patient?' Pearl left Rowena being rocked on that crackling bosom.

She had agreed to stand godmother although it would put her under the disadvantage of having a god-relation named Harold. She continued to refer to the 'Clay baby' without admitting the necessity to raise a smile. She would have said there was absolutely no malice in it. Then she found that they spoke of the child as 'Harry'. 'They might just as well have christened him Henry,' she said. 'Harold Clay is such a sequitur, if you know what I mean.' The Dutch Portuguese looked sulky: it was to be the last logical conversation they had. Shortly afterwards they brawled and parted.

From a big bland baby Harry grew to a big affable toddler. His every crease and dimple shone with the milk of human kindness, he was the embodiment of Rowena's own pristine charity before the facts of life spotted it. Pearl made a point of remembering his birthdays and allowed for his development, though she did not actually witness it. She sent teddy bears and cuddly dogs, then building blocks and a cowboy suit, action men and, when he was ten, a model yacht kit.

She was herself occupied with the interior furbishing of a Victorian castle in Wiltshire. It was the home of a prosperous meat-pie manufacturer who was physically and mentally nauseated by meat. He felt the dichotomy between his civilised life-style and its beastly provenance. He could not bridge it. His sensitivity was such that the sight of animal products, however refined and restructured – his own suits and shoes, his wife's handbags, the bone china on his dinner-table, even stringed instruments playing a Haydn quartet – reminded him of steaks and kidneys.

Pearl was sympathetic. How different it would be, she sighed, if he were in the business of making fruit-pies. Apple and apricot, gooseberry and pear were so sylvan. But someone had to cater for the public's carnal appetite and it would be irresponsible and selfish as well as uneconomical to abandon the empire he had built up. Of course, said Pearl, he did not need her to tell him that a man in his position was not answerable for himself alone. There were hundreds, indeed thousands – taking into consideration the eaters, as well as the makers – whose livelihood and happiness were in the production of his meat-pies and he owed it to all of them to learn to live with his sensibility and try to resolve it. Impressed by her perception, he installed her in a suite in the castle.

Pearl and Rowena met occasionally in town. Rowena said that London was no place for a child and tirelessly sought to entice Pearl out to Chiselhurst where they now lived. Pearl countered by urging them to come and stay with her in Wiltshire.

'There's masses of room. Basil's given me the governess's flat in the east tower. It's self-contained but there's a private staircase behind the panelling to the master bedroom. The Victorians liked to get their money's worth.'

Rowena blushed. She had become a little quicker on the uptake. 'I don't know, it's a long way and we haven't a car.'

'There's the train,' said Pearl. 'And you'll like Basil. He's Meadow-Sweet Pies, you know. I mean literally. He owns the whole show and I don't have to tell you he's got a lovely golden crust.'

They came for a weekend. It was not a success. Rowena was intimidated by the castle and confused by Pearl's thirties decor. Clay broke one of her Lloyd Loom chairs. Harry was an identikit schoolboy in grey flannel knickers and one of those awful little soft caps with a badge bearing the words *floreamus igitur* or something like. He was cheerful, good-natured and unimpressionable. Only a male child, Pearl thought, could be at once completely at ease and utterly inelegant. Young Harry managed to combine and make a strength of his mother's innocence and his father's uncouthness. Basil came by after dinner but did not stay long. As he left, he said to Pearl, 'I'll see you tonight,' and Rowena turned to Clay who took her hand and held it protectively to his chest. Pearl was amused and greatly irritated.

The next morning they walked in the castle grounds and while Clay and Harry explored the shores of the lake Rowena said shyly, 'Pearl, I wish you would marry and settle down.'

'Do you?'

'I wish you could know happiness like mine.'

'Well, I shan't. I'm sorry, Roo dear, I haven't your potential.'

Rowena sighed. 'Being clever must take it out of you so.'

'That's the general idea, to take out what's there.'

'Pearl –'

'Look, Roo, you have your life, Porty and Harry, and I have mine –' She extended her hand towards the castle. 'All this, and Meadow-Sweet Pies too.'

'But how long will it last?'

'As long as I want.'

Harry was making engine noises and swooping round Clay with arms outstretched, pretending to be an aeroplane. Clay shuffled round and round on the same spot, keeping the boy in his sight.

Pearl said, 'He doesn't mind, then.'

'Mind?'

'Harry not being a girl.'

Rowena smiled. 'Why, he adores Harry. They have such fun together. Porty's just a boy at heart.'

'More like brothers than father and son?'

Rowena's soft lip trembled. 'Why do you say it like that?'

'Like what? I think it's lovely. Just lovely.' Pearl took her arm and pressed it. When they turned back towards the castle, Clay came lumbering after them. Harry ran, roaring and swooping, towards the lake.

Times changed for Pearl. Her battle with the Meadow-Sweet syndrome began to pall. Basil's sensibilities, she felt, had had their day. It was time he learned to accept the facts. As she said to Take Yamatura who had come down from London with some modern Japanese prints, 'I appreciate the ethics of turtle-soup but I must be allowed to use sable brushes without question. I mean, he doesn't can pine-marten, so why should I have to search my heart every time I paint?'

'Come back to London,' said Take.

Pearl sighed. 'I gave up my flat when I came here. I've nowhere to live.'

'I have very nice apartment,' said Take, taking off his glasses and polishing them. 'Room for very nice lady.'

Subsequently they went to Japan, and Pearl stayed in Tokyo for a year. She came back with a beloved vagabond who wore hand-tattered silk shirts and washed his beard in rosemary-water. They lived in rooms above a bizarrerie which Pearl ran with success in the Fulham Road. The vagabond worked every day on his portrait of himself and had no occasion to leave the flat. Pearl shopped and cooked for them both between selling her bizarreries to provide the money to shop and cook. It was a predictable cycle. In the evenings the vagabond required entertainment and his friends came to the flat bringing Algerian wine which they drank after they had finished Pearl's vodka. She was shrewd enough to know that she had reached the time of life when she was going to have to pay for her fun. She believed she could still afford to discriminate, although eventually, of course, she would just have to take what she could get.

62

She decided that the vagabond was not beloved enough nor fun enough any more. She sold the business at a realistic profit without taking him into her confidence, and moved out one a.m. while he slept, with little more than she stood up in. She had always lived light and she left enough for the vagabond to pawn and stay alive for one week more before he had to take up vagabondage again.

She gambled on the lease of a place under a stand-by demolition order: it might not be demolished before the year 2,000, or the bulldozers might arrive next spring. She went ahead and made it into a profitable, privileged small hotel. She was not yet forty and had no intention of being a Madame: she shared the privileges as well as the profits.

She seldom thought about the Clays. What could she think about such ordinary people? She was incredulous when, one night, Clay turned up. She found him in the foyer of the hotel, hatless, coatless, sitting with his hands between his knees just as he had sat, years ago, in the hospital when Harry was born. The receptionist said that he had asked for 'Mrs Schenck'.

Pearl went over to him. 'Porty?' It was probably the first time she had ever called him by that absurd name. He looked up and she thought that some people are born with a built-in comprehensive minus mark and could never make up the shortfall. 'It's *Miss* Schenck.' The area of dark between his eyes made him less stimulating to meet than a sheep. 'You'd better come in here.' She went into her private sitting room.

It was late, she had had a tiring day and was looking forward to taking the vodka bottle with her into her bath. 'Is anything wrong?'

He said, 'I thought you were married.'

'Mr Schenck married my mother, not me.'

She poured two whiskies, she really did prefer to keep the vodka for her bath.

He drank his at once. He looked disarranged, roughed up, but then he usually did. One could never be sure whether he was under stress as well as socially lacking.

'Why didn't you bring Roo?'

'She doesn't know I'm here.'

'Have you quarrelled?'

'No.' He thrust out the empty glass. Refilling it, she noticed that the knuckles of his other hand, bunched on his knee, shone white. 'It's Harry.'

'Is he ill?'

He shook his head. 'Sometimes I could kill him.'

'Well,' said Pearl, 'I expect every parent says that. But I thought

63

you two got on so well together.' He made a sound between a groan and a sigh and she thought of her bath. Vodka and hot water went so well together, provided, of course, they were kept apart. 'Surely you're not going to let a child get the better of you? If he's disobedient, give him a hiding.'

'I can't.'

'Why not? Didn't you ever get one?'

'He's not disobedient. It's the way he looks at me.'

'He's cheeky? Laughs at you?'

'I never minded that.'

'Well then?'

'He's nearly twelve years old, growing up, and he's beginning to look at me like –'

'Like what?' He was moving his head to and fro, swaying, his whole body denying, refusing something. 'You're not holding his sex against him? As I remember, you wanted a girl.'

'I never meant, I never wanted to have children.'

'Well, everyone makes mistakes. It's up to you not to let Harry suspect he's one of yours.'

'I love Harry.'

As he stared at her along his trumpet nose, his nostrils blown wide, she thought he was going to throw back his head and bellow. 'When in doubt, think what your own father would have done. Oh, but I forgot – you were brought up by your uncle. Good old Uncle Charlie?'

He seized the bottle and helped himself to whisky. 'He was my father.'

'Not your uncle?'

'He was my mother's brother. And my father.'

'Well, well.' Surprised and pleased, Pearl considered that her interest was vindicated. Hadn't she always felt that there was more to him? There had been little enough, in all conscience, to meet the eye. 'Well, well,' she said again. 'Of course it was quite the thing at one time. The ancient Pharaohs married their sisters.'

'He didn't marry her.'

'Bad old Uncle Charlie.' It might explain a few things – the way his features and his limbs refused to co-operate, or even to acknowledge each other. Those woolly eyeballs. It might explain everything. 'Does Roo know?'

'I couldn't tell her.'

'You've told me.'

'You're her friend.'

'Do you want me to tell her?'

64

'No. Unless – if anything happened.'

'What should happen?'

'God help us,' he said, without expectation.

'I think you ought to tell her.' But he sat with his hands palm up and looking at them as if he'd just realised they weren't a pair. 'Are you afraid to? It won't make any difference to her.'

He lifted his eyes. 'I'm afraid, yes. About Harry.'

'Harry? Oh, Harry! I see. I don't think you need worry on that score.' Actually she was thinking that his eyes never let anything through unscrambled. So how did Roo manage, not knowing? 'Harry's genes have worked out. He's a normal, healthy boy.' Of course not knowing was the only way Rowena *could* manage. With her, ignorance was more than bliss, it was the way of life. 'Well, isn't he?'

He shook his head. 'You don't understand.'

'I'm trying to.'

'When he looks at me like *he* used to –'

'Like Uncle Charlie?'

'I could kill him.'

'Just because he takes after his grandfather?'

'You don't understand. I hated him.'

'Your own father?'

'My mother's brother.'

Old, unhappy, far-off things. 'It's time you forgot and forgave. You'd never harm Harry.' Pearl smiled. 'Blood's thicker than water, yours and his must have a higher than usual density.'

A week later, on Harry's birthday, Pearl drove them all to Hindhead. Rowena had packed a picnic lunch and Pearl was to stand tea at the Punchbowl Hotel. Harry sat with her in the front of the car, Clay and Rowena were in the back. Pearl could feel Clay's knees pressing against her seat. When the car hit a bump it was like a personal attack.

'Harry's dying to see the Devil's Punchbowl,' said Rowena. 'I do hope it's still there.'

'Why shouldn't it be?'

'I don't know. They keep building. Pearl, do you remember those lovely gardens we used to walk through on our way to school?'

'The rec.,' said Pearl. 'What times we had in the gardeners' hut.'

'Did you?' Rowena sounded wistful. 'I used to think it was a bad place.'

'The Devil's Punchbowl must be pretty bad,' said Harry.

'Is that why you want to go there?' said Pearl.

'I'm more interested in the gibbet. Where they hanged murderers and witches. I hope that's still there.'

'Afraid not,' said Pearl. 'But there's a stone cross to mark the spot.'

'I do hope it's not going to rain,' said Rowena.

Harry turned in his seat. 'Don't worry, Mum, it's going to be a lovely day.'

Obviously Clay had not yet told Rowena his ugly secret. It would have gone straight from her head to her heart. She was so transparent it would have been possible, thought Pearl, to watch it bolt down her jugular vein and across her thorax. Certainly it would be seen darkening her pretty pink ventricles.

'It wasn't bad, the gardeners' hut. We had a midnight feast in it. There was nothing to eat, but we lit a fire and roasted hyacinth bulbs. They tasted foul.'

'I wasn't asked,' said Rowena.

'Jack Rigby and I stayed the night.'

'Oh Pearl!'

'Can I drive?' said Harry.

'You know you can't.'

'I could if I tried.'

Pearl looked at him sharply. In profile something showed through his pudginess. She was not, at that moment, disposed to like it.

'Darling,' said Rowena, 'promise me you won't try. Not yet.'

'Why?'

'It's against the law –'

'The law!' Harry hooted with derision and in the driving-mirror Pearl saw Rowena, dismayed, turn to Clay. He took her hand.

As they drove through Milford it started to rain. Pearl said, 'Only a shower,' and switched on the windscreen wipers. By the time they arrived at the Bowl it had settled to a steady downpour.

Pearl parked the car just off the road to Hindhead Common. 'It's a nice view. On a clear day you can see Farnham Castle. You'll have to take my word for it.'

Harry peered through the window. 'Where's the Punchbowl?'

'The picnic's off, I'm afraid.'

'Oh Pearl! I've brought egg and cress sandwiches, sausage rolls and coffee and cream buns and chocolate biscuits and a seedless navel for each of us –'

'I have my own navel.'

Harry burst out laughing. Rowena blushed. 'Oh, Pearl –'

'I'll buy us lunch at the hotel and you can eat your navels on the way home.'

'We'll have our picnic in the car. It will be fun!' cried Rowena.

'Does the Devil still use it for punch ups?' said Harry.

'Punch is a drink,' said Clay.

'Some drink. Some bowl. It's full of dirty old bracken.'

'There's a lot of wild life.'

'Can we go and look?'

'If the rain stops.'

Harry drew a grid in the steam on the car window and he and Clay began to play noughts and crosses. Rowena unpacked the lunch. Pearl received a green-whiskered sandwich and a sausage-roll on a cardboard plate. She thought of the gin and lime waiting for her in her little room back at the hotel. 'Why is it that hardboiled eggs smell of sulphur?'

'Oh Pearl! They're quite fresh – I always buy from free-range chickens –'

'It tastes delicious.' Pearl slipped her sandwich into the map pocket on the car door.

The rain stopped. Over Blackdown a sliver of blue appeared. Harry demanded to be shown the gibbet.

'There is no gibbet.'

'Where it used to be.'

'It was up there, just above the bend on the road.'

'Will you come?'

Pearl wound down the window and lit a cigarette. 'I don't think so. I've already seen it.'

'*You* haven't,' Harry said to his father. He jumped out and opened the rear door of the car. Clay seemed to divest himself of the car rather than to get out of it. He stood in the road, his clothes bagging out in the wind. Pearl missed the pressure of his knees in her back.

Harry said to her, 'Are you any relation?'

'What to?'

'That thing up there, that used to be there.'

'How do you mean?'

'Mum calls you a flibbertigibbet.'

'Harry!' cried Rowena.

'It's all right, Mum, just trying to establish the connection.'

'There is no connection,' said Clay. Putting his arm about the boy's shoulders he led him away along the road.

'I suppose I am a flibbertigibbet,' said Pearl.

'Oh Pearl, it's just that you're so unsettled. So alone. I do wish you had someone permanent. Life is so full of meaning!'

'The meaning isn't the same for everyone. I couldn't be happy with your way of life.'

Rowena could be seen reluctantly accepting that. She gazed at Pearl with alarm. 'What could you be happy with?'

'Every day something different.'

'Don't you ever think about the future?'

'Why should I?'

'You're not getting any younger –'

'But I am! Every day. I'll be in my teens soon. Where will it end, I wonder? In the absence of a womb to go back to?'

'Pearl –'

'Look, the sun's shining. I simply must stretch my legs.'

The Bowl was now steaming. Every raindrop blazed. As Pearl started down the track to the bottom she felt the wet heather flick at her ankles. It was still preferable to being confined to the car with Rowena in one of her idealistic moods.

The track was tortuous and she soon decided not to go as far as the bottom of the Bowl. When she came to a small plateau she stopped and looked back. She could not see Clay and Harry on the slope beyond the road, but Rowena was starting to follow her down the track.

She waited. Rowena, momentarily hidden by a bluff of gorse bushes, could be heard unvaliantly descending, with gasps and cries and a rattle of falling stones. It was too bad how she had let herself go. Pearl could honestly claim to look years younger than Rowena and in the final analysis she must feel it. There was such a thing as youth of the spirit. What Rowena had, had always had, was a sort of infantilism, absolutely non-spirituous.

'Bravo!' she called.

Rowena appeared round the bend of the track and scrambled down to join her. Her hat had slipped over one eye.

'Oh Pearl –'

'Take a breather,' said Pearl kindly, straightening the hat.

'It's so beautiful here –'

'Isn't it! Like a pot of cabbage coming to the boil.'

Rowena's bosom swelled. 'I love the country.'

'Of course you do.'

'It's so peaceful –'

'Not really. The noises are different. Bellowing birds and whistling cattle and combine harvesters and electric saws.'

'I love living in the country.'

'In Chiselhurst?'

Rowena's lip stiffened. 'It's the Garden of Kent.'

'Are you happy?'

'Oh it's lovely here. Of course it's wilder, but I love the coun –'

'I mean are you happy all the time?'

'Oh yes! Pearl, aren't you?'

'No, thank God.'

Rowena's face blurred, it was surprising how quickly her features lost what identity they had. 'I never thought, when we were girls together – you were so pretty and clever, I always thought you'd be the one to marry and be happy ever after.'

'My dear Roo, that is, or was, strictly for children. And even they won't swallow it nowadays. In any case it's humanly impossible and socially undesirable. And being happy ever after is definitely not a corollary of getting married.'

'Oh Pearl –'

'On the other hand, I can't think of anything more awful than total, unalloyed, permanent happiness. If that's what the old fairy-tales were getting at, they're smarter than we thought.'

Rowena's face had dissolved into anonymity, a general statement of dismay.

Pearl laughed. 'I'll go back to the car and fetch a rug. We might sit here, it looks like being a nice afternoon.' She left Rowena without another glance – one more would have overtaxed her patience – and started back up the path.

'Oh Pearl!'

She did not stop. Absurd as it seemed, she felt obliged to put distance and time, if only a few minutes, between Rowena and herself. It was not Rowena's reaction, predictable and simply tiresome, that bothered her: it was her own. She sensed a discrepancy, and more than that she was not prepared to admit to. Women, as a sex, were penalised. They carried around a lot of outdated instincts and unlocalised fears: one simply could not answer for the way one was put together.

When she reached the car she picked up the rug but decided not to go back with it immediately. Whether she liked it or not, she had to accept that she had some aboriginal tendencies.

An awful thought occurred to her. If her personality, her Pearlness could be boiled out, would she be qualitatively the same as Rowena? Quantitively – oh there must be a difference in degree!

She lit a cigarette and leaned against the car. The strip of blue sky had widened, a noisy biplane was labouring from cloud to cloud. She heard nothing else until the sound of footsteps on the road. She turned and saw Clay running towards her. He was hatless, his hair stood up as if with fright. When she saw his face rocking and rolling on his shoulders she remembered how she had thought that it never showed anything of his emotions. What it showed now was a fight, raging as he ran. He, it seemed, was trying to run from it. His chest laboured, wolfing the air, she heard it rasping in his throat. He ran towards her, not looking where he was going nor expecting, she could see, to arrive.

She was unsurprised when he passed her and the car without a glance and pounded away along the road. An approaching motor-cyclist swerved to avoid him. The rider's heel struck sparks in the grit. Clay ran on, over the brow of the hill. 'Get himself killed!' shouted the motor-cyclist as he roared past Pearl.

She thought not, on this exposed stretch of the road. There might be more brakings and some frayed nerves, but for a mile or more visibility was good.

She looked up at the scrub on the higher side and saw Harry jumping down into the road. He too ran towards her, cramming his cap into his jacket pocket.

'I say, have you seen Dad?'

'What's happened?'

'Did he come this way?'

'Yes.' Pearl held him by his coat tail as he made to run past her. 'Tell me what happened.'

'Nothing. Well almost nothing. We found the sailor's stone – you know, the sailor came off his ship at Portsmouth with a pocketful of money, all his pay –'

'Why was he running?'

'You'd run if there were a couple of murderers behind you.'

'I mean your father.'

'Dad? He was just fooling.'

'No.'

'We were fooling about up there. Look, I'm meant to go after him!'

'No. Wait.'

'We were laughing – not about the poor old sailor. About you, as a matter of fact.'

'Me?'

'You and the roast hyacinths.'

'I've never seen him laugh,' said Pearl. 'I didn't think he could.'

'Of course he can.' Harry blinked up at her, his fringe of hair pricking his eyelids. 'You don't like my dad.'

Pearl frowned. 'I think he's someone you have to like a lot, or it's no use. Do you know what I mean?'

'You mean you don't like him.'

'I can't accept him. Harry, something happened to make him run away from you. What was it?'

'He wasn't running away from me. We were laughing and he just went.'

'Laughing about me. How did he look?'

Grinning, Harry made two rings with his thumbs and forefingers and held them up to his eyes. 'He just looked.'

70

'Did he say anything?'

'No. Can I go and find him?'

'I'll do that. Take this rug to your mother. She's waiting down there on the hillside.'

She got into the car and switched on the ignition. As the engine fired she glanced through the window. Harry stood with the rug bundled in his arms and on his face an irrelevant look. It was not relevant to a schoolboy or to anyone she knew – or would want to know. And it passed so swiftly she felt that she had surprised it as much as it had surprised her.

'Bring him back!' shouted Harry.

As Pearl said to herself as she drove away, 'Better not.'

Watch It

At the beginning of February Reresby retired from his job as Chief Clerk to a firm of ships' brokers. He had been with them for fifty years. The change in his circumstances was immediately and chiefly remarkable between 8.00 and 9.30 a.m. and 5.00 and 6.30 p.m. Reresby remarked it then because those were the times he had commuted between his office and his home.

He continued to rise at the same hour each morning and to eat breakfast with the *Financial Times* propped against the black salt-glaze teapot. Afterward he went to his room instead of walking to the station. He sat at his desk and wrote as he always had in his office, the index finger of his left hand supporting his temple. He was taking a correspondence course in Local Government and another in Law. These subjects did not especially interest him, they were chosen as a discipline rather than an education.

His wife brought him coffee at eleven and tea and biscuits at four. At one o'clock he laid aside his pen and ate sandwiches while he essayed the crossword. Just as he always had done. The arrangement was convenient, leaving Mrs Reresby, who had not retired, free to do her work about the house. They were accustomed to dining at night and neither of them wished to change to doing so in the middle of the day. But when spring came in the second week of April Reresby instituted a slight variation. He took a stroll each morning for the sake of his health.

Their house backed on a shabby municipal heath called The Plats. For most of the natural year the vegetation did not appear to be growing so much as planted, in the sense of having been strategically placed. The bushes looked as unalive as they did on the plastic model of the terrain in the Borough Surveyor's office.

But at the beginning of spring even The Plats was sensitized, even the impermeable grass and the petrified trees, and there was tenderness about the bus-tickets and bottle-tops, in the scrupulous light they were a kind of flora. Reresby tended to think of them thus, he was not a nature-lover, to him the countryside was an under-privileged area.

He took a walk each morning, the weather being clement. After the second week in April it could be expected to remain reasonably so. He walked on The Plats because it was convenient to open the door in the wall of his garden and step on to the grass. He found it pleasant, which was a small bonus – he did not as of right anticipate pleasure.

He had often been on The Plats in the past, he knew the paths to the telephone kiosk, the bus-stop, and the Star of India. In winter they were a dirty walk.

Mrs Reresby called The Plats ' a waste land' and Reresby agreed. Asked to what use the land should have been put she would probably have said that it would have made 'a nice park'. Reresby would have deliberated, seeing the reverse side of each advantage. Not caring for lawns and flower-beds nor wanting to be overlooked by houses or deafened by traffic he would probably have said it should never have been left unmade. He believed unquestioningly that pavements were progress.

For the sake of his health he walked with shoulders back, chest out, arms swinging, as he had been required to do on parade. He recalled the Sergeant-Major bawling, 'You're free men, you bastards, free as the skin on a sausage, but by God you're going to move like clockwork!'

There were definite signs of life on The Plats. The bushes clinging like grim death to the rusty ground put out mitres of green, the blackthorn blossomed all over as if it were wreathed in steam. And once Reresby heard the cuckoo, just two or three 'cucks' and an 'oooo', but recognizable. When he mentioned it to his wife she said he must have heard someone fooling about.

'Must have?' He did not accept the imperative. Yet how was he to explain the airiness the sound had intimated to him? Or that it was the pure absurdity which had caused him to smile?

'No self-respecting cuckoo would come to The Plats,' said his wife.

He sometimes paused by the pond. He found the pleating of the water comforting and was surprised because there could hardly be anything more pointless than the wind ruffling this large puddle. Perhaps the absence of point and of any conclusion accounted for the comfort? At his age – and constantly reminded as he now was – suggestions of immortality, even in a puddle, were comforting. It was nice to think that even after sixty-five years he didn't know, and that the cuckoo was not a respectable bird. Should he call it a-respectable?

His thoughts had never tended so erratically. Having so much more time to think he trusted that his mind was merely flexing itself for the task.

But the little girls were more than a bonus of pleasure. He supposed – he preferred to – that other people did not see them. Or did not see them as he did. They were a private, secret joy, and there was no need to share it, nor any means of doing so.

There had been a bad moment when Varenna realised that she was not invited, that Claude, aged six, was to go alone. Varenna's cheeks burned.

'It doesn't become you to make a scene,' she was warned.

Why was it never becoming nowadays to do what she was about to do? Life was getting impossible to live up to.

'You're a big girl and must learn to contain your feelings.'

She was fit to burst with her feelings, it was all she could do to keep from flying apart. Surely a scene was preferable to a burst child?

Claude said, trying to put things right, 'I shall have to wear my accordion dress and you know I don't like it.'

'You'd have to anyway, whether I came or not.'

'It's Claude's birthday and only Claude's. Great-grandmamma wishes to honour her.'

'When it was my birthday everyone went!' cried Varenna. 'Even Daddy!'

Her mother nodded. 'It was appropriate. Remember, you're the eldest. Now go and call for Christabel and come back here, all of you, for biscuits and milk at eleven.'

Claude said as they went into the garden, 'Proprate? Is that why we had fish?'

'Don't try to change the subject. I can imagine the scene! You and Great-grandmamma at that enormous table. Will she put you at the opposite end, or beside her? How ridiculous!'

'I shan't mind if we don't have fish.'

'What will you talk about? You're such a child. In the awful silence you'll sound like a little horse munching. Promise me you won't eat a rusk.'

'Remember,' their mother called, 'you're not to speak to strangers.'

'Great-grandmamma keeps the rusks for herself.'

Varenna put back the hair from Claude's forehead. 'It will be awful for you, poor baby.'

'Will I have to say prayers?'

'You'll have to say grace. "Give us this day our daily bread and make us truly thankful . . . ." And Claude, Great-grandmamma really means you to be.'

'I wish you were coming!'

'Then we'd both have to eat fish.'

Christabel, their cousin, lived next door and was waiting in her garden. Claude ran to her crying, 'I'm to go to lunch with Great-grandmamma! All by myself!'

Christabel's brows shot up into her fringe. 'What for?'

'For my birthday!' Claude cried impatiently. 'Isn't it wonderful?'

'It's mad!'

'I assure you our Great-grandmamma is absolutely sane,' Varenna said coldly.

'But what will they talk about?'

'About Claude of course.'

They passed in silence through the garden door to The Plats. People chalked on the other side of the wall and each morning they looked to see if there was anything new.

'What is "National Pot"?' said Christabel.

'Ask me when you're older.' It was a reply which Varenna had herself been given and now found useful. She also found that Claude's advancing years advanced her own and said percipiently, 'It's her birthday, she'll be six years old and Great-grandmamma will talk about her future.'

Claude felt alarmed. The future was a capacity in which she foresaw she would either not be herself or would be herself in constant difficulties. She could not imagine coping, as Varenna did, beautifully. If Great-grandmamma offered her a future would she have a choice? Could she refuse it and remain as she was? She was so afraid that talking about it would not mean taking or leaving it but taking it only. Great-grandmamma had a way of piling herself up when annoyed and looking down from the top.

'Does she know what she wants to be?' said Christabel.

They often spoke of Claude as though she were not present. Sometimes it made her feel more important, sometimes less.

'She can't be anything, except a secretary or a nurse. She has no talents, we don't hear her playing the piano or see her painting pictures –'

'I do paint pictures!'

'They'd have to be marvellous at your age and they're not. Great-grandmamma will tell her what to do.' Varenna used Claude's shoulder to help her get up on her toes and added calmly, 'Of course, you don't have to do it.' Claude was startled and relieved. 'Now I'll show you the dance of the little swans.'

They ran to the edge of the pond, lifting their knees, fluttering their hands, and laying their cheeks on their shoulders.

They appeared to have no viable connection with the world. They were simply there or not there by the tilted white water when Reresby looked. It became a conviction of his that they did not exist anywhere else. If he regarded them as coming between fairies and angels it was because they were outside his experience, outside his concepts, even. For when had he conceived such something and nothing?

Mrs Reresby asked why he had such a fancy for The Plats. 'You used not to like the place much, what do you do there?'

'Do?'

'You could walk all round it in twenty minutes, and you're gone for more than an hour every morning.'

He told her the truth. 'I watch the children playing,' and thought what an under- in fact non-statement it was, and pitiably dull.

She pitied him. 'Poor dear, you miss George and Connie. Never mind, they'll be here at the weekend.'

Reresby smiled to himself, though with compunction because he loved his children.

At first he had been a little affronted, he considered it a frivolous and irrelevant pleasure and of no benefit. Sitting was not as beneficial as walking and what was to be learned from the antics of these little creatures?

Only that he had an idle side to his nature.

Afterwards, at his desk or as he was falling asleep he would see with his inner eye a vision of them so radiant and faultless that he was humbled. He knew then that he was receiving what his unconscious wit had sought, a straw to grasp and stay afloat on.

'The man's here.'

'What man?'

'The man on the seat. There, that's enough dancing,' said Christabel. 'Let's look for primroses.'

'Here?' But Varenna ran as hopefully as the others to a glimmer of yellow under an elder bush.

'It's banana peel!'

Sometimes they saw clouds like elephants in the water of the pond and this had led Claude to respect it. She was the only one still at the assiduous phase of making-believing. The other two gave her goblins lip-service, their own were different now.

Joining hands they circled the pond and Claude gravely chanted, 'Monster, monster, monster, don't come out and eat Venna and me and Christabel.'

'You silly, what else can it eat?'

'And it has to have very *little* girls because it has a weak stomach.'

Claude cried, 'It won't eat me because I know about it!' Their voices came to Reresby much as the voices of clocks come from another room. He might, with a little effort, have identified what they were saying, but was content to catch the sound through the thunderous Spring breeze. Their cries descended or floated away and sometimes seemed to come out of his head – something which he remembered or wanted to hear.

He could not remember seeing anything like them before but he had undoubtedly wanted to. Through a long life he must have wanted to see them and grown tired of waiting. And when it was over, even though he couldn't say to anyone, 'What about *that*, then?' it was going to justify all the brown years.

He didn't particularly like children and he hadn't liked being a child. It seemed to him a tedious way of procuring adults. George and Connie had been – well, children, with jam on their faces. He was relieved when they grew up.

These little creatures would grow up, too, and no one would remember how perfect they had been. He might forget, but he would always know that perfection was possible.

Connie, at the weekend, asked how he liked retirement.

'I find plenty to do.'

'We haven't changed our routine,' said Mrs Reresby. 'It keeps us in trim.'

'If it was me,' said Connie, 'I'd turn routine upside down. How else can you be free?'

Reresby smiled. 'There are other ways.'

'Your father takes a walk each morning.'

'Everything has its price you always say, don't you, Dad?'

Reresby had said that and at first, at the very first, it was a challenge. Then an assurance and, latterly, an inescapable fact.

'You've certainly paid,' said Connie. 'Fifty years hard labour! But how awful if you never *feel* free.'

Reresby reflected that 'freedom' must be the most overworked word in any language. It was also the most ambiguous – to a nonsensical degree – but for want of better it must be the word for what he was experiencing.

You could call it something else, he told himself, knowing full well that he couldn't, with only broker's terminology to do it in. He couldn't define or even confine his experience because the white water and the clear air and the very season were part of it.

So was the lack of time, knowing that each day might be the last and could equally well have been the first because one glimpse would have sufficed. And should have, as it turned out. What was he doing every day? Not stocking up glimpses or getting clearer ones; he was just being greedy and eating them up with his eyes.

Christabel knew that she was being eaten. People often looked at her and she liked it, when faces turned to her she felt like the sun.

But this old man! 'He has no right to stare at us so.'

'He's not doing any harm. What harm could an old man like that do?'

'Old men and rabbits have nasty habits,' sang Christabel, lifting the hair from her neck with a gesture which enchanted Reresby.

Claude was talking about her birthday lunch. To her surprise she had enjoyed it, every minute, even saying grace which Great-grandmamma had seconded with a loud 'Amen!' When Claude arrived home and Varenna asked her, 'Poor baby, was it awful?' she had said proudly, 'I had a lovely time!' at which Varenna smiled, 'Silly baby, no one would blame you,' and turned away, leaving Claude checked and puzzled.

'We had eggs in pockets for our lunch,' she told Christabel.

'She means *oeufs aux poches*.'

'I mean eggs in pockets! Great-grandmamma said so.' Claude added out of consideration for Christabel, 'Of course they're not really.'

'You had them because that's Great-grandmamma's favourite lunch.'

'It's mine too. Then I had banana and chocolate ice-cream and Great-grandmamma had plonk.'

Christabel burst out laughing and Varenna cried irritably, 'What? What?'

'That's what Great-grandmamma said it was.'

'Great-grandmamma this, Great-grandmamma that – can't you talk about anything else?'

Claude couldn't, not yet. 'She gave me this.' She showed Christabel a brooch shaped like a butterfly with wings of iridescent blue. 'They're real butterfly's wings and Great-grandmamma says it's exting. That means there aren't any more.'

'It's beautiful!' cried Christabel. 'Isn't it beautiful!'

'It's my first piece of jewellery Great-grandmamma says. She says when I grow up I shall have lots more, pearls and diamonds and rubies –'

'She says anything!'

'And if I keep them next to my skin they won't run away like money and friends. . . .'

Christabel laughed and with instinct laid the blue brooch on a strand of her corn-gold hair.

'I'll never be poor, Great-grandmamma says –'

'Great-grandmamma, Great-grandmamma!' mocked Christabel. 'You little parrot, how can she possibly know?'

Reresby wondered what they were talking about. They constantly drew together and as constantly parted, with an aerial motion which he must have seen somewhere else though not, he thought, in anyone else. Such gestures were beyond grace, which had to be achieved, where the defect had to exist to be made good. These creatures had but the perfect way of doing anything.

Varenna, turning to join Christabel and Claude, made them momentarily a heart, a knot, a flower in Reresby's not very long sight, with an eye of blue and gold at its centre.

'My Great-grandmamma is nearly ninety years old,' Varenna said statelily to Christabel, 'and we expect her to know more than you.'

Vindicated and, she thought, authorised, Claude joyfully re-possessed her brooch. 'I shall wear it on my skin!'

She held it against her forehead and to Reresby it was a blazing blue wound between her eyes.

Varenna said, 'It ought to have been given to me.'

They became still, Christabel's hand stayed half-way through her gesture of lifting and spreading the long hair on her neck. They stared at Varenna but neither of them was as surprised as she.

Why had she said that? She supposed because she thought it a little. She heard herself say, 'I'm the eldest and should have it,' with alarm, as if her body was acting independently and awfully and had come out in sores.

Claude shut her fingers over the brooch. She was beginning to feel dismay, to go soft. Claude's way was to melt and then harden into despair. Claude's despair was impregnable.

Varenna knew this, yet she could say, 'Great-grandmamma intended me to have it.'

'Oh, Venna,' said Christabel.

Varenna was shocked too. She didn't understand herself, she didn't even like the brooch, she thought it rather common. Claude's eyes beseeching her strengthened her disgust.

'As the eldest I have a right to it. Give it to me.'

Claude, at the soft nadir of dismay, opened her hand and let Varenna take it.

'I don't think you should do that,' said Christabel. 'I think you should let her keep it.'

'I don't care what you think.'

Varenna did not know why she did these things when she so hated doing them. It was as if she had to drag into the light something in herself which was only just there, which other people wouldn't have mentioned, wouldn't have owned to.

'The beastly thing's mine now.' She stabbed it into the collar of her coat.

Then Claude despaired. She wept for her loss and for the injustice which crushed her, but mostly she wept for Varenna. That, she knew, was grave. She opened her mouth and bawled. Reresby was too shocked to get up and retreat from the sound.

79

'Venna, give it back,' urged Christabel. Varenna, looking at herself in the pond, thought that there was a monster in it after all.

Claude put her heart into her weeping, in fact her heart seemed to be flying out of her bosom with every breath. She let it fly, it would have choked her to keep it.

Reresby saw and heard but could not leave now that it had gone wrong any more than when it was perfectly right. He had to stay while the child pitilessly demolished it.

The sounds of her distress carried across The Plats to her mother in their garden behind the wall. She hurried out, concerned because this was no burst of rancour but a torrent of feeling.

And it alarmed her when she came in sight of the group and saw that neither of the older girls was making any effort to comfort Claude. Varenna who was always so good and kind to her – it was somehow ominous that Varenna was not looking at the child but was calmly gazing across the pond.

'Claude! What is it? Whatever's the matter?' Claude was now misshapen with tears like a candle that has guttered and spread in its wax. 'Tell me what's upsetting you, my darling!'

Claude turned her face to Varenna whence her help usually came.

The mother looked from her niece to her elder daughter. 'You know what it is?'

Christabel gazed at her shoes. Varenna, as she turned away, took the brooch from her coat and dropped it into the pond.

Claude was gathered into her mother's arms, her tears dried and the hair put away from her crumpled face. 'Tell me all about it.'

It was impossible. Claude could not tell her mother, she could never tell anyone. She didn't really know what Varenna had done, except end the world.

'Did something frighten you?'

Claude was still frightened, she hid her face in her mother's shoulder.

'What was it?'

What could Claude say? That the ground had opened? And that so far as she could see it was never going to close again? She would at once have been asked who opened it. Varenna was not looking at her, even to warn her to say nothing. Varenna kept her face averted, she had deserted Claude, abandoned her to that future which Claude could not cope with.

'You must tell me!'

Claude saw that she must. 'Him!' she cried wildly, and her mother, looking round, saw Reresby on his bench, watching, stooping forward because he was anxious and did not want to miss anything. 'It was that old man!'

Her mother set her down and knelt before her. She took Claude's hands. 'What did he do?'

Claude was telling a lie but she thought, she hoped, that if she told it hard enough it might true. 'It was him!'

'What did he *do?*' She was held and ungently shaken for an answer. 'Tell me what he did!'

Claude, who could think of nothing more to tell, cried 'Nasty rabbits, oh nasty rabbits!' and wept because her powers of invention had so soon run out.

Dragons

The morning after they came back to Paris from their honeymoon he told her that Sunday lunch was *en famille*.

'Every Sunday?' she asked.

'To Maman,' he said, 'it would seem like the end of the world if we were not all at her table at twelve o'clock to eat the meal she has been preparing since daybreak.'

'Daybreak!'

'It is a tradition.' He smiled. 'You will see, you will eat well.'

He did not ask her if she minded conforming, and on that first day she did not mind. She wanted to belong. She went, joyfully, to Sunday lunch with the Villeneuves.

The family was not rich, but they were in good circumstances. The parental apartment was the major portion of a big house in Vincennes. It was furnished with a useful mix of heavy old sideboards and wardrobes, cane chairs and an imperishable Brussels carpet as bright and chaste, they said, as the day it was put down, thirty years ago.

The kitchen was stone-floored and iron-barred like a strong-room. It was indeed the room of a special sort of strength, for in the small hours of Sunday the red light on the cooker glowed like an altar lamp and the sacrament began.

Dedicated and alone, Madame Villeneuve worked through vegetables and fruit, ribs, legs, hearts, livers, eggs, butter, cream, to fill the family stomach. And every Sunday, so that the world should not end, the family went to lunch.

When they had been married a month – a month of Sundays, Caroline said, 'Couldn't we not go? Just for once?'

It was rash, it was foolhardy, and she saw the folly of it as soon as she had spoken. Not that Pierre was angry, or even surprised. He simply said they must go.

'Why must we?'

'Because I am hungry. Besides, Cousin Bertrand is coming today.'

At least two facts emerged from that, facts which Caroline had hoped would cease to exist if she did not admit their existence. First, Pierre was unaware of her finer feelings which were, she sometimes thought, so fine as to be positively rare; she wept, since she could not laugh, at her own absurdity.

The other was, in its way, just as heavy with disaster: Pierre was

82

not getting enough to eat. He was obliged to go to his mother for the kind of meal he was used to and had a right to expect. The kind of meal his wife could not give him.

She tried, was always trying, but she couldn't cook, she couldn't even cater. She forgot to buy what was needed or she bought things she did not need and which would not marry in any recipe. Like green peppers and vanilla pods.

Her own mother had warned him, 'You French are so practical.'

'You English are not?'

'Yes, but someone like Caroline, with no earthly idea . . .'

'I shall be practical for us both, then.'

'Caroline has a very small appetite,' concluded her mother, not thinking it necessary, or expedient, to pursue the subject. She was not to know that Caroline was marrying into a family which assembled every week as a solemn ritual, to consume a huge meal, elaborately prepared and presented.

Pierre, too, had tried. The first time Caroline was obliged to confess that there was no bread in the house but there was cake, he laughed and called her his Marie Antoinette. The next time, he pulled a face and said, 'Is there a famine? Is there a war?' He told her, 'You have been dreaming again.'

It was true, she did dream. Or rather, she stopped thinking coherently, stopped putting two and two together and let things add themselves up. Sometimes they subtracted and she was left with a beautiful simplicity. Encounters confused her: people in shops, in the street. She sensed complexities she could not control and possibilities she dared not explore.

She had come to dread all encounters because of the one inexorable, annihilating encounter, Sunday lunch at the Ville-neuves'. She could not tell Pierre. He was sure that his family had fallen in love with her, as he had.

'Bertrand doesn't like me,' she said, on the fifth Sunday.

'He adores you. They all do.'

It would have been enough if they would just let her be. All she wanted was to be taken for granted.

Outside his parents' house Pierre extended an impatient hand, as to a dawdling child, 'Dreamer!'

She wasn't actually dreaming at that moment, she was casting about for something to think of through the long hours ahead, a charm, a saving grace. And there came to her a strange and lovely thing she had seen days before.

Slowly, along the Cours la Reine, writhing, thrashing, rearing, and still as the dead, had come dragons. They glided under the trees, breaking the lower leaves with their horned heads, their eyes upturned, blind as eggs. In the reflected light from the river their scaly skins seemed to ripple, and the great combs to rise on their necks. They were the colour of honey, carved out of sandstone, bright and warm and blunted with age. They rode on a lorry which turned and crossed the bridge. She had stood entranced, watching them sink out of sight among the traffic.

'Maman will make an onion tart,' said Pierre. 'It is Bertrand's favourite.'

'Pierre, have you ever seen a dragon?'

'Certainly. You must never say to Maman that I criticise her onion tart.'

'But Pierre – a dragon? Really?'

He lifted her chin. 'And do not speak of it before Bertrand.'

How to describe, let alone justify, her emotions as she entered the house? Who would believe that without enemies or enmity she could feel so threatened? That on Friday and Saturday, even on Monday, she panicked because there was only one day in the week? Because all the other days led to it, and before her was a lifetime of Sundays.

However engaged she was in the kitchen, Madame Villeneuve always welcomed the members of her family as they arrived. She came to the door, as impeccably turned out as if she had been free to spend hours on her toilette. It quite unnerved Caroline.

'Caroline, how pretty you look. But so pale. You are like a wand.' They touched cheeks.

There was no nonsense about aperitifs, the Villeneuves' appetites did not need stimulating. On the stroke of twelve they moved, as one, to the table. Madame Villeneuve took one end, Monsieur Villeneuve, solid as a sofa after years of her cooking, the other; between sat their two sons, their son's wives, their daughter and her husband, and the son of Madame Villeneuve's sister.

Bertrand had an affliction of one eyelid, causing it to droop and to give him a leer which was far from his nature. He was a cold, contained man. He brought his lawyer's manner to the table, invariably approving, but accepting nothing without due deliberation.

The ritual began. Bertrand inserted a corner of his napkin between his throat and his collar. Caroline was dismayed to find that he was seated next to her. He draped the napkin across his waistcoat to ensure maximum protection.

'Do you wish to be disembarrassed of this?'

He indicated Caroline's handbag which was balanced in her lap.

'Oh no!' She held on to the bag with both hands. One day it would surely happen, someone would take away the only thing that stood between her and disaster. If they only knew what she carried in her bag! The food that she could not eat, the pasties, terrine, pancakes, gateaux, she shovelled, under cover of the tablecloth, into her English handbag . . . and smuggled away. She wept for shame every Sunday evening when she shut herself in the bathroom and flushed the mess down the lavatory.

She had to choose between this private shame and public dishonour. Sunday lunch was a sacrament partaken of by all the family. It would be considered heresy and a direct insult to Madame Villeneuve to leave anything edible on one's plate. Once, Caroline had left a spoonful of rice and a lengthy inquest had followed.

Madame Villeneuve ladled soup as Pierre announced, 'I think we shall go to Morez to ski.'

It was the first Caroline had heard of it. But Pierre often chose to announce his intentions at the Sunday lunch. She was used to not being consulted; it was not being told that made her disconsolate and unhappy.

'But you've never been skiing,' said Henry.

'I shall take lessons. I shall learn. You will see, I shall fly free as a bird!'

Caroline tried to believe that there had been nothing to tell until the family gave their approval: if they condemned there was nothing doing and no need to mention it anyway. She convinced herself that in any event she must be the last to know.

'Caroline is not eating her soup,' said Madame Villeneuve.

She would have to, of course. Soup could not be carried away in a handbag.

'Will Caroline learn?' asked Monique, and Pierre said quickly, 'Of course. She has a natural aptitude.'

Had she, wondered Caroline. For what? For freedom? Was that what he meant?

'It would be wise to insure yourselves against accident and fatality,' said Bertrand.

'Doubtless it will be an experience to walk like penguins,' said Madame Villeneuve, and with a gesture called in the empty soup plates. 'One must experience in youth in order to reflect in maturity.'

'Who wants to reflect on a broken collar-bone?'

'I shan't break my collar-bone,' Pierre said firmly. 'I shall break the pure white snow. I shall soar like a lark and swoop like an eagle. That will be something to reflect on.'

'Caroline, we are waiting for you to finish your soup.' In the last spoonful was a slice of leek. She dared not leave it, although she hated leeks.

Madame Villeneuve carried away the soup plates and returned with a tray on which was a fire-red dish and piles of toast.

Bertrand raised his brows and touched his lips with his napkin. 'What have we here?'

'A little pâté de campagne,' said Madame Villeneuve.

Across the table Pierre smiled at Caroline. He was pleased about the skiing. She hadn't known that he wanted to soar like a lark and swoop like an eagle. The family discussed Monique's new job, as a fashion buyer. The pâté was delved into, spread, received and welcomed on the tongue. They raised their voices above the crunching of toast. Caroline managed to slip her portion into her bag but the pâté clung to her fingers. She sensed a distaste which was not her own. Looking up, she saw Bertrand's empty eyelid.

The next dish, a salad, was brought to the table and Madame Villeneuve announced: 'To cleanse the palate.'

'Chablis will do it better.' Monsieur Villeneuve filled up the glasses.

'Caroline should eat red meat and plenty of green salad. And take liver extract every day.' Madame Villeneuve had apparently reached this conclusion and was instructing Pierre. 'She is too pale.'

'Maman, she has good health.'

'But no substance.'

Neither of them looked at Caroline. Pierre smiled as if recollecting her. 'She will not become gross, she is a little string person.'

'She must not have little string children,' said Madame Villeneuve sternly.

'Caroline is silent.' Monique, who dared to smoke between courses, lit a cigarette. 'We talk so much she can never get a word in.'

'*Enfin*, she is stringy and pale and silent, so what have you done to her, Pierre?' said George.

'Caroline will speak when she is ready.'

'We are ready.' Monique blew a smoke ring.

'Perhaps she has nothing to talk about.'

'She has as much as any of you.' Pierre frowned.

'Why shouldn't she have?'

'Caroline, *ma petite*,' Madame Villeneuve spoke kindly, 'tell us what you have been doing.'

Now they were all gazing at her: Monique smiling, Berthe chewing, Pierre anxious, Bertrand with his wide-open eye. It was her nightmare, the moment when they all, simultaneously, became aware of her. At that moment, as Madame Villeneuve said, she had no substance. She felt it drain away.

'She has been shopping,' said Pierre. 'We went to that big –'

'Let her tell us,' said Monique.

There must be something she could say to stop them staring at her. If she said she had done nothing they would shrug and smile and afterwards Pierre would say, 'Couldn't you at least try?'

She tried. She said, 'I saw dragons.'

'Dragons!'

Why had she said that? Because she hoped the word would be enough and the family would be charmed, would turn away, dazzled.

'Dragons?'

Across the Sunday lunch the beautiful gallant ghosts appeared. Of course it was the very word to hold their attention. Only a small explosion could possibly distract them now.

'Where?'

'They were going along the Cours la Reine.'

'Walking?'

'Dragons don't walk, they undulate!'

'They were on a lorry.'

'A lorry!'

'Were they breathing fire?'

'They were stone dragons.' Their ghosts, having hovered briefly, vanished, and she could not describe how beautiful they were because she could not now remember her joy in them.

'Caroline is young for her age,' observed Berthe.

'So are all women.' George grinned. 'But they usually choose to be too old for fairy-tales.'

Caroline bent her head, afraid she was going to cry and be seen crying. She groped in her bag, pulled out a handkerchief and with it a piece of toast. A lump of pâté sprang greasily into Bertrand's lap.

In that hollow moment she heard, she could swear, the small explosion she had wished for – fixing, not distracting, the family's attention on her. And she remembered that dragons are monsters. They had bewitched her with their seeming beauty, the dragons had engineered this squalid fate.

Their magic in the Cours la Reine had brought down upon her the Villeneuves' derision, and Pierre's humiliation. The family would never forget and he would never forgive.

She looked up into the pewter eye under Bertrand's drooping lid. She heard Madame Villeneuve say, 'Caroline has imagination. That also is a natural aptitude.'

Bertrand stirred, and with thumb and index finger took up the morsel of pâté, grey and slightly sweating. He placed it at the side of his plate.

'It is possible that what Caroline saw was from an old mansion at

Neuilly.' He forbore, and she had a strong impression of the effort of will it cost, to dab at the mark on his trousers. 'The house is being demolished and the garden statuary has been bought by a dealer to be shipped to Baltimore. A pity. We shall not see their like again.'

No one spoke. There was a profound creak as the Villeneuves, solid people, sat back in their chairs. George winked at Caroline, Monsieur Villeneuve raised his glass to her in silent salute.

'Caroline has been privileged,' said Pierre, and smiled at her.

'Naturally.' Madame Villeneuve rustled away into the kitchen and returned with the next course.

'Onion tart!' cried Berthe.

'It is in Bertrand's honour.'

'You are too kind, aunt.'

Bertrand received the first portion. He took a crumb on his fork and placed it on his tongue. He nodded. 'It is excellent.'

Caroline looked at the piece of toast still in her lap. If she put it on her plate everyone would see her do it. If she returned it to her bag, Bertrand would see her do it.

Madame Villeneuve cut the tart into slices. Caroline's heart missed a beat, two beats. She thought if it were to stop altogether she might be said to have died of Sunday lunch. But who would say it? Who would know what she had endured because of veal and beef, sheeps' brains in black butter and duckling with cherries, crêpes and soufflés and –

'Caroline.' Madame Villeneuve was holding out a plate.

Because of onion tart. She drew a deep breath. 'No, thank you.'

Something passed round the table, starting with Monsieur Villeneuve. It was less than a murmur, more than a sigh, and it ended with Madame Villeneuve crying: 'Caroline!'

'I have had an excellent sufficiency,' Caroline said, and folded her napkin.

'Bravo,' said Bertrand.

A Considerable Speck

How happy they were when they were first married. She could remember if she sat quietly, first clearing her mind. It was like looking through a keyhole. She could see only a very little, only a circle of light, tiny and charmed. Everything had been magic! Not that they were unaware, they knew that there was still sorrow and pain about, and plenty of it, but they themselves were scatheless, there was not a scathe could touch them. They had each other, together they made a perfect whole. They were not blithe, they were enraptured and somewhat amazed and when they found time from all else they were feeling, they were grateful. It was as if they were the first to enter the state of bliss which was the true, ultimate state 'whereinto', as she said, smiling at them as if they were distant children – as indeed they were – it seemed that 'everyone else must soon come'.

Each time she looked through the keyhole she saw the same scene, or rather, the same moment. And she did not exactly see it, she was admitted to it, one eye at a time. That eyeball had to supply the rest of her. It was quite pitiable, the way she squeezed herself into the keyhole. She was beginning to understand that it was all she was going to get, there were no other moments, before or after. In fact it wasn't even a moment, it was an intimation which lasted a moment, an intimation of the purest blessedness. She could say that was how it was, believe it or not, and really it did take some believing. But for how long? Would she, one day soon, find herself unable to remember even that? She had taken, lately, to saving the memory, not using it for dreaming, but for really desperate occasions.

The worst, she sometimes thought it the lethal thing, was that she dare not ask how *he* felt. She was so terrified of the answer. Any answer. Although perhaps if he said he felt the same it would be ever so slightly better, they would be within shouting distance. But if he said he was all right, 'super-deluxe' was what he would actually say, even if he said it just so as not to upset her or because he did not know what she was talking about, it would put them utterly out of reach. Once and for all. What are we now? she asked herself. The answer was that if she asked and he answered, then it would have been admitted, tacitly or otherwise. What would have been admitted? That she was not smiling but weeping. 'Happy?' some cynic had said. 'It is better to be comfortable.' And perhaps, she thought, immensely sensibly, she was expecting too much to expect it to go on and on without a break. The fact was, it *had* gone on, and now anything else was a fall from grace.

She was not actually remembering at this moment. With the smell of Bendick's chocolate melting, there was no desperation. She was making a mousse for supper and reflecting, as well she might, on her dependence on the memory. 'I have nothing to last me,' she said, and looking round her kitchen saw the cooker rusted, the fridge gutted, the dishes in pieces. No one knew better or feared more than she that the memory, too, would go, and all she would be left with would be the hope that things had been different.

She broke an egg and passed the yolk back and forth from one half of the shell to the other, letting the white drop into the bowl. 'Dear God, that it should come to this!' She was not a believer, but someone or something was to blame.

It had started in Italy. She could identify the actual moment. Of course she hadn't seen it then. All she had seen then was their sublimity, the shining armour wherein they trusted. She, certainly, had trusted in it. She had firmly believed that nothing ever again could touch them to harm them. Naturally, things were trying to get through, unaccustomed as they were to not being at liberty to smudge and blemish and ultimately crumble every kind of happiness. She had marvelled and joyed in her serenity and when laughter was in order she had laughed. Italy could be said to have begun it, but of course it would have happened almost anywhere. She saw that now. At the time, in Italy, she had simply laughed.

Beating the egg-yolks she thought that a spoonful of Grand Marnier would give originality to the flavour of the mousse. Chocolate was so bland, even bitter chocolate. She would have made a face once and said that a sweet should be sweet. Once, she had been in no doubt as to what she liked: strawberry jam and meringues and sugared almonds. And she had known what was good and what could be relied on to transmit goodness: silver-haired old people, Members of Parliament (any party except Communists), green vegetables and Liberty's store in Regent Street. And she had never been in any doubt as to what would endure: love, truth, beauty, honour, she would have said.

The melting butter when she dropped it into the yolks looked incompatible and as if it would never blend. She battered it with her spoon into spangles of golden grease. She wondered if she was about to like celery. Not only her tastebuds were changing: she had reservations, she was less trusting. It was foolish, had been shown to be foolish, to think the best of everyone. And she was no longer sure what the truth was. As for love . . . she sighed, without resignation. It had been many-splendoured but sometimes now it was distinctly shabby.

Of course, she was older now, rising twenty-three, and could be said, could be expected, to be maturing. How unpleasant it was, and arbitrary. She had not asked for maturity, wholly happy as she was she did not expect, certainly she did not covet, a higher degree of bliss. Given the choice and knowing what she knew now, she would have passed up maturity. But she must hope and believe that she would eventually know more and achieve a superior quality of happiness.

They had gone to the Italian Lakes on their honeymoon and from there they drove – it seemed they floated – down to Naples, stopping and staring at whatever took their fancy on the way. In Florence he said, 'Let's go and have a look at Fysole.' 'At what?' 'I believe there's a good view from up there.' 'Up where?' 'About three miles from here.' 'Is it spelt F-I-E-S-O-L-E?' 'Fysole, that's right.' She laughed, they both laughed. He continued to call it 'Fysole', even to the English schoolteacher staying at their hotel. She continued to laugh, and when the schoolteacher reddened with annoyance she said gaily, 'We saw such a funny old picture in the church at San Domenico.' A few days afterwards, looking at the map, he spoke of passing through 'Fross-in-one' en route to Naples. She smiled and lightly bit the lobe of his ear. It wasn't until they were home again and had been married some three months that he referred to 'the Bulky Parsnips or whoever'. She twitched her lips the first time, and when it happened again she said quickly, 'You know very well their name is Bulkley-Parsons.' 'That's what I thought I said.' 'And her father is a Lieutenant-Commander.' 'Commands a fleet of ballpoints at the Admiralty.' 'I don't see the relevance.' 'He's a desk sailor.' 'I honestly don't see how it matters. It certainly doesn't entitle you to be offensive.' 'Offensive? Me?' He laughed but he laughed alone. She was beginning to anticipate his refusal to admit liability. 'It was just a joke,' he said.

Madge and Ted Carmody who were coming to supper were in their forties and could be expected to be fully matured. One wondered – one might try to find out – what quality of happiness *they* had achieved. It wouldn't help much because everyone had a different way to go and would get there sooner or later, and some would not get there at all. She would have expected a show of serenity. Madge was not excitable, that would have been out of keeping with her build. What she did have was a kind of monu-mentalism, one was very sensible of her presence. Ted was trans-parent and *his* ripeness could be merely prejudice confirmed.

91

She was finishing the mousse when she heard his voice in the hall. 'Kate? Are you there?'

Yes, she was here, she had chosen this of all places in the world. It was not, as she had once thought, her destiny: it was a highly significant choice.

'Where else would I be?'

She had now to discover what the choice signified. When I know that, she thought, I shall know what I hope and when I know what I hope I can try to achieve it.

'Kate – there you are.'

He came into the kitchen and kissed her. His eyelids drooped, he tightened his arms and purposed to kiss her again, urgently. She recognised the preliminary frisson and turned her cheek.

'Dickie, I must get this stuff into the fridge.'

'What stuff?'

'I've made a chocolate mousse for supper.'

He brushed his lips deep into her hair, then released her. He had never been difficult about that sort of thing. She maintained that it would become tiresome if they were not both that way inclined. But if they were, she said, even a slight inclination could be encouraged into a positive riot. And she preferred the circumstances to be propitious. There was no longer the need to seize or to make opportunities. They were sure of having the time and place, the marriage service had given them that. 'Bed, you mean,' he had laughed, and agreed.

She carried the tall glasses to the fridge. 'It's chocolate and orange mousse. With a dash of Grand Marnier.'

'Lovely. What's for pudding?'

'Madge and Ted have a weight problem. I can't embarrass them with apple pie and cream.'

'Of course not. You think of everything.'

He sounded wistful and she said, 'Someone has to try!'

He was not aware of any such need. His own mother had said, 'Dickie takes life as it comes,' which was another way of saying that he didn't think. She was prone, now, to wonder what relationship existed between thinking and feeling. Just how much, and what, did Dickie feel? She was thinking of course of the higher feelings, the emotions. She had never seen him in agony of mind, not even when they thought that their car and all their luggage had been stolen in Naples. Joy he was always showing but to be specific about the sort of joy one would have to call it high spirits. Animal spirits. She was alarmed at her own perception.

'I remembered the wine.' He was looking at her longingly. She used to find that irresistible, however cool and remote she might have been feeling. Now she asked herself did it pass with him for love? 'Plonk-de-plonk from the sunny banks of the supermart, between the currants and the cornflakes.'

'As soon as they arrive you can put it in the fridge to chill.'

'Would you care for a glass now.'

'I haven't time. There's the table to set.'

'Can I . . . ?'

She held her face in her hands and laughed. 'With the kitchen knives and the pottery condiment set your Macclesfield aunt sent us?'

'And the cloth with the beetroot stain.'

'And the Jacobean tumblers I got from the milkman.'

'And the mustard pickle.'

'And the tomato ketchup.'

'Only if we're having chips . . . . '

He laughed, she was already past it. She cried silently, 'My love, where are you?' and ran past him into the dining-room. This was fast becoming a desperate occasion and she could not, with all she had to do, invoke the memory to help her through. She flung open the windows, letting in the stiff breeze, tempted to make things uncomfortable. Why should everyone else, unaware, enjoy themselves while she, in true agony of mind, stood at the crossroads of her life?

'Honey –' he had followed her, 'is anything wrong?'

'Naturally not. I adore Madge and Ted, I would gladly work my fingers to the bone for them.'

'Is that necessary?'

'Of course not. I happen to know they're crazy about sea air.' He watched her dealing out table mats, flanking them with silver and with wine goblets crowned like bishops with mitred napkins. 'It does matter.'

'What does?'

'Remembering people's likes and dislikes.'

It gave her no satisfaction to observe Madge's shudder as she came into the house and the sea wind lifted the pictures on the walls. She ran at once to close the windows, crying, 'Who wants us to perish!'

Madge and Ted were physically two of a kind. They were both big-boned and well-fleshed and when they moved they stirred rather than used their limbs. Thereafter the resemblance was not so marked. Madge was insular and proud of it. If she was to be believed, she had a far from still centre. Ted, who was a local bank manager, was expert at delegating. He had fingers in a great many pies: they were, however, second-hand fingers. He knew his business but was never seen busy at it. People who mistook his calm for indifference did so, Dickie said, to their cost.

'Children, when are you going to get your approach road made up?'

'Oh Madge, we're not. All that beautiful willow-herb and mallow – we love it! It's so sylvan.'

'All those potholes – like riding on a cakewalk.'

'After rain, you should see the birds bathing. Why is the sky always bluer in a puddle?'

'We were afraid for our back axle.'

Ted put out his arm and drew Kate to him. 'You're the only girl I'd drive out here to see.'

He made overtures in his wife's or Dickie's presence. He and Kate had never been alone together but if the chance offered she believed he would take it. She had said as much to Dickie. Dickie blitherly declared that Ted was a great-hearted chap. 'Would you think that if he seduced me?' 'He never would, it's just a graceful compliment.' 'Graceful?' Dickie had looked at her and reddened and said hastily, 'I mean he wouldn't –' 'You mean he's great-hearted and graceful.' 'He wouldn't do anything to upset us.'

Madge was wearing a long dress which made her look tentish, if not marqueeish. Kate remembered that she was great-hearted too.

'Your side of the bay is all that's left.' Madge took Dickie's arm and bore him with her towards the dining-room. 'Our side is all hoverport and sewage effluent.'

'I thought we'd have drinks first,' said Kate.

'We're not drinking. Doctor's orders. "You can drink or you can eat," he said, "you can't do both." '

'That was you,' said Ted. 'I'm acknowledged to be as fit as a flea.'

'We chose eating,' said Madge. 'But don't let us inhibit you.'

'No differentials, we'll share a glass of lemon juice with you,' Dickie said cheerfully.

It was thoughtful of him but why hadn't he thought a little more and realised that Kate was in need of a sherry after working all afternoon in the kitchen?

'I could eat a horse,' said Madge.

'Not on the menu,' said Dickie. 'But moose is.'

'Moose!'

'It's all right, Kate's taken off the antlers.'

'Why don't you show them the garden?' cried Kate.

'Do you mean venison?' said Ted. 'Madge, Kate's roasted us a haunch of venison!'

'With cranberry jelly?'

'Where did you get it? Clever of you, Dickie –'

'Darlings! Lead me to it!'

'He didn't!' cried Kate. 'And I didn't! We're having steamed turbot and chocolate mousse. M-O-U-S-S-E!' There was a silence. Kate burst into tears. 'Dickie, how could you!'

'Honey, it was only a joke –'

'Are we laughing? Are we?'

Dickie's ears went back and his grin faded. Ted made a jollying noise. Kate ran away from them into the kitchen. Madge said, following her, 'Childie, don't take it to heart.'

'Where else should I take it? I feel so humiliated!'

'Why? We're going to have a delicious, thoroughly civilised meal –'

'And hurt!'

'Only your pride, and that'll soon recover.'

'You don't understand! It's not pride with me, it's self-respect.' Hers was being systematically undermined. Dickie did have a system. It wasn't deliberate, he didn't even realise he was using it, which made things worse. At this moment, in tears, she believed that it made things impossible. 'Oh Madge, what shall I do?'

'About what?'

'I'm losing my self-respect!'

'Childie, when you've been married as long as I have you'll find your self-respect's been reinforced.'

Kate looked up, eyes brimming. 'How long –'

'Ted and me? Twenty years.'

She stopped herself crying 'Oh God!' which would have been impolite but couldn't stop herself repeating 'Twenty years!' in a tone of blank dismay.

Madge laughed. 'The first five were the worst.'

'Oh please don't joke about it.'

'I'm not. During those five years I was casing the situation.'

'Casing the situation?'

'The marital situation. Frankly, I wouldn't expect it to take you as long as it did me. And once you've done it, you know just how much room you have to manoeuvre, how far you can go and you can begin to experiment. That part's quite fun. Afterwards –' Madge sighed. 'You don't have to worry about afterwards yet.'

She supposed that Madge had some idea of what she was talking about, it could be only an idea; teased out of the woolly nonsense it probably meant that Madge had been deceiving Ted with someone else. It was of course irrelevant and immaterial and she certainly did not wish to hear Madge's guilty secrets.

'It's not like that,' she said. 'I know all about marriage and how far I can go. I don't want to go anywhere.'

Madge, smiling, seemed to accept the rebuke. 'Dickie's a dear. There isn't a speck of harm in him.'

'Who said anything about harm?'

'Childie, I think I might have that drink. After all, fish isn't really *eating*, is it?'

She thought how impossible people were, especially one's own people. One considered them, tried – to the extent of putting oneself in their place – to cater in every sense for their needs, emotional, intellectual and physical, not expecting gratitude or even recognition, but co-operation – surely one could expect that? And what happened? They made a mockery of one's sensibility. Madge, she feared, would make it a talking point: 'Inviting us over, a ten-mile drive, for dinner which turned out to be the veriest snack.'

The fish she served with a herb and cream sauce in the French manner. She gave Madge and Ted the largest portions and they speedily emptied their plates. Ted cleaned his with a piece of bread which he then popped into his mouth. A little less gusto would have been kinder, to say nothing of common politeness. her eyes filled again with tears.

'Heavenly sauce,' said Madge. 'What's in it?'

'Some tarragon, chervil and shallots.'

'Chervil?'

'It's a pot-herb, smells of aniseed and has tiny white flowers. I found it in the little wood at the end of our lane.'

'You'd better transplant some of it,' said Ted. 'That land's under offer.'

'Under offer?'

'At the moment one of those bargain-break builders is fighting a consortium that wants to build a marina there.'

'Oh no –'

'Childie,' said Madge, 'you're going to be approached, potholes notwithstanding.'

'Oh Dickie!' As she turned to him, the earlier tears resolved and spilled down her cheek.

'It's all right, honey. We're a long way from the road, it won't affect us.'

'It's *my* wood! There are bluebells and wild damson and chanterelles growing there!'

'You could put in a bid,' said Ted. 'Starting in five figures.'

'Dickie said we'd always be alone here.'

'Kind of creepy, isn't that? On our side of the bay we do see life.'

'Mind you, it's natural,' said Madge, 'wanting to be on your own. So make the most of it.'

'But if they won't let us?'

'Then make the most of the wanting.'

'How long does it take you to get to town?' Ted asked Dickie.

'Two hours.'

Ted whistled. 'Four hours' travelling five days a week. And half of that is just for getting round the bay. Whose idea was it to live out here?'

'It was when we were on holiday,' said Kate. 'We hired a boat and came over and found this house. It was empty and the funniest thing was there were huge hollyhocks growing all up the path and we walked underneath them – it was like walking under the swords at a military wedding and I said to Dickie, "I'll marry you if we can live here."'

'Because of the hollyhocks?'

'We bought it because it was secluded,' said Dickie. 'To have a bit of privacy. That was the idea.'

'It's certainly private,' said Madge. 'We stopped in the village and asked the way to Gull's Cry and they hadn't heard of it.'

'Just open its beak and look down its neck.' Dickie grinned and stroked a tear from Kate's cheek.

Their first significant difference had been over the naming of the house. To her it had ranked as significant: to him, as became terribly obvious, it was not noticeable, was not even a difference. He simply didn't realise that anything was wrong. He smiled and teased, tenderly teasing and touching her, as he was at this moment, never noticing her stiffness, unaware that he was uncovering a barrier between them.

She had decided to call the house Gull's Cry and Dickie said he couldn't see the Department of Inland Revenue putting that on their tax demands. The name had come to her the first time they saw the house. They hadn't known it was for sale and they were walking round the garden, peering in at the empty windows. She heard the gulls wheeling overhead and thought I want to live in that sound. It was a wild, lonely sound. She would never be lonely, of course, she had Dickie. He said was it to be Gull's Cry or Gulls' Cry. She said to him, 'Listen, just listen!' They stood there, the wild lonely sound blowing to them on the sea wind. Dickie, mock serious, said if it was Gulls' plural, it ought to be Gulls' Cries and HM Inspector of Taxes would think he was really putting the screws on.

She could hardly believe her ears. She had turned and run away from him. He caught her up, she was in tears, at the end of the lane and it took him the rest of the afternoon and all his tenderness to comfort her. She knew now that the barrier had always been there: their closeness, their seeming to feel and to think as one – a perfect fusion, it had seemed, of two minds and bodies – all that was illusion.

'You hear gulls crying in London now,' said Ted. 'There was a pack of them going over the Mall and it sounded all wrong somehow.'

'Everything's mixed up,' said Madge. 'Look at clothes. People wear frilly blouses and jackboots. We went to a party where a girl turned up in one of those knitted granny squares.'

'Gulls? In London?'

'Thousands. You can see them any day in Green Park. They make more noise than the buses.'

Kate, her eyes wide, turned to Dickie. 'You didn't tell me!'

'About the gulls? Can't say I've noticed them.' He grinned. 'I'm conditioned to the noise they make.'

'But you knew – you knew what I had named the house! And why!'

'Tell us why,' said Madge. 'We have wondered.'

'Doesn't it matter to you that the whole idea – the concept – is lost?'

'Honey, they're not the same gulls. They're not from here –'

'Childie, if you'd seen the looks we got when we stopped and asked where Gull's Cry was.' Madge laughed. 'Finally, Ted flatly refused to ask the way.'

Ted winked at Kate. 'I re-phrased the question and said could they tell me where the peachy little brunette lives, the one who looks like Audrey Hepburn, only prettier.'

'People are funny,' said Madge. 'They think you're playing games. One man said were we on a treasure hunt and another said ecology bored the pants off him.'

'It peeved them,' said Ted, 'to be asked the way to a noise.'

'You don't understand!'

'I do, childie. When I was your age I was crazy about names. I had an old Ford Pop and I called it Armitage, heaven only knew why.'

'You lusted after Chris Armitage, that's why,' said Ted. 'When you couldn't have him you named the car after him and drove it like a demon.'

'Utter rubbish!'

'It's applied psychology.'

'Applied lies!' cried Madge. 'The boot – and I'm really talking about another part of your anatomy – was on the other foot. It was you who followed Chris Armitage around like an adoring dog. I had grave doubts about you in those days.'

'We called it Gull's Cry because it's sort of wild and private,' said Dickie.

'Women can't understand a real relationship between men,' said Ted. 'They always bring sex into it. We were mates, Chris and me, in the best sense.'

'It *was* wild,' said Kate. 'Then.'

'Nothing's changed –'

'The best sense?' Madge said to Ted.

'It's not wild now because you cut the banks and the hedges and chopped down the hollyhocks.'

'That had to be done, honey, that was a clearing operation.'

'We were on the same wavelength. There was nothing bent about it,' said Ted.

'And it won't be private, they're going to sell the land and build houses.'

'They won't build in the lane.'

'I never had to say "OK with you?" because if it was OK with me it was OK with Chris.'

'Why didn't you marry him?' said Madge.

Unable to bear it, Kate cried, 'It will never be the same again!'

It was the very truth of the matter and she was not surprised at the sudden silence. She would have expected it. She waited for their dismay, it seemed to her that she was uttering a fundamental – *the* fundamental truth, which annihilated them all. For however overdue, however cut and long ago dried it was, it was still a revelation. They could not fail to see it, they were indeed seeing it, she thought, they were sitting there shocked. She heard in her heart the mourning cry of a gull. It was actually she who cried, on all their behalfs.

Then Dickie said, 'Honey, of course it will –'

'No it won't,' said Ted. 'She's right, thank God.'

'God?' cried Kate. '*God?*'

'When you get to our age the last thing you want is to be young again.'

Madge nodded. 'All that emotion – it's mandatory, you're not human unless you feel everything – but what a relief when you can stop.' She blew a kiss. 'Never mind, children, your turn will come. And now I think Ted and I could be allowed another little drink.'

That night when they were in bed Kate said, 'I'm not like Madge, I don't know if I'm not like other women, but I'm not like her. I shall go on feeling everything if I live to be a hundred.'

Dickie, leaning over her, said, 'Honey, you're a one-off, you're unique.'

'Agony and ecstasy, fear and joy and pain –'

'And love.'

'I have always felt everything. I feel for other people as well as for myself. And for animals, I can't bear to think of fox-hunting and vivisection. I even feel for insects.'

'So long as you keep on loving me.'

'When I was a little girl I used to go round letting flies out of webs. And my father said, "The spiders will starve." ' And she had been afraid that she might not be able to change things. Of course she immediately forgot and continued, like everyone else, to try, and sometimes she believed she had changed things. It made only plain logical common sense and justice that everyone should be able to do that, otherwise, where was the point? Where, she asked herself, were things like conscience and God?

'I can't promise.'

Dickie pushed himself up on his elbow and stared down at her. 'What do you mean?'

With him of all the world she wished to be absolutely truthful. 'You've seen what's happened, how can we be sure of anything?'

'What's happened?'

'Oh God!' Of course it was useless to appeal to the very one who had let this happen and she cried out in anger.

'Tell me what's happened.'

'Why should I? I shouldn't have to. If you don't know, if I have to tell you, there's no point. It means there's nothing between us, we're just two separate people.' She buried her face in the pillow.

Dickie took her by the shoulders and turned her face up. 'Don't say that. Whatever happens to you, happens to me. But I'm thicker and coarser and some things don't happen to me so much or so soon.' In the dusk he looked fierce, his eyes glittering, his hair standing up, his brows bristling. 'Hell, I'm a man!'

She had to laugh although she was nearer to tears. He it was who had said it, but she was the first to realise the truth of it. The unfunny, ultimate, irreversible truth. Even if he could have taken on her quality, how could she ever have supposed she could take on his?

'We can at least change the name of the house,' she said.

'The house? At least?'

She sat up, smiling to his face. 'We can't change anything else, can we? And it will never be Gull's Cry to me again.'

'My God.' It was his turn, but she noticed that he spoke as to an associate. 'So that's it.'

'We must call it something general, like Hilltop or Lane End or Sea View – you can see the sea from upstairs.'

'There have always been gulls in London.'

'Of course there haven't. It's part of the new syndrome, everything's mixed up, you can't be sure of anything any more.'

'Hundreds of years ago, before London was started, do you think they didn't come up to the marshes?'

'I don't care what they did then, they're in the City now.'

'We called it "Gull's Cry", one lonely gull, not a whole flock –'

'That's how they go about now, in flocks, screeching above the noise of the traffic. When do you ever see a lone gull?'

'You said you wanted to live in that sound.'

'I was so naive! Why didn't you tell me how naive I was?'

'I like the name, I always did.'

'We could plant some more hollyhocks – not along the path, of course – and call it "Hollyhock Cottage".'

' "Gull's Cry" still sounds wild and kind of private to me.' She felt him put out his hand in the dark, though he did not touch her. 'Isn't that what you want to be – private?'

She laughed. 'Those gulls, do you think they commute? Do they go up to town sitting on the roof of the eight-fifteen?'

Almost an International Incident

'Six o'clock. We'd have been in Rimini now.'

'And I'd be in my bath. Did you know there's only one *bagno* to each floor? Five times I tried the door on ours and each time a different voice was singing "Carmen".'

'Wouldn't we, Harold? Wouldn't we have been in Rimini?'

'Men – at least I think they were – singing the "Toreador" song, but the last one sounded high and reedy.'

'It was the same guy washing himself away.'

'I know it was Rimini we'd have been in because I cast my travel diary according to the itinerary and after lunch I was all set to write up the Mandrioli Pass.'

'The steam was coming out of the keyhole. I tell you that door was wet *through*.'

'Right after we left Florence I knew we wouldn't get over those hills.'

'When we were riding down from Lenslebourg the bus gave a shudder right on the edge of one of those drops and seemed to lose herself. An old Buick I had did that, just rolled over and died.'

'The guy's a lousy driver.'

'Wouldn't you expect them to have more than one bathroom on each floor? I mean, it's styled a hotel, not a pensione.'

'I guess we're lucky to be here without booking or anything.'

'Did we know the bus was going to break down? We booked a tour, not a mosey-round.'

'I expressed myself before we started. "This is a cheap package," I said to Harold, "and it'll be trimmed to the bone, there's no way else they can do it for the price," and he said, "So long as they provide the fundamentals," and I said, "What we call fundamental they call fancy."'

'Well I'm glad to be here. It's an opportunity we would have missed if that cotter-pin hadn't broken.'

'Opportunity for what?'

'For seeing this place which is an unscheduled stop. We never would have known it existed. We'd have rushed on by – and for what?'

'For a bath at the Bellavista.'

'Everyone gets to Rimini. We've got the chance to experience some place else and I think we should make the most of it.'

102

Pearl Rubinsky thought so too. She and Bennet always agreed about these things, the first time she ever heard Ben he was voicing her thoughts.

'Did you see those holes in the rock? People are living in them. Real troglodytes!'

'The water in the whisky tastes like real river,' said Vic Farrar.

'We came on this trip to see something outside ourselves and I'd say this place is right outside us.'

Plump Wilma Borg said it wasn't what she came for.

'We've a real chance to get to know people. The danger as I see it is of being encapsulated in that bus and never contacting reality.'

'I think it's nice stopping over in the mountains,' said Pearl.

'Everyone else will be down at Rimini.'

'You making it out some kind of privilege, Pearl?'

'Not to be in Rimini now? *Not* drinking at Morissey's?'

'Give me the Bellavista any time.'

'Pearl, don't put words in my mouth!' Bennet was pink and a little mortified. 'Don't do that, Pearl, it's how wars are started.'

'Let's go and eat.' Vic picked up a handful of his wife's long hair, he often invited her with a tug. She made no objection, shook her hair back on her shoulders when he let go and looked with her pale eyes askew – Bennet had said he felt he wanted to align them for her. 'What are they giving us for dinner?'

'String soup in a tureen painted with the story of the Fall.'

When Vic and Nell Farrar went to find the dining-room the others stopped talking generally among themselves. Ben worried because Pearl's ankles were puffy. He made her sit down so that he could touch them and gauge her discomfort.

Wilma Borg talked to the Harold Harpers, Mrs Harold was scoring through and through 'FRIDAY – Rimini' in her travel diary. It was no longer possible to know what they were thinking, or rather it was not possible to stop them thinking the wrong thing.

'They don't want,' Pearl said sadly, 'they just don't.'

'Never mind about them. Are *you* all right?'

'I'm fine.' She was seven months pregnant and they had debated exhaustively whether they should come on this trip. But it would be years before they could contemplate it again. 'We'll go out tonight, won't we?'

'Maybe you should rest with your feet on a pillow.'

'Ben, we did say we'd never let it restrict us –'

'This side of risk I said, Pearl.'

'My ankles will be down in the morning, they always are.'

Vic Farrar had carried his whisky into the dining-room. The bottle stood bald and functional beside the wicker-covered Chianti flask. Nell Farrar was composedly eating spaghetti and Vic was trying to snatch the ends of it out of her mouth.

'I wish he wouldn't horse around,' muttered Pearl.

'He drinks too much.'

They wanted to sit over away from the Farrars but Vic beckoned them.

'Come on, you two, this is where they cook the string and save the chicken but I've had them untie the knots first.'

Bennet and Pearl sat down at the next table and Bennet put up the menu between themselves and the Farrars. 'Someone should tell him it reflects on us all.'

'But not you, he's older than you. Also he's bigger. Harold Harper should speak to him.'

'Or Wilma.' They smiled at each other. Wilma Borg was bigger than Vic.

Pearl felt hungry, she usually did now, and there were savoury smells from the kitchen which opened out of the dining-room, and from the windows which opened on the piazza came a smell more pungent which enlivened senses deeper than those of taste. She asked Bennet if he could smell the olives.

He sniffed judiciously. 'I didn't think olive trees smelt.'

'They do, I know they do. I know that smell from way back, it seems like from before I was born.' Pearl said wonderingly, 'My great-grandmother was Italian. Do you think it could be in my blood? And that's why I feel at home? I do, Ben, I feel I belong here.'

'It's well known, Pearl, that women in your condition have queer fancies.'

'This is absolutely nothing to do with my condition, this is with me, Pearl Rubinsky, Pearl Patten that was, or just Pearl or just that was and am and will be again when the condition's over.'

'I'm glad –'

'Also,' said Pearl, really liking the place – the check tables and green vines and even the cheap pictures of big-breasted girls – as she knew she wouldn't like any other place on the trip and as she would probably never be able to like any other place again, 'I feel that the people here are my friends. They may be more than that, I'm not sure whether it's a blood-tie –'

'Hey,' cried Vic, 'Nell's going to show how the contadini drink wine!'

Nell picked up his whisky-bottle and put it under her chair.

'Wine for my wife – in a goat-skin!'

'Signor, we have no goats.'

'It was a joke,' Pearl said, gently smiling to the girl who was serving them.

The girl looked into Pearl's eyes and the frown vanished from between her own. She set down the great tureen which she carried from table to table and asked pleadingly, 'Signora, is everything all right?'

'Everything's fine!' cried Pearl. 'Isn't it, Ben?'

'You surprise me,' Vic said soberly, pouring Chianti into his soup. 'No goats? There were always goats in Arcady.'

'This is called Quattro Santo, signor.'

'Four saints, no less. Couldn't you get one good one?'

'They are all good.'

'And this place is four times blessed. Do you think some of it will rub off? We certainly can do with a little blessing.'

'Scusi?'

'He means we're sinners,' said Pearl, 'all of us here, all of *us*, he means. We don't know about you, do we, and anyway it's none of our business.'

'He means we hope to benefit from our stay,' said Bennet and Vic laughed and punched him on the shoulder.

The Harold Harpers and Wilma, coming in from the street, said they had been round the piazza from which there was a view of the Adriatic and that the trees, all the trees, were full of electric light bulbs.

'What kind of soup's that?' said Wilma, looking into the tureen.

'Tagliatelli in brodo, signora.'

Of course the girl might not know what it was all about but she had to know what Vic's manner meant. Her face coloured darkly as she served Bennet and Pearl with soup. Pearl touched her hand.

'You mustn't mind, Gilda, we were only fooling.'

'That's right, Gilda,' said Vic. 'I'm an uncouth bastard.'

The girl hesitated, clasping the tureen in both arms she seemed about to turn and walk away. Then Vic leaned over and gently patted her hip. She smiled, the dark colour in her cheeks turned rosy and warm.

'Si, signor,' and she went to serve the Harpers, signalling with her bottom like a little white duck.

After that the dining-room filled with people from outside as well as the hotel guests and Cipriani, the proprietor, in flannel suit and grubby sneakers rolled from table to table asking was everyone happy.

Everyone was. There had been a change of heart like a change of wind and happiness went right through them. In fact Pearl felt that it went through the door and down the mountain for miles, though perhaps not as far as Rimini.

The meal was delicious, Pearl had second helpings. Gilda filled her plate and told her she must eat for two.

'I'm such a pig!'

Gilda smiled. 'A pig must eat for twenty.'

Vic picked the biggest golden peach out of Nell's hand and gave it to Pearl. 'That's for Higham.'

'Who?'

'All babies are Higham, born and unborn.'

Pearl's sense of belonging in this place was getting stronger, she couldn't remember having such a definite sense even back home.

'Not "back home", honey,' Ben corrected her, 'don't say "back home".'

'Well, I don't remember having it so much.'

'It's the Chianti. You're not used to it and you just drank up a whole glass.'

Pearl was sure that the looks she was getting from the big Italian women and the little Italian men weren't Chianti. She wasn't imagining, she was conditioned to indifference which was what one generally received and generally gave and she was as surprised as anyone that people she had never met and who didn't know her name should be nodding and smiling as if they knew *her* since before she was called Rubinsky or Patten or even Pearl.

'Will you look at that!' cried Wilma. 'They've switched on all the tuttifrutti lights.'

Everyone looked and cried out. In the square the trees signalled red, blue and orange as the breeze shook the light bulbs. And behind and above all the other colours was the luminous golden green of electrically lighted leaves.

'How lovely!' breathed Pearl.

'There will be dancing tonight,' said Cipriani. 'Tomorrow is the fiesta of Santa Lidia.'

'A fiesta! Oh, can we stay for it?'

'I think not. We're behind schedule and they're working overnight to fix the bus so that we can leave in the morning.'

Pearl asked Cipriani who Santa Lidia was.

'A good nice girl.'

'What was she sainted for?'

'For curing warts.'

Bennet said he had had an aunt who cured warts with fuse-wire but she was never canonised. Pearl pointed out that Lidia wouldn't have had the use of fuse-wire.

'We'll go dancing tonight, won't we? Under the trees?'

'Maybe.'

'Oh, Ben, it's the best thing we ever did, breaking down here!'

'Pearl, I want you to remember you're going to be a mother.'

Although she didn't say so, tonight Pearl intended to forget it. She already had. The past had brought her here and the future did not exist either for her or for the being inside her. For him too, especially for him, there was only the present which she was living in and he was – not yet, not quite. He was still part of her, not invulnerable in that womb place because he had to be home when she was home, here when she was here, dancing when she danced.

While Ben wasn't looking she poured herself another glass of wine. 'Higham's going to dance,' she said, and drank. It tasted of wet iron and she grimaced approval.

They were setting off fireworks in the square. Probably there was too much light for the ground display to show up, but everyone enjoyed the noise.

'Do let's hurry and go out!' fretted Pearl.

'It sounds rough. Maybe you'd better stay inside.'

'Oh, Ben, please! There won't be another chance like this and you were glad of it you said. We should take this chance to break out of ourselves you said –'

'I did not say so, Pearl.' Bennet frowned as a great peppering of crackers ran across the square and finished, amid shrieks, under the hotel windows. 'If there's anything that bad in us we should try to change for the better, not run out on it.'

'I think so too,' said Pearl. 'But this is the first and last time I'll be here and every minute's important, I've got to really spend each minute. You brought me here, you brought *me*, not just Mrs Bennet Rubinsky and the mother of your son.' Pearl laid all ten fingers on her breast. 'Remember me, Ben?'

She certainly didn't know herself, looking at him like that, and all she put into the look – she didn't suspect she had it in her. She caught the reflection in his eyes, there was a short sharp battle of Bennet Rubinsky which Pearl won and then felt sorry and reasonably guilty but unrepentant.

'All right, but not until we've had our coffee,' he said. 'It'll give them time to simmer down out there.'

Pearl thought they were more likely to boil over. She sat patiently while Bennet drank coffee and smoked a cigar. She was recalling how they had ground into Quattro Santo in bottom gear, the driver hanging on to the wheel. When the bus stopped in the square she had stayed in her seat while the others got out to stretch their legs. Their driver and guide went off to negotiate a night's stay at the hotel for the passengers while he took the bus into Forli for repair. She was tired, the roar of the engine had deafened her and Quattro Santo looked no different from any of the villages, hill or plain, that they had come through. It was perched among terraced fields and the same black cypresses and rusty chestnuts. It had white and yellow walls, crazy shutters and archways and pots of geranium and narrow streets with washing laced from house to house. She had been seeing Quattro Santo all day. It was as if a long-running movie had jammed and become a still.

Pearl did not much like the arriving on this trip. After hours of blundering at speed past brandished faces and places, when the bus finally stopped and set them down she felt she could get out of time the way she could get out of step. Well, it was feasible, with her it was feasible and she couldn't make much sense while part of her was still coming. She had been happy to stay in the bus for a while after they got to Quattro Santo.

Little by little, the place took on identity. The first thing she noticed when her ear-drums recovered from the battering, was that someone was practising on the church bell. An unusually light and silvery peal it was – perhaps because of the altitude – and very sweet and homy to listen to the ringer trying his carillon and never getting it quite right.

Then she noticed, on a twisted iron balcony no bigger than the fenders of their Plymouth saloon back home, an old brown woman tending a great lily with petals like the wattles of a cock. She was sponging its fat stem and its swollen leaves as if they were the body and hands of a sick child.

Then Pearl noticed how the stones in the road were worn, and the steps where people had put their feet going up and coming down to the same places for years. It shouldn't have engaged her, none of these trifling details should, because after all this was Europe and she was supposed to be absorbing only the best of it. But somehow they signified, very definitely.

She held Ben's hand across the table. 'I shall always remember tonight.'

'Pearl, if I refuse you anything it's for your own good.'

'I know.'

'And you'll let me be the judge?'

She was willing, had always been glad, in fact, for someone else to judge what was good for her. She couldn't herself have reached some of the conclusions, let alone acted on them. But if Ben was the judge tonight there would be only early bed and hot milk to remember, and a digest of the *Swiss Family Robinson* which they had started yesterday on the beach at Spezia. Could she really relish Papa Robinson's sturdy philosophising tonight?

She was spared any reply by Wilma Borg's coming to their table.

'Imagine, we're going to have a ball and all! Are you changing, Pearl?'

'Not my dress, but I'll put on some flatties so I can dance.' She got up, calling back to Ben, 'Do you know, Higham's looking forward to a dance,' and got away upstairs before he could say anything.

The girl Gilda was folding down the sheets in their room.

'Isn't it exciting?' cried Pearl. 'The fiesta and everything?'

Gilda smiled.

'To think we wouldn't be here if the bus hadn't broken down. We'd have gone right on to Rimini. We do keep going right on, you know. I didn't think about it before we came on this trip but it's so – encapsulating.'

'Signora?'

'You know, like space travellers. We should get down and make contact. That's what we're doing tonight.'

'Rimini is very fine. There are fine shops and hotels and beautiful villas. Here there is nothing.'

'Oh, you're wrong!'

'Here there is nothing,' Gilda repeated. It was a joy to watch her plump up the pillows and tighten the sheets. 'Here are still women who wash in the river with stones. Like this.' She seized up an ash-tray and beat the bedclothes with it.

Pearl sighed. 'I guess I like it for what it hasn't got as much as what it has. Don't do that, please!' The sky was an amalgam of blue and gold – platinum to the half-averted eye – the mountains were mauve, the villages sprinkled on them like crumbs. Pearl had not had time yet to look at it. 'Please don't close the shutters.'

'You like mosquitoes? These we have.' Gilda briskly slapped the shutters to. 'Of course if you like all night –' she bared her teeth and uttered a piercing whine from the back of her throat, 'and this –' she slapped her own cheek and pretended to pick a dead insect out of her bosom.

'I guess not.'

Pearl sat down with her shoes in her hand. She liked the wheaten colour of the sheets – unbleached linen, she supposed – and they smelled like new bread. She wondered if they were laundered in the river.

'I was going as chambermaid in the Grand Hotel where are one hundred and fifty rooms,' said Gilda, laying out Pearl's nightdress.

'But my mother died and I stayed to keep house for my father and brothers.'

'What a shame.'

'Then I marry Nino, my third cousin.'

'Oh then it's not a shame.'

'Shame?' Gilda shook out Ben's pyjamas which he had rolled up and thrust into the overnight bag. She folded them and put them on the pillow next to Pearl's nightdress. 'Nino and me have been married three years.'

'So have we, almost. If my reckoning's correct our baby will come on our wedding anniversary.'

Gilda turned swiftly. 'Nino and me, we have no baby.'

'But you will–'

'We never have– I never have . . .' As she gazed at Pearl the colour rushed up her throat to the roots of her hair and was gone, leaving her strong white skin faintly glistening. 'Not once.'

'There's plenty of time!' cried Pearl. 'We didn't actually plan this for now. We were coming to Europe first and we were going to fix the house and we thought maybe after that we'd start a family. It happened right out of schedule. Ben says Nature breaks her own laws to achieve her ends.'

'My mother had three children when she had been married only two years.'

Pearl was going to say she must have made an early start, but thought better of it.

'I am a good Catholic, I ask the Virgin to give me a child, I make the pilgrimage. She hears other women, she hears cats, dogs, pigs!' cried Gilda. 'Me she makes barren!'

Pearl said firmly, 'Nonsense. You're the sort that has crowds of babies.'

Indeed she was, full-bosomed, wide-hipped, passionate dew on her skin, ripe, exactly ripe for procreation.

'Nino wants a son and I am barren!'

'Oh stuff! You're not at all. It might be his fault, your husband might be the one – you know what I mean?'

'Nino?' Gilda drew herself up with something like a smile but no fun in it. 'He is not the one!'

She was so vehement that Pearl blinked. 'Well, if there's any reason besides luck – good or bad, depends how you look at it – why you haven't conceived, it probably means you need a small operation, or hardly that – just some slight adjustment.'

'Adjustment?'

'Look, if you're worried you should see a doctor, have a check-up.'

110

'The *dottore*? He is good only like this –' Gilda pinched her own bottom and laughed, turning up her chin. Her bosom shook with laughter, her throat pulsed.

Peal laughed too. She had a vision of a Restoration comedy scene, a skinny old man in rusty black chasing the rosy-cheeked maid-servant.

They laughed until tears came and then Pearl wiped her cheeks. 'Gilda, you will have lots of sons.'

'I will have lots of sons, you will have lots of sons.'

'We'll have a baseball team! But tonight –' Pearl kicked off her shoes and they flew across the room, 'tonight I'm going on the town.'

'Signora?'

'I'm going dancing in Quattro Santo in honour of your Saint – what's her name? – the one who cured warts?'

'Tomorrow is the day of Santa Lidia, the saint of little children.'

'Oh.' Pearl said softly, 'Shouldn't you pray to her?'

Gilda nodded. 'I light many candles. Nino too, he stops at the church on his way to work and lights a candle to Santa Lidia. He does not know I have seen him.'

'And I'll light a candle to her before we go! For you! She won't mind me not being Roman Catholic or anything, will she?'

Gilda shook her head, seeming not quite sure whether it was the done thing.

'It's not as if I'm an unbeliever,' said Pearl. 'I just happen to believe differently.'

When she bent to put on the flat shoes for dancing Gilda went on her knees and took the shoes from her. She gently drew on each one, smoothing Pearl's stockings over her ankles. '*Dolcemente*, signora. You should be careful of yourself.'

'I should mix in. A pregnant woman is a power-house not a glass menagerie my paediatrician says.'

'Scusi?'

'He means we're tough, extraordinarily tough, I guess. I will light a candle for you.' Gilda was still kneeling and Pearl couldn't resist touching her cheek. The flesh bloomed – that was the word for it. What joy she must be, so many different joys. Pearl shyly lifted on her finger the strong blue-black ringlet in front of Gilda's ear. 'I'll pray to Santa Lidia to give you a baby.'

It seemed such a happy thought and might have helped in some way not apparent to themselves and anyhow it could do good, Pearl felt it could only do them both some good.

But Gilda moved her head aside. 'You are very kind, Signora,' and Pearl, who had been feeling wonderful, was confused by the way she said it.

111

Then Bennet came looking for her, asking was she ready, was she all right?

Gilda stood up in one swift movement and with lowered eyes went out of the room.

'What was that girl doing?'

'Putting on my shoes for me and I want to do something for her.'

'Like what?'

'Oh, I'm thinking,' Pearl said vaguely. It would only embarrass Ben, he spoke about the importance of getting outside himself but he wouldn't wish to get even a little way inside anyone else.

The band had arrived in the square and was setting up under the chestnut trees. There were half a dozen of them, middle-aged men in shirt sleeves and one, the tympanist, in waistcoat and no shirt. They had no music stands and no chairs. They stood or sat on the steps of the fountain. Only the saxophone player, a very fat man, wedged himself into an old basket chair and thereafter stood up and walked with the chair clamped to his hips. It seemed doubtful whether they would ever perform, they were so emotionally involved with artistic temperament or their own disharmony. So much arguing, shouting, pouting and shrugging surely could never put forth a concerted effort let alone a chord of music.

'We'll look around while they make up their minds,' said Bennet and he and Pearl walked away from the coloured lights and through an arch into a street that tipped right down off the mountain.

'How ever do automobiles get up here?' said Pearl.

'They don't, this is for foot passengers only, on two feet or four.' Bennet pointed to a cigar-coloured donkey bringing up crates of canned beer.

'Ben, look – cobbles.' Pearl had to feel them with her fingers as well as the soles of her feet. 'They're warm, like just-laid eggs, aren't they like just-laid eggs?'

She began to see so much and wherever she looked was more, the eye couldn't get away for seeing.

'Come *on*, Pearl!'

'Ben, look. . . .' She hadn't expected to see grass growing out of a street and just had to have it between her fingers to be convinced. 'Look how it's growing!'

'Pearl will you please stand up!'

The houses leaned towards each other and scarcely beyond the heads of passers-by was the washing stirring in the breeze that came up, Ben said, warmed from the sea. Ben said the sea was like a griddle warming up the air all day.

The shops spilled out to their feet, so did the people, it was necessary to step over and round and wait for the women to move their chairs and the children to roll out of the way. What Pearl liked best was when the shutters weren't closed and she could see into the houses. Back home she wouldn't have thought of looking, she wouldn't have wanted to.

'How poor are these people?'

'By US standards too poor to live.'

'The way they do live,' said Pearl, 'they've got style.'

'You shouldn't confuse it. There's more than one way of doing things and theirs is mostly the oldest way. That doesn't make it the most efficient.'

'I think so too.' Pearl was watching a woman buying live eels, running each one from her chin along the length of her arm.

'What you're calling style is what the Rubinskys left behind in Poland. It's how your great-grandfather made out in the Catskills and if they'd all stayed home you'd be bringing up the beer on a donkey.'

'We wouldn't have met. Did you think of that?' She tucked her hand into his armpit and they jolted over the cobbles and Pearl's full stomach rocked from her hip-joints.

Then they came to a clearing among the houses and in the middle was a church. Light streamed from the open door, the white-hot voltage of hundreds of devotional bulbs. They looked into a shell of pure glory. From the nave to the altar each grain of wood and stitch of fabric was glorified. Pearl felt slightly repelled and so probably did Bennet because he said, 'It's no place to bring your sins.'

Pearl wondered if Santa Lidia had a side chapel of her own, there was sure to be a statue and sconce. It would be only a gesture to light a candle in that blaze. Pearl was going to make it, but preferred not to in Ben's presence. His family had been Catholic and his recoil was total.

'It's clinical, I guess that's what they want from Confession.'

Bennet smiled. 'They won't confess tonight, they'll wait till after the fiesta.'

He led her away and Pearl made up her mind to come back first thing in the morning before he was awake. Perhaps there won't be so many lights on in the church, she thought, and my candle will show up.

An old woman in cinder-black passed them, surprising Pearl because her big feet were bare and the way they plunged in and out of her skirts seemed not directly to belong. It struck Pearl that the difference here would amount to much more than doing things one old way and she liked that, she liked the thought, she found it

113

exciting. Yes, it was exciting to go on taking off layers, expecting and not caring that she could never get to the heart of it.

They came to a street of round arches with shops in them. The shops were still doing business – fruit and meat and fish and an ice-cream parlour – but there was no getting away from the cold smell of stone. Three men sat round a marble slab playing cards. Stacked against the walls were new white tombstones and at the back of the shop a giantesque marble angel with wings outspread. How will they get it out? Pearl wondered. There were only these old vaulted doorways not much taller than a man's head.

The things to eat started her salivary glands working, she frankly coveted the sides of white salted pork, the strings of dark sausages, the butter in batons, the tubs full of olives. The bread too, sticky and spiced, and trays of rich bright things too small for cookies and too big for candies – she'd have taken them all if they'd have travelled and never mind the bibelots.

Bennet bought some of the cookie things packed in a cone of thin brown biscuit. They ate them right away, walking under the arches, it was the first time Pearl had eaten the wrapper as well.

She hadn't seen so many birds in cages before either, packed in, wing to wing.

'Why, they're wild birds,' she said distastefully and put her finger on the bars and at once every one of the wretched little prisoners panicked and tried to fly. There was such a whirring and struggling and beating of wings in the tiny space that she snatched her hand behind her back with a cry.

It was over in a moment, they fell on each other panting and dishevelled, a heap of tiny brown and black feathered birds with gaping beaks and legs no thicker than pins.

'They're wild birds!' Pearl said again, this time with dismay. The shopkeeper came out all smiles and tapped the cage, but the birds were too exhausted to do more than flutter feebly. 'Isn't there any law about that?'

Bennet shook his head. 'The wonder is that there are any left to catch by now.'

'But it's awful!' The shopkeeper was talking earnestly to Pearl, winking and nodding and several times he plucked at his shoulders as if he were pulling off wings. She shuddered. 'Whatever is he saying?'

'I think he's telling you they're good to eat.'

'To *eat*!'

'That's so. They roast them on sticks, sort of a kebab.'

'Oh no!'

Pearl's revulsion was obvious even to the shopkeeper. He turned away, shrugging and spreading his hands, palms up.

'I guess it's some more of their style,' Bennet said, smiling.

'It's awful, and it's not as if they haven't plenty else to eat.' Pearl pointed to the cage and asked the man, 'How much do you want for them?'

'Signora?'

'How much? *Quanto costa?*'

'Pearl!'

'Tre cento cinquanta lire.'

'Three hundred and fifty? Ben, that's only a dollar for the lot!'

The Italian held up one finger. *'Una, una,* signora.'

'He means each. Pearl, you're crazy if you're thinking what I think you are.'

'Ask him how much for all of them. *Tutto*!' cried Pearl to the shopkeeper. Whereupon he began to do sums on his fingers.

'Pearl, it's madness. What are you going to do with them?'

'What do you think? I'm going to set them free.'

'Cinque mille lire,' said the shopkeeper.

'Pearl, he's having you on. I'm not paying twenty dollars for a cage of birds!'

'Ben, please!'

'No!'

The shopkeeper, watching their faces, smiled knowingly. He put his hand into the cage, took out a bird, dropped it into a paper bag and gave the bag to Pearl.

'Signora, *prego*!'

'But I want them all!'

Ben took her arm. 'Pearl, he's giving you the darn thing. Stop arguing and come away.'

'Giving it to me?' Pearl looked at the smiling man. 'It's not his to give, it's a free creature.'

'Prego, signora!'

'Look, Pearl, if you bought the cage full and set them all free you know what would happen? They'd be caught again tomorrow.'

'But how?'

'I don't know. With bird lime and snares.' Bennet said bitterly, 'What chance do they have?'

Pearl sighed. 'I suppose I'm a phoney wanting to buy sausages and wild birds.'

'What?'

'Never mind, let's get away from here.'

As they went, Pearl gingerly carrying the paper bag, the shopkeeper laughed and made fluttering gestures with his hands.

'That man's a brute.'

'He's no St Francis,' said Bennet. 'Who is?'

They went to the end of the street and found a courtyard with an acacia-tree and one side open to the scrubby start of an olive-grove.

'It's quiet here,' said Pearl, 'and the bird can fly up into the tree.' She opened the bag. Nothing happened, the bird did not move. 'Why doesn't it fly out?'

'It can't. Also it's scared.' Ben took the bag, took the bird in his hand and threw it into the air. It fell to the ground, not like a stone so much as a leaf drifting and Pearl exclaimed in dismay. Then it opened its wings, sprang up and was gone.

Pearl laughed. 'That one won't get caught again, it's a wise bird now.' She was relievedly, enormously happy. 'Wasn't it nice of that man to give it to me?'

'You're crazy like a fox, Mrs Rubinsky, and I love you.' Bennet kissed her and they walked with their arms round each other as they used before they were married – and after, though not very lately because Pearl was sensitive about putting her big stomach in front of Bennet.

They found their way back to the hotel by following the direction of general noise pent up in the piazza. It was hard to believe that the place had been quiet when they saw it first. Bennet estimated there were about a thousand people there, counting those on the balconies and roofs and leaning out of windows, all noisy in themselves or in their musical instruments or anything they could bang or blow or twang on. And they were all in motion round the piazza like the stuff breaking and rising, flashing and rolling in a fast-boiling pot.

'My, what a scrimbash,' said Bennet.

'Look, Vic and Nell and the Harold Harpers are over there. Let's go to them.'

Pearl plunged into the crowd. Bennet, protesting, followed. It was quite a battle getting to Vic Farrar and the Harpers. Vic saw them and came to help Pearl.

'Isn't it fun?' cried Pearl.

'It's Walpurgis night,' said Vic.

The staid Nell was dancing with herself, her arms clasped about her shoulders. A boy perched in a tree played his accordion for her alone.

'Pearl, take care!' cried Bennet, temporarily penned behind a string of girls who had joined hands.

'Take care of Higham,' said Vic.

'Higham wants to dance.' Pearl too clasped her arms around herself – across her stomach not her chest – and waltzed to Nell's music. She felt wonderful, light as air and warm as wine and roses.

The boy smiled at her as he played and the breeze rocked the silly bare light bulbs in the chestnut tree.

Then there was no more dancing, they were pushed back against the buildings to accommodate a procession coming into the square. A phalanx of children led, boys in rough white robes and girls in dusty black carrying long peeled sticks with which they struck out, not too much in fun, at people as they passed.

After the children came an old man staggering under a heavy embroidered banner, then a company of nuns followed by boys carrying cardboard lions on sticks and a papier mâché dragon draped over the heads and shoulders of two men on bicycles and riskily lit by candles from inside.

The tail of the dragon clowned around, catching up with its head, riding beside it, pedalling madly past or darting from side to side honking an absurdly falsetto hooter. It was miraculous how he avoided crashing or setting himself alight. The crowd roared slavishly at his every antic. The trumpets and drums of the band following him in blue and silver uniforms were drowned in shouts of 'Bigallo!'

Finally, on a kind of silver cake-round carried by two men came a big plaster figure. It had just been repainted, the colours were bright and sticky, red where red ought to be – white, blue, green, yellow, scrupulously laid on – the map of a girl. Vic said it was Lidia, one of the four patron saints of the town.

'Reminds me of a Chev I had once, I put so many skins of paint on her she was wholly sealed up, you couldn't open the doors or lift the nose or turn the wheels for paint.'

Pearl felt sorry for Lidia. The bearers tilted her so that her chaplet of flowers slid down to her nose. She wasn't getting any reverence. In point of fact, Pearl was thinking, the tone was altogether temporal. Everywhere she looked was this down-to-earthness: the ancient was ancient with years and use and still was being used; the beautiful was something else first – a lot of other things first – and beautiful in the last resort. And so holiness, if there was any, would have to be earned and not just seen. Presumably Lidia earned hers sometime.

The dragon was bringing the tone down further, or its tail was. Its tail certainly was. One of the wheels of the rear bicycle became wedged and amid shouts and laughter the rider fell off. Everyone shouted 'Bigallo!' but the procession moved on without him, the dragon steadily cycling and pulling its empty tail.

Of course he had fixed to fall off so that everyone should see him. He was everyone's fool tonight, a wedge-shaped man with a big head and shoulders tapering to a pair of legs bowed like a baby's. He wore

117

only a waistcoat and shorts and a string of cobnuts round his neck and was either very swarthy or very hairy – he didn't stay still long enough for Pearl to get a good look at his face. The act was to try to mount the bicycle, and as unrehearsed slapstick it was pretty good. His ferocity undermined every move, he employed enormous guile which recoiled on himself; the bicycle defeated him simply and calculably by falling the way he did not expect it to fall, or refusing to go forward with him when he was already launched and in motion.

Round and round he chased, snatching, tripping, piling up with his face in the spokes and his baby-doll legs kicking and the crowd jeered and laughed and stamped and egged him on. If he did manage to mount the machine and began to wobble away someone would reach out and hold the back wheel until he lost his balance and keeled over on his back, the bicycle on top and his feet still furiously pushing at the pedals.

Finally he lost his temper, or pretended to, and tearing off his necklace of cobnuts threw them at the crowd. Women retaliated with flowers which dropped at his feet and then boys aimed olives at him. He pantomimed fury, shadow-boxed the crowd and charged it and fell flat in the best custard and whitewash tradition.

'We could use him to warm up our ball games,' said Vic.

Pearl had never liked clowning, she worried about the mess. Her instinct was to cover up for anyone making a fool of himself, she was sorry for this man. He was filthy from rolling on the ground and his chest and shoulders were scraped raw. She wondered at the work he put into it, the unkindness to himself. Wasn't there a greed about the way people shouted and gestured – as if they couldn't get enough? Was it worth being popular so? Wasn't it too close to being *un*popular?

Suddenly Bigallo picked up his bicycle and rode away. He had either had enough or he wanted to catch the procession. Then the crowd began to move, the bulk-up broke into private eddies. People began to laugh their own laughter and call to each other. But while there was still space around Pearl and Bennet and Vic and Nell and the Harold Harpers, the throwing started.

Vic was the first to be hit. It was nothing worse than an applecore and he grimaced and smiled as he brushed it away. Then Harold uttered an exclamation and put his hand to his face.

'Who threw that?'

Who indeed? People were strolling, talking, singing, some were dancing with their arms across each other's necks. Urchins they suspected but those in sight were scuffling among themselves on the ground.

Then Bennet was struck on the chest. He picked up a small hard olive and even as he straightened he received another full in the face. At the same moment Nell, who was twirling again to the music of the boy in the tree, looked mildly round, rubbing the back of her neck.

'It's from over there,' said Vic. 'Behind the fountain.'

Pearl had already seen. Among so much movement, a group of faces steadily turned were as alerting almost as a streamer. And she was aware of something outcoming across the crowds to them. They were all at the receiving end – Ben and Vic and Nell and the Harpers – why did she feel that she was the focal point? Did she feel that?

'Isn't that the girl from the hotel?' said Vic.

They were all young people and probably it was the holiday, the occasion more than anything they had drunk which had put them in such spirit. Probably they could do as much for each other as the rusty red wine of the hillside and what they did was probably harmless and the germ of harm was slipped them halfway. They were laughing and aiming at the Americans with rubbish from the basin of the fountain, mostly rotten fruit and balled-up cartons, wet and unpleasant but not dangerous. Gilda, the hotel-maid, was with them. Or they were with her. They encouraged each other with their throws and with their hits, but the source was this girl, white-skinned, black-haired, hanging on the arm of a heavy-browed young man – her husband, probably. She was excited, her cheeks flaming, her full lips laughing, crying out or pressed to her wrist in delight.

'Goddamit,' said Vic, ducking to avoid a soggy orange rind, 'what started this?'

'Why don't we do something?' cried Mrs Harold Harper.

'It's only in fun,' said Pearl, 'we should try to understand that.'

She was thinking that it might take a little more time than they had. Not that people here were so complicated or so different, just that she had other expectations, so did Vic and the Harold Harpers, everyone did. And Bennet, of course, knew what she meant – he had meant it, first, anyway.

'Pearl's got something. We shouldn't try to apply our standards.'

Vic picked wet pith off his lapel. 'I don't know if I can go along with some of theirs.'

'You don't have to. Just suspend judgement and take back collateral impressions.'

Pearl saw Gilda quite clearly. Gilda was laughing, she looked like those ripe glowing girls the old masters loved to paint. The sulky-browed young man stooped towards her, his hand possessively on her neck. Gilda turned and looked directly at Pearl. She raised her arm, Pearl was just about to wave back when something struck her full on the forehead.

The blow was as sudden as a clap of darkness. Involuntarily she must have shut her eyes. She opened them and everything was pouring with light – red, green, gold, even Bennet was ablaze. She cried out, held out her hands, she couldn't see who took them and she was terribly afraid of falling and pulling that person down with her.

'Pearl!'

'She's been hit!'

'She's bleeding!'

'No,' Pearl said sharply. 'It's not blood, it's the lights, something happened to the lights.'

Bennet was looking at his palm. 'Here's what they threw. A stone – they threw a stone at her!'

'Nell, help me get her into the hotel.'

'I'm going to find who threw this and give him the hiding of his life!'

'Leave it!'

'Leave it? Till when? Till they make a killing? I'm going to beat hell out of them!'

'Someone should do that!' cried Mrs Harold Harper.

'Don't be a fool.' Vic seized Ben by the back of his jacket. With one twist he had the jacket off Ben's shoulders and pinioned his arms in it. 'Do you want to start a riot?'

'I'm not scared of those hoodlums. . . .' Wrenching and squirming, Bennet fought Vic's hold. He dropped to his knees to try to break it. 'Damn you! Let go!' Vic was stronger than Bennet and all Bennet could seem to break was the buttons off his shirt.

'I'm not thinking only of that bunch,' said Vic. 'The whole town's lit up and God-happy and ready for anything, including mayhem.' He shoved Bennet before him towards the hotel. 'Nell and Mrs Harper, please bring Pearl and let's get the hell out of this.'

And Pearl was frogmarched away too as if she was tending to be troublesome, she who had never felt less like troubling anyone. She just wanted to be in some dark place years from now, with a cold coin on the middle of her forehead. There was a burning hot one there, she was going to have a long, long headache.

And she was upset about what was being done to Bennet. He fought Vic every inch to the hotel, with people laughing and calling heaven knew what at him. They thought he was drunk.

When they reached the lobby he stopped struggling and went quiet and stiff. Vic held his arms and his shirt collar gapped and he looked ready to burst into tears. Cipriani came forward with cries of concern as well he might: they hadn't made much of a carnival night re-entry.

Nell and Mrs Harold took Pearl upstairs and made her lie on her bed. They bathed her forehead: the skin was broken, Nell said, but not to worry. Mrs Harold said she didn't understand anything and wished someone would explain. Pearl wished the same, but who was qualified to do it?

Bennet came and took her hand. 'Pearl, is it bad? Does it hurt?' He gripped and shook her fingers, he was primarily very angry. Anger was a primary feeling and came before love, thought Pearl, way before love.

'No, it isn't bad. I was just surprised I guess.' And surprised for a longer time than that minute. 'It's stopped hurting.'

'Why should they *start* to hurt you? You of all people!'

'I'm not special,' said Pearl.

'You wouldn't hurt a soul!' Bennet indignantly crumpled her hand and then sandwiched it gently between his. 'Pearl, are you going to be OK?'

'She's going to have a headache,' said Mrs Harold.

'We should get a doctor to check her over –'

'In this place?' said Mrs Harold. 'What kind of doctor do you expect to get here? Let her rest and take a little aspirin if she must. I had it through pregnancy without ill effect, but strength of mind is the only recommendation I really care to give.'

Mrs Harold and Nell left soon after and Bennet went at once to the window.

'That bunch is still down there fooling about among themselves. I don't see the girl.'

'What girl?'

'From the hotel. She was with them.'

'She wasn't.' Pearl shut her eyes. It wasn't true, either, that the bruise had stopped hurting. In the middle of her forehead she felt every contour of the stone that had hit her. 'They were strangers, all of them, and they were only fooling.'

'The blood on your face wasn't fooling.' Bennet soberly buttoned his shirt. 'I was ready to take them all on. I could have, Pearl.'

'I know.'

'Vic Farrar said that's what they wanted, to provoke us. I didn't care if they did or not, it was what *I* wanted.'

Against her eyelids Pearl could see the bruise. It was X-shaped, a cross of purple fire. 'I'm glad you let them go.'

'Vic stopped me. He had a jackhold, but if I could have broken it I'd have gone for them. I'd have broken Vic's arms, Pearl, and gone for them.'

121

'I'm glad you didn't fight. I think I'd have died.'

'A man has his feelings.'

'I know.' She said softly, 'I know about your feelings.'

'He was right though, Vic was right to stop me. Why, it was nearly an international incident.'

Pearl raised herself on her elbow and reached towards the dressing-table. She was going to look in the hand-mirror at the mark on her forehead. 'You mean there could have been a war about it?'

'Now did I say that? Did I mention a nuclear holocaust? You're putting words in my mouth again, Pearl. It could get us in serious trouble. This isn't America, this is Europe and they're jumpy as hell.'

It brought tears to her eyes and a lump to her throat. 'I wish we were home!'

'Look at it this way. We're ambassadors here, I'm not putting it too high to say that. What these people think of us is what they're going to think of America. Vic could see that, he thought for all of us. It isn't everyone can do that, Pearl, at a time like that.'

'Nell wasn't hurt.'

'I just wonder if I'd have had the foresight to hold *him* back if she had been. We can only hope so.' Ben looked at her soberly. 'It's not so much of a bruise.'

It was more of a graze really, where the sharp edge of the stone had broken the skin the threads of blood had dried already. There was no point in saying that it had broken much more, that she had the sensation of a great star-shaped fissure. In what? The window of my soul, she thought. Oh my!

'No, it's really nothing.'

'Are you sure you feel – in yourself –' Ben gingerly touched the blanket over her stomach, 'in the essential, I mean, you feel secure?'

'I feel fine.'

'Rest is what you need. Rest and quiet.' He closed the windows on the sound of music from the piazza. They were dancing now, crammed together, back to back. Pearl wondered if Nell's little soloist had found someone else to play to. 'I think I'll go and talk to Vic. Will you be OK, honey?'

'I'll be fine.'

'I'll be right back.'

He went out, gently closing the door. He was going to talk to Vic, acknowledge Vic's responsibility, give him best. Bennet was ready – anxious, in fact – to do that when he believed it was due and he was going to think a lot of Vic Farrar from now on. Vic had just got himself that distinction.

Pearl put down the hand-mirror and lay back on the pillows. She started to relax the way she had been taught, toes first – tightening and letting go, ankles, calves, knees, thighs, right through her body to her scalp. Her scalp was where she should have finished, but she could neither tighten nor slacken her forehead. She had no muscles left in her forehead.

'It's localised anyway.' She patted her stomach. 'You're all right, Higham.'

She wouldn't be getting up early tomorrow to light a candle. She didn't wish anything for the girl, good or bad. She was sorry for her, but that was only a quarter of the story because besides Gilda and her need was Gilda's husband and his need. And besides sorrow which Pearl had now, there was splendour which she had had for seven months. This evening, right up until the almost international incident, she had felt very, very splendid. Perhaps it was the splendour that the stone had broken.

Had she been responsible, like Vic, thinking of other people and not just herself, she would get up tomorrow early and light two candles for Gilda. Gilda certainly could use them. I would, thought Pearl, if I believed they'd do any good, if I thought they'd really do something for her – it did not seem illogical to insist on that now, whereas before the gesture had been nice enough and the thought sufficient – but of course it's nonsense. I wouldn't be justified in contributing, morally I'd be wrong, playing at responsibility. I should ask her point-blank why she threw a stone at me, make her say why so that she understands it herself.

Was that what she should do? But she wasn't like Vic and she didn't have to study to be like him. She rolled over, but nowadays it was pretty uncomfortable lying on her side. Groaning, she rolled back and found herself looking up into Gilda's face.

It was a physical shock and Pearl's body reacted at once. It bore down on the bed, absurdly trying to shrink its stomach, and she had a half-second to observe this. Of course she had known that she would almost certainly have to face Gilda again and she had accepted it that way. She didn't think – she didn't even think it would be more fitting to think – that Gilda would almost certainly have to face her.

She must have cried out with alarm because Gilda said, 'Signora?', inclining her head on her strong white neck.

Pearl pushed herself up on her elbows. She had not expected the facing to be like this, with her stretched out, disadvantaged, on her bed. She would have slipped off and got to her feet, but Gilda put a hand on the bed on either side and leaned over Pearl.

'Are you not well, Signora?'

Pearl's heart beat uncomfortably. She was sweating, which she practically never did, and quite independently her right arm went across her stomach which she had been taught never to try to hide but to carry in pride and joy. She was scared, her instinct was not to trust this girl and a purely animal instinct it was – nothing to do with reason. Reason urged Pearl to challenge the girl, make her think what she had done, why she had done it.

'I have a headache.'

What was it that Pearl instinctively feared, apart from the capacity to throw stones? Of course Pearl would never have that capacity herself, she wouldn't want to do anyone that kind of harm. But of course that wasn't the harm Gilda wanted to do Pearl, not stone-throwing, not really.

'A headache?'

She was a beautiful girl: presently she would coarsen and fatten and this she would let happen and in her heavy white body would be the same fear and rage. But she was beautiful now and the fear and rage could be forgiven.

'Gilda –' Pearl said softly, but Gilda cried, 'A headache?' and leaned over and ungently touched the centre of Pearl's forehead. When Pearl flinched and tried to turn her head away she laughed.

'Why do you want to hurt me?'

'Hurt?' Gilda's throat arched and her tongue curled back between her teeth with laughter. 'Here we lie down for a man, not a headache!' She ran to the window and with a thrust of her arms burst the shutters apart. 'You should dance. All night. We shall all dance all night, every man with every girl until the feet bleed!'

Pearl shuddered. The noise of the band came brassing over the noise of the crowd, her head throbbed to a strict tempo, the lights jazzed in her eyes.

'Please shut the window.'

'You are not sick! Women have babies all the time.'

'Yes,' said Pearl, 'don't they?' and they gazed at each other, Gilda with her back to the window and the fleering lights, Pearl on the bed, propped on her hands behind her spreading stomach. It wasn't international, it was their own incident.

Gilda suddenly came back to the bed and dropped to her knees. Pearl cried out in alarm as she pulled away the blanket.

'What are you doing?'

Gilda put her ear to Pearl's stomach. 'I am listening to the life.'

Noon

Perhaps no one else appreciated what a decisive time it was because each thought that he or she was the person doing something different. The little ones did not think about it at all, they came from the beach intent on sand messes and scotch eggs, this year they were absolutely dedicated to scotch eggs for lunch. At noon the parents – the 'husbands and wives' Davina Saye-Hennessy was calling them – met together in the hotel bar for drinks; the curtains of the bungalow on the cliff were closed one by one and the skuas flew off their rock for a destination unknown.

Looking up at the bungalow Davina said to Jane, 'I shouldn't fancy it at the same time every day, it's so automatic.'

'Mother says if you make a point of going to sleep always at exactly the same time it becomes as automatic as switching off the light.'

'Animalcule, who's talking about going to sleep?' Davina had grown up since last summer and her amusement was now quite private.

Noon was the time she chose for her sun-bath. She took off all her clothes and lay among the rocks at the far end of the beach, and that too was since last summer. Then she had been a tomboy, salty and ubiquitous. Now she was languid and withdrawn, her rare bursts of energy tumbled Jane as the foam tumbles a cork.

'You can be judged by what you are found to be doing at noon.' Davina scooped a hollow in the sand for her shoulders. 'No other hour is so significant.'

Jane was to be found standing guard although this was hardly necessary since no one else came to the beach at noon. Davina herself wouldn't have bothered but Jane did, Jane fretted.

'Why do you do it?' Even as she asked she suspected that Davina would tell her such a small fraction of the truth as to constitute a lie. 'Don't pretend it's just to get brown all over because I know it's not.

'Suppose someone sees you?' To Jane that would be as shameful as if someone were to see herself naked on the sand. She couldn't explain but she was furious with Davina for exposing them both. 'What would they think?'

Davina leaned back on her elbows, her eyes shut against the sun. 'You're a damned prude.'

Was that what Jane was? Was it damnable to rather – infinitely to rather – *not* look at naked bodies? And was she permanently damned if she never got to like the sight?

'Don't show how absolutely without it you are, Baby Jane. Nudity is normal.'

'You're only two years older than me.'

'Three. And environment counts.'

'What's wrong with my environment?'

'The question is, are you going to live now, good child, or in the past? You're a hundred years out of date.'

'I am not! I just don't like that sort of thing. I –'

'It isn't any sort of thing,' said Davina, '*it's my* thing and you couldn't understand.'

'Sitting in the sun makes my head ache.'

'Then go and have nursery lunch with the other babies.'

'But suppose someone comes? Suppose someone sees you?'

Davina may have wanted someone to see her. The thought, coming of Jane's ridiculous concern, interested her. If someone were to see her would she ever do this again? If someone were to see her it would be a conclusion, yes, a logical one, but it wasn't the reason why she stripped, or rather it wasn't the only reason. There were many reasons, all intricate.

She rolled on her face. Here was one: arching her quaking stomach she gently lowered it to the burning sand. With fingers and toes she scrabbled until, under the surface, she found icy cold and wetness. To experience this extra hotness and coldness at the same moment was indescribably important. How could she possibly describe it? Or the feeling that she was full of sea, that she was the quick of the sea, that pierce her and pain would run out into the Indian Ocean? Or the sounds which she did not so much hear as transmit? Which came up through the sand and sounded through her bones? At best they were a kind of music and she the one instrument it could be played on, but generally they were intimations of something else entirely going on. Life at another level. How could she tell anyone that this was her essential private history which poor little Jane would try to forget?

In the hotel bar Tommy Wilsher said, 'This is the best time of the day,' and some of the others agreed. To some the mornings were rather a strain. Their working days were full of occasions to rise to, but the weather had become too hot for golf and unless they were dedicated sea- or sun-bathers they had three hours of nothing particular to do. Some of them didn't enjoy that and since they were paying to enjoy themselves it weighed on their consciences and they kept trying to get their money's worth. There should be some keener pleasure than dozing in deck-chairs.

'This is my finest hour,' said Tommy, 'and it's regular.'

'Isn't that a double negative?' his wife said to the Flessatis. 'It cancels itself out.'

'This is when I begin to be human again.'

'It's when you begin to drink.'

'We're on holiday, woman. Aren't we?'

A curious situation when thought about, and a few of them had thought about it while watching the sea rolling and unrolling. Lots of time, food, drink and scenery were the authorised version of bliss but some one or two of them had heard a voice crying, 'I don't know what more you want!'

'Tommy's been on holiday all his life,' Netta Wilsher told the Flessatis, 'which is not such an achievement because nothing kills a holiday so stone dead as having everyone else kicking around too.'

'You don't know anything about me,' Tommy said to her. 'After fifteen years of marriage you should have picked up a few specifications. For one thing, I like people, I need them. With people I come alive. . . .'

Netta laughed. 'I've done my best,' she told the Flessatis. 'I keep coming in in different hats and I say "rhubarb, rhubarb, rhubarb" to encourage him to talk – like mothers, say "wiss, wiss, wiss" to get the baby to go pee-pee.'

'People!' shouted Tommy. 'I need warm-blooded human people, not a cold tin bitch!'

'What are you drinking, Netta?' said Ellyott. 'Gin and French?'

'I'm not drinking. We can't afford both to.'

'Am I hearing right?' Tommy appealed to the Saye-Hennessy's who came into the bar then. 'Or am I stoned already?'

Netta stood up and with a Huckleberry gesture dived both hands into the pockets of her jeans. 'This morning we're three gins to the good and that's thanks to me.'

'Do I beat you? Or starve you? Do I go to another woman for satisfaction? I don't know the meaning of the word any more –'

'Be quiet, Tom,' said Mrs Saye-Hennessy. 'We've had a long, long morning on the beach and we've come in for some short, short drinkies. No sexual recriminations, please.'

'We're not drinking. My wife says we can't afford to. Will the barman give a rebate on this whisky which I've only looked at, or can I interest any of you in a second-hand Scotch? At auction – going, going – in a good cause – to keep my wife from starving.'

'Netta's drinking with me,' said Ellyott.

'She can't accept charity. She's got principles, she's got them all over. I tell you, hedgehogs don't have prickles where she has principles.'

'It's not charity –'

'That's how there can be little hedgehogs!'

Ellyott put his hand on Netta's shoulder. 'It isn't charity, it's my privilege and pleasure,' and steered her on to the balcony. She was trembling but her smile was tight. 'We'll make it a large gin,' he said.

'I haven't even got the excuse that he's drunk.'

'He is in a way. After a drink or two he'll sober up.'

When he came back from the bar she was gazing out to sea, her chin in her hands. He was glad to see that the smile had gone and she had stopped trembling.

'We heard a strange sound last night,' she said. 'It was about eleven o'clock, we were walking along the beach and the sea was very dark – you know how enormously dark it can be. We were very happy. We often are,' she assured him sharply as if he had questioned it. 'We heard something, I can't describe it but it was low and sweet and we stood still to listen because even the shuffle of our feet on the sand drowned it. Tommy said it was mermaids singing.'

It never ceased to surprise Maurice Ellyott what men said to women, how out of character it was. He put the gin into her hand. 'This is a haunted shore.'

'Is it?' she said, 'Is it?' as if it mattered. Perhaps it did, if she wanted mermaids she would want ghosts.

'I suppose one can expect it of any shore – if one is disposed to expect anything of the kind. Not, perhaps, of Brighton beach, though there have been drownings even there.'

'Isn't that your Jane?'

He shielded his eyes and looked. The small dissolving figure in the heat haze was unmistakably his Jane, unrelaxed as a squirrel, on a big loaf-coloured rock below the headland. He smiled at the Janeness of her.

'Tommy blames me for not having children,' said Netta, and he was brought back into the thick of that.

'Tommy doesn't want children,' he said. 'He told me.'

'He doesn't want them as such – if you know what I mean.'

She drank half her gin and twitched the base of her glass round and round on the stone parapet. It made a slight gritting sound which emphasised for Ellyott the unpleasantness of the incident.

'I think women over-estimate the importance of procreation to a man – the function, that is, not the act,' he said carefully. 'They are congenitally unbalanced on the question. I think a woman is more likely to blame herself, often quite unjustly.'

He was also thinking about Jane. Why was she there? She was passionately inconspicuous by nature, sitting alone on a rock on a deserted beach in the noonday sun wasn't like her.

Netta said, raising her glass to him, 'Thank you, Ellyott-with-a-y,' and he complained to his wife afterwards about people who asked for sympathy and then mocked the sympathiser.

'She wasn't mocking,' said his wife. 'She once told me she envied me. "Your Maurice is stamped right through," she said, "Like a stick of rock." '

'I don't care for her analogy.'

'Oh my dear, take it from whence it came. Netta can't trust Tommy even to handle their domestic finances. Do you wonder that she envies anyone with confidence in her husband?'

'I didn't care for Wilsher's, either. Some things are private and incommunicable, it's embarrassing when people try to communicate them. I resent being given innuendoes to translate.'

'Don't you think she felt that too? She was grateful to you for stopping it.'

'I hope they don't make a habit of it, I shan't make a habit of my part. By the way, what was Jane doing on the beach at noon?'

'On the beach?'

'I saw her from the balcony. She was sitting on a rock, all alone.'

'Alone? She usually goes with Davina. Today I was too busy with the babies' lunch to notice what she did.'

'What I find surprising,' said Ellyott, 'is the time and place. The beach at noon is an odd place for Jane to be.'

'She really should have her lunch with the little ones and take a nap while we have ours. She shall tomorrow.'

But by tomorrow Jane had a blinding headache and sickness and was so miserable that she lay in a darkened room and wished to die. The light hurt her terribly. It was stored up in her head and broke into scalding splinters except when her mother's hands covered her eyes. The doctor diagnosed a touch of the sun.

'She's delirious,' said Ellyott. 'She's had more than a touch, I should say she's had a thump of the sun.'

'She appears to have something on her mind,' agreed the doctor. 'Can't you reassure her?'

Jane's mind indeed seemed to be giving her as much trouble as her sickness. Her face was pinched with worry.

'Don't go to the beach, Daddy, don't let *anyone* go to the beach.'

'But Jane, they're all on the beach, as happy as sandboys.'

'When they come up,' said Jane faintly, 'don't let them go back. Promise –'

'But why, Jane?'

She was about to be sick again and wailed in her misery.

'Just promise,' his wife said sharply. 'That's all you need do.'

'How can I?'

'Because the child's ill and she asks you to!'

So Ellyott promised and Jane leaned retching over the basin.

'Poor little sweet,' said her mother, 'she's worried that the others might get sick too.'

Ellyott doubted that. He was not denying his daughter's goodness of heart, he was remembering the outline of her on the rock. Why did she sit up there as if to the crack of a whip?

His wife laid the child on her pillows and gently touched the wide-open eyelids. 'Rest now, darling, everything's all right. A promise is a promise.'

Jane looked at her father. He was not to know what passed between them but it seemed to satisfy her and her eyes blinked shut as tight as a doll's.

There was nothing more that Ellyott could do. He went slowly downstairs, pausing on the landing to look through the medallion window at the sea. He took these pictures with him when he left, these locket pictures of a small sea – the depth of glass it was, perhaps, that minimised it. On choppy days the foam creamed along the shore, in calm weather the sky and sea were cracked with a fine hair crack and the boats, when there were boats, inched along the radius and vanished. Ellyott liked to remember the views from the landing window. He had formed the habit of stopping to add to them whenever he could.

It was now eleven o'clock, the sky was white hot. Red and blue children like confetti were dotted over the sands. Sighing, Ellyott went downstairs and out on to the terrace. He noted that they had just watered the paving stones and swept them. The stones steamed as he watched. Really it was unseemly and if he had wanted brass heat he could have gone to Spain.

He found a chair in the scant shade of a wall. Here, everything was battened down, pinned back and put away from the wind and rain, there was no provision for prolonged heat-waves. At night now, after days of unmitigated sun, the old rocks sweated but did not completely cool. Ellyott's trousers dragged at his damp knees as he sat down, he picked them up between finger and thumb and shook them free.

He could only suppose that Jane in the blaze of noon had meant to mortify her flesh. Since she was of his flesh he had some idea of what she had suffered. Children, other children, were primitives. He excepted Jane, but he knew that she was devoted to her principles and some of them, necessarily, were childish.

Tommy Wilsher shambled past wearing wet bathing trunks and a sandy towel over his shoulder. Seeing Ellyott he came back and flopped down beside him.

'Got a cigarette?'

Ellyott gave him one and Tommy hugged his knees and smoked strenuously. He had plump round knees covered with golden fuzz like babies' heads.

'Don't believe all you hear.'

'I don't think I've heard anything,' said Ellyott.

'She – Netta – told you I was a drunken sod.'

'No.'

'That you can believe. I am. But I'm not bankrupt.'

'She didn't say you were.'

'She'd like me to be, she'd like me really down in every way so she could raise me up. Women all want that.'

Ellyott could see that it might be true in Wilsher's case. Whatever he did to himself he looked like a damped and tidied boy.

'I can't complain about the profit margin. In my line of business it's never staggering, but it's steady.'

'That's nice,' Ellyott said politely.

'I daresay I'm worth as much as anyone here. I *do* say it!' Pink rushed up out of Tommy's collar into the roots of his cornstalk hair. 'I'm worth more than Saye-Hennessy on his Army pay and Flessati with his pickle-works.'

'Flessati's in the wine trade.'

'And he drinks on an expense account. And his Mercedes is a company car. Well I couldn't live like that, what's mine's my own.'

'It's odd weather we're having for this part of the world,' said Ellyott. 'This long hot spell has changed the character of the place.'

Tommy glared. He looked maternal with those twin baby heads clasped to his bare chest.

'I could lend *you* a card or two.'

'No doubt.'

'You're full of doubt!' Tommy's rage suddenly gave out. He flung himself on his back with a winded grunt. Looking up at Ellyott he was a size smaller but had become privately content with himself. 'You're right to be. And Netta's right to watch our outgoings, though God knows what good it can do. We wouldn't be here if she weren't paying, she said we had to have a holiday. "Let's try to get back where we started, let's try to be friends again." Friends! What the hell does she mean?'

Even Tommy did not expect an answer to that. He employed himself smoking his cigarette upright like a funnel and making train noises. Ellyott flexed his damp knees preparatory to getting up and going.

'We never were friends. I used to tell her as much as I thought good for her and the fact is, nowadays the less she knows the better.'

'I assure you I've forgotten the incident. I imagine everyone else has too.'

'Poop, poop!' said Tommy, and moved his arms like pistons.

'Excuse me. I find it uncomfortably hot out of doors at this time of day.'

'You're excused, old Ellyott-with-a-y.'

'Why do you call me that?'

'Because it's your name.'

Ellyott went back into the hotel. His wife was not in their room. She looked up when he gently opened the door of Jane's room and put her finger on her lips. Jane was sleeping.

The time was eleven thirty-five. Ellyott lay on his bed and watched the clock. He heard them come from the beach, the children first – their voices like the chatter of sparrows on Sundays. Then came the adults, the Flessatis hauling their fibre-glass boat over the pebbles and Saye-Hennessy who cracked his towel like a whip, all of them who kept the noon ritual.

He lay until the door slammed on the last voice. He heard the skuas go over, circling round as was their custom before flying away. Then he put on his hat and went down to the beach.

He and Jane were much alike. She had her principles which were sacred to her, and horrors which he recognised as young versions of his own. He grieved sometimes for the offences which she would be caused. She was going to grow up to a series of shocks, a blow-by-blow destruction of what she in her innocence held dear. He wished her a thicker skin and a less passionate heart.

The spring tides had thrown cordons of pebbles up the beach. They were like mountain ranges, the valleys between being deep enough not to be able to see over. Ellyott, standing at the bottom, watched the peaks bleed off into the white sky. He began to see the same sly motion everywhere, it was all slipping in the heat. He could smell dead crabs and stranded fish which would undoubtedly have reached a high degree of putrefaction. His tongue tasted foreign to his mouth, but he was scrupulous in his repugnance. He picked up and fingered the texture of one of the pebbles. It was sticky with salt. He put it back where he had found it and climbed on up the slopes, lifting his feet as if to negotiate eggshells.

Jane must also have disliked this. She would have disliked it more, tender Jane could not have expected to enjoy herself alone in the wolfish heat of this utterly inhospitable place. And if she had found herself here by accident she could have upped – the word was appropriate to her manner of departure – and left. Why hadn't she? Why not, with the glare making her head throb and the smell and feel unpleasantly affecting her? His hope of finding out was minimal because probably Jane herself could not have told him. Probably it was incommunicable.

When he should locate her rock he proposed sitting there himself – briefly, he stipulated, wiping the triangle between his upper lip and his moustache – he would then either see what she had seen or, if great minds think alike so surely must blood-related ones and he would get an idea how her thoughts had tended.

He didn't find Jane's rock because he found Davina first and it was a measure of his dislocation that from then on he scarcely remembered Jane's part. He thought at first that Davina was a mermaid. They exist! he thought, without tenderness or enchantment. But the idea did have significance and seemed, even in his confusion, to presage radical alterations.

He was horrified. In a fractional moment he experienced fear, revulsion, dismay – and indignation on account of supposing her a monster half human, half fish, which would create confusion in scientific circles. There was also the implied insult to the human form.

He objected to being personally involved with such a discovery. Mermaids were not only legendary creatures, they were seaside low comedy, picture postcard jokes of the order of the fat lady in a striped bathing-suit.

Then he saw that she had two legs like everyone else. She lay with her head towards him and her feet to the sea and her face being upside down it was by her long poker-straight hair that he recognised the Saye-Hennessy child. He groaned and stirred in his stiff clothes.

Davina had heard him coming over the beach. She had been unsurprised, knowing that he must come. The end had been ordained – if that was the word and was not merely what was done to clergymen – from the beginning. She had to be seen, heaven knew why – heaven must know, no one else did.

Calmly she turned to look, not particularly concerned about identity. But when she saw that it was Jane's father she was furious. Hell, she thought, oh bloody damned hell! Aren't there any *people* here, only parents?

She glared up through her eyelids. She wasn't going to move or try to run away, anyhow she couldn't now without his seeing her. Perhaps if she lay still he would politely look the other way. He was a very polite person. Where was he going? Down to the sea for a private paddle while the beach was empty and no one would see his bare feet?

He never swam or sunbathed, he sat in the shade in his linen suit doing crossword puzzles. In Davina's unconsidered opinion he might as well be dead except for the use he was to Jane. His footsteps over the pebbles sounded like a horse munching. Davina, wondering what Jane would make of the development, sniffed with laughter.

The crunching stopped suddenly. She arched her neck and looked backwards. He was about twenty feet away, at the top of a ridge of pebbles and though he wore dark glasses she knew that he was looking straight at her. No man had ever done what he was doing, not even her own father. What a foul trick of fate that someone's *father* should be the first!

'Go away! Shoo!' she said aloud, but of course he went on looking through his medicine-blue lenses, he probably thought she didn't speak English, probably he thought she was a big blue shrimp.

She relaxed her neck muscles and lay flat again. Apparently things could go wrong even when they had not been planned, nor sought, nor entirely understood. What she meant was, there had seemed to be a reason for what she experienced on this beach, it had all seemed to be getting her somewhere. How stupid and pointless and stultifying if it had to end with Jane Ellyott's father.

Ellyott feared she was going to scream. He would suffer complete disintegration if she did. At present he was shattered, though not widely, and held himself together, just. Seeing her mouth move and open he waited with skin crawling. But she uttered no sound, or none that he heard. She flattened on the sand and the soft-shoe shuffle of the sea, passing for silence, kept him from falling apart.

After a physical crisis people need just to sleep. He needed just to look. He realised that if he were to get decently by this – he could never get over it – he must be allowed to look. He stood as sharp and still, had he known it, as Jane on her rock. He didn't give Jane a thought, not Jane or anyone, with Davina shining full in his face.

The naked women he had seen in rooms, among beds, chairs, tables and the universal tooth-glass, had not prepared him for this voluptuous child on a stark white shore. Remembering those women wouldn't have made her any easier to look at. He did not remember, he gazed like Adam on his converted rib.

Davina was going to be big. Her mother had told her, 'Men like big girls and Army men prefer them. Remember, it's the men who matter, I'll not have a girl of mine left on the shelf.'

'What a quaint phrase. Lots of people don't believe in marriage.'

'You do. And you believe in God.'

'What's God got to do with it?'

'It's part of the same thing.'

'I may not stay in the Army.' Davina had said. She meant to have a career, she wanted to taste all sorts of life – eventually she would have to eat some of it. 'I'm not interested in men *per se*.'

'What?'

'As distinct from women.' But Davina's mother maintained that she would be when the distinction became apparent. Davina privately contested that, and on the beach with Mr Ellyott considered that she had disproved it. In the first analysis, Jane's father was a man.

She remembered the bottle which Alice had found in Wonderland, bearing a label – 'Drink Me'. She needed no label, the sun drank her up through to her backblades and when she turned on her face she was dry as a leaf. Mr Ellyott stood absolutely still, as still as death. She felt a twinge of interest.

Ellyott had been holding his breath. When she moved he allowed himself to exhale. The sun leaned on him and sweat ran over his lip and down the backs of his legs. He noticed nothing. He was simply a seeing eye, seeing the girl tapered solid as a fish from her waist to her upcurled toes. Seeing her for five minutes? Ten? He could not have gone farther or forgotten more in a lifetime of travelling.

He came to himself as if a switch had been pulled. Davina heard him leave. She did not lift her face from her arms. Punch, punch, punch! went his feet on the pebbles, walking away fast.

As they sat at lunch Ellyott's wife asked him if he had found anything.

'What should I find?'

'When you went to the beach.'

'I went. Why not?'

'I was wondering why Jane was so anxious that you shouldn't. I thought you might have found out.'

'I went to find out, if I could, why she should choose to stay there until she made herself ill.'

'Netta Wilsher says Jane regularly sits on the beach at that time of day. She can see her from her window. When the heat's really unbearable, Netta says, there's Jane bolt upright on a rock.'

Ellyott found that he preferred not to think about Jane on the beach. He preferred not to think about the beach at all.

'She won't tell me anything,' said his wife.

'There's probably nothing to tell.'

'I shall ask Davina Saye-Hennessy if she knows.'

'It will be best if we simply drop the subject. I don't believe it will happen again.' At the moment of speaking, he did not. It was unquestionably an isolated incident. His wife stubbornly crumbled her bread. 'It will be kinder to say no more,' he said, rebuking her.

Davina, at table with her parents, considered Mr Ellyott through her sunglasses: as from this p.m. she had taken to wearing them indoors. She found him better-looking than the other men, though not nicer: Ted Cotterell was nicer looking but he almost always overdid everything and this Davina found pitiable. Jane's father was actually handsome, actually his paternity was irrelevant she now realised. He was not as much a parent as her own father – or as Mrs Ellyott for that matter.

He has redeeming features, she thought, looking at his profile, he has not coarsened himself with family living.

He appeared uninvolved even with Mrs Ellyott – or *particularly* with Mrs Ellyott. Although he sat at a table with her they did not make a pair.

He did not look at Davina, not once, not even in her direction. It would have changed the whole complexion if he had. Tommy Wilsher would have looked at her, had it been Tommy Wilsher who saw her nude on the beach he would have brought her nudity right back into the dining-room with him. And expected to flip the secret between them. Tommy Wilsher would wink and wave, she could picture him waving two fingers at her across the tables.

'Take off those glasses, Davina,' said her mother. 'It's harmful and rude to wear them indoors.'

I suppose it could have been worse, Davina thought resignedly, laying aside her glasses. Without them she saw that Ellyott's cheekbone, where his beard would be if he did not shave, was lavender blue.

Next day Ellyott discovered that he was prepared to go to the beach at noon. He stood patiently in a corner of the terrace, a non-shady spot but one of the few places where he would not be noticed. He would not allow himself any reaction, he was like a man with a tricky beast which needed to be given rope before it could be finger-tip controlled.

People were still spread among the rocks and bobbing about in the sea. It seemed impossible that the beach would ever be vacated.

The old Downeys were the first to move, they had weak hearts and could not hurry. Then the Cotterell boys went, kicking a beach ball, and Saye-Hennessy strode up from his swim. The children ebbed and flowed and finally leaked away and at the cliff bungalow the curtains were drawn over the windows like the thin eyelids of a bird.

Who had instituted the exodus? Was it only this summer, an uncharacteristically hot summer, that everyone got up and left the beach together? Why did they do it? Not to escape the heat of the day, many were back on the beach by two o'clock when it was appreciably hotter than at twelve. Just to drink or to get ready for lunch or because, like the children, they were made to?

He saw Davina wearing a green dress and walking among the rocks and so sharply turned from the sight that he pulled a muscle in his neck.

Perhaps last year he simply hadn't been aware of the exodus at noon. Perhaps there was no significance in common, perhaps it was simply a habit which everyone happened to keep to and any time now someone would break.

He began to walk slowly down the beach over the intrusive pebbles. He did not wish to intrude. Once he saw a green flash like a flag among the rocks and went cold with anger. But he kept on, lifting and gently placing his feet. The noise of the stones lacerated him.

Davina thought, I shall never understand why I did not understand that it had to be him. There's no other possibility, they're all too old or too young. He stands out like a sore thumb – no, not sore, he's too collected, and not a thumb, he's a long middle finger.

She remembered how Mr Ellyott had looked at her on the day she arrived at the hotel. When she went in to dinner he had put his chin on his hand and looked, but he hadn't seemed to see her after that. He's seeing me now, she thought.

She hadn't been sure that he would come to the beach again today. Suddenly it had begun to matter, before she could turn around it mattered intensely. When she undressed last night she could see no reason why he should come. She wasn't the shape yet. Her breasts were like kitchen cups, they should be pointed like pears: she couldn't keep her stomach in, it positively pouted, and she had almost no shadow between her thighs.

If he did not come to the beach and she did, she would have to live with the knowledge. There was a distinct possibility of its poisoning her life. Then she saw him waiting on the hotel terrace, wearing his bread-coloured suit and his cap. He was so *fully* dressed!

He came down the beach and stood in the same place as yesterday, already she thought of it as his position. He has taken up his position, she thought, but of course they were not playing a game. At least not a children's game. She believed it was the word 'play' she objected to.

Ellyott had gone through the time between, through meals, conversations, encounters, appearances of rest, pretences of sleep and gestures of habit, passing the hours until noon. Everything he did, appeared to do, was cover for that – yet it wouldn't have mattered, either, if there were no cover, he believed he would simply have come to the beach and looked, or simply stayed on the beach and looked. Simply, simply, was his cry from the heart.

And looking was so soon unbearable. The glare hurt his eyes. He shut them and girl-shaped blood blazed under his eyelids. He opened them and she was glutted with light.

So much ultra-violet brought on prophylactic tears. He did not attempt to rub or blink them away, he turned and climbed blindly back up the beach.

He asked Saye-Hennessy, 'How old is your daughter?'

'Davy? Going on thirteen.'

'She's – tall for her age.'

'We're all tall for our age. I'm six foot three, my wife's five-nine and my son's six foot four and a half.'

He delivered the information with zest. Ellyott sensed that it was an integral part of his philosophy.

'Davina's bright with it,' said the major. 'Tell me, is it still waste to educate females?'

'Still?'

'It always was. And biologically they haven't changed, they've pushed themselves but they're still the only ones that can proliferate.'

'Excuse me,' said Ellyott, but the Major held him with a plain stare.

'I don't think women are inferior, I think their minds are different. No daughter of mine's going to be educated beyond her capacity.'

Ellyott averted his eyes from the tuft of hairs in the hollow of the Major's throat. He had hoped the confrontation with Davina's father might restore his sense of values, but he found himself unable to accept that the girl on the beach had the remotest connection with Major Saye-Hennessy. He could not even connect her with Davina Saye-Hennessy.

'She'd make a good nurse, she has the brain to count swabs and the brawn to lift the incontinent sick. She wants to be a doctor, of course.'

Davina Saye-Hennessy was still a child. Dressed, even partially, in that avid summer, he recalled that her body was not serene. It filled out her clothes like soft fruit filling out a paper bag.

'Or a lawyer because she can argue the toss.'

The girl on the beach was more original than a child and she had existed long, long before Major Saye-Hennessy.

'It's important to know your limitations.' The Major complained to his wife afterwards that Ellyott's expression – when his face had any – did not synchronise with what was being said to him.

In the morning the sea had a skin which did not break, even on the last wave up the beach. All along the shore it lifted and lapsed without a crease. There wasn't a cloud in the sky and it was hotter than ever. The black hand of the barometer moved backwards when the glass was tapped.

Ellyott watched them go to the beach. The small children were fretful and buffeted each other. Their wails mixed with the cries of the skuas which could not settle on their usual rock.

'The weather's breaking,' said old Mr Downey as he came by. 'The birds know.'

'It's not that,' Tim Cotterell told Ellyott. 'There's a hawk about.'

Hand in hand the Wilshers passed Ellyott without a word. He watched them walk into the sea. Their heads remained precisely the same distance apart.

He played clock golf with the other Cotterell boy. After several rounds Ted Cotterell suggested a swim.

'No. I am definitely not going to the beach today.'

'Well, I am.' Ted dropped his shirt and trousers on the terrace and vaulted on to the beach. He already wore his bathing trunks.

Jane was much better, she was sitting up in bed, reading. Mrs Ellyott had had rather a bad time with her.

'Nursing a sick child in a hotel, one is made to feel like a criminal.'

'I suppose they were afraid she might have something catching.'

'Like Bubonic Plague?'

'Why don't you lie down for an hour before lunch?'

'What I'd really like is a drink. Jane won't need me for a while.'

Ellyott looked at his watch. 'No one will be back from the beach yet.'

'They really have been disobliging about Jane. The trouble it was to get her a little iced water! With children in the place there should be some sort of room service at night.'

'I suppose a hotel must run on the assumption that everyone will be normal.'

'Every morning I had a fracas with the chambermaid. She wanted to turn out Jane's room and if I hadn't been there she'd have turned Jane out with it.'

'We shan't come here again.'

'But you like it here.' She too paused at the medallion window on the landing. 'So do I.'

'There's no need to make a habit of it.'

'None of the children have ever been ill on holiday before. It might not happen again.' She said, looking through the window, 'How much more pleasing a view is when it's framed.

'I admit it's a very clean hotel,' she said. 'The girl was telling me she has to turn out every room every other day. Thoroughly. The manager's Swiss and of course there's no other work for people here.'

'We shan't come back.'

He had a whisky while he waited for noon. When the time came he

stood up and put his bar stool into place and announced to his wife
that he was going for a walk.

'A walk?'

'Why don't you come?' He was without compunction.

'This is the hottest time of the day.'

'It gets hotter later on.' He touched her hand in leave-taking and
left her at the bar.

'Maurice!'

He did not look round although he smiled at Netta Wilsher as he
passed her.

He was so prompt that Davina hardly had time to undress. She
threw off the last of her clothes and lay back on the sand as he came
round the rocks.

She had to hurry for him but good heavens, she thought, she had
him in the hollow of her hand. Did she want him there was not the
question. Mr Maurice Ellyott was a secret if ever there was one, her
own father did not know what he thought about. 'Is he clever by any
chance? Is that what's the matter with him?'

Mr Ellyott came at her bidding, a man of thirty, forty or fifty. She
could have been born and died three times at least in his life-span. He
came at noon because she took off her clothes at noon: if she chose to
take them off at some other hour, in some other place, he would come
just the same. He would come running. Between yesterday and today
was this difference: yesterday he ran away from her, today he ran to
her, crash, crash, crashing over the beach regardless.

He was behind her in his position, waiting before the last pebbles
had ceased to slide from under his feet. They were suddenly both
dead still, like lizards flickering and freezing into immobility.

Her own heart was beating from somewhere it certainly couldn't
be – in her throat or her head – but there was no sound from him. He
was noiseless, odourless and she could probably call him 'an
acquired taste' of life. This morning the sea was quiet too, easing into
the land with no more sound than the water in a swimming-bath after
the last swimmer has climbed out.

No doubt she could have fainted from just whatever came into her
head at that moment had she been fanciful or nervous. She stretched
herself taut and with her fingers began secretly to dig for coolness
under the burning sand. By pressing back her head and pushing up
her chin she was able to see his face. Today he wore no hat and no
sunglasses, he was staring at her with black eyes, somehow he had
lost the whites of them.

He took a step nearer. The relief was enormous. She had been
afraid he would do nothing. There was nothing *she* could do and they
could be stuck like this for ever on the beach at noon.

One step at a time he lifted his legs and set his feet down with infinite care so as not to disturb the pebbles. He looked so funny and bread-coloured, bread suit and bread face and two burnt currants in his head. Did he think he was deceiving her? If she sprang up and cried 'Boo!' she could reduce him to crumbs.

A little avalanche ran down from the crest of the pebbles. She stopped herself from crying out as something hit her face, she must not frighten him.

He *was* frightened, he froze into stillness, his foot lifted, waiting for the subsidence to cease. Davina, with her neck arched, watched him upside down. This she had to see. It occurred to her – she liked to see in the round – that the scene was set. The quiet sea and the empty beach had been setting it all morning. She felt like a patient wheeled into the operating theatre where everything has been got ready and she wanted to stand up and shout 'Crumbs!' but she knew he would not crumble.

He lowered his foot, negotiating for somewhere to put it, moving with fearful deliberation. When he reached the shelf of pebbles immediately above her he began to tremble as if the weight of the world were on him. His hands met and locked on his chest – Davina had seen men contending with their two right hands, each hand straining to bring the other down, but these were his own hands contending with each other. Under the weight of the world he broke up above her very eyes. Bits of him floated down, his jacket first. His jacket dropped over her and he climbed back up the beach.

A Love Affair

Markheim had not wanted to go to the party. 'A wine and cheese party. The wine will be red and terrible.'

'You should put in an appearance.'

'As a spectre at the feast? It won't inhibit them, they are disposed to like spectres.' He rang his spoon against his cup. Treble at the rim, it spoke of teatime pleasantries, buttered toast and sandwiches of whiskered cress. 'It's not my envelope, Nan.'

' "Scene" is the current word.'

'I believe there is a wine actually called "Barbarossa" –'

'You should get out of your envelope occasionally.'

'– a supermarket mistake.'

His wife smiled. The day they first met he had been playing cricket with someone's children on Wanstead Flats and had knocked the ball into one of the ponds. Turning, he had seen her smile, only the smile, not the face, not even the lips smiling, and thought at once, I am safe.

Outside Crosby's flat, bicycles were impaled like martyrs on the railings. The party turned out to be a vehicle too, wheels are not the only things that can carry you away.

Markheim was probably the only one destined thereafter to apply the definitive – *the* party. It could not have become that to anyone else. At least, not for his reason.

'I'm glad you could come.' Crosby, meeting him in the hall, divested himself of the girl who was draped about him. 'Is Mrs Markheim with you?'

Markheim considered that the occasion did not warrant an excuse, certainly not a lie, but Crosby and the put-off girl were waiting, the girl to be put on again, Crosby with the faintly dissident smile he wore at lectures.

'No.'

'Now that's a shame. Still, you know everybody. And if you don't, they know you. *Magister publicus homo est.*'

'Oh,' said Markheim, 'no –' but Crosby, moving away, pulled the girl about him as if she were a cloak.

'I'll get you some wine.'

Jardine and Faulkner, of the faculty, stood together. It was not the line of least resistance but of none, for they were close friends. Jardine the joker was flourishing a stick of celery. Faulkner drew himself up, filled his lungs and let the air out, smoking almost. He could be seen to sigh.

In the crowd were many of Markheim's students. To others he would be known as a talking head. It was early and they were not yet serious. Later they would discuss life and, from their safe distances, death. They wore each other: one beauty had a boy over her wrist, another at her feet and a third buckled round her waist. Sex had this simple format, not old and thick with gods and monsters. No Aphrodite, no Minotaur. Markheim thought they could not know what they had missed. Nan would have said no, they could not know what *he* would have missed.

Crosby returned with a glass of wine. 'There are cheese and biscuits on the table behind Professor Jardine. I bet on you, you know.'

'On me?'

'It was generally agreed you wouldn't come. So I win a fiver.'

'Why?'

'Because here you are.'

'As to the general expectation,' Markheim said, 'I'm not sure, myself, why I came. I am not gregarious. Why, I meant to ask, were you confident that I should come?'

'I gambled on your being enough of an individualist not to stick to your own rules.'

Markheim frowned. If he managed to be fundamentally private, he had to believe he could see out as well as in, without – unlike Janus – being seen looking both ways at once. 'I'm glad you won.' He glanced about for somewhere to put down the glass of wine and forget it. The room was hot, the noise rebarbative. Jardine, leaning his back against the table, had tipped up a plate of biscuits: cream crackers were being dealt round his feet like cards.

'You will mingle? Talk to the girls? To this girl,' said Crosby.

That was the first Markheim really saw of her. She was made real by Crosby's lifting her off his neck and handing her over. There was a significance in the lack of impact which Markheim began to appreciate even at the time. At the time he thought that she should never have looked like a coat. Afterwards, he thought it impossible.

'This is Ruth Sobiescka,' said Crosby, leaving them together.

She was not what Markheim called pretty. He preferred blondes, almost any blonde he would have called pretty. Her hair was brown and she had, herself, the quality of brownness. It was sensible behind her pale skin and in the guarded way she looked down her nose, and it tempered the bright industrial orange of the dress she wore.

He had no small talk, 'chatting up' it had been called, implying an element of preparation which he could dispense with. Wry at his own thankfulness, he inclined his head and braced his lips. And realised,

too late, that she might interpret it otherwise. She did, in fact, toss back
her long hair, like a horse disclaiming the bridle, and thus early the
fallacy, which was also the crux, of superiority, came up between them.

'Good evening.' In other circumstances he could have ushered her
to a seat. They stood facing each other, she alerted, he aware of the
discrepancy, but thinking it merely the gap of knowledge between
strangers. Their only point of contact being this room. And Crosby.
Why Crosby? 'May I offer you some wine? It was brought for me but
I haven't touched it. Yet,' he added, not to appear ungrateful.

'I don't drink. Wine,' she added in her turn, though whether from
mockery or nervousness, he could not tell.

They were silent for so long that he feared she would go away. Her
going would announce his failure. In no uncertain terms. These
young people – their youth was ethnic – were brutally certain in their
terms and she would leave him abruptly and obviously. Of course she
was not nervous, so she must have been mocking him. An elderly
man, one of the inferior race. He had been willing to allow her that as
presumption, not letting himself be touched or much amused by it,
believing that both races held trump cards but that age, being the
testament of youth, held the rest of the suit.

She stood with hands locked and hanging to her thighs, squinting
at him with the narrowness of her gaze, for all the world as if she were
receiving censure and defying it. A tendentious pose, tending to show
up his want of the social graces. Jardine and Faulkner, though not all
of his world, were a significant part of it: enough to put about his
reputation as a stick.

'Is that your bicycle on the railings outside?'

She slightly turned her head away, but not her eyes, narrowing her
gaze the more. 'I don't ride a bicycle.'

'I beg your pardon.'

'But you *are* a public man.'

'To my students, yes.'

'So why did you deny it?'

'Did I?'

'In Latin, yes.'

'It was not the statement I took exception to, it was the use of
"*magister*" in the context.'

'Why?'

It was on the tip of his tongue to say that it did not matter. But they
were having a conversation. 'There are other interpretations.'

She smiled and suddenly he was nowhere in her brown gaze and he
knew that she knew it was stick talk and experienced a quite
disproportionate dropping of his heart.

'Some of them frivolous.' He looked at his watch. What o'clock was immaterial, it was time to go. 'How hot it is.'

'I am cold.' She plucked at the silk scarf tucked into the neck of her dress and it fell to the floor. Markheim bent to retrieve it but she cried 'Don't touch it!' so sharply that people looked round.

He watched her pick the thing up and knot it round her throat, which she did with violence, as if she had half a mind to strangle herself. A young man, also watching, said something to the girls he was with and they all laughed.

'I must be going,' said Markheim.

She said, 'I am learning Latin. And Greek.'

'Yes?'

'Teaching myself.'

Marginalia for enterprise: it was a small old dodge, some hopefuls believed it could procure a difference of degree – between getting and not getting.

Markheim, taking a sip of wine, was at once reminded of a medicine of his childhood, rich and red in the spoon, raw and rusty on the tongue. Like wet iron.

The bicycles on the railings, the wet iron railings, had put him in mind of martyrs. Why? What could be less like suffering flesh?

Obviously the party – the prospect of it – had unsettled him and Nan was right, he should more often exchange his contentment for this dismay. In order to become undismayed. By student parties, anyway. But wasn't martyrdom a bit steep?

'Markheim is a German name,' she said.

'And Sobiescka is Polish.'

'You are German?'

'Not for a long time. My grandparents came to England a hundred years ago. We have lived here ever since.'

'Herr Doktor.'

'Professor.' He smiled. 'You too must have been born here.'

'Why?'

'You speak with no trace of accent, no nuance even. But of course, I beg your pardon, you are a linguist.'

'My grandparents are buried in a cesspit.' She said crisply, 'So we have been given to understand.'

'A cesspit?'

'At Treblinka. With several thousand others. Dung to dung, wouldn't you say?'

'No.'

'One day it was ordained by God and Himmler that a certain infected area of Lodz should be reclaimed. Purged of the Waldheims,

Lamarcks, Radoms, Sobiesckas. There was no warning, but some escaped, my father among them. He hid in a drain. A sewage drain – it ran in the family, wouldn't you say?'

'No,' said Markheim, but he felt bemused. Martyrdom, it seemed, was not so steep. He had been as it were preparing to meet this girl, this Ruth.

'My father said that two rats, if one were to stand on the head of the other, would have been as tall as he was. It is possible, he was small for his age, but rats cannot be made to stand on each other's heads. So how would he know?' She sounded vexed, as if the objection had often been raised and never resolved.

Markheim now saw her long nose as a variant of an Assyrian profile. Something dark and accipitrine had been modified to European proportions. But she was still capable of a fierce, indeed a barbarous, aspect.

'And after he came out of the drain?'

'He walked to the Gulf of Danzig and got on a cattle boat going to Stockholm. He had to disguise himself as a girl and act the part – leaving, he said, nothing to the imagination – of the Captain's new young wife. Can you believe that?'

'Yes,' said Markheim.

She said furiously, 'He was twelve years old and boys are such liars.'

She would allow – was in fact inviting – Markheim to condemn the story. A silly enough little trap. But it was her rage which had the inconsistency of truth, directed – he could see it was – wholly against the boy, her father.

'It happened a long time ago,' he said.

'What has time to do with it?'

'Morally nothing. A bad thing is no better because it was done last week or last century. But I'm afraid time is the best we can do.'

She mimed a laugh, putting up her chin, pursing her lips, inhaling sharply through her nostrils.

Markheim looked for somewhere to put his wine. Walking out of the room, carrying a full glass, would be an admission of defeat, and if he approached the table he would be obliged to speak to Jardine and Faulkner. In other circumstances he would have had no objection to speaking, would by now have joined them. But all he wanted was to get away. The boys and girls were beginning to sing and strum guitars. He could not bear their music.

'I'm afraid I . . .' Could he put the wine on the table, briefly salute Jardine and Faulkner and return to the girl as if she were waiting to continue a conversation? Would she wait, once his back was turned?

'I want to show you something.' She took his free hand.

He cursed under his breath. Her touching him was a breach of faith, wasn't it she who had rejected even his fingers on her scarf? Thereby pledging them to eschew physical contact?

'Another time.'

'There won't be another time.' She held him, palm to palm, and drew him into the hall.

Of course it was not Crosby's house, Crosby rented a room, or rooms, but for tonight he had the freedom of the stairs. Every tread was occupied, boys and girls lolling, crouching, squatting, humping or propped with feet against the wall and backs against the banisters. It showed how much a staircase was needed in a sitting room.

Ruth Sobiescka obviously purposed to go up it, and Markheim believed she would have broken through legs and heads and trodden, if need be, on chests and thighs. Hauling him after her. Quite ruthless: was her name then a warning, or a cry of despair?

He stopped in his tracks, stopping her at their arms' length. She turned on him the face of a saint, the brown wood face of a Radegonde or Cecilia, even the eyes were wood. Then she dropped his hand and ran away along the passage.

He might have gone out through the front door. At his leisure, and pleasure, carrying the glass of wine which he might have left on a windowsill. To be found and returned sooner or later. But it would be an act of rejection, and if only for the evening, if only for the moment, she might bear it in mind where, perhaps, she was least able to bear it. How was he to know? The reason he gave for not walking away, walking out on her, seemed to him scrupulous and he allowed himself some credit for it.

At the end of the passage was a flight of steps and he could hear her running down them with the same urgency as she would have run up, through legs and thighs and treading, if need be, on the faces of her friends. What was there to justify it – except the fear that there was nothing?

He found her in the basement kitchen. The light was not switched on, a lamp in the street outside diffused the darkness enough to show that she was at the window with her back to the room. He picked his way to her side. The window gave on to an area of dustbins and coal cupboards. At eye-level the pavement began.

'Rather a weird effect, those bicycles hanging on the railings.' He was thinking, too, of the effect of seeing her like this, long hair coalescing her head with her shoulders. He had said once to Nan, 'They all try to look like nuns. Of course,' and had added, 'It doesn't matter.' What he meant was that they succeeded. Nan had smiled, as if she knew what he meant. Only now did it cross his mind that almost certainly Nan had not known. 'I noticed it when I came in and it was still in my mind. You must have wondered why I asked if one of them was yours.'

She shook her head. 'Bicycles are weird anyway. They're shaped to our extremes.'

He still had the confounded wine in his hand. But in every kitchen was a sink and surely he could empty it away. 'What was it you wanted to show me?' He gestured into the dusk. 'Not that you can, here. I'm sorry, but we couldn't very well unseat all those people on the stairs.'

'People?'

'Shall we switch on the light?'

'There is no light. The bulb's blown.'

'In that case –' He turned into the room and reached out, groping, towards a sensed rather than seen solid. His arm struck something which teetered, rolled and crashed to the floor. 'Oh dear, that was a bottle–' Judging by the reek of wine which rose up from their feet it hadn't been empty. 'How very unfortunate.' But he found a space in which to leave his glass. 'I shall have to own up, and pay up, for the spilth. Of course.' He waved fretfully in the dark. 'Do be careful where you tread.' She had turned towards him, he could now see the long blur of her face, finding to his surprise that he could supply most of the features of it. But not the eyes, not the expression. 'I shall try to find a light of some sort.'

'There's light enough.' He was aware of movements, and rustling, as if she were screwing up ball after ball of paper. 'What I want to show you, Herr Doktor –'

'Professor.'

'– doesn't have to be seen to be believed.'

He saw a larger blur of white, shaped and with details such as his eyes could only have conjectured. She was naked to the waist. Could pure surmise be so explicit? She came close, he noticed no change of perspective. Impure surmise, he thought wryly, was supplying the details.

'Do you believe?'

Her flesh had as much substance as the nimbus of a candle, but he was aware of the wick at the centre. It must surely be significant how often and variously he compared her. To a nun, a horse, a coat, and now a candle.

Her flesh smelled of wine, but not the stuff spilled at his feet. She it was who had a bouquet in the pores of her skin, and would have, long after this red rubbish had been mopped up.

She stretched out her arms, linked them round his neck and by their weight drew down his head. She tightened her grip and his ears roared as if he were listening in to a sea-shell. She was tall, he found himself slipping into the hollow of her throat.

He waited, his forehead wedged against her breast-bone. Her breast-bone was silent, she was not excited, not even disturbed, just determined. As for him, he was ridiculous. Of course, to be out of one's envelope was to be at risk, ridicule being the least of the risks. He felt a cold apprehension of what else might come and tried to relieve his neck which was bent at a painful angle.

The girl suddenly let him go. She dropped her arms and stood back. He lifted his head, rubbed the muscles of his neck, knowing that it was up to him to say something. He ought to explain his act of rejection, make it acceptable. What explanation was there which was not in itself offensive? She was up against more than she knew: to hint at too much could make Nan absurd as well as himself. Besides, he was still human. How futile to fear his own humanity!

'Will you teach me Greek?'

He could hardly believe his ears. He thought she must be laughing silently. Perhaps she had found her own way to reject him.

'I'm afraid I can't'

'Why not?'

'You should ask Professor Jardine.'

'I'm asking you.'

'I'm sorry.'

'Why won't you?'

'Be careful – the broken glass –'

'It's because I'm Jewish, isn't it?'

He stared at her grey nimbus, smiled into the dark. 'It's because I'm writing a book and can't take on more extra-mural work.'

'I'm not talking about that, I'm talking about why you couldn't bear to touch me just now. Because it would defile you to defile me. You can't stand the thought of your pure Germanic seed spilled on a Jewish whore.'

'You over-estimate your importance in that respect. It is natural and absolutely right that you should. At your age one should have great expectations. Even an under-valuation is a cry to be contradicted. At my age, we have all our yesterdays as appraisal.'

She stretched herself, yawning. He could see her arms lifting, pictured the tabula of her upturned chin, her throat arching, her breasts rolling back over her breast-bone. A gesture, as he saw it, of profound relish.

He felt an obligation – to her, of course – to add, 'As for me, I am married and content.'

'With the Frau Doktor?'

Nan asked him how the party was.

'As I expected.'

'Who was there?'

'Students, Jardine and Leslie Faulkner.'

'It was still your envelope.'

'I talked to a girl. Crosby introduced us.'

'Didn't you enjoy that?'

'Not much. She had an obsession about Nazis.'

'And?'

'She was Polish. Her grandparents went to Treblinka.'

'That was before your time.'

'She couldn't see that.'

'I'm sorry I persuaded you to go.'

He feared she might have done them both a bad turn. But the only reason he could think of for his fear was that he couldn't tell her so.

'She believed that the time element was cancelled out. And between us, I suppose it is.'

'So is any other element. She wasn't there at the material time and nor were you.'

'I think she wanted to pick a grudge-fight –' for old, unhappy, far-off things and battles long ago. 'There was no battle for them.' Nan looked over glasses. As she might if he had complained of an indigestion. 'Those people were always the victors. She wanted me to put up my fists for a won cause.'

Markheim remembered when the town was quite small. Twenty years ago he could look out of his window in college and see the boat-shaped town anchored in the lee of the hills. Since then it had broken out into estates and put forth tower blocks. It was fast losing its identity. It might, of course, acquire some other which he would not fit into.

Figgis was waiting, having delivered his bomb, Figgis was, justifiably, waiting for the shock waves. They had in fact started, but Markheim was being careful. He was never prepared for this sort of thing and sometimes worried that he asked the questions which would produce only the tenable answers. Different questions might show up the paltriness of the reasoning, people might be moved to re-examine their motives.

Figgis, now, might be made to see that he was committing a crime against money. Even though it was ratepayers' money: perhaps – if one knew the colour of Figgis's politics – *because* it was ratepayer's money. The boy was sitting with his hands between his knees and his head bowed.

'Why?' said Markheim. Figgis spread his hands and examined his fingernails. The gesture was uncharacteristic, he was not given to gestures but to absolute quiescence. He seemed at a loss. 'You knew I'd ask,' said Markheim.

Either he had known and not cared, or he had not cared to know. Markheim felt his anger rising. Not at Figgis but at the capacity to dismay: they all possessed it and, he thought, cultivated it.

'*Nil admirari*. Is that it?'

Figgis looked up. 'I wonder at everything.'

'So you will not finish your course?'

'You could say I'm cutting out because I don't mean to end up with a dead weight of knowledge round my neck.'

'Indeed?'

'Let's say I'd rather go out and get just what I need to know. Just enough, that is, not just exactly.'

'Revert to the primitive?'

'Begin at the beginning.'

'Which beginning? The Iron Age? Earlier? The cave-dwellers? Plato's prisoners saw only the shadows on the wall of the cave, remember. And where will you find the cave? It moved with the mountains, millennia ago.'

'I'll go further back. To the womb.'

'Dear God.'

Figgis grinned. 'I know the idea's been around a long time and I shan't be the first to try.'

Markheim pressed the buzzer on his desk which connected to the refectory. 'Tea, please, for two. And biscuits.'

'I shall question everything, examine everything. I do mean everything: why the water runs out of the pipe, who's the I who's not me. I want to reach a conclusion before I die.'

'Plumbing and psychology – either could take a lifetime.'

'I'll work fast.' Figgis, who was plain, was plainer when he smiled. His big china teeth shone with spittle.

'How will you survive in a complex society?'

'I'll enjoy trying.'

'Why won't you be honest with me?'

'I am being. Up to a point.'

'The fact is, you can't be bothered.'

The tea came. Markheim lifted the lid of the pot and poked inside with a spoon. 'Four tea-bags. I was afraid they might put in only two.'

'I can't be bothered for what you're offering,' said Figgis.

Markheim sighed. He was sorry, though not specifically, not for the curtailment of Figgis's academic career. It was a general sorrow he felt, general weariness perhaps. One did get tired of this sort of thing. He heard his voice, as if from the other side of the room. 'Do you know Ruth Sobiescka?'

'The Maypole?'

'I beg your pardon?'

'Yes, I know her.'

Figgis did not take his tea. Markheim pushed the cup across the desk. 'Biscuit?' He was shocked at the way her name had come to his lips. He doubted if he could have stopped it, indeed he appeared to have been waiting for the chance to utter it.

'Which department is she in?'

'She's not a student.'

'Not? I was under the impression. . . .' She had not given it. It was, he supposed, his envelope again, and thought that therefore the impression she had given must be subject to his limitations.

'She's a barber.'

'A barber?'

'At Vladimir's, in Russell Street. It's a unisex saloon. She will shave your beard and perm your wife's hair.'

The Frau Doktor. 'I had no idea.'

'Why?'

'It didn't occur to me –'

'Why do you ask about her?'

'She expressed a wish to learn Latin and Greek.'

'She's got a lot of strings and a lot of dancers.'

'What does that mean?'

'Figure of speech. I can't think what she'd want with the humanities.'

'A dead weight of knowledge. An albatross to hang round her neck?'

They stared at each other. Figgis looked ugly, his face reddened, his eyes glittered. 'More like a Sainsbury's broiler.'

He did not wait for dismissal or utter a goodbye. He blundered out and the door banged open behind him.

Markheim sipped his tea. He was not angry. He should, at least, be ashamed of his detachment. Of his callousness. The boy had a brain, was the most promising of his class, and Markheim had said more than once, 'I foresee a straight run for Figgis: industry, cybernetics, management, politics. A portfolio in some office where rough edges are an asset.'

Figgis might achieve all that without completing his university education. The point was that for Markheim there was no point. Not even of contact. He had taken Figgis's defection in his stride and knew that he was making, had made, progress in some unidentified direction: nowhere did it approach his academic affairs.

From a far corridor came a snatch of pop music, a multiracial voice sang 'Jes' you wait an' see, everything gonna be all right.'

He got up and closed the door. 'There's no hope in their music,' he had said to Nan and she, the comforter, had smiled. 'They don't hope for the same things as we do.' Nor in the same way. The hope of young people was in the heart, not the head. The hope of children was in the alimentary canal. It would seem a logical progression.

'He had made up his mind to tell me nothing. I had no opportunity to raise the moral issue,' said Markheim. 'It was all over in a few minutes. He didn't even wait to drink his tea and I had ordered a pot for two. I shall have to pay for it, of course.'

'He was too upset to think of tea,' said Nan.

'Upset? He was thoroughly tiresome.'

'What did he say?'

' "I am cutting out." Those were his words. To cut out is to overtake, to supersede, to surpass, to eviscerate.'

'To detach.'

'To default. To renege. I wonder will he tell the chancellor that what the university offers is not worth his taking?'

'You think he believes that? For whatever reasons?'

Markheim looked at her bleakly. 'For whatever reasons, he may. As for me, I can confidently expect to hear from the chancellor that one of my students is dissatisfied.'

'How absurd you are. Figgis is obviously in the process of making out his case. He cannot do other than present a cogent argument which he is probably relying on you to demolish.'

'He has always been totally serious and absolutely sure of himself.'

'And the more likely to an attack of absolute mistrust. Still totally serious, but tiresome for everyone else.'

'A *folie de doute*?' It occurred to Markheim that as he went away Figgis had looked as if he were about to weep, with rage and tears.

Nan took his hand in both hers. 'What has happened?'

'I've told you.' He looked at their three hands, clasped, speckled each with the same brown spots, the pigmentation of age. Grave marks.

'There's something else.'

'Nothing.' He had it on the tip of his tongue to say 'I don't give a fig about Figgis.'

Their two hands, palm to palm: Ruth Sobiescka's he had never actually looked at, but knew it to be long, childish and tender, the knuckles pearly, the veins threaded between her fingers like blue cotton. He wished he could tell Nan the joke, but not giving a fig for Figgis was no joke.

'He is doing the right thing. They all do the right thing who give up. It is for the others, for whom the question never arises, that there is any question.'

'Dear –' said Nan.

'He owes me nothing. I owe him an education and he won't accept it. The debt is cleared.'

'He owes you an explanation.'

'I shan't play God.' He touched his lips to the brown spots on her hand.

'A girl came here today.'

'Girl?'

He asked from pure shock. An instinctive back-hander. He was not yet sure what there was to hide.

'She said you met her at Crosby's party.'

'She came here?'

He was as dismayed as if he had suddenly encountered a stranger in a place where he fancied himself alone.

'Are you going to coach her?'

'No.'

'Did you promise to lend her books?'

'No.'

Nan plunged in her needle. 'Let's see, what is her name?'

'Ruth Sobiescka.'

This time it did not fly to his lips. It uncurled in his throat like a wave in the sand.

'She wanted to borrow the Clayton *Aeneas* and Maldwyn's *Catullus*. She asked for those specifically. Recommended reading, she said.'

'Not mine.'

'I'm glad I didn't give them to her. I said I didn't know where they were.'

'And then?'

'We chatted.'

'What about?'

'Her work mostly. She is a hairdresser.'

'Yes.'

154

'You knew?'

'Figgis told me.'

'I think she may be dangerous.'

'In what way?'

'Not to us.' Nan smiled at the idea.

Again he asked, 'In what way?'

'My dear, she is a constitutional liar.'

'How do you know?'

'Not with criminal intent, I am not saying that. Although those books are valuable.'

'And you knew where they were.'

'That was an excuse, not a lie. This girl can't help herself, she needs to believe whatever she says and people like her do great harm.'

His urgent need was to stop talking about her. There was danger in that.

'Ruth Sobiescka may not even be her name,' said Nan, biting off a thread.

In Russell Street, on the wall of the supermarket, a blue plaque claimed the site of the Old Boar Tavern and – mistakenly, Markheim believed – an *auto-da-fé* of Huguenots in 1583. It was more likely that such a show would have been put on outside the city wall where there was plenty of room for burning and dancing.

How often did she look at the plaque? Nan would say once would be enough to set the world alight, she would say it began on Tesco's wall, the people queuing up to die, the boy hiding in the drain, the sodomite in the captain's bunk. He did not have to entertain Nan's doubts.

Vladimir's decor of fusc and scarlet embarrassed him. So did the blown-up photograph of a china doll in the window, androgynous, scalped, with white satin erupting from the hole in its head.

He turned his back. It was possible to watch the place reflected in the plate glass of the chemist's opposite. A woman came out, touching her helmeted hair. A man stood on the threshold, combing a toupee held on his palm like a small mammal. The time was 5.25.

Markheim toyed with the idea of writing about fashions in persecution; not a history, an examination of the accessories before the fact, demand and supply, and how persecuted and persecutors complemented each other. It might appeal to one of the quasi-scientific weeklies.

At half past five the chemist came to close and lock his door. He glanced at Markheim who continued to gaze at weedkillers and stomach-powders and to see reflected upon them the shadowy comings and goings at Vladimir's.

He stood a long time there, in abeyance rather than waiting. The grey evening space between one side of Russell Street and the other was a bubble and inside it was all of Ruth Sobiescka that mattered. All that could matter – to him. It should be enough, her actual physical presence would be a complication, most likely a calamity. He ought sedulously to avoid it.

Chilled, he wondered was this the measure of his years? Was he at that time of life of natural shrinkage, loss of involvement, concern, consideration – love? His envelope, now, the final self-engrossment?

Not quite yet, for he was unable to move away. He had to stay until the bubble burst, he was, in fact, here for the bursting.

A young man came out of the hairdresser's and crossed the road. Markheim turned to face him. He was wearing a wide-awake hat and smoking a cheroot. His trousers were skin-tight, he had a crotch like a ballet-dancer's.

'*Buenas noches,*' he said.

A lot of strings and a lot of dancers. Markheim smiled, reminded of a harmless pretty story he had heard about a ballet-dancer's crotch. He felt no animosity, no jealousy, had no natural reactions, thank God. No old man's envy. What he did have would defy looking into. He should not be such a fool as to try, even for conscience's sake. There was nothing that Nan should, or could, have had.

Ruth Sobiescka came out of the shop. At once he crossed the road, a busy road, and only as he stepped on to the opposite kerb did he realise he had barely escaped the wheels of a bus.

'You were nearly dead! Don't you look before you cross the road?'

Thus the bubble was burst. And took years off him. For a nick of time he was a child being scolded. With fear, and love. How absurd, how bathetic. To sum up, and in a word, how *old*.

'It was bloody stupid.' She was shaken and resentful. 'I could have done without it.'

'I know.'

'It's just that I've had a bloody awful day – what do you know about that?'

'I'm sorry –'

'Stuff it!'

He would have liked to consider her anger. It was real, but disproportionate, related only functionally to him. She had turned and was already walking away.

'Couldn't we –' he said, behind her elbow, and was cut off by a knot of people descending from the bus. He broke through them using his arms like a swimmer. 'Can't we take coffee together?'

'I don't drink coffee.'

'Tea?'

'A vodka and lime.'

'I thought you didn't drink alcohol.'

'Not wine, wine is bourgeois.' The wind sprang her long hair and wrapped it round her throat. 'Oh, why don't you stop me?'

'Stop you?'

'Talking like that. What could be more bourgeois than vodka and lime?'

She might be twenty years old, barely twenty. With preserved or overstepped pockets of naivety. He knew that it happened, they couldn't keep up with everything.

There was a smart bar on the corner of Russell Street. Markheim had been there once with the Dean and had felt his own lack of smartness. With Ruth Sobiescka he felt nothing: of all its intents and purposes the place had only one for him – being inside as opposed to out.

He ordered drinks of the barman, carried her glass to a bench, sat on a stool in the midst of people and there was no substance in any of it. Faces were as fluid as the shapes under his eyelids. Except hers, her face ruled straight on either side of her nose. Her hair falling straight on either side of her head. Her neck, perilously long, driving straight into her shoulders. The Maypole.

'I wasn't coming back,' she said. 'For the books.'

A lot of strings. Why had she elected to attach him to one? As a matter of expediency. At twenty, anyone might prove useful.

'I wouldn't have pestered you.'

'No.'

'I just want to learn.'

'Greek and Latin. Why?'

She drank the vodka, she seemed to open her throat to it, banged down the empty glass and said cheerfully, 'I needed that.'

'I'll get you another.'

'No. You shan't subsidise my necessity.' She sprang up before he could move and went herself to the bar.

He could have met her need, he thought it might be the only chance he would have. At sixty. Although he had had what no other man could have – his private vision of her, supplying in the dark glories such as he might never see in daylight. Not at sixty.

She came back and sat opposite him. She had, apparently, a sudden wish to identify him, or simply for the want of better to do, looked round his face, feature by feature, down as far as his tie. Then she said, 'Why are they called the humanities?'

He thought, she is looking for philanthropy. 'It is what they are, unique to the human race. It is all we can be sure of.'

'Sure of?'

'Animals and plants, animate and inanimate matter can, conceivably, do everything else we do.'

'I call them the hilarities.'

'Why?'

'Could be for the same reason.' She tossed her hair back over her shoulder. 'I liked your wife. She's not a Frau Doktor.'

'No.'

'She's not German.'

For her it was the crux, and held them together. At least – at most – it held her, and for that he should be grateful. Would she have bothered with him otherwise?

'I feel about the whole German race – you know? They're poison, every one of them. For evermore.'

If Nan was right and she was a congenital liar, how would she have bothered had he simply been English? The question was idle, he might as well ask who would she have bothered with if Crosby hadn't introduced them. Who she was currently bothering with was what he wanted to ask. The many strings.

'Why did you – suggest yourself?'

'Suggest myself?'

'To me. On the night of the party.'

'God, you *are* German,' she said loudly, and looked round the bar. 'Who else would ask?' she asked of them all. Men glanced across at her and smiled.

He accepted her scorn, if not for the one thing, for another: for the husks of envy, the dry fidgeting which she was right to despise.

'I ask because I am an old man.'

'You simply don't know what I'm talking about.' She flung out her hands, taking, inviting in, the men across the bar.

He said sharply, 'I know enough, I think, to carry on a private conversation.'

'My father wrote it all down. About his parents, their friends, their friends' children, how they were rounded up and taken away and gassed. It was very tidy and quiet, they waited their turn. They were already dead, he said, just waiting to have it made official. He had some funny ideas.'

'Funny?'

'About what was important.'

Such clumsiness was lamentable and he lamented it. 'I should like to read what your father wrote.'

'I'll see you damned first.'

She had seen that anyway, his damnation was quintessential. He could feel it in his bones and, not sparing himself, laid his hand on the table. The big green ramulous veins reminded him of some bad old plumbing.

'Tom Figgis –' he said, unable to preface or connect it, thinking again of the many dancers, of whom Crosby was assuredly one. And who else?

'What about him?'

'He is a student of mine.' He waited, she made no comment. She looked under her brows at one of the men across the bar. He, drinking and talking, was at the same time openly appraising her. 'I will lend you books, but I wonder are you ready for Clayton and Maldwyn? The rigour of the thought complicates the language. Of course I don't know how advanced you are.'

'It doesn't matter. Scrub it.'

'No, no, I won't be instrumental in keeping from you the finest languages on earth. God knows they're closer to heaven than anything else we have done, or ever shall do. You still haven't told me your reason for wanting to learn them.'

'I just want to.'

'Have you read any Greek or Roman history?'

'Look, I don't need to know what happened. It's no good knowing, it's actually bad if you're going to do your own thing.' She was talking to the man across the bar, though not looking at him. Smiling into her fingers, she was communicating. 'Freedom is not doing other people's things.'

Markheim reflected what a nicely psychosomatic humiliation he had found for himself. Tailored to his need. If he needed to be taken down a peg or two or three, there could be no finer instrument than this girl. He was obliged to appreciate, and covet, her fineness for the job. It was so much his that he could not bear the thought of its being blunted on someone else.

'I know what happened once,' she said. 'That was other people's.'

'Figgis –' again he put up the name as something, anything, to come between her and the man across the bar, 'Figgis advanced much the same argument in favour of dropping a formal academic training.'

'Figgis is dropping everything. He thinks he's dying.'

The man across the bar waved to her as he went out. It was not a farewell gesture.

'Dying?'

She stood up. Markheim's outflung hand dared no more than to take up and hold on to her empty glass.

'You can't mean – really dying?'

'I don't know about really. People can die of thought,' and she turned to the door.

As he said to Nan, 'These young people can't forgive history for getting it all over before they were born. They can't wait. What will happen to them if they can't wait?'

'Nothing,' Nan said, smiling.

The Little People

'I should like to go. A real castle!'

'A gothic folly at East Grinstead.'

'Chelwood, actually. It's in the Forest.'

'We've been to Bodiam and Corfe and Drumegg and Knocknelly and Schloss Wurlitzer and I've seen enough battlements to last me a lifetime.'

'But not my lifetime!' cried Elvira.

'You don't even know these people. It's inconsiderate, not to say gormless, to invite you to dinner in the wilds without an introduction or even a recommendation.'

'Sussex isn't wild, it's a home county.'

'It takes personal distinction to make up for the lack of gorm. Do they have any?'

'Sir George Carteret is the managing director of the Cassiopia Press.'

'Ah, ah, ah!' cried Victor, not quite laughing. 'But Cassiopia don't deal in your sort of stuff.'

'Stuff? My work is not a barrel of molasses.'

'Where should we be, where would the bitter world be, my dear, without its sweeteners?'

'I *have* wondered why they asked me.'

'I checked their list. They publish unexpurgated editions of naughty classics, memoirs and pantry-books by eighteenth-century parsons, East European poetry, and political cartoons. *Haute couture*, my love!' He was a lion in the china-shop of her sensitivity, crash followed crash, and then an explicit tinkle: 'Theirs is a prestige imprint.' She did not agonise about the damage because he could break nothing she valued. Each knew where their interests lay and she was content that his should be wholly practical. 'Perhaps Carteret is thinking of extending his list to supermarket sales. An introductory offer of an Elvira Corteen paperback with every jumbo-sized carton of mild green Fairy Liquid.' Victor, grinning, revealed not the yellow canines of the king of beasts, but the expensive crowns of Harley Street.

'I would prefer Mr Cube,' said Elvira. 'Whatever happened to him?'

'An outdated advertising gimmick – there's nothing so dead. We must think of your future.' Victor pulled his nose, a largely ribald gesture with him. 'Why shouldn't you immortalise Fairy Snow as the supremo of the elfin world?'

'There is – there always has been – Knuckleberry,' Elvira said soberly.

'He's not exactly a cult figure.'

'As King of the Elves he has certain responsibilities.'

'Ah, but Fairy Snow would be totally involved with the human race. A kindred spirit.'

'With a name like that I would expect her to be standoffish.'

'I see her as a harlot with a heart of gold.'

'A harlot?' cried Elvira.

'She ought to have a little fun, don't you think?'

'But I'm writing for children!'

'That's what I mean.' Victor giggled. 'I wouldn't be surprised if Carteret has worked it all out.'

'I would rather he left that to me,' Elvira said coldly.

'Of course as merely the husband of a famous writer I don't expect to interest them, but I should have been asked out of common politeness.'

'Could we regard the invitation as mutual?' Elvira unfolded the letter and read aloud: ' "Dear Miss Corteen, Sir George Carteret and his wife, Lady Carteret –" '

'Who else would she be? Baronets don't have morganatic marriages.'

' "– have pleasure in inviting you to dinner." Nothing can come of it, of course. I've just renewed my contract with Dickory Books.'

'The fundamental principle of a bargain is that it can be broken. Otherwise you've got a top without a bottom.'

'I don't wish to be known as an unprincipled opportunist.'

'We could carry it off,' Victor said, twinkling, 'if we got a good enough offer.' He would, she knew, welcome the stigma which would enhance his reputation for hard-headedness. 'Take the Rover. They'll see you're not being undervalued.'

Elvira would have been happier in her little Fiat which roared bloodthirstily at every incline. Victor's car ran so silently it made her feel conspicuous. 'Like the last pea in a pod,' she told Knuckleberry as they drove through Purley. He, of all people, would know what she meant. She had not quite located him, but trusted he was in the bean of light which danced between the nearside wing mirror and the silver flower-holder in which Victor had put a single white rose.

On one score she could, indeed she should, feel sorry for Victor. What he so patently lacked, and could not know, was the supreme joy of creation, motherhood without the squalor. She thought of herself as a mother, giving or withholding life. Victor was not in any but the most random sense a father. Any but the most randy sense, amended Knuckleberry, and she blushed scarlet. 'You mustn't suppose,' she rebuked him, she knew he did suppose it, 'that we should be riding in this luxury if it were all up to me. On what I make I couldn't afford to run even the Fiat. A moped, perha ., which you would find very blowy. Virtually impossible for you to stay on, I should lose you and you'd have to catch a swallow home. Or a pigeon.' She remembered having heard that swallows mated on the wing. It would never do to expose Knuckleberry to that sort of thing. 'Victor is a very successful business man, he makes pots of money.' Knuckleberry could raise pots of fairy gold but, as she had often told him, it would not be valid currency. 'It isn't a question of getting more, though he likes money and believes in it. This is something he wants for me.' She touched the petals of the rose. 'Cassiopia Press is such an eminent firm and he knows I should feel –' She paused because Knuckleberry was as imitative as a child and it was important that he should get the right impression. Happy, proud, flattered would be too much for her to feel, and pleased was not enough. 'I should feel *bucked* to be one of their authors.'

While it was true that she had made a name with her fairy-books she had not had recognition from the literary weeklies. They carried advertisements of her publications, which they were paid to do, but reviewed her en bloc with the baby books at Christmas. One of them invariably spelled her name as if she were some sort of car.

'Victor is the most considerate of men.' Knuckleberry doubted this. He thought that Victor did not properly appreciate her. It was dear of him, he was the only person against whom she found it necessary to take Victor's part. Victor would smile at the idea, but she could truthfully say that Knuckleberry was more real to her than many flesh and blood people. She could talk to him, although he did not always stay to listen, he was a restless spirit. Occasionally he came out with things which she did not remember putting into his mind, remarks which were quaint and refreshing. Sometimes he rather shocked her, but she did not blame him. She was an educated woman and knew about the tricks of the subconscious.

As she negotiated the Godstone roundabout she exclaimed, 'Fairy Snow! I ask you! Of course I wouldn't dream of taking away your position, even to please Cassiopia.'

But later, as she sat sipping gin and tonic – she had stopped at the Felgate Manor Hotel '*pour encourager elle-même*' as she put it – she found that having asked Knuckleberry, she was getting a considered answer. Surprised and touched, she looked where he had briefly alighted on the handle of the beer-pull. 'You really mean it? A partnership? You and Snow? But it would have to be regularised, she would have to be your consort. What about Etain?'

Knuckleberry, who was as knotty as an oak and about three inches high, promptly vanished. Elvira felt rather flat, sitting there with her empty glass. She bought herself another gin and thought how lovely it would be to have a signed limited edition bound in green morocco and lettered in gold – she was so fond of green, and of course it was the fairy colour – which one day would be auctioned at Christie's: 'An Elvira Corteen autographed copy has a rarity value impossible to assess in this day and age.' What made anything rare? Who, or what, decides? If it was a question of scarcity, her books would stand an excellent chance. If it was a question of uniqueness, although she had not been the very first in the field, she *had* made the field her own. No one else had such an affinity with the world of faery. Gin made her wistful and she sighed. The truth of the matter was that rarity was love. If enough people loved and desired a thing it was logical to assume that there was a universal, or at any rate a very considerable love and desire for that same thing.

Knuckleberry reappeared to tell her that Etain had no talent for leadership. She was, he said, strictly a ring fairy. He was obliged to deputise for her on State occasions, she shirked responsibility and was bored by protocol. Etain, he said, went off dancing and playing the dandelion clocks with her light-minded friends when any official ceremony had to be performed. 'I didn't know that,' said Elvira, 'you should have told me.' Knuckleberry said he wasn't one to tell tales but since she had raised the question . . . 'Etain is a dear little creature,' said Elvira, 'and terribly sensitive. I won't have her upset.' It was the reverse of a euphemism, for Etain's equilibrium was that of a moth round a candle-flame. She had been chosen for her looks, not her intellect. All the fairies were pretty, even the bad ones, but Etain was sweetly pretty, just like Elvira at twenty who had been an English rosebud, dewed and pure. Knuckleberry was the ruler of Fairyland, but to Elvira, Etain was the quintessence of fairy.

'It would be against my principles to penalise her for being herself.' Elvira knew, of course, that other writers did it all the time, they manipulated their characters to suit their own purposes. She had a special relationship with her people. Tiny they were and she it was who called them into being, but once in being they had thisness and thatness of their very own. They were individuals, as was clearly shown by the fact that she had not been aware of Etain's short-comings.

'I'm afraid you'd find Snow the diametric opposite of Etain.

Northerners are so adamant, such sticklers. You only have to look at Freesia.' Knuckleberry sniffed so hard that his whiskers flew up to his ears. Freesia, Queen of the Icelings, was a brilliant rigorous spirit and something of a thorn, or rather an icicle, in his side. Elvira hid her smile. He seemed tough, but actually he was very vulnerable.

'That's another thing. Freesia's bound to see Fairy Snow as a rival. Oh I shan't depose her, she has absolute authority over all the icebergs and fields and floes – and every last particle in domestic fridges and freezers. She has no jurisdiction over snow, but she might, she just might, claim it on a technicality as melted ice. We don't,' said Elvira – it must have been the gin putting the thought into her head – 'want a cold war on our hands.'

She had a talent for losing her way when driving, so perhaps it was also the gin which led her infallibly to the castle. She had noticed that there was a period between her second and third drinks when her efficiency was at a peak – one hundred per cent, not just her own rather dubious best – and she wished she could have held on to it for the evening, the encounter with the Carterets. Sir George threatened to be commercially-minded in his approach to her work. He would despise it but he would be ready to make a profit from it. She hated the Fairy Snow gimmick, linked as it was with washing machines and nappies. She envisaged a dreadful television jingle, a crude cartoon figure engaging the fickle fancy of the media and going down in history with Mr Cube and the Esso tiger. The faery world which she had created, the dear familiar spirits she had brought into being for the delight and edification of a privileged minority of children and a few more privileged adults, would drown in a tide of vulgarity and ignobility. Only as she turned into the lime avenue leading to Carteret's castle did she remember that Fairy Snow was not, as far as she yet knew, Sir George Carteret's idea. It was Victor's.

Victor was mistaken, too, about the castle. It was not a sham, it was real, hundreds of years old, with round towers flying little pennants and a moat full of hydrangeas. Set, indeed it appeared to float, in meadows thick with moon daisies, it was utterly enchanting. As Elvira said to Knuckleberry, anyone who lived in such a place could not be a Philistine.

She parked the car in one of the little aprons marked out for the purpose on the drive. With the engine switched off there was an unequivocal silence which Elvira recognised at once. She had heard it in her mind's ear, the breath-taking hush, a finite quiet finishing with the call of a late lamenting cuckoo in some far-off forest glade. It was nothing more nor less than genuine faery time. As she remarked to Knuckleberry, one habitually had to put up with less, but what more could one ask for?

She stepped out of the car. The only encroaching sound was the crunch of her feet on the gravel. She would have liked to think she was the first to step that way for a hundred years. She would have liked to have been thirty years younger. She would have liked to be Beauty in the enchanted castle and Sir George Carteret, perhaps, a sad, sophisticated Beast. She would have liked a crystal carriage where the Rover was, and to be going to a fairy revel instead of dinner with a publisher. She would have liked never to hear again such words as 'diminished potential' and 'audience evaluation'.

It suddenly struck her as she stood before Sir George's castle that she had never had or done what she would have liked. Except in imagination. The thought had always had to suffice, taken – pressed, squeezed dry! – to its illogical conclusion. What a presser and squeezer she had been. What a searcher, going like a bee after nectar, for the hidden sweetness, the fundamental purity of mankind. She believed it existed, she believed it was the crux of the human condition. How else should one interpret the story of the eviction from Eden?

She blinked, bemused. It might still be the gin. More likely the place, said Knuckleberry, it was a highly instrumental place. 'You mean influential,' said Elvira. But did he? Could a building, even a castle, an inanimate object, *exert* – that was the operative verb – influence? Whereas it might well, oh very well, be an instrument of magic.

How still it was, not a bird, not an insect, not a shadow stirring, not a blade of grass bending. Grass did not bend under fairy feet.

A manservant opened the door to her knock and waved her in with a hand in a grubby white glove. 'Miss Elvira Corteen,' he at once declared, not waiting to ascertain that she was. Something about him reminded her of a pantomime policeman.

But really she had eyes only for her surroundings. This, she thought, was how it was. She had always known that somewhere it must be a fact. Here is your actual magic, she said to Knuckleberry, suspended like a spider on a thread about six inches in front of her nose. They gazed at each other and she saw that he was clean-shaven whereas she had confidently supposed him to be bearded. His ears, pointed and luminous, leapt up above his head like flames, then stooped and shrank into his cheek. He said something which she didn't catch and immediately faded away.

He it was, it must be, who had brought her here to Sir George Carteret and this perfect rapport. A rapport, as Knuckleberry undoubtedly knew, for he had a practical streak, destined to be founded on a sound and prestigious economy. The Cassiopia imprint would take her hobs and goblins, pixies and boggarts, all her aerial creatures, straight into the classics. Her dear devoted Knuckleberry, her brainchild, her own fairy godfather, had arranged it all. She marvelled, with a slightly chilled sense of awe, at the power – omnipotence one could surely say, for it was wellnigh heavenly, of the little people.

'I understand,' she said aloud, and then remembered the man-servant but he was nowhere in sight. She was alone. That, too, was perfect. She was quite unaffronted at not being received, she asked nothing better than to be left to herself at this enchanted moment.

The great thing about Sir George's castle was that it wasn't authentic inside: no tapestries and mouldy flags, no armoury displays, no jugular beams, mantraps or fald-stools. The walls were panelled in silver-lime, from the ceiling depended chandeliers of Venetian crystal, innumerable full-length mirrors gave them back sparkle for sparkle, perpetuated every vista. The general effect was of an infinite spectrum of purest daylight. The furniture was Adam at its most aerial, stuffed Borzois lounged elegantly on the moss-green Wilton. At least Elvira supposed them not to be real, but was startled when the muzzle of one quivered with finesse.

She had heard that Lady Carteret's hobby was interior decorating. What a privileged couple they must be, having the taste and the power to impose it. One had to insist in this day and age, when vulgarity was obligatory. They would understand what she had always tried to say. That small was truth as well as beautiful; that to discover ourselves we must turn away from the global and the simply colossal – as evolution had turned from the dinosaurs – and look, each of us, for our own infinitely complex grain of perfection. She believed it to be self-evident, entirely logical. Wasn't the grain how mankind began? In the first and final analyses each one of us was a nucleus, and personal aggrandisement was personal loss. One should not seek to enlarge, but to master the art of diminishment. She believed in the recontainment of ultimate beauty and eternal truth. But when she tried to explain this to Victor, he had said it was asking too much of the Pill.

At the far end of the hall was a huge stone goblet full of white and gold arum lilies. They blazed a joyous but dignified welcome and Elvira went towards them with arms outstretched for an embrace. She did in fact kiss one of them, nosed passionately into its calyx and touched the others with her finger-tips. 'Darlings!' she said, and thought how wonderful if the Carterets turned out to be no more than these, if Sir George and his lady had transformed themselves into pure dreamy, exquisite flowers.

She felt, rather than saw, a shadow, of something like a large moth which slid away out of the corner of her eye. Turning, she saw the manservant. With one gloved hand he motioned her towards a small arched doorway. She went through it into a circular room in one of the turrets. There were bookshelves from floor to ceiling, a desk-table and a chair. There was no space for any more furniture and Elvira experienced a strong claustrophobic qualm.

The manservant followed her in and sat himself at the desk. Elvira was left standing facing him three paces away, which was as far as she could get without backing into the bookshelves. His was the most unindividual face she had ever seen. In fact, if one looked uncharitably, as she was disposed to do, it was geometrical. Such a face as one would immediately and irretrievably forget.

They stared silently and Elvira, who could think of something to say, for some reason could not say it. She turned to look at the books, Cassiopia editions, slender and laced with gold, or bible-fat and richly marbled: *The Madrigals and Mottets of Orlando Gibbons*; *Morall Songs and Light Conceits*; *The Life and Loves of Sophonisba, Duchess of Corinth*. She visualised a spine of emerald snakeskin bearing the legend, Elvira Corteen, in Romance lettering. But standing there with her back turned, she felt increasingly unwieldy. As if the man was concentrating on certain parts of her anatomy and actually causing them to expand. She swung round, resenting the perversity of the situation, that he, the employee, should sit while she, the guest, stood before him like a prisoner, an interrogee. Was he, she thought, about to 'screen' her?

'Please tell Sir George and Lady Carteret that I am here.'

'It is immaterial.'

'I beg your pardon?'

'Your being here is immaterial to them. For they are not.'

'Not?'

'They are in the tropics.'

'The tropics!'

'Cancer or Capricorn. That too is immaterial.' He made a face which she knew she *would* remember, for each symmetric feature, slightly skewed, evidenced something quite specific. She could not decide whether it was jocular or hostile.

'But I was invited to dinner – I wrote accepting the invitation over a week ago.'

'You had no choice.'

She could and did, choose to ignore that. 'I have driven down from London!'

'I have observed that quite well-nourished people will travel considerable distances in the expectation of a meal. In your case, of course, the expectation was of something more.'

It occurred to her that he was definitely not a manservant. 'Who are you?'

'You may call me Snow if you like.' Elvira gazed at him with the dismay of one whose likes are being misunderstood. 'Without the prefix, please. It is irrelevant in any of its contexts, but we have to remember who we are dealing with.'

'We?' It was only one of several questions she needed to ask.

'In order to communicate, we have to use your language, but we do not have to subscribe to its imperfections. The invitation came from us. We could have summoned you in any way and at any time. I would have done so with less ado, but certain elements favoured a little entertainment at your expense. There will be no dinner, Miss Corteen. None of your expectations will be fulfilled.'

Elvira, who wished very much to sit down, could find nowhere but the edge of the desk, and to perch there would give the impression that she was co-operating: even, she thought faintly, that she was trying to flirt. She closed her eyes and he rapped sharply on the desk. 'You have given considerable offence.'

'I have? I don't know what you're talking about. I don't know what any of this is about. If it is a hoax I shall most certainly take it up with the Carterets –'

'The Carterets know nothing. It is no hoax, it is an operation.'

'Are you kidnapping me? I'm afraid there's no money for my ransom.' Although she experienced a normal spasm of laughter it came out as a squawk. 'You should try Barbara Cartland!'

'She does not write about fairies.'

Looking at him made her head swim, but Elvira forced herself. 'What's that got to do with it?'

'Everything. There is great exception to the image you give us. Although you have no public to speak of, you inculcate a ridiculous and obnoxious idea in immature minds. They receive it, retain it without question, and pass it on to the next generation. There is no surer way of perpetuating a lie than by telling it to children.'

'A lie? What lie?'

'This.'

He lifted two fingers in neither a bishop's blessing nor a rude gesture, and up from the surface of the desk sprang Knuckleberry in his dear little green hat. Elvira cried out, pleased and frightened. The fingers tapped Knuckleberry's side. Slender as a dragon-fly, white-gold and iridescent, emerged the exquisite Etain. 'And this.'

'They are my dear, dear fairies –'

'They are lies. So are the gnomes and brownies, the sprites, goblins, hobs and boggarts. Do you really suppose that such pathetic minima have a place in the universe?'

'How dare you!'

'It is not a question of daring.' To her horror and dismay he clapped Etain between his gloved hands and she vanished. 'These things are calumnies.' He held his hands either side of Knuckleberry ready for the clap. Elvira cried a warning, Knuckleberry smiled at her. His smile was the last to go. The white gloves were held out for her inspection. They were grubby, but the grime was in the fabric and not so much as a pinch of dust remained. 'For thirty years you have made us a laughing stock.' He held up his hand like a traffic policeman as she opened her mouth. 'I am aware that Andersen and the Brothers Grimm began it, and the mawkish element was introduced by Mrs Herbert Strang. But you, you have not merely perpetuated it, you have brought it to the peak of banality and made us risible and totally negligible. We will not wear this image in the eyes of the human race.'

'Who? What?' cried Elvira wildly. 'Who is *we*?'

'The little people.'

'Little?'

'This,' he said, splaying his fingers across his chest, 'is an adaptation. For the sake of convenience.'

'Whose convenience?'

'We are none of us more than four inches tall.'

As if at a given signal Elvira heard rustlings in the air and caught, in the twinkling of time between motion and stillness, the ends, the very extremities of movements. She blinked, angry with her own two eyes, and saw a face no bigger than her thumbnail. In vain she told herself that it must be a regression, due to her disturbed and distracted state, to a childhood pastime of drawing faces on her fingernails. She could see hundreds of tiny faces, all symmetrical, cold and blank.

'Had I retained my natural size I should have been obliged to shout. Tiresome.' He was definitely concentrating on certain parts of her anatomy, she could feel them swelling. 'We especially object to your choice of names. Elvira, for instance: you adopted it because it means "elf-counsel". You saw yourself as guide and mentor of all the hop-o'-my-thumbs. And Knuckleberry.' She heard a sound, more effervescence than hiss, but just as inimical. 'A feeble parody of Mark Twain. You see, Miss Corteen, we know all about you. What you cannot see is that we are not concerned with the things that concern you: money, sex, appearances –'

'Sex? I'm not – I have never –'

'Indeed you are.'

'I am concerned,' cried Elvira, 'with the over-emphasis, the squalid physical, moral and commercial exploitation, the gross publicising of what should be a sacrament between two people. Wholly private, wholly pure, an indefinable emotion which should never have been defined, a secret which cannot be divulged –'

'Exactly.' He nodded. 'It is a subject which never ceases to dismay you. And repudiation is a conscious act.'

Elvira, who no longer cared what impression she gave, was about to lean against the desk for support when she realised that the surface was occupied, every inch. Tiny figures stood in ranks, watching her. She thought they were nude, then she saw that they wore uni-garments like children's sleeping-suits with feet, the colour of plasma. She retreated against the bookshelves. 'Are they –'

'They are we. Is that grammatically correct?'

'I think it ought to be "us" – I don't know – Oh God!'

'That,' said the man at the desk – was he man or manifestation? – 'is the original fairy story. The first cognisant act of mankind was to find a culpable creator. Someone to blame. An exerter of undue influence, ergo, man could then claim total exoneration from frailty, mismanagement, lunacy and sin. That is the theme of all fairy-stories.'

Elvira said bitterly, 'You like to talk, don't you!'

'I am here to talk, you will do well to listen. At this moment you are being better informed than your philosophers and scientists. You are in a position to confirm the fears of the fearful and the dreams of the dreamers.'

'I am?'

'You are looking at what you call the secret of the universe.'

Elvira said wildly, '*You?*'

'Us.' Again there came the sharp effervescence from the waiting multitude. 'We have taken over the universe. Never mind from whom, though in view of your egomania I had better say that it was not from you, because you do not possess even your own planet. Mankind is merely an element in an everlasting state of flux. There have been, and will continue to be, other takeovers, and the life expectancy of the human race is too minimal for consideration. Suffice it to say that we need this planet for our own purpose.'

'And what,' said Elvira, trying to repossess herself, 'might that be?'

'Your lease has run out. It won't be long, in your chronology, until we have the place to ourselves. Time has no significance for us, but it may mean something to you if we say that we have been waiting since the first viable conglomeration of atoms and molecules resulted in the first living entity.'

'It means nothing!'

'Then we shall put it bluntly. You are on a crash course, Miss Corteen, you and your fellow men. Your system – I am speaking generally – is governed by the simple mechanics of acceleration. The rate of progression increases in direct proportion to the factors involved and we need hardly tell you there is no point of return.'

'You need not tell me anything!'

'If we consider the all-important financial factor –'

'It is not all-important to me!'

'People,' he said, and there was no doubt that he was not in that category, 'have a strictly limited understanding which reaches its apogee, such as that is, in the understanding of money. If we say that eighty years ago wages were seven shillings a week for a typist and five for a dock-hand and now they are in the region of one hundred pounds, even you can see that you are on the verge of an economic explosion. A similar stage has been reached in all other spheres – technical, social, biological, ecological, and what you are pleased to call intellectual.'

'I don't believe in you!' Elvira raised her clenched fist to the little multitude on the desk. 'I don't believe you exist!'

As she spoke, they vanished, and there was the tooled leather blotter and the silver inkwell and the polished pearwood under an intact film of dust.

'It is immaterial what you believe.'

'It's your favourite word, isn't it? Immaterial – *that's* significant!' She put up her hands to clap him as he had clapped Knuckleberry and Etain. He did not move, but the room did. The circular room spun round like a top. Sick and dizzy she fell against the bookshelves.

'You will cease writing about us.'

'I don't write about you.'

'Cease writing. Yes, that would be best.'

'But I must write! I live to write –'

'Then write about something else.' He made his specific grimace. 'Sex, for instance. Anything, provided it does not concern, or try to concern, us.'

'It has never concerned you. I write about the true fairies and pixies and gnomes and the tiny folk who live in cockleshells and ride on butterflies' wings –'

'It has to stop.'

'But why?' She felt like Tosca: 'Love and Music, these have I lived for, nor have I done aught to harm any creature. . . .' Well, not exactly music, though she had once thought of becoming a concert pianist. And Love had been painful, she preferred to forget Love. 'Why me? I'm not the only one who writes fairy stories.'

'Surely you don't expect justice?'

'I couldn't write about sex. The idea is totally repugnant –'

'There will be no further warning.' Suddenly They were back, and now there were more, shoulder to shoulder on every surface, whether it was flat, oblique or perpendicular. They hung in bunches from the ceiling. She could not turn anywhere to escape the thumbnail faces. 'We have already taken appropriate action.' He raised his brows, making no alteration to his expression. 'Most appropriate.'

Chilled, she asked, 'What have you done?'

'We have put a changeling in your place.'

'A changeling!'

'We use changelings when the situation warrants. They are ephemeral, we cannot rely on them for long or indefinite periods. They soon revert to the state of flux from which we take them. They are of course the dead –'

'Of course,' Elvira said faintly.

'– waiting for rebirth. Only the life-force, which has been a complication but is soon due for annulment, can consolidate them. Changeling Corteen has presented herself at your home with a plausible story to account for her return. She is even now closeted with your husband.'

'What do you mean – closeted?'

'She is of course your exact double. But, if I may say so –' he paused to let her see that there was no one to stop him, 'of a quite different disposition.'

Elvira, who knew all about changelings, could only cry, 'This isn't a warning, it's a frameup!' and blench at the absurdity.

'We knew you would refuse to do as we asked.'

'Of course I refuse! I'm an artist, nobody tells me what to write.'

He nodded. 'It is true that your decisions were programmed at birth. We had only to look at the print-out.'

'Computer jargon!' She thought she saw a glimmer of hope.

'Used merely as an analogy for your benefit. A computer, as you call it, is a clockwork toy by comparison with the organisation of a single living cell and you are quite incapable of understanding your own working patterns. To revert to the subject of the changeling Corteen: she is, as you might expect, indiscreet, silly, possessed of the lowest cunning and a particularly vulgar manner. She is the type calculated to do most harm to your public image.'

'You're behind the times!' Elvira cried, trembling with anger. 'The only harm to be done nowadays to a public image is to keep it out of sight!'

'You mean all publicity is good? Perhaps. Provided that if one audience is alienated you are able to satisfy the more liberal tastes of another.'

'Really –' she clung to the word, 'really this is utter nonsense! I have never heard such pretentious claptrap, such – bull!' It was one of Victor's words. His commonsense, his sturdy scorn – barbaric she had thought it, but she needed barbarism now.

'Unbelief, too, is illusory. Humanity does not know anything, so must believe everything. If I may quote from recent research on the subject: "Air Chief Marshall Dowding, after investigating hundreds of reports, came to the conclusion that there was sufficient intelligent evidence for people to believe in fairies. . . !"'

'It's not fairies I disbelieve in, it's you! You're some sort of faker and these creatures are the illusion. I don't know how the effect is achieved and I don't care!'

She turned her back. One of Them was astride the door-knob. She set her teeth and thrust out her hand. Yet when she touched nothing and, at the last second, saw nothing, she felt as sick as if she had crushed the creature between her fingers.

From the doorway she looked round. The man she had supposed to be a servant still sat at the desk, alone: the creatures had all vanished. He *looked* like a servant.

She went through the hall of the castle. It was dazzling, all the light and emptiness. As if for a scene prepared. And focused. In the infinity of mirrors she saw herself at once enormous and dwindling, an accurate great map of pores and veins, and a pilule of moving dust. She shut her eyes, her foot touched one of the Borzois. It groaned.

How gentle the air when she ran out of that place into the twilight. How soft and woolly. And how homely the car. She bundled behind the wheel and slammed the door. The stale scent of Victor's cigars comforted her, and there was his rose in the vase on the dash. She took it and held it to her lips. Of all the white clinical light inside the castle not a glim could she see from here. It was solid dark. How odd that was, and ominous.

She switched on the ignition, started the car, but turned it too sharply and stalled the engine. Panicking, she trod on the accelerator. The car shot into a flowerbed. The wheels whirred, sinking into soft earth. Her heart leapt in her chest, a crazy leap that sobered her. She engaged reverse gear and backed the car on to the drive. There she forced herself to stop and buckle her seat-belt and switch on the headlights. She tried to think logically about what had been done and was still to do.

She was weeping a little when the car moved off, the tyres crunching richly on the gravel. When she turned into the lane and saw lights across the fields she cried thank God for those people obstinately and demonstrably living their lives. So God was a fairy-story. . . what could be purer and more magical? What else did one pray for?

Unsure what she was seeing, she dashed her hand across her eyes. There was something in one of the wing mirrors. Surely it was too big for a moth. Surely the shape was familiar. She cried, 'Is that you? Oh is it? Aren't you dead?'

Knuckleberry reminded her that he was immortal.

'Of course you are! But my dear, I was afraid that terrible man would have done something, put you under a spell.'

Knuckleberry pooh-poohed the idea so fiercely that he blew his beard up round his ears – how glad she was that he had his dear little spade-shaped beard again. The man was a charlatan, he said, and as to spells, he probably could not spell his own name.

'Fairy Snow!' cried Elvira hysterically.

For one thing, said Knuckleberry, the changeling business was not based on the dead. It was, and always had been, a matter of assembling the right constituents, but with people becoming more and more complex changelings were hardly worth the trouble now. They took time to make up, it wasn't done – didn't she know? – with the wave of a wand. Besides, changelings were always discoverable by the nearest and dearest: in fact, it was a measure of nearness and dearness how soon the substitution was spotted. Certainly it would not be possible to deceive Victor for more than a minute.

'I never thought it would. Dearest Victor! It wasn't that that upset me –'

How badly she was driving, said Knuckleberry. She should stop and dry her eyes, he had no wish to end up in the ditch. She thought of calling at Felgate Manor for a restorative, but he reminded her that she had not eaten for hours and although a double gin would work wonders, the internal combustion engine was not receptive to wonders.

It always touched Elvira when Knuckleberry, who was of the air, airy, was so considerate about the weaknesses of her flesh and blood. She stopped the car in a layby but left the engine ticking over while she dried her eyes and blew her nose. 'I can never feel the same again. I'll never understand. Of course it was all a put-up job, but who by?' Her eyes filled afresh. 'Who could be so *cruel*?'

Only one person, Knuckleberry said cheerfully, and couldn't she guess who? 'I certainly cannot!' cried Elvira. Well, it wasn't Sir George and Lady C, said Knuckleberry, for they were somewhere in the Spice or Sugar Islands, and it wasn't the manservant, he was merely the instrument – the mouthpiece you could say – 'Oh you could!' cried Elvira – and it wasn't the thumbnail people, they were just part of the illusion. So who did that leave? 'You don't mean – No, no I'll never believe it!' Knuckleberry tutted crossly and pointed out that no one was asking her to. With all due respect, due, he meant, to her, Victor simply didn't have it in him. Which left one possibility. Herself. Yes, declared Knuckleberry, blowing up his whiskers, *she* was the one, she had brought it all on herself. 'But that's absurd! How could I? I couldn't . . .' What it all boiled down to, said Knuckleberry, was a bad case of self-doubt. So profound that she had not been conscious of it. Dismayed, she declared, 'But I was happy!' Not really, said Knuckleberry, really she was unsure and confused, and in revolt her subconscious had staged the whole thing. Elvira could not credit it. 'That dreadful man? The things he said? Those – plasmic creatures?' Oh yes, said Knuckleberry, the human mind being what it was and the creative mind being creative – yes. It had all started sensibly enough: the Carterets and their letter inviting her, the castle itself, Cassiopia Press, the man who was really only a servant, some kind of major-domo, those were facts. The rest was an accessory after. At some stage reality had drifted into fantasy and she had waking-dreamed it all. She might, and perhaps she should, enquire what had become of reality. But not just now. At this moment she should see that her self-respect, nay, her very faith, was in jeopardy. Elvira protested, 'But I have no faith!' He was referring, Knuckleberry said, to her faith in her work. She had been warned. It had taken a daymare to do it and she ought to be grateful. 'Oh I am!' sighed Elvira, 'but who to?' To the power that was and always would be, he said solemnly. To the Good Fairy. He was referring, of course, to Faculty X, the power which unites the conscious to the sub-conscious. 'I'll be eternally grateful,' promised Elvira, 'but was it necessary to be so – so callous? Some things I won't ever be able to forget, or to remember them merely in the context of a dream.' Being morbid would get her nowhere, said Knuckleberry, she should talk it over with Victor. She agreed that that would debunk the dream. 'But will it resolve the doubt? Suppose,' she said fearfully, 'it helps to confirm the doubt? Suppose the doubt is meant to be confirmed? The point is' – really it was the starting point as she saw it, as anyone would see it – 'if the Carterets were going abroad, why would they invite me to dinner?' She had better find out, Knuckleberry said huffily, and when she asked how, he shouted Questions! Questions! 'It *is* material,' she reminded him gently, whereupon he danced all over the car in his rage. (He was of course directly related to that Rumpelstiltskin who had stomped through the floor when he couldn't get his own way.) Elvira waited meekly. One had to remember that fairy tempers, like fairy gold, were evanescent.

They drove the rest of the way home in silence. Elvira hoped it was companionable. As they crossed the river Knuckleberry flew up to the fairy lights on the Victoria and Albert Bridge.

Alone, she reflected how dependent she was on him. Although Victor was only aware of his existence on the printed page and had no idea that Knuckleberry shared her daily life with her, he had once referred to him as her alter ego. She would have liked to believe it. Knuckleberry had many qualities she envied: honesty, sturdy sense, fearlessness, an unsqueamish delicacy of nature and a delightfully gnomish humour. He also had a will of his own and came and went as he chose. Sometimes he would reappear when she could well have done without him, and if so minded would pop in and out of the scene, or would unsettle her by staying just outside it, invisible, and uttering derogatory bleeps. She hoped he would not turn up while she was telling Victor about her experiences. He had a disconcerting way of measuring Victor's reactions against her own. Indeed, he spoke in her ear, though not, of course, in Victor's, about feelings which she could wish, sometimes, not to have had.

Was she going to tell Victor? Could she hear herself describing the thumbnail people, or the manservant's philippic, or how the castle which had seemed so pure and lovely had turned sinister and demoralising? Victor would laugh with tears in his eyes – Victor wept with laughter, never with grief.

She reached home and drove the car into the garage. Finally it was the rose which reassured her. A chivalrous gesture, and Victor was not given to chivalry. She could have sworn that he was constitutionally incapable of thinking of anything so graceful, eloquent and superfluous. The flower spoke to her of beauty, the perfection of the unman-made world and its continuance. The rose was not merely a message of hope, in its delicate but invincible fashion it was a guarantee. She took it from the vase and held it to her lips. So how clever, how wonderfully subtle of Victor to have chosen, for a gesture so alien to his nature, one which yet expressed the practical side of it.

When she let herself into the house and heard voices she thought damn, someone's come. She did not feel up to explaining away her return, dinnerless, from the Carterets. It would look as if she had been snubbed, and perhaps she had. She did not want any of their friends reaching that conclusion. She decided to go quietly upstairs and wait for the visitor to leave. Then Victor laughed, a sound so full of delight that her blood stirred. And immediately ran cold.

This was not gaiety, it was impure joy of a certain sort. Arising from certain unmistakable conditions.

She stood gripping the banister rail and staring at the half-open door of the room where they were. It seemed that her questions were about to be answered, that there was one odiously simple reply to all of them. Victor laughed again, and in that moment the evening's episode acquired a new and totally credible meaning. She could almost hear the links linking up. And this time she did not think, why me? That, too, was answered.

She wanted to turn and run. What prevented her was finding in herself some spark of honour. She moved towards the door. Already she was sickened by the thought of what she would see.

She pushed open the door. Victor was facing her. He was nuzzling into the neck of a woman whose head rested on his shoulder. Her arms were round him, her stockinged feet perched on his. Glued together they were swaying in some kind of dance. Or was it the early tempo of an orgy?

Elvira watched, for a few seconds or long minutes she did not know, she was trying to limit what she saw and contain the ruination. She was also, she discovered – and found time and emotion enough to despise herself – curious about the method. She had never been very good at that sort of thing. She observed, with revulsion, the winding and folding, the almost *culinary* action of the woman's flesh, as if it were, or would become, an emollient lump to be spread over the man's. Over Victor.

The devastation was entire. There is my work! she thought wildly, there is always an end in that, and a beginning.

Victor looked up and saw her. With his chin deep in the woman's hair he looked into Elvira's eyes. His own widened, she saw astonishment but no consternation. He blinked, lifted his head, staring. The woman went on twining and swaying him with her.

'I'll be damned,' he said, and withdrew one hand from whatever it had been doing to rub his eyes.

Elvira said, 'Yes, it's me.'

Victor said, 'I don't believe it.' He was, she saw, about to laugh. Then he thought better of it, and frowned. 'Is this a joke?'

'If it is, I don't think I'm going to be amused.'

'No?' He seized the woman by her shoulders and swung her round with a swift, unceremonious movement. She staggered. Steadying herself, she leaned against him and looked at Elvira.

Nobody gasped. Elvira, when she began to understand, plainly heard the reverberations of disaster. And as she was obliged, forced, into further understanding, the sounds became a coherent roar.

What finally demolished her was seeing the runestone. It was a piece of polished porphyry carved with letters from the runic alphabet. Depending from a fine silver chain, it lay in the generous cleft between the woman's breasts. Victor had given Elvira a stone and chain exactly like it, she was wearing it at this moment. She had on a dress exactly the same as the other woman's, a rather expensive silk jersey in pale blue and French grey, eminently suitable for dining in the country with a prospective publisher. Her good but outmoded diamanté watch was duplicated on the woman's wrist, her wedding and engagement rings on the woman's fingers, as was the colour of her nail varnish. The woman had kicked off Elvira's blue Tuscan sandals, but the marks of the straps showed across her instep just where Elvira's, too, had puffed up. Elvira's hair was the same sustained chestnut, styled, surely by the same hairdresser, who gave her credit for more symmetrical features than she had. And Elvira knew, without being close enough to see, or needing to be told, that this woman had a fine raspberry pink thread – the first, it was feared, of several across the bridge of her nose.

Elvira not only wore identical clothes and did her hair the same way, she was the living image of the other woman. But shouldn't she say, she thought in fear and anguish – surely she should! – that the woman was the image? How fully she was living there in Victor's arms, holding his arms about her, seeking even at this moment to rub her cheek on his! She smiled lazily at Elvira. No one spoke.

Elvira did the sensible thing, kicked off her shoes, went to the drinks cupboard and poured herself a gin. She drank it and poured another.

'Hey –' said Victor.

Elvira had gained enough strength to say, 'Who is this woman?'

Victor laughed, out of key. '*You're* asking?'

'She's not me.' Remembering the woman's gross lechery, Elvira cried, 'I am not her!'

'Who are you?'

'You know very well.' Elvira drained her glass and replenished it again.

Victor put the woman aside none too gently and came to pick up the gin bottle. 'Look here –'

Elvira, looking, saw that it was nearly empty. 'I'll buy the next one.'

'Is this some sort of joke?'

179

'You have already asked that, and so did I, an hour or so ago. The answer seems to be yes.'

'It's certainly comical.'

'The joke's on us. On you and me.' Elvira finished her third drink. She did not think that she had the situation in hand, nor had anyone else present. She sat down on a handbag which lay on the settee. The bag was identical with her own and it afforded her a small, sharp satisfaction that if it contained the same things as hers, some of them would undoubtedly be broken.

Victor sat down facing her. The woman dropped into his lap and there they were, the three of them, sitting together Elvira thought angrily, as if this was an ordinary social occasion.

'Have the goodness,' she said, attempting icy scorn, 'to put that creature down.'

'Why should I?'

'Because she is an impostor.'

'She's my wife.'

'*I* am your wife.'

'Can you prove it?'

'Do I have to?'

Victor pulled at his nose, his largely ribald gesture. 'One of you has to.'

'Surely you can see what she is? She's a changeling.'

'A what?'

'She looks like me and dresses like me, I daresay she sounds like me, but she won't act like me. They never do. That's the point of the exercise.'

'What exercise?'

'The changeling exercise.' Elvira glared at the woman who seemed to be getting brighter all the time. Cruder. She seemed actually to be cheapening and vulgarising Elvira's own looks. 'Changelings are the reverse of whoever they are impersonating.'

'Changelings? Pshaw! There are no such things.'

'I assure you there are. And always have been. How else do you account for schizophrenia? Dual personalities? Or things just going wrong?'

'Crap,' Victor said rudely. 'Keep it for your readers.'

'My readers? So you admit I am – who I am –'

The woman laughed and rolled deeper into his lap.

'She's not real!' cried Elvira.

'Oh she is,' said Victor, putting his face down into the woman's neck.

A Picture from an Exhibition

'No, I wouldn't call him dedicated. If there was something else to do he would always do it.'

'Something else?'

Laura who had known what she meant, was aware of the improbability of communicating it. 'Going to parties or picnics, visiting friends, or painting the bathroom.'

'The bathroom?'

Someone laughed. 'It was a question, perhaps, of liking a quiet life.'

'You mean that domestic pressures' – the woman with the spyglasses leaned on the words – 'were brought to bear?'

'Oh no. It was quite voluntary – to the extent of being involuntary. He always did what he wanted.'

'And he didn't always want to paint pictures?'

'I think he was always ready to. He just hated missing anything.'

'He's awfully good,' said the girl from the Slade. Laura realised how glad she was for the present tense. 'That's what I feel when I look at his skies – awe.'

The woman with the spyglasses let them drop on the silver chain about her neck and looked nakedly round the room. 'For a small show, in the middle of August, at World's End, you're doing very well.'

Laura had thought otherwise. A trickle of people, steady, still but a trickle, had crept through the gallery all the morning. 'I really don't know what to expect.'

'Why did you decide to show your husband's paintings here and now?'

'I want to sell some. I need the money.'

'Indeed.' The spyglasses took, or rather completed, Laura's measure before being borne away on a tour of the room.

'You shouldn't have told her,' said Hansen at Laura's elbow.

'Why not? It's true.'

'She thinks money – the lack of it – is obscene. If she buys now she'll beat you down.'

'I won't be beaten down.'

'God, look – it's Joe Tadema!'

'Is that bad?'

'Dear girl, you are sublime. Joe is nearly the most influential art critic in London.'

'Who is quite the most influential?'

'Waterboy. You won't see *him* here.'

As Hansen billowed away with his diva's welcoming gesture, Laura said apologetically, 'My husband didn't know about the art world, either.'

'If he had,' the girl from the Slade said, 'he wouldn't be the artist he is.' Again the present tense, and again Laura was comforted. 'Tadema's the Jesus man in the green suit. He claims he's Alma's cousin's boy.'

'Alma? Oh! Yes.' Tom would be forgiven for being out of touch, he would have been expected to be, even with the past. But not Laura. She would have to try harder.

'Lots of people know a good thing when they see it. Where Tadema's really clever is the way he always gets to see the good things.'

Laura realised that Dendy had arrived before she actually saw him. He changed the circulation of the air, there was always a bit of a breeze where he was.

'How's it going?' And he kissed her on the lips, in front of everyone. He could do that now, for her consolation, to which the world would agree she was entitled. He looked round the walls. 'Is this all?'

'He didn't paint many.'

'You should keep a few,' said the girl from the Slade. 'They'll fetch a lot of money one day.'

'We can't afford to wait till we're dead,' Dendy said cheerfully.

'I suppose not.' The girl glanced at his hand which rested on Laura's hip, and turned away.

'I've been longing for you to come,' Laura said to him. 'It's gruesome waiting here while people peer and prod at Tom's things.'

'Prod?'

'There's a woman with spyglasses –'

'My God, what's that?' He had seen it of course, and if she had hoped otherwise she ought at least to have moved away from it. She found that what she had hoped was that if he saw it he would not look at it. But he now planted himself, rocked on his heels, seethed softly through his teeth and examined it. 'What a picture!'

'It's called "The Paradise Garden".'

'You bet it is. The old devil!'

It was a small picture, about a foot square, but it overtopped all the others, had alternately drawn and turned away every visitor to the exhibition. There was more than a hint that it was too hot for these walls to hold.

The scene was formal, of fanciful yet well-trimmed yews, the topiarist's art set against a predictably blue sky, and old roses depending from the branches of a tree. The grass was a luminous green, in the shadows quite blue, and here and there, to marry the unsubtle difference, were scattered the coracles of white rose petals, blown and a little rusted by the heat.

There was nothing formal or predictable about the figures in the foreground. One was a satyr, of old igneous stone, scabbed with yellow lichen. It had no face, as a face was looked for, but Laura had glimpsed, or supplied, the shape of the very worst there could be in one, and ever since she had feared that she was about to recognise whose.

The other figure was living. No shadow of doubt. The textures of stone and flesh were an exultant contrast, the naked woman clinging to the statue in a passionate, a lascivious parody of a crucifixion. Her arms hung from the outstretched arms of the satyr, her legs were pressed into his thighs, every hollow of her body was cupped over every convexity of stone. And there was scorn in the abandonment of her pose. It was at once rejection and solicitation.

'I wouldn't have thought he had it in him,' said Dendy.

Hansen brimmed towards them, arms outflung to skim Laura from the rest. 'Laura, this is Joseph Tadema, London's – nay, Europe's – greatest and most percipient critic of the visual arts. Joe, allow me to present Mrs Tom Bevis.'

Tadema clicked his heels and ducked his head. His whiskers twitched, presumably he smiled.

'And this is Dendy Green, a close – an intimate – friend of Tom's.'

'The greatest critic?' said Laura.

'Darling, he won't eat you! Talk to him about Tom. I must go and focus Lady Gorman's eyeglass on the right pictures.'

The three of them stood looking at each other. Tadema absently scratched his beard, as he might the head of a dog he was fond of.

'Will my credentials suffice, Mrs Bevis?'

'I didn't mean!' Laura said hastily.

'Tell me about him.'

She felt herself panicking. She could not talk to this man about Tom, she could not talk to anyone about him. He was more than private, he was, he had come to be, integral. This she understood without surprise, except at its not having been apparent to her before. She could no more tell Tadema about Tom than about any of her other private sources. 'There's nothing to tell.'

'A non-person? Or is it you?'

'I expect so,' said Laura. 'I expect there's less to me. Or there was. Now, I suppose, there's more. I don't know –'

'Look here,' Dendy began, but Tadema held up a quelling hand, and addressed himself to Laura.

'I should like to look round his studio.'

'He didn't have one. He worked just wherever he happened to be.'

'He was a Sunday painter?'

'Saturdays too, and evenings if there was nothing to watch on television.'

'Tom was a simple chap, straight as a die. The last one you'd expect to take up art,' said Dendy.

'Simple?'

'At school we called him Jelly. He was pretty transparent, you know.'

'No I don't,' Tadema said coldly. 'I do not know Tom Bevis to be a simple man, Mr – ah – Green. I find that a man who paints with a palette-knife invariably has something to hide.'

'Tom painted with brushes. From Woolworth's,' said Laura.

'Idiosyncratic,' allowed Tadema. 'However, there were occasions, especially in his sea and landscapes, when he used the knife to a degree of impasto, to get an immediate, daunting effect. He often did wish to daunt. As well as dazzle.'

'He was an open book, old Tom,' said Dendy.

'The question is, who can read him?'

'He had nothing to hide,' said Laura.

'I believe I may fairly describe myself as addicted to artists,' said Tadema. 'I believe I may also claim to have, in my way, experienced some of their problems. Not entirely at second hand. I see the dichotomy between the man and the artist, the eternal struggle which – in this picture – appears to have reached a kind of compromise.' He approached 'The Paradise Garden', and with his long white forefinger pointed out the details as he spoke. 'A quite different technique has been employed, starting with the grain of the canvas, which is finer than he was accustomed to use. It was – you are right, Mrs Bevis – painted with brushes. But not from Woolworth's. He would have invested in hog and sable for the fluid treatment of these greens, and the brilliant mass of the sky. Note how he has blocked in the shadows under the leaves of the tree, using black straight from the palette, a full black for the high light of noon. Do you see how it encroaches on the figure of the woman? There is a purely or, I should say an impurely, local darkness between her shoulder-blades. Whereas the statue does not rate the dignity, however qualified. The statue is the colour of a bad plum. For a non-figurative painter he has done not at all badly. The subject, of course, is dramatised allegory, even to the little grey viper, symbol of deceit, coiled about the nude's ankle-bone.'

'Deceit?'

'The snake is not so treacherous nor two-faced as we humans are. The whole is executed, if I may so, with a deliberation which renders the picture quite nondescript.'

'How can you say so?'

'Slavish application to detail was not within his gift. Was it Ruskin who said that only the imaginative truth is precious, all else, mathematical and scientific, is truth only of the husk and surface? You might regard this as probably the huskiest picture your husband ever painted, Mrs Bevis.' Moving away, Tadema's farewell flip of the fingers, was permissive and slightly frivolous.

'Husky?' Dendy peered, nose to the canvas, as if to smell it out.

'When Tom showed me the picture I asked what it meant. He laughed and said it was a dream he'd had.'

'It's you. You know that, don't you?'

'Me?'

'The nude. I'd know the backs of your knees anywhere. And the rest.'

'I never modelled for him.'

'He had opportunity to refresh his memory.' Dendy sounded cheerful.

'Do you think he knew about us?'

'Of course not. Why should he?'

Why indeed. To Tom she had been cool and faintly disparaging about his lifelong friendship with Dendy Green. To Dendy, in Tom's hearing, she had been on the defensive – defending Tom, the heavyweight, against the bantam blows of his friend. Dendy had continued to tease, to rib, to ride, and at the same time to carry Tom, just as he had done at school. And Tom had seemed content, he was constitutionally a contented man, not so much making the best of things as simply not being open to anything less.

'I'd like to stay,' said Dendy, 'but I've got to get back to a board meeting. I'll pick you up here at six.'

'I think I knew that the snake is a symbol of deceit. It comes as no surprise, so I must have known, subconsciously. And if Tom knew like that, even if he *only* knew like that, he must have known, like that, about us.'

'I don't believe it's a snake. It's her garter that's slipped.' Dendy put his arms round her for anyone who happened to be looking to see. 'I don't believe he knew then, and I believe that if he knows now, he's glad for us.'

When he had gone she was alone, or rather, not talking, for the first time for hours. Her face collapsed, she felt that it did, into its own shape. All the uttering and listening and smiling and taking in and giving out and not giving away, had made a nothing of it. Her face had been a puddle blown upon, whipped up and walked in.

She stood in front of the picture, her back to the room. She had the absurd feeling that Tom had got her there, that he had got her to get herself there by putting on the exhibition and by every step she had taken and every word she had spoken. And now here she was, faced with what he knew, what he had made of the knowledge, what he had made of her.

She had not needed to be told that the naked body was her own. Recognition, when first she saw the picture, had been immediate. It went beyond the merely representational which might or might not be a faithful likeness. She knew who it was meant to be and Tom knew that she knew. 'I bet you didn't think I had dreams like that,' he had said, with the great grin that split his face in two.

And yet, what was there to know? That she could, and did, love two men at once? Surely that was nothing but good? It *was* good, she told herself fiercely. There could not be too much love, and she had been a true wife. Yes, true: not the husky truth Tadema talked of, but the real, enduring truth of marriage. She had always been there when Tom needed her, whichever way he needed her. He had lost nothing to Dendy, their needs were different, they did not clash, did not even overlap. It had worked out so well: the mechanics of being in two places and seeming to be only in one had been so simple and natural. It had not even been mechanical. If she had thought about it that way, she could have said that his insistence on the best had played into her hands. But she didn't, she thought herself lucky, thought herself blessed, being able to live two lives.

She found that she had been hearing, without listening to, a voice which had started up somewhere behind her right shoulder. A woman's voice, ineradicably Upper Fifth, travelling, as it must have done, across hockey-field and form-room.

'It's the Delameres' garden, somewhat glamorised, of course – they never managed to get their yews decently trimmed – but the give-away is that awful priapic statue the Reverend's grandfather brought back from Pompeii. I'm broad-minded, but really, I went hot all over when I first saw it. Canon Bawtree declared it was pagan and had no place on Christian ground.'

'But it's still there,' said a man's voice. 'Isn't it?'

'The old Canon died and no one turns a hair about that sort of thing any more. What liberality we've achieved!'

'Who's the woman?'

'Oh that's no mystery, either. It's Faith Delamere, the Reverend's unmarried daughter.'

'Sings, doesn't she? Rather a pleasant mezzo, as I remember.'

'Tom Bevis didn't paint her for her voice.'

'Sang "I will kiss the hem of His garment" at the Easter service, didn't she?'

'My dear, I rather fancy they'd got beyond that.'

Laura swung round, but they were already walking away. She did not know their backs, she was sure she would not know their faces. She felt at once glad, and distressed, and relieved. And what she needed was to sit down, it would not have taken a feather to knock her over.

She turned to the picture. 'Tom?' she said, 'Tom?' as if it could answer.

It did, it gave her a straight answer. His going, weekends in summer, to his friends the Delameres – 'Might as well,' he'd say, not seeming keen, 'I can watch cricket, if nothing else' – was the way things had naturally worked out. 'Why don't you come? They'd like to see you,' and she had always found a reason why she didn't – 'It's not my scene, church and cricket. Besides, I must wash the curtains.' She kept those Saturday nights and Sundays for Dendy. And Tom had Saturday night and Sunday for Faith Delamere. . . .

Was it possible! Yes, the picture told her, yes, the naked woman was Faith: no, Tom did not have dreams like that. It was for real. New vistas opened, strange and slightly absurd, and the absurdity had the ring of truth. In his playing her own game, taking a lover, taking the Vicar's daughter – making the best? – there was, there had to be, that touch of the incongruous. Tomness she had called it, and thought she knew it all.

Was she glad there was more? She should be, to be consistent. Hadn't she wanted the best for him? Should she grudge him the kind of happiness she herself had had? She might not believe that he had reached the same degree of joy with Miss Delamere as she reached with Dendy, but she should not deny him the chance. The chance had been a fine thing, and he had taken it. And now he was gone.

She couldn't weep here. She mustn't. But weep she did, hot splitting tears, and the picture, the damnable picture, swelled and broke and reshaped itself with merciless clarity. She put her face down into her hands, trying to press away the sight with her fingertips.

'Mrs B? If you'll pardon the expression, being what I've always thought of you.' She did not recognise the voice so much as the suggestion, the merest whiff – to do him justice – of the salt and fecund sea. 'A little less formal, meaning no disrespect, now or at any time.'

She blinked away her tears, and there was the fishmonger from the corner of their street, arrayed in a black jacket and striped trousers like a one-time solicitor, and somewhere, surely, there was one silver fish-scale, clinging and redolent.

'Mr Mitcham, how nice of you to come.'

'I wouldn't miss it for anything.' Holding his bowler vestally between his thighs – 'He was a gentleman, was Mr B.'

Gentle, yes. A man without violence, without even the rage in the blood that made for a passionate lover. She had thought.

'Many a chat we had in the Star of Asia. About art, and life.'

Tom had never mentioned it, but to say so would diminish Mr Mitcham's sense of his own importance and she ought not to do that because he might have been important to Tom.

'An artist to his fingertips, he was.'

She would not have said that, either. He did not argue or pronounce or take up attitudes about art, his own or anybody's. He was ready, always, for someone to know better than he did.

'I'm going to possess myself of one of these.'

'I beg your pardon?'

'Buy a picture.' Mr Mitcham advanced on Laura. 'I haven't made up my mind which one.' He put the bowler behind him so that he could get closer and speak confidentially. 'It all depends on the price.'

'And on finding something you like.'

'Mr B used to say a picture ought to speak to you. If it doesn't, you should leave it and find one that does. You won't remember the old song that was all the rage when I was young.' He sang, in a bold, tuneless treble, ' "If I had a talking picture of youooooo, I'd play and play it over, all throughooooo, I'd give ten shows a day, and a midnight matinée, if I had a talking picture of you." '

Hansen, at the far end of the room, whirled round, and Lady Gorman aimed her eyeglass at them.

'Perhaps you'd like a seascape,' said Laura.

'It would be talking shop to me, would that. I have enough of the sea. I know what I like.' He brought the bowler up to his chin and looked at her over the brim. His eyes grew misty. 'Are there any – did he ever – paint any girls in the – you know, the altogether?'

'Nudes?' Laura backed until she touched the frame of the Paradise Garden, blocking it completely from his view.

Mr Mitcham twinkled at her, with a frank admission of weakness. 'If you'll pardon me saying so, that's the kind of sweet talk would take my mind off fish-guts.'

'I'm sorry. He didn't paint people.' The nude and the satyr were under her left shoulder-blade, making their mark right through her, as if she were a stick of rock.

'Well, he had his artistic licence, he had pretty models, girls only too happy to pose in the altogether. It would be just a job of work to get them down on the canvas. No more to it than filleting a plaice is to me. Pity for him.'

Laura said sharply, 'You need not feel that.'

'I said once how nice it was to be able to paint what he saw and keep it in cold storage, like, and he said it was better to be able to paint what he didn't see.' Mr Mitcham laughed. 'That wouldn't do for me because I don't see nothing. Well, I'm sorry there aren't any girls, but I'll take a look round.'

She watched him walk away, respectfully biting the brim of his bowler, passing one by one the pictures of things which Tom had not seen. Moors, mountains, seashores, cornfields, churches.

'Tom?' she said. 'Tom?'

Lunch with the Chairman

'I need hardly remind you how important this rapprochement is –'
   'Why can't he use words we understand?'
   'Or words he understands.'
– 'not merely to this department, but to our enterprise. We have been chosen to make this first unofficial contact with our new Chairman –'
   'Person!' called Mrs Arkwright.
   'What did you say?'
   'Chair-*person!*'
There was a mirthful murmur, it had not been known that she was a feminist.
   Teague glittered, his version of a smile. 'I don't think there is any doubt as to his lordship's sex. The fact that we in Attire will be the first to meet him is a strong indication of the regard in which this department is held.'
   'We all know it's being done alphabetically,' muttered Deever of Men's. 'One lunch a month right through the store, and when he gets to Wrought Iron and Wicker he'll know us like ABC.'
   'Poor old bastard,' said young Housego, fresh from comprehensive and entirely without respect.
   'I should like' – Teague was coming to the crux – 'to think that the Chairman will recall this meeting with our department, his first with staff, as the most enjoyable. It is up to us to set an example which will be an inspiration and a challenge to the others. As you know, it is to be an informal occasion and I am sure I need not remind you that, appearance-wise, we have a standard to maintain. I trust we shall achieve the right balance between informality and good taste. Lounge suits, gentlemen, please, and I must ask you, Housego, to wear a collar and tie and leave that tee-thing at home. Ladies, your nicest *afternoon* frocks – I am myself very appreciative of the plunge neckline and slit skirt, but modest is also beautiful and we shall do well to remember that his lordship's brother is an Archbishop.'
   'So bosoms are out,' said Miss Calthorp of Children's, looking at the busty young student who was doing vacation work in Gloves.
   'Don't you mean in?' said Deever.
   'He doesn't drink either.' Teague grimaced, his private opinion showing. 'No alcoholic beverages will be served during the meal.'
   There were cries of dismay. Teague held up his hand, smiling with more than a hint of masochism. 'We must make a gesture of respect for his lordship's principles.'

Mrs Hagan said to Mrs Emlee, 'That settles it. I shall have a migraine. You'll be all right, you've got your mother.'

Mrs Emlee knew what was meant. Her mother was ninety-two and it was quite expected that some time or other Mrs Emlee would have to stay at home. She had never used her mother as an excuse for absenting herself from work – nor legitimately needed to do so, for the old lady was strong as a lion – and she did not propose to now.

She was the only person present who had as yet said nothing, audibly or inaudibly, about the Chairman's lunch. It was ridiculous how frightened she was. She would have thought that after fifty-five years of life, to say nothing of twenty years of marriage, she would have acquired resignation at least. But it had always been the same: from girlhood she had been shattered by social encounters. Indeed, it was to combat this known weakness that she had taken a position as a saleswoman. She had supposed that she would thus be obliged to face up to and handle people. In the event, she had learned to handle herself, to recognise the point at which her disorientation would become obvious. She was able, now, to hide it under a collected exterior, and had been told that she was never ruffled. She believed that to outward appearances it was true. No one knew the struggle she had to open her mouth.

'I can suit myself,' said Mrs Hagan. 'I'm not dependent on this Company or its Chairman for my living.'

Mrs Emlee *was* dependent, so was her mother who was not entitled to a full State pension and as a senior member of the department it was incumbent on Mrs Emlee to attend the lunch.

Her difficulty had always been in translating herself into words. Not that she had anything complicated to say: she would have been happy, she would have been wholly content, offering the everyday remarks which came so naturally to other people. But she couldn't get the words right, let alone the tone of voice. So she clung to such formulae of her trade as 'What lovely weather for the time of year'; 'Would you care to try something else?'; 'Brims were never really out'. When something less official was looked for, she fell silent, and suffered.

'Mrs Emlee!' They all looked at her, Teague held up two fingers in a papal gesture. 'As the most senior of our ladies you will be seated on the Chairman's immediate left.'

'Many are called, only one is chosen,' said Deever.

Mrs Hagan, perhaps, was close enough to see how Mrs Emlee blanched, but must have thought it was with triumph because she said sharply, 'He's only a life peer.'

'He is a multinational,' said Teague.

One person knew all about Mrs Emlee's difficulty, and that was her old mother. She blamed it on an aversion Mrs Emlee had had as a child to showing her teeth, which were bad. They had long since been replaced by nice white dentures, but her mother well knew that she was a creature of habit.

'What shall I talk about? To a man like that?'

'You must find out what are his interests.'

'How? How can I possibly –'

'Try *Who's Who*.' The old lady had not been around for ninety years for nothing. 'Avoid philately and the occult, they're too absorbing and he won't talk to anyone else.'

Mrs Emlee thought that unlikely, but she did as her mother recommended and consulted his lordship's entry.

Elevated to the peerage in the 1960s, he headed companies, commissions and consortiums all over Europe. He was, or had been, president of a national conservation trust and of a long list of societies – charitable as well as self-seeking. He served on advisory councils for hospital and penal reform. He was married, had four sons, a house in Rutland Gate and another in West Byfleet. He was a Freeman of the City, but did not appear to have recreations.

'Let *him* talk,' said the old lady. 'That will be best.'

But Mrs Emlee knew that she would have to say something, and of all the things in the world that might be said, not one seemed suitable for her. Perhaps she was too conscious of her position. She had always believed that being Head of Hats carried a certain distinction and required a quality midway between panache and elder statesmanship. She knew she did not have it and the Chairman was bound to see that.

'A man like that,' said her mother, 'won't expect you to talk, he will expect you to listen. Wear your blue foulard, blue is a good listening colour.'

By the day of the lunch Mrs Emlee had memorised an opening remark which she hoped would open nothing, and a tone of voice in which to utter it. As she lined up with the others in Teague's office, converted for the occasion into an executive dining-room, she could not quite be seen rehearsing her line. There was a frown of concentration between her eyes but her lips were tightly compressed.

'Our Emlee looks worried,' said Deever.

'Understandably,' said Mrs Arkwright. 'She's not exactly a dazzling conversationalist.'

'Housego, remove that gum,' said Teague. 'And smile, everyone, please.'

'Here comes the birdie.'

192

The Chairman was among them. He had brought his aide-de-camp, a young man wearing a suede suite and a Viking moustache. The Chairman was huge and unkempt, but big as he was, his chalk-stripe was bigger, the jacket actually swivelled on his shoulders. His nylon shirt, by contrast, was too tight, and showed his mammary glands to advantage.

He shambled in, smoking a cigarette, brushing ash off his lapels and not looking anywhere. All a-glitter, Teague sprang to his side.

'Your lordship, this is a great pleasure. We in Attire are deeply sensible of the honour. We regard it as a recognition of the not inconsiderable contribution this department has made . . .'

'Mother of God,' said Mrs Hagan.

'What contribution?' Deever asked out of the side of his mouth. 'We're 30 per cent down on last year's figures.'

'His lordship's here to see to that,' said Mrs Arkwright grimly.

'May I present the members of my staff?'

The Chairman fished a cigarette out of his pocket. The cigarette was bent. He stuck it, angled upwards like a stack-pipe, in the corner of his mouth. Housego was seized with a fit of giggles. The aide, in one swift, balletic movement, produced a lighter and a flame for his lord. Teague, looking daggers at Housego, snapped his fingers for Deever to step forward and be introduced.

Mrs Emlee, with beating heart, kept her gaze on her hands which she had decided – mistakenly, she now thought – to hold clasped in front of her. She felt that she looked prim, but not in the right sense proper. When Teague called her name she unclasped her hands and nerved herself to look up.

She need not have bothered. His lordship was not shaking hands, he had his in his trouser-pockets and was merely nodding as each person came before him. Mrs Emlee resisted an instinct to curtsey. She said how glad she was to make his acquaintance. He grunted.

The introductions over, Teague switched his smile to full head-lamp beam. 'I know I am speaking for everyone here when I say that we hope that after this happily informal get-together our Chairman will think of it as his first meeting with the people who are the backbone, the lifeblood of this Company. Indeed, I go so far as to say that it is we, the staff –'

'Lunch,' said his lordship. It was the first word he had spoken. He made for the table and took his seat at the head. The waitresses, who had been told that Teague's speech would take at least ten minutes, were thrown into panic. There was a scuffle for places, young Housego put himself on the Chairman's right and was hauled out of his seat by Teague. Mrs Emlee, thinking to hide herself at the bottom of the table, was sharply summoned to the top.

His lordship spread a napkin across his chest. He sat, a still centre, spoon held upright in his fist.

'Hurry! Hurry!' cried Teague, clicking the fingers of one hand at Mrs Emlee and the other at the waitresses. He had hard thumbs and could produce a sound like castanets.

It seemed to Mrs Emlee an appropriate moment to speak her piece. It would bridge the hiatus, until the table had settled.

She took her place at the Chairman's side. She unrolled her napkin, which in itself was a calming gesture.

'I see you have been instrumental in saving much of our national heritage. . . .'

It wasn't right, and would not have been even had she said it as she intended – lightly, interestedly, admiringly.

'So much is being lost, not only to us, but to our children. . . .' It sounded, she thought wildly, as if she were referring to children of hers, fathered by his lordship. 'I mean of course the next generation. . . .'

He turned and stared at her. She had to assume he was staring, no glimmer of an iris showed between his narrowed lids. His was a monumental face, of the sort seen on plinths, in parks, squares and echoing halls. His jowls would look well in stone and his nose was marbled already.

'I mean I read – somewhere . . .' she could not say she had looked him up, it was too premeditated, 'that you do – you are – on various committees. I think that's . . .' floundering, out of her depth, she could make no effort to save herself. As she went under she was heard to utter something which might have been – surely to God it was not! – 'nice. . . .'

The Chairman opened his mouth and by accident or intent his cigarette dropped from his lip. It went straight into his soup-plate. A flustered waitress, harassed by Teague, came with a tureen and started to serve the soup. She stopped, the ladle dripping in her nerveless hand when she saw the cigarette afloat on the brown windsor.

Teague gave a roar like a wounded tiger. He was and always had been an opportunist, and before the stub had swum once round he whipped away the plate and replaced it with Mrs Emlee's.

Trembling with shock, the waitress delivered a statutory three ladlefuls. The Chairman tapped with his spoon to indicate that he wished for more. The plate was filled to the rim. He started supping at once.

Mrs Emlee never did get any soup. It seemed to her like justice. She sat crumbling her roll, burning with crimson shame which she believed was apparent to everyone, whether they had heard her gaffe or not.

Teague, on the Chairman's right, talked about his concept of supranational trade. His lordship finished his soup and felt in his breast pocket for another cigarette. When the aide had lit it, he propped his huge head in his hands and puffed strenuously and rhythmically, like an engine ascending a gradient.

'We cannot afford frontiers,' Teague was saying. 'It is no longer a matter of nationalities or ideologies, it is a matter of survival. World resources are being used selfishly and unscientifically – they are being plundered. As I see it, there must be a convocation of business heads from every country in the world to decide how best to allocate and deploy resources for the universal good. And such people must have power, absolute power, to impose their decisions –'

He was interrupted by the waitress coming between him and the Chairman to serve the next course which was roast sirloin, baked and boiled potatoes, sprouts and individual Yorkshire puddings. His lordship removed his elbows from the table and helped himself to gravy, horseradish sauce, mustard, salt and clouds of pepper. The aide poured him a glass of orange juice and placed beside it a silver pill-box.

Teague leaned forward and continued beneath the shelf of the waitress's bosom. 'As I see it, neither territorial size, population or power politics would have any influence. It is now the small sheikhdoms which have the whip hands –'

'Pardonnez-moi,' said the aide who had brushed against Mrs Emlee's shoulder.

His lordship cleared his plate while the rest were still eating their soup. Mrs Emlee placed a crumb of bread between her lips. Mrs Arkwright called across the table, 'How nice your blue looks. Real silk lasts and lasts.'

'The EEC is simply not enough. I would go so far as to say it was never enough, what do you think, your lordship? You have had,' said Teague, visibly bowing to it, 'invaluable first-hand experience. . . .'

Some vast subterranean disturbance – possibly a sigh – passed through the Chairman's frame.

'Did you make it yourself?' persisted Mrs Arkwright.

Mrs Emlee gave the briefest affirmative nod. But his lordship, sensible no doubt of the chronic deficiency seated next to him, swung his great face round to her. She thought he said 'Harg?' It was not a question she could answer.

Teague stopped talking and watched her. They all watched, the whole table waited on her as the one who had engaged the

Chairman's attention. Only the waitresses, desperate with haste, went on dishing out beef and vegetables.

The crumb of bread tickled Mrs Emlee's throat. She coughed. It was not enough, she would have to say something, have to utter. It was her responsibility, her duty as Head of Hats. And, if Teague could be said to be host it could be said that she was hostess.

With iron calm, giving no hint of her inner turmoil, she said, 'I beg your pardon?'

The Chairman was not disposed to grant it. He grunted, without question. Mrs Emlee saw profound dissatisfaction in the way he swallowed his pills, three bright green ones chased down with orange juice. A rustle went round the table, not so much a sigh as a return to tempo. People could be heard picking up their lives again.

Mrs Emlee thought that hers could not be picked up, at best it could only be scraped up.

'The view from the roof of this building is quite something,' ventured Mrs Hagan. 'We could have a garden up there. Not so elaborate as Selfridge's, just somewhere green and flowering where people could relax.' She looked boldly at his lordship. 'Staff as well as customers.'

'Gimmickry, gimmickry!' chided Teague. 'Let us remember that this is a serious business based on traditions of the highest quality, value and service. Fair dealing comes before vulgar display.'

'A garden's not vulgar,' said Mrs Hagan. 'A garden is lovesome.'

Teague addressed himself to the Chairman. 'This department is known for its enthusiasm. Our ideas flow – our mature reasoning comes a little later.'

Well ahead in the lunch stakes, his lordship was served with the sweet; pastry balls filled with something brown and sprinkled with chopped pistachio nuts. He attacked them with his spoon. They skidded off his plate and shot across the table. He picked up the remaining one and tried, unsuccessfully, to break it. There was a definite ringing tone when he dropped it on the plate.

Teague summoned the waitress who was in the act of giving Mrs Emlee her first course.

'What's this supposed to be?'

'Profitrolls, sir.'

'It's inedible!'

'Oh no, it's quite fresh – straight from the freezer.'

'It's frozen solid, you idiot!'

'It's the special sweet you ordered –'

Teague bared all his teeth at her. 'Take it away and bring something his lordship can eat!'

The girl burst into tears. She ran from the room, taking Mrs Emlee's vegetables and leaving the profiteroles. The Chairman and his aide lit another cigarette.

'I really don't know what to say. It's ludicrous –' Teague essayed a man-of-the-world laugh and invited his lordship to share it. 'Kitchen staff, of course – typical of the mentality. Had I known, had I dreamed, anything like this could happen, I would have been out there supervising every detail myself. One does not expect to have to, but it is the only way to get things done properly. The matter will be reported to management, I shall make the strongest possible representation. . . .'

'Point of fact,' said the aide, 'we don't eat pastry.'

The Chairman rose to his feet. 'Lumbered' was a word that came to Mrs Emlee's mind, though obviously it shouldn't. Flakes of ash, frail as moths' wings, drifted down on the slices of beef which were all she had yet been served.

'I shall organise something else at once!' Teague was crying, alarmed.

'Afraid there won't be time,' said the aide. 'We have an appointment with Moscow.'

'Moscow?'

'A trade delegation from the Soviet Union.'

'But he hasn't finished his lunch –'

'One doesn't keep the Russians waiting,' said the young man in the suede suit. He was, thought Mrs Emlee – her thoughts were getting out of hand – a suede young man.

In the doorway the Chairman paused. They all thought he was going to say something. He stood plucking at the seat of his capacious trousers. It was a gesture which suddenly transported Mrs Emlee into the past, to her schooldays. She had attended what was called a primary school, where boys and girls were taught together. There was a boy in her class from an unfortunate family. He was obliged to wear his father's old trousers cut down at the knee, and was forever pulling at the big empty behind. There had been something quite desperate about him. As if he was trying – and Mrs Emlee had known even then that it was hopeless – to disassociate himself. Of course no one took him seriously, children were so unkind. And not only children. . . .

Would the Chairman have said something if someone had not been there to do it for him? Mrs Emlee doubted it. She did wonder how he managed on his committees, and how would he communicate with the delegation from Moscow? She supposed that the less said to them the better.

The aide sent his smile round the table with a practised sweep. 'It has been a great pleasure to his lordship to meet you all. We have enjoyed our lunch. Thank you.'

Then they were gone, Teague leaping at the Chairman's side, escorting them to the lift.

The table came to life. People stuck out their elbows, spread their knees, laughed – the women indignantly, the men defensively.

'It wasn't our fault,' said Mrs Arkwright.

'Do you realise he never said a word?'

'He did – to Mrs Emlee.'

'What did he say?' they asked her.

She said she couldn't remember.

The Dream of Fair Women

'Is it really called that?'

'Why not?'

'Couldn't you have found somewhere else!'

'You asked me to suggest somewhere Janine wouldn't find you and you could rest up. This is it. The landlord owes me a favour. Are you going to quibble about a name?'

'I can't stand women. I've done with them.'

'You? You won't be done till you're in your wooden overcoat.'

'I mean it. So far as I'm concerned it's not a dream, it's a bloody nightmare.'

'It's a poem by Tennyson.'

'So it's a poem by Tennyson, but if Janine tracks me down . . .'

'Beach, he's the landlord, will see her off.'

'I tell you she's sworn to kill me. And she'll do it.'

'It beats me how you get into these situations.'

Selwyn grinned. 'That's because you don't know the power of love.'

He made Miller take his key and go to the flat and check that Janine was out. Then he went in and got his things together. She had locked the wardrobe but he had no qualms about breaking it open. He took the whisky and gin, he liked whisky and she liked gin and he reckoned she deserved to suffer for illegally impounding his clothes. He frisked the mattress, felt in the space under the Sleepeezie label. It was empty, as half expected, seeing that he had removed some cash from there only the day before. But it was worth a look, she was such a creature of habit. He could say that twice, he could say anything boring about Janine twice.

'She's mentally unbalanced,' he called to Miller who was keeping watch from the front window. 'If she's crossed she goes bananas.'

'Find yourself a nice homely girl with money.'

'All women are crazy, I've definitely done with them. Come on, let's get out of here, I don't feel safe.'

In the car on the way to the pub Miller said, 'Beach isn't exactly mild-tempered either. He's an ex-Commando, so don't start anything unless you want your neck squeezed.'

'Is he married?'

Miller nodded and grinned, showing his eye-teeth. 'I'd be surprised if you started anything there.'

199

It turned out to be a Victorian-style red brick hostelry in a mini-minor road, not much more than a lay-by, off the motorway. Miller could be right, Janine wouldn't come looking for him here. Selwyn, observing the thick carpets, claret-shaped lamps and claw-footed chairs, guessed that it was pricey. He needn't mind, he had the money Janine had been putting by for a new cooker, it would see him through the week and he was entitled to a spell of comfort – morning tea and newspapers in bed, full English breakfasts, three-tiered lunches and brandy after dinner.

Beach, the mine host, looked out of character with the place. He was beetle-browed, no longer young, but big in hams and fists, with a hot hard eye and hairy nostrils. Miller introduced Selwyn as 'this friend who's having trouble with his life-style and needs peace and quiet to sort it out'. Beach finished what he was doing, wiping the bar counter with a piece of mutton cloth, before he shook hands. It was like being saluted by something cold, damp and powerful: a boa-constrictor. Miller said, 'If anyone comes asking for him, he's not here, you've never seen him, or anyone like him.'

Selwyn, who was wiping his shaken hand on the seat of his trousers, put in, 'Especially if it's a woman asking.'

'What sort of woman?'

Miller said, 'Tall, slender, thirtyish, foreign-looking.'

'Blonde or brunette?'

'Dark brunette.'

'That goes for a lot of women that come in here.'

'Home-dyed,' said Selwyn. 'And built like a racehorse, she's got the same twitchy skin.'

'Money?'

'Excuse me?'

'Do you owe her money?'

'Certainly not.' Selwyn had perfected the art of clearing his face and retracting his ears with a boyish openness which most people – women, anyway – found irresistible. Beach found it totally resistible and gave him a non-complicit stare. 'It's an emotional entanglement, you know what I mean. She'll get over it. But she's liable to say and do things she'll be sorry for later on.'

'I'll put you at the back,' said Beach. 'If you see her coming you can get away down the fire-escape.' He wasn't smiling and there was no twinkle in his eye.

Selwyn thought it politic to laugh, so did Miller. 'You'll be OK, Sel. Call me if there's anything else I can do.'

'You've done enough,' said Selwyn. Later he might need to borrow Miller's car, but as of now Miller was welcome to go. Selwyn clapped him across the shoulders. 'I won't forget it, sport.'

He was probably doing Miller a favour. The inn, tucked away as it was, couldn't be much patronised and whatever Miller owed the landlord would be covered by the introduction of a paying guest. At present, anyway, Selwyn was prepared to pay. If he became unprepared by force of circumstance there might have to be a reappraisal.

A little old man with legs like a jockey and wearing button gaiters carried his bag upstairs. He opened a door on the first landing. 'Here we are, sir, I hope you'll be comfortable.'

'If I'm not you'll soon hear about it.'

But he approved of the room. It was dignified, full of solid, well-polished furniture and good old Turkey carpet, not Janine's plastic wrought-iron chairs and skid-mats on bare parquet. The bed was double, well-sprung, noiseless, the pillows plump, the eiderdown billowy and pink satin.

He lay down, closed his eyes and summoned a few erotic memories. When, sighing, even soulful, he got up, the short winter dusk had set in and the room was full of substantial shadows.

He was not, and never had been a fanciful type. His school reports complained 'lacks imagination', but in the one and only important respect that was not true. He had plenty of imagination when it came to the little old three-letter word that made the world go round. One of those shadows looked uncommonly like a woman. Wishful thinking, of course.

He switched on the light and the shadows vanished. There was a sort of tallboy with a vase on top which could have looked like a figure, a woman's if he was sufficiently wishful. Whistling, he unpacked his clothes and hung them in the closet, he was of a sanguine disposition and fate, or Nature, or the law of averages would provide.

He filled the bath and tipped into it half a bottle of Janine's bath oil which he had taken more to annoy her than because he liked it. It made the gloomy old hotel bathroom smell like a sauna and streaked the bath bright green. Afterwards he put on his dressing-gown and drank Janine's gin. This was the life and he was grateful to her for putting him up to it.

While he shaved he took a good look at himself. He had not been born with money but he had the remote next best, a thoroughly prepossessing exterior. In fact women were too damn prepossessed and couldn't wait for the property to become vacant. Which was how the trouble with Janine had started, over some wretched girl who thought she owned him.

He stroked his nose. Roman, Janine called it. It wasn't, it was

Greek. And his skin, olive and warm, with greenish shadows after his shave, had positively obsessed her. He watched his smile light up his face and he couldn't wonder, he honestly couldn't, at the damage he inflicted. He couldn't be blamed for it either.

He dressed and went down to dinner. The tables in the dining-room were all set, white cloths and sparkling glasses, cutlery for three courses, bread baskets and napkins folded into bishops' mitres.

But company, though expected, did not arrive. He ate with a thousand of his selves reflected to infinity in the mirrors that lined the walls. The food was above average, country paté and toast, followed by veal cutlets, creamed potatoes and button sprouts, then a nice apple charlotte with clotted cream, cheese and biscuits.

The woman who waited at table was as black as the ace of spades. He asked her what her name was.

'Rosanna.'

'That's two names, Rose and Anna.'

'Just the one. Like glory.'

'Glory?'

She drew the cork from his bottle of wine with a report like a gunshot. 'Hosanna in the highest.'

He watched her take her big hips away between the tables. She was majestical, even stately. In her own country she would rate as a beauty. But looking at her was like looking at a newly black-leaded grate.

When she brought his veal chops he raised his glass to her. 'Bottoms up.'

She inclined her head and smiled, not the melon grin of her kind, no more than a quirk of her lips. 'I hope you enjoy your meal.'

He saw her afterwards serving behind the bar. He didn't stay long. There was nothing to interest him, executive types talking about 'demand-promotion', elderly housewives, and a man with a smelly dog.

Anyway, he had demands of his own to promote. He was thinking of getting away somewhere warm for the winter. It would need a miracle to stretch Janine's cooker money to pay for his bed and board here *and* buy him an air ticket to Cyprus or Benidorm or wherever. He needed to think, and take a look at the fire-escape.

On the way up to his room he met a woman. He was deep in thought and didn't see her until they came face to face, or rather, knee to knee. It gave them both a surprise, wholly pleasant for him. As she stood on the stair above he was close enough to follow the blush that ran swiftly and softly from her neck to her temples. He did not stand aside, his hand went out to the banister rail and his arm barred her way. He smiled deep into her eyes and that again was a wholly pleasant experience.

She was young, but not too young, mid-thirties perhaps, he could see tiny scarlet threads under her skin. He could also see that she was a natural pure blonde. But she had raven black brows and lashes which, contrasting with her corngold hair, stopped his heart as well as his eye. Over her blue silk dress she wore a frilly apron, decorative rather than menial.

'I do beg your pardon,' he said warmly.

She lowered her eyes and made a movement, not quite a curtsey, nor yet a bob, but it acknowledged his status as a paying guest – and a promising male. All without a trace of coquetry or coyness.

He would have handed her down the stairs but she drew back and stood against the wall so that he could pass.

'Mrs Beach?' She lifted her chin, smiling. 'My name's Selwyn.'

She nodded and next minute was gone, slipping away down the stairs and along the passage to the bar. Whistling, he went up to his room.

But he couldn't settle to his own affairs. He kept thinking about the woman. It was the old story, he was about to start something. Only this time he had a feeling that a start had already been made. Who by? Mrs Beach? He had only seen her for a couple of minutes but he could see she wasn't bold like Janine, nor forward. She had class, something he tended to forget women could have. It was in the way she looked at him, sure of her quality and expecting his to be up to the same standard. Well, he wouldn't disappoint her, there was a best in him, let her bring it out and see how good it was.

'Mrs Beach, you're a peach.' He went to the window and looked at the fire-escape. His plans had changed, he might be staying longer than first budgeted for, and there were other emergencies besides fire that he might want to escape from.

He decided to go back to the bar and have another look at Mrs Beach. But she wasn't there. Beach and the black woman were getting ready to close. She was rinsing glasses, Beach was re-arranging chairs. He stood, a chair in each hand, and stared at Selwyn, eyes as hard as bullets. Selwyn did not ask him where his wife was, he disliked the idea of talking to Beach about her.

Hopefully, he thought, he might find her upstairs. He hung about outside his room and when he went in, left the door ajar. The dress she wore made a whispering sound when she moved and he would certainly hear if she passed by.

All he heard was Beach's heavy tread going along the passage and up the next flight of stairs. Selwyn shut the door and went to bed.

Next morning he was wakened with tea and newspaper, brought not by Mrs Beach, as he had confidently expected, but by the old fellow with elliptical legs.

'I hope you slept well, sir.'

'Where's Mrs Beach?'

'Gone shopping.' The old fellow drew back the heavy curtains and let in a blaze of light.

Selwyn flinched. 'Hey, I ordered the *Sun* newspaper, not the bloody solar system. Leave the curtains.'

'I beg your pardon, sir.'

'Another thing, Barney, I want a pot of tea in the morning, and biscuits, not one cup going cold.'

'My name's Sidney, sir. I'll see about the tea.'

'Ridden many winners, Barney?'

'Sidney, sir. Winners, sir?'

Selwyn pointed to his legs and the old fellow put his hands over his kneecaps with the gesture of a girl covering her modesty. 'That's the arthritis, sir.'

Selwyn burst out laughing. There was no point in getting up right away, so he ordered breakfast in bed.

He looked through his newspaper. News didn't interest him, girlie pictures did. He had once gone so far as to cut out the best ones and stick them on the wall in the bathroom at the flat, but Janine and the steam between them soon curtailed that little show.

It was after eleven when he strolled downstairs. He left the inn and walked along the road, thinking he might meet Mrs Beach coming back from shopping.

The sun had gone in, the clouds were building up for rain or snow. This was marginal country, the fields still spattered with clay from the excavations for the motorway, the hedges broken down and a dredger like a dead dinosaur rusting in the ditch. He could hear the roar of traffic on the M-road, but the only traffic in this lane was an orange mini, driven by Rosanna. She lifted her hand to him as she passed. They had it made over here, he thought. A car to come to work in! In her own country she'd be walking barefoot with a bundle on her head.

Chilled to the bone – he hadn't put on a top-coat – he turned back. The name of the inn still narked him. 'The Dream of Fair Women'. Whose dream? Not Beach's, that ape wouldn't have the delicacy to dream. Though he did have one of the fair women. Selwyn found that he actively objected to the notion that he and Beach had the same tastes.

He was the only one for lunch and again he was served by old

Barney, creaking across the dining-room with his thumb in the soup. Selwyn sent it back. 'When I want a taste of horse in my brown windsor I'll say so.'

'Sir?'

'Is Mrs B back from shopping?'

Barney picked up the plate and his thumb went under the soup to the base of his nail. 'Mrs Beach is in the kitchen.'

Selwyn went to the lounge after lunch. He kicked the fire into a blaze and stretched himself on the Knole settee. It was sleeting outside, the room was twilit and warm and he fell asleep.

A sound wakened him, a sort of remote whispering. He knew what it was before he opened his eyes. It deeply and deliciously disturbed him. He sat up and saw her walking slowly to and fro in the firelight.

'Hello there,' he said, sounding surprised, though he was not. He believed his luck, he was lucky in love, only when he was out of it did his troubles begin.

She stopped, turned to him, and now that the whisper of her dress had ceased he was left with the astonishing contrast between her black winged eyebrows and golden hair. It could have been a mistake, but Nature did not make that kind of mistake and it was an unqualified triumph. The skin of her lips was so fine and full of warm blood that again there was a contrast, almost fierce, between the redness of her mouth and the pallor of her face.

'I waited for you,' he said, and another voice, not the one he used every day but one which he reserved for private and primary communications, said, 'I've been waiting all my life.' And he knew that if he never spoke another, he had just spoken something which was a whole truth.

Standing before him, head bowed, her hands clasped in front of her, she too seemed to be waiting, for his wishes – his pleasure. He felt himself go hot, then cold, then hot again, and put up his hand to her. But his reach wasn't long enough, or his aim wasn't right, or his timing, and he did not quite touch her. 'I don't even know your name.'

She raised her head, and with that slight movement her dress whispered. He had not yet heard her speak. Perhaps she was dumb? Was that what Miller had been getting at when he said he would be surprised if Selwyn started anything?

Selwyn could have laughed out loud. Words he could very well dispense with when he started anything, words and clothes. Smiling broadly, he stood up to look deep into the neck of her dress to the beautiful shadow between her breasts.

'I'm called Alice.' She glanced up from under her lashes and as quickly lowered her eyes.

'In your Alice-blue gown.' He made a move towards her but she
bent away from him like a flame in a draught. 'You're not scared of
me, are you?'

'No. It's my husband I'm scared of – he is so terribly jealous.'

'I don't blame him.'

'So terribly jealous,' she said again. 'It is terrible to kill someone
out of jealousy.'

'Kill?'

She drew herself together, clasped her arms about herself,
suddenly cold perhaps, or fearful, or in pain. 'A young man, a
student, he was just a boy. Years ago. He came here to work in his
vacation and my husband murdered him.'

'For God's sake!' said Selwyn. 'Why?'

'He thought he was my lover.'

'Was he?'

'I never had a lover.' She raised her face to his, opened her eyes
wide, violet eyes, the only colour he had ever seen to match it was in
one of those old-fashioned carboys in a chemist's window. 'I only had
my husband.'

Selwyn felt quite dizzy. 'How could he – I mean, how did he get
away with murder?'

'He strangled him and hanged him from a beam in the cellar. He
made it look as though the boy had killed himself, you see.'

Selwyn, who did not see, said, 'Why should he kill himself?'

'Because of unrequited love. That's what everyone thought. But
my husband thought I had requited it.'

'How can you go on living with someone like that?'

She smiled. Selwyn sensed an awful lot in that smile, but was
unable then to appreciate just how much, and how awful. 'Next time
I shall make sure there's a witness.'

'Next time?'

'Next time he kills someone.'

He flung out his hands with the impulsive gesture which had
endeared him to so many women. 'There's no reason why it should
happen again! Don't be scared on my account. I'm not a boy, I'm a
man of the world, I can take care of myself.'

'Ah, you –' She uttered a sigh. It said plainer than words that she
knew the difference, and all the other differences there would be
between a man and a boy.

But instead of taking his hands, her own flew to her throat. She
murmured, 'Tonight.' Any of the women he knew who still
remembered how to colour up went blotting-paper pink and puffy.
Alice Beach blushed the tenderest shade of rose.

206

'Where?' he said eagerly. 'What time?'

A sudden gust of wind hurled heavy rain, or hail, against the window. He had turned his head to look, and in that moment she slipped away. When he turned back the room was empty.

'Damn and blast!'

'I beg your pardon, sir?'

That was Barney, bringing in an armful of logs.

'Where did Mrs Beach go?'

'I came in the back way, ain't seen nobody.'

Selwyn was joined in the dining-room that evening by a gang of commercials. They were having a reunion and kept Rosanna busy fetching wines from the cellar and chasers from the bar. He wanted to ask where Mrs Beach was, but decided not to prejudice anything. For all he knew she had made arrangements which would not bear enquiring into at this stage.

He sat at his meal, scarcely aware of what he ate, going over in some detail his expectations for later on. He was able, because of many past encounters, to vary the opening gambits. He couldn't make up his mind which he would prefer. One thing was certain, Alice Beach was intended for him. And he for her. The mutuality was going to make it a memorable experience. His bones, as well as his flesh, melted at some of his expectations.

When the salesmen started singing a smutty song to the tune of 'Annie Laurie' – it wasn't even original, just the same old smut from his schooldays – he got up and went into the bar.

It was still sleeting outside, there weren't many drinkers in the 'Dream' that night – the man with the smelly dog which was wet-through and smellier than ever, and some girls and boys getting stoned on vodka and cokes. They looked under age, Beach probably couldn't afford to turn them away. He was leaning on the counter reading a newspaper.

Selwyn got himself a double whisky. He sat quietly taking it between his teeth and his tongue and turning over in his mind the question of whether Beach could have done murder. He had been wondering – not all that often, having better things to think about – since Alice had told him. The man was certainly an ugly customer and had plenty of bad coming to him. But on the whole Selwyn was inclined to think she had exaggerated, kidded herself. A woman, any woman, loved the idea of murder being committed on her account.

The salesmen came in from the dining-room and at once the bar was in an uproar. They had had a skinful, they were all in the same hairy skin together, jolly old pals, auld acquaintance never to be forgot, buddies, all for one and one big headache for all. They were singing another worn-out classic, about the nun and the undertaker. Beach was kept busy as they ordered and counter-ordered and forgot to pay, and spilled their drinks. Selwyn had to laugh, watching him run to and fro, wild-eyed and sweating, trying to cope. A beerpull jammed and he lost his nerve and started bellowing.

Barney appeared, none too readily. 'I told you to fix this bloody thing!' shouted Beach. 'Get Rosanna. Where is she?'

'Got a headache.'

Selwyn wasn't surprised to hear that. He strolled over to the bar and watched Beach wrestling with the beerpull. 'Give me another whisky.'

Beach looked up with hatred. 'You'll have to wait. Can't you see I'm single-handed?'

'So was Rosanna.' Selwyn winked. 'It's your turn now, sport.'

He went upstairs after his third whisky. He knew when to stop. Alcohol was good, was practically medicinal at such times. It was a guarantor. But only up to a point, beyond that point was no return, only rapid deterioration. He meant to acquit himself perfectly tonight, for her sake as well as his own. 'I never had a lover,' she had said. He was filled with the pure and uplifting spirit of selflessness.

It was also reasonable to suppose that the first place she would look for him would be in his room.

He undressed, put on his pyjamas and dressing-gown, tucked a silk cravat over his pyjama-collar. She was a creature of refinement and delicacy. There would be no time to waste, but she would require a little dalliance and – he rinsed his glass and put it ready beside the remains of Janine's gin – a little of the guarantor.

An hour passed. He had left his door ajar and a dozen times went out into the passage to look for her. He heard the salesmen go, packing into their cars, engines roaring and tyres screeching as they belted along the lane. They'd be lucky if they ran into nothing worse than a squad-car and breathalysers. Afterwards, all was quiet downstairs. He looked at his watch and saw that it wanted but half an hour to closing time.

She wasn't coming. Either she had been prevented or she had been teasing him. Even ladies could be teases. Especially ladies. He cursed her aloud. 'Damn and blast you, Alice Beach!'

'No – please!'

He swung round. She was there in her Alice-blue, holding out her arms to him, her golden hair ablaze, her cheeks shining with tears.

'My dear – I didn't mean it!'

He started towards her, but she put her finger to her lips. 'Shhhh –'

'I thought you weren't coming!'

'Oh, nothing could stop me now!'

'Why did you leave it so late?'

'Late? If you knew how long I have waited!'

It was more of a wail than an exclamation. He went cold, and did not immediately go hot again. 'What about Beach? Won't he be coming up soon?'

'Not yet, not just yet.'

It occurred to Selwyn that she didn't even know how long a love-making would take, how long it *could* take.

'We don't want to hurry anything,' he said, and went to close the door, 'but I've been waiting too.'

She flung up her hands in a quaint, old-fashioned gesture of protest. 'Not here – it cannot be in this room.'

'Why not? It's the safest place. I'll lock the door.'

'He has a pass-key, he'll come looking for me. We must go somewhere else.'

'Where?'

'Come. . . .' She slipped out of the room and was gone. When he went into the passage she was standing at the point where the stairs went up to the second floor.

'Not up there,' said Selwyn. 'He sleeps up there.'

'You must trust me.'

He was close enough to see how her eyes shone and her parted lips. She was breathing fast, and so was he, but her breasts moved in perfect rhythm as if there was a soft little motor under them. And the Alice-blue dress whispered to him.

He said hoarsely, 'I don't care where we go so long as it's now!'

'It is now – I promise.' She ran up the stairs and opened a door. He followed, found they were in a room, in darkness. He could just make out the shape of a bed, the clothes tumbled, a mound of eiderdown. It looked promising.

The time for delicacy was past. He threw off his dressing-gown and cravat, stood in his pyjamas. There was a movement on the bed, she was waiting for him.

'Alice . . .' he groped among the bedclothes.

At once several things happened. A light was switched on. Selwyn blinked, dazzled and disbelieving. A black face was looking up at him from the pillow. At the same moment he heard Beach's voice in the passage below. There was no one else in the room, no Alice, just himself and Rosanna. She raised herself on her elbow, her eyes rolling white with alarm.

'What are you doing here?'

He might have asked her that, but Beach's footsteps were on the stairs. He cried, 'Where's Alice? Where is she?'

'Alice?'

'Alice Beach – Mrs Beach. . . .'

It wasn't possible, yet Rosanna's skin seemed to darken. The shine went out of it. She said, 'That Mrs Beach has been dead a long time.'

'Dead?'

'Killed in a car accident four, maybe five, years ago.'

'Goddamit!' cried Selwyn, 'That's crazy, up the creek! She was here a minute ago. She's framing me, why I don't know, but it doesn't matter now. . . .' It was a matter, now, of self-preservation. 'Beach is coming –'

'He is coming here.'

'You've got to help me – Rosanna, I'll make it worth your while – I'll have to brazen it out – he can't object – it won't look – I mean it's not as if you're his wife, is it?'

'I am his wife.'

'What?'

'His second wife.'

Selwyn's jaw dropped. His mouth fell open and dried. Then Beach came into the room, and there was a moment of crammed and unpeaceful silence. Beach took in the scene – Selwyn in his pyjamas, Rosanna in the tumbled bed. A moment was enough, even for Beach, a man of not especially quick intelligence. He was also a plain man, and in that moment became downright ugly.

He made for Selwyn, unstoppable as a tank making for an enemy trench. Selwyn ran round the bed, shouted with all the strength of his lungs. He found he was trapped, his back to the wall, but, desperate, kept shouting for help, for understanding – for a little more time. Beach's hands gripping his throat stopped him at last.

He didn't see Barney come running as fast as his crooked legs would bring him. Barney arrived in the doorway, stood and gaped. It was really all he was required to do. Had Selwyn been the fanciful type, and had the opportunity – which, naturally, he had not, he might have recalled at least one promise Alice Beach had kept: 'Next time I'll make sure there's a witness.'

A Fairly Close Encounter

The flight was delayed. Novalis, a reasonable man, reasoned with himself about air space. One would not wish to rise and find it fully occupied, one would prefer to remain on the ground. Indefinitely, if need be. He sighed. He was too often disadvantaged by his habit of seeing through to the logical conclusion.

If Miranda and her aunt had travelled overland the journey must have taken a couple of days instead of hours. Was he prepared to sacrifice any of her time, to say nothing of his own – of which he had everything to say? It was now three months since he had seen her. We are to be married in the Spring, he had taken to explaining, she is a patriot, it is her wish that we be married in the centenary year. Asked about her, he would say she is dark, petite, and wears her hair long. Sometimes he volunteered the information without being asked, in order to speak of her. She was in no danger of becoming a formula while he so vividly recalled how her hair clustered about her neck but fell clear of her shoulders and her small exquisite bosom. It was the contrast between secrecy and boldness which enchanted him.

He had now to resign himself to losing one and possibly two hours of their precious time together, but reasoned that safety is not guaranteed, even on the ground. Railways are not infallible and boats even less so.

He was occupying one of the airport chairs, the two bouquets positioned across his knees; red roses for Miranda, freesias and nemesia for her aunt. The flowers were tastefully presented in trumpets of regency-striped paper twined with silver gilt lace.

He had gone to the best florist in town, Gucchi's, an establishment of the utmost sensibility. Serene white colonnades, a lily pool, a Cupid fountain, love-seats, pergolas, surrounded but did not overwhelm flawless blooms of all denominations, from orchids to anemones. Recalled in the noise and heat of the airport it seemed the nearest approach to Paradise available to metropolitan man. Miranda, he thought, would make a perfect Eve.

As a huge woman went by pushing a trolley laden with pigskin cases, he was reminded of air and the treachery of it. A casual wind could send Miranda's plane off course, a pocket could drop it into the sea. He worried about her, suspended above the earth.

He worried about their separation – how to resolve those three months without a kiss or a whisper between them? In Gucchi's, among the lilies and roses, it could have been pure artistry. The flowers he had brought were a fragile link, a promise which Miranda might not perceive. Here among crying children and sweating pigskin, how was he to promise her anything?

It seemed to be a matter of quality of promise rather than inhibition, for seemingly it was possible to deliver something, even among the children and pigskin. Opposite him, two people were implementing their promise to each other. Indeed, it looked as if it would be fulfilled, here and now, on the airport chairs.

Novalis turned his head away. He mistrusted demonstrations, even scientific ones. There was in this one some of the ancient science of love-making.

The indicator-board signalling 'Rome – delayed', revived his angst. He became concerned about the condition of the bouquets. How long could they remain fresh and presentable in this over-heated, overtaxed atmosphere? Inside the cones of paper the roses still sustained beads of water on their velvet petals. But the freesias had darkened slightly and the nemesia let fall a dry floret. To this least of his worries he might apply reason. And did so, to occupy his mind, other thoughts being unproductive and defeatist.

If the plane were delayed a further hour, the roses would be presentable, the freesias less so. Another two hours and the aunt's bouquet would have suffered visibly but the roses, if not subjected to close scrutiny, might still pass muster. He reasoned that in the fuss following a delayed landing, Miranda would not be looking intently at her flowers, or at anything – with the exception of himself. The aunt's flowers he must be prepared to abandon in the wastecan, Miranda's look he could not prepare for. It might happen at the moment of encounter or just before, or at some time or times afterwards. It must be expected when he least expected it.

Nothing was due to the aunt in the way of propitiation or douceur. The bouquet had simply been a nice idea. Hyper-anxious, he now foresaw that Miranda and her aunt would have their hands already full with the sundry items ladies carry on journeys. Added to handbags, hats, scarves, magazines, the bouquets would be unnecessary encumbrances. Any look he received from Miranda would surely contain an element of disapproval.

The couple opposite claimed his attention – not that they had any use for it, they were engrossed in each other. It was the engrossment which drew his eye.

In their late teens, neither children nor adult, they were currently coping with the problem of sex, and doing so with the rashness of children, which was preferable to the lewdness of adults. Novalis

212

wondered at their indifference to their surroundings. In a limited sense it was sublime.

The boy was long armed and something of a contortionist. He had his arms about the girl, his legs knotted. Knee over knee, ankle over ankle. His face was hidden in her neck. Like that, faceless and entwined, he was her setting. She spilled over him, lavish rather than large: she had more than enough of herself and could afford to be generous. Novalis registered her, without blame, as a slut. His had been a strict East European upbringing and he expected little or nothing from the West.

This girl was wearing a sun-top with the word 'Happiness' blazoned across her bosom, a form of advertising carried by all consumer goods. Her skin had become a bright crude pink with injudicious exposure to the sun. She might well be suffering from first degree burns. The boy's caresses were puppyish and rough and caused Novalis to wince for her.

It was announced that the flight from Amsterdam was landing, the provisional time of arrival of the flight from Rome was unchanged. A man with a rucksack on his back blocked Novalis's view of the couple and he fell to thinking about Miranda's aunt who disapproved of him on the grounds that he had no sense of humour. He believed that gravity was a virtue, but as the aunt was rich and childless and Miranda was her only niece, he was prepared to make an effort. He would present the bouquets with gallantry and some light-hearted remark such as 'Flowers for the fair'. Not that the aunt was fair, but he hoped she would take it in the spirit intended.

The man with the rucksack moved away in time for Novalis to see the boy taking the girl's neck in his hands. His thumbs met over the windpipe. Novalis experienced a sudden strong desire to see them sink deep into her flesh, and to see it change from pink to scarlet to dark purple under pressure. He was of course having a conditioned reflex: just as the sight of a gun provoked thoughts of its lethal possibilities, so must the sight of hands about a throat.

It was questionable whether these two were serious – the question must be what constituted seriousness for them. One did not know if horseplay was their nature or a protective cover. Protecting what?

The girl was watching Novalis. Her senses were no doubt permanently male-alarmed, but he got a mild shock when he realised that she was displaying for his benefit. Somehow she was contriving to relate her movements to him without his co-operation or approval. Certainly without his approval. He considered that she was vulgarising the essentially private and delicate exchange between man and woman.

With distaste he observed how she wallowed about on the airport chair, her knees in black fishnet tights spread wide and mocking, her breasts rolling under the scanty sun-top, her neck arching so that the colour was strained out of it. Her eyes glittered at Novalis from under their lids, her lips parted to reveal the darting tip of her tongue. She pulled the boy's head down and bit his ear, said something which caused him to look round at Novalis and laugh.

Novalis turned away. The flight indicator now estimated the Rome arrival time as 15.00 hours. There was time for a cognac which might disperse thoughts which had become expendable. But what to do with the bouquets whilst he struggled through to the crowded bar?

He vacated his chair, positioned the bouquets across it and crossed to the bookstall. He made a quick classification of the publications on offer: travel and leisure guides by the score, women's interest pulps by the dozen, juvenilia for all ages, girlie art, political cartoons, horoscopes, language dictionaries, handbooks on health, antiques, bonsai gardening, hatha yoga. Nothing to command his interest. The display provoked thoughts on the sin of profligacy which had always seemed to him the most insidious vice.

Abstemious by nature and nurture, he deplored the current tendency to over-production. In his opinion too much of even a good thing resulted in loss of virtue and benefit and detracted from the quality of life. If small was beautiful, less was mandatory. He remembered his old professor in Prague asserting that world government could best be achieved by simple equations, one for each hemisphere.

Before going to the bar he glanced back in the direction of his chair, and saw the girl in the act of taking up one of the bouquets. She held it to her face, elevated her shoulders, swelled her bosom, clowning a mighty inhalation. Novalis envisaged the flowers shrinking, devitalised. Then she laid the bouquet along her arm and walked towards the exit, kissing her fingers to the air as she went. The boy laughed, men halted their luggage trolleys and stared.

Novalis hurried after her. 'Excuse me, I think you have my flowers.' She looked round. At close quarters hers was a soft spreading face, lacking East European bone structure, a florid English rose, unlike Gucchi's shapely blooms.

'Yours are over there, on the chair.'

'I have two bouquets, and plans for both of them.'

She put her head on one side, quizzed him with uncalled-for familiarity. 'Are you going to a funeral?'

'These aren't the sort of flowers for dead people.'

She had of course taken the roses, Miranda's roses. It disturbed him to see her with them. This girl was overpowering, she overpowered his thoughts, including his thoughts of Miranda. Facing her, he was unable to be aware of anything else, was compelled to remark the consistency of her skin, as thick as cream, and as moist. The sun had coloured but not dehydrated it. Her lipstick was smudged by the boy's kisses. Her eyelashes, spiked with mascara, signalled inanely – her eyes were as bright and empty as an infant's.

'Findings keepings.'

'You did not find, you purloined and I shall be obliged if you will return my property.'

'If I don't?'

'I shall call the police.'

He found it impossible to guess what she was thinking, if she was thinking at all. She seemed entirely blameless, probably because she was mentally unreachable. Physically, of course, she was reaching for him. Hastily he dropped his hand which he had extended to take the flowers.

'What's going on?'

The boy had come to her side. A head taller than Novalis, he had the lean and hungry look mentioned by William Shakespeare: these two might indeed be described as English bumpkins.

'He says he's going to call the cops.'

'If I have to.'

'Who says you have to?'

'This young lady has appropriated my flowers and is unwilling to return them.'

'It's just a game she plays, to see how much she can get away with. She doesn't want your flowers.'

'I do. They're lovely.'

There was tenderness in her voice. The boy winked at Novalis. 'They only die.'

'You never bought me flowers.'

'I didn't know you wanted any.'

'They don't only die.'

She was staring at Novalis, and something quite independent of their surroundings and circumstance, and of themselves, passed between them. It threatened to engage them at an unplumbed depth. Novalis had no wish to plumb it, or to be engaged. It was unwelcome and quite unjustified by this chance encounter.

The indicator board was scheduling the Rome flight as landing and at once his anxieties returned. Everyone knew that an aircraft was most at risk on take-off and landing. The flaps could refuse to open, the wheels might lock, the brakes might fail, the plane overshoot, hit the airport buildings and catch fire. Miranda could be snatched from him in the very moment of her coming down to earth.

And there was the question of his own sufficiency at a time when he would be expected to have enough for them both. It was reasonable to expect that after they were married their relationship would be such that each would supply what the other lacked. But it was unreasonable to expect Miranda to supply all that he lacked at this moment.

'My flight is landing. Please be so good as to give me my flowers.'

'I only wanted to hold them.'

'You just did,' said the boy. 'Now give them back.'

She pouted, which did not become her. Novalis, who had seen Miranda wrinkle her pretty nose and purse her lips and look utterly charming, marvelled at the malice of Nature which could provoke the same impulse with such different results.

'I'll give you a flower,' said the boy, 'one you won't buy in the shops.'

Novalis turned away and moved towards the arrival barrier. She would arrive, Miranda and her jocular aunt who considered him a stick. Miranda was minutes away and here he was, undeniably sticklike, empty of emotion.

'Hi, you forgotting these?'

He looked round. The boy was attempting to wrest the flowers from the girl. She held them on high, teasing, using them to beat him about the head.

'Keep them,' Novalis said bitterly.

Laughing, the boy parried her blows. 'I don't let my girl accept presents from strange men.'

'I have no further use for the flowers.'

'I'll pay you for them.'

'That will not be necessary.'

The girl said, 'I was going to give them back anyway.' She was unbecomingly damp from her horseplay. Sweat shone in the creases of her arms, in the cleft between her breasts.

The boy held up a coin. 'If you paid more you were done.'

'I don't require payment.'

The boy bent down and dropped the coin into the side of Novalis's shoe. Entwined, they went, the girl cradling the flowers on her arm. She turned and blew Novalis a kiss.

Miranda saw him at once. For him she had a seeing eye which dispelled the obtrusive people between them.

They moved towards each other, she with serene assurance, he stiffly, his heart risen into his throat. They met, she took his hands, her ungloved fingers warm on his. She kissed his cheek. 'How cold you are!'

'I have been waiting.' An absurd comment when the airport lounge was stiflingly hot.

'I know – we were late taking off and when we arrived there was nowhere for us to put down. Darling, you are so pale!'

'The excitement of seeing you.'

'I hope you aren't going to faint,' said Miranda's aunt. 'It's really not necessary.'

'I'm quite well, thank you.'

He was glad that he had left her flowers on the chair. It would have been improvident to present them. She was a tall, well-structured woman, carrying a well-structured handbag, an umbrella, and a carrier bag containing duty-free purchases.

'Allow me—'

'Save your strength for the luggage. Let us go and find the carousel.'

'Darling,' Miranda took his arm, 'has it been awful – waiting?'

He knew that she was referring not merely to the airport delay, but to the time they had been parted. They looked into each other's eyes. Then and there he should have said yes, oh yes! It was the moment: if he could have found the voice, the warmth and closeness must have come as surely as day must follow night. 'I have been watching people.'

'How dull!' cried the aunt. 'People are so predictable.'

'Things happen.'

'What things?'

The prospect of describing the incident of the girl and the flowers dismayed him.

Miranda said helpfully, 'Little things.'

'In the context of an international airport minor incidents tend to be exaggerated.' He knew that he sounded pompous and was aware of the coin in his shoe. It was cutting into his instep.

The aunt cried, 'Oh do look at that woman! How ridiculous to wear a caftan for travelling! Miranda, have you decided on your wedding dress?'

'Almost.'

Novalis said, 'We have almost exhausted the subject.'

'Indeed?'

'We have discussed it at length.' Seeing an opportunity for a little light relief, he added, 'In fact it is only the question of length which remains unresolved.'

'What do you mean?'

'We cannot decide whether the fabric could sustain a train.'

'I shouldn't have thought that need concern *you*.'

'I am concerned in all that concerns Miranda, we are concerned in each other.'

'Take care. One must beware the imposition of one's own opinions on one's nearest and dearest. I have been married and I know.' Perhaps it was the sight of the relentlessly revolving luggage on the carousel which provoked the aunt to fatalism. 'It is asking for trouble to assume that another person is having your same thoughts and emotions at precisely the same moment as yourself.'

'I like to think that Miranda and I complement rather than duplicate each other, that we are the two halves of one whole.'

'One whole what? A lemon?' The aunt burst out laughing. 'What a droll fellow you are!'

Miranda smiled. 'He can be very funny when he chooses.'

Happy Event

I don't expect you to believe this story, I should not believe it had it been told to me. It happens to be true, but I have found that truth is largely a matter of expedience. In my capacity as a doctor, people tell me every day about themselves, their families, their friends, their circumstances, and it suits them to believe that they are speaking the truth. The woman who tells me, 'I never eat bread, only toast,' is an opportunist, not a liar.

I have learned to use my wits and my eyes and form my own conclusions which, if I am lucky, will be a degree or two closer to the facts. If I say that this story is as true as I can make it, you will say, quite rightly, that this is no guarantee that it is not a complete fabrication. No matter. You will be better for not having dreamed of it in your philosophy.

I am a GP in a place which I shall identify only as a country town west of the Pennines. My practice is a large and demanding one. My work has supplanted, if not fulfilled, the need for wife and family. Some people choose to think – again as a matter of expediency – that because doctors are intimate, in a cerebral sense, with the human body, they have no need to be intimate with it in any other way.

I satisfy my needs as discreetly as possible, but there is always an element of luck in such transactions, and mine was out when I first encountered a woman calling herself Mary Tobias. It was not her real name, but she used to say that it was as good as any, and I now suspect that it was a great deal better than some she answered to.

She came to me first as a patient, and subsequently I was unfortunate enough to run into her again, in Vienna.

There is no need to describe the details of our relationship, it would probably never have developed as it did had we been in England. Vienna is still a heady city. Suffice it to say that this woman was in possession of information which I knew she would not scruple to use against me.

She turned up in my surgery one day, about a year ago. I had not heard from her since we parted in Vienna and the long silence had lulled me into a sense of security. I hoped she had forgotten me; I wished her well, so that she would not need to do me ill. But I knew there could be only one final solution. I hoped, and had dared to believe, that she was dead. Certainly I did not give her a thought that fine June morning when my receptionist announced a Mrs Montalban.

The sunlight bounced off the chrome of my steriliser unit and spilled lozenges of light over the surgery walls. I was thinking of curtailing my afternoon round and getting in some golf.

'She's a new patient,' said the girl.

'What is she like?'

'Oh, she looks like an actress.'

I was mildly intrigued. The people who came to me were mostly shopkeepers and farmers and housewives from the industrial estate. I did not suspect how preferable any one of them would have been.

She might indeed have been an actress, doing rather well in repertory. Her clothes were good – chosen to produce a certain effect. I was familiar enough with that effect to recognise it even before I recognised her. She had changed the colour of her hair from ash blonde to chestnut brown. It added depth to her eyes and I gazed a full minute before I said 'You!'

She looked at me with a faint smile, missing nothing, I dare say, of the changes that time had worked in me.

'You didn't know me, did you? The name should have given you a clue.' The Montalban had been our hotel in Vienna, run on English lines by a Prussian Jew with a Dutch wife and a Spanish staff. 'Aren't you pleased to see me?'

'Of course,' I lied. 'I'm glad you're looking so well.'

'Is that a professional or a personal opinion?'

'How did you find me?' I had in fact moved from one end of the country to the other during the last few years.

'Oh that wasn't difficult.' I suppose I sighed, for she smiled. 'My dear, if you wanted to be private you should not have become a doctor.'

I wanted to ask why she had come – not that I was in any doubt. I knew where I stood, and I knew I was not well placed. But I remembered how she used to amuse herself at my expense and, as our relationship deteriorated, her teasing changed to a malicious and, at times, quite dangerous irony. I did not care to listen to that again.

'Least of all should you have stayed a GP.' She looked around her as she spoke, taking out a cigarette – from the packet, I noticed. No gold or silver case, no palm-fitting lighter, she used a match. Now that I observed her more carefully there were small but unmistakable signs that trimmings had had to be abandoned. Perhaps it was why she said, with a mixture of impatience and satisfaction, 'You don't seem to have got any farther.'

'I still have to get up at 3.00 a.m. to usher justifiably reluctant human beings into this over-crowded world.'

'More fool you. You might have been a top-flight gynaecologist, consulting at five hundred guineas a time if you had handled yourself properly. If I'd had your advantages!'

'What advantages?'

'That, mainly.' She pointed to my degree in medicine which hung framed upon the wall.

'It isn't an open sesame.'

'Opportunity doesn't knock,' she said. 'You have to grab it by the throat.'

'Let's get to the point. Why have you come?'

'I wanted to see you again. Can you think of another reason?'

I did not reply. She held the weapon, I had no intention of running on it.

'Another – almost expendable – question, then. Are you married?'

'No.'

There was no ashtray in the surgery and she tapped her cigarette into my spider-plant. 'With your proclivities it would be a mistake.'

'I really don't know what you mean!'

'My dear, greying temples become you, but if handsome is as handsome does, you would be a very plain man. Aren't you going to offer me a drink?'

'This is a doctor's surgery, not a cocktail bar.'

'I have often wondered,' she said, smiling, 'at what point do the private whims of a professional man become unprofessional conduct?'

Even a man who has studied pathogenics will on occasion seek to avoid facing an unpleasant fact in the vain hope that it will go away.

I turned the pages of my appointment book. 'I'm sorry, I have several calls to make.'

'The sick and needy must wait, you have some ministering to do here,' and she removed her gloves and untied the foulard scarf at her neck.

'I didn't realise you had come to consult me professionally.'

'Not about my health, about my future.' She little knew that I would have been content, happy indeed, to hear that she did not have one. 'It's not particularly rosy at the moment.'

'Whose is?'

'Ah, but I am not dedicated to the service of humanity, like you. I am only concerned about my own future.'

'What do you want.'

She sighed. 'How ungallant you've become!'

'I'm a busy man –'

'Well, then, busy man, I need money.'

'I have none.'

'But isn't the National Health Service a doctor's jackpot? Every cough, every pimple, every streak of nappy-rash has its price! Provided the supply of human ailments never runs out, your income's guaranteed. Doctors can't get fired – although of course they may get struck off. It sounds so much more dramatic.'

'I don't know what you are talking about.' I did of course know. I am not an especially benevolent man, despite my profession. Indeed, because of it, I see more to dislike and despise in human nature than most people. But I have never felt such ill will towards anyone as I did towards Mary Tobias at that moment. I knew what it was to have a murderous impulse; my hand was suddenly made aware of a particularly solid brass paperweight on my desk. 'You had better be careful,' I warned.

She laughed. 'How absurd you are! It was you who was so rash and very very careless at the Montalban Hotel. Do you remember Spiegel, the manager? I assure you, he remembers you, so does Madam Spiegel. And Katrine, the chambermaid, was so surprised when I told her you were an English medico who looked after the sick. "After what happened here," she said, "I cannot believe it." People are so naive!'

'Be sensible.' I gripped my hands together on the desk.

'Sensible?'

'Don't drive me too far.'

She looked at me sharply, she was no fool or she could not have lived so long by her wits.

'Very well, I'll stop teasing. Obviously you haven't got the sort of money I'm interested in, and life is getting too short to bother with chicken-feed. I mean to live like a peacock while I'm still young. But you may be able to help tide me over.'

'You must understand I can't afford to do anything which might jeopardise my position.'

'And *you* must understand that you can't afford to make stipulations.' She crushed her still burning cigarette into my potted plant. 'I've had a run of bad luck; some things have not turned out as I had a right to expect, and someone – a very different kettle of fish from you, my dear – let me down quite badly. I suggest you advance me a couple of hundred, in the short term.'

'Pounds?' I said stupidly. I felt as if I was pulling the waters over my head. 'Short term?'

'I wasn't thinking of kisses. But two hundred pounds can't be expected to last for ever.'

'I haven't got that sort of money to give away.'

'Think of it as an insurance rather than a gift.' She was again looking about her as she spoke, openly appraising. Some of the rings had come off the curtains screening the examination couch, and patients' feet had worn the carpet from my desk to the door almost through to the canvas. I wasn't sorry, at that moment, that my small surgery was a little shabby.

'Whatever I give you – five pounds or a thousand – won't be the end of it,' I said bitterly.

'My dear I'm not vindictive. If I really thought you had given your all I shouldn't drop you in the dirt because you had ceased to be useful. Perhaps we should look farther ahead. You might find me a job.'

'A job? You?' It was my turn to make an assessment and I noticed that those fingers on which she habitually wore some very good rings – her collateral, she had called them – were bare. She was thinner; it suited her, but I surmised that she had reached an unprecedented low in her career. 'What sort of job?'

'Oh it must be very light, very well paid, and congenial. I see myself as private secretary to some lonely tycoon, his sole confidante, his alter ego. He must, of course, be in a very lucrative line of business.'

'What on earth can I do about that?'

She shrugged. 'Have you no one of the sort among your patients?'

'I can't help you there.'

'There I am not in a position to help myself.' She took out another cigarette, making sure that the packet was empty before she dropped it on my desk. 'To tell you the truth, I don't much want to. I should prefer to be independent as long as I can. It will be up to you' – she smiled in a way I had cause to remember, which revealed her rather long incisors – 'to pay your premiums.'

It was then that I had a thought, nothing brilliant, and certainly no inspiration. It seemed to have been waiting at the back of my mind. Perhaps it had, for staring up at me from the notepad on my desk was a name which had been there all the while Mary Tobias was talking and, in fact, for some days before she came. The idea wasn't even conclusive, I just hoped that it might be a way of staving off her demands for a while. Beyond that, I felt no more than a perfectly legitimate malice.

'There are no tycoons among my patients,' I said, 'but I do know of someone who is looking for a nurse-companion.'

'I am not prepared to give blanket baths and carry bedpans.'

'This person is very rich, probably one of the richest people in the country, if the truth were known. But there,' I said, 'I don't suppose it ever will be.'

'What does that mean?'

'He is a recluse and lives alone except for a woman who looks after the house. She is not exactly a talker; there's a saying in the village that if you had a shilling for every word she's been heard to utter in the last twenty years you'd still be short of a pound.'

'Family?'

'He has none. His wife died years ago. There was a son who quarrelled with his father and went away. I believe he was killed in the war.'

'One would need to be sure.'

'I beg your pardon?'

'What is the old man's life expectancy?'

'Not much.'

'You'll have to be more definite.' She watched me through cigarette smoke. She was still amusing herself at my expense, but I could tell that she was interested. It would serve her right I thought, or rather it would serve her a degree of wrong which I swear I did not believe was anything like that which she was ready to do me.

'Six months,' I said. 'A year at most.'

'How do you know?'

'Those advantages you spoke about – I am a doctor. The post wouldn't suit you, it requires nursing experience.'

'I could soon acquire that, and put up as good a show as a devoted daughter.'

'He is –' beneath the name on my pad I had drawn a two-legged black cross, 'rather a difficult case.'

'I should need to be sure about the son.'

'What do you mean?'

'In the event, his blood would be thicker than mine.'

I did not ask her what event. I could guess, and I thought, fool that I was, that it was my turn to be amused.

The name on my pad was Thomas Levi's, and to say that it was synonymous with unpleasantness would have been a bit of a euphemism. Indeed, some simple people went so far as to point out that his surname was an anagram of something worse. At the time I dismissed that as merely fanciful. To me, Levi was a difficult patient by reason of his condition, and his temperament. He had made his money by high-powered usury. Many were the stories of the mighty whom he had brought low and the humble he had simply liquidated. If gossip were believed, his own wife, when she was surely old enough to be past such passion, had killed herself in a particularly flamboyant manner. But that was long before I came to the district. I neither believed nor disbelieved. Thomas Levi's past did not interest me, his diminishing future did.

He had an inoperable tumour, already far advanced when I first examined him, and to tell truth I was surprised and even puzzled that he was lasting so long; especially since his vigour appeared unabated and his capacity for mischief as unique as ever. Sometimes I felt he was waiting for something.

Only a day or two before Mary Tobias turned up, Levi's professional nurse had come to me in a state of hysteria. She was leaving, she declared, had in fact left, nothing would induce her to go again into that house. 'Never, never, never!' she cried, and beat on my desk as if to combat my insistence. 'Very well.' I said I was not unsurprised, for she was the fourth in as many months to find Thomas Levi too much of a handful. But this time I intended to find out why. None of the other nurses had been able to give me any account: one had departed without a word, one had fled during the night and had not so far been traced, and the woman before Nurse Croxley suffered from an unpardonably weak heart. She had been only a few days in the job when she had a cerebral embolism which left her paralysed and speechless.

I treated Nurse Croxley for shock. She was patently very shocked, and there was a deeply ingrained L-shaped mark on her left cheek which puzzled and bothered me. It looked as if it was not going to fade. When I had seen her before she took up her duties she was a brisk, sensible woman with a face like a horse and the constitution of an ox. Quite capable of coping with old Levi, I thought. Now I perceived her peasant origins, for as she grew calmer she moaned and rocked herself in a most unprofessional way.

'Tell me what happened,' I said, and when she hugged herself closer and uttered what I can only describe as a keening cry I said sharply, 'Nurse, please control yourself. I must know what this is all about.'

'Never, never, never!'

I do not think she was refusing to tell, I think she was unable to. She seemed to utter the word with desperation, as if it were a spell in which she placed but little hope. At any rate, I never did learn what had actually passed between her and Levi.

I asked him of course. I was angry; trained nurses weren't easily persuaded to come and bury themselves in this country district and I did not relish having to cast around for a replacement.

'What did you do to her?' I said.

He grinned and told me he had done nothing. The dry skin stretched on his skull until I thought it would split. 'The woman was a fool.'

I reminded myself that she had a face like a horse and it was quite possible to frighten a horse by some harmless act which would have been of no significance to a superior intelligence. I chose to believe that, I refused to speculate about the mark on her face. I had decided to try to engage a male nurse and I told myself that the difficulty would soon be resolved for soon old Levi would no longer have the strength to make trouble.

None of this did I convey to Mary Tobias. She would only have laughed. I had convinced myself that Levi must have made some highly improper suggestion to Nurse Croxley which had thrown her right off her old-maidenly balance. Mary could find out for herself, I thought. She supposed he was a sick, tetchy old man whom she could woo and wind round her finger, and I let her suppose. She had her price, which was high, but Levi could afford to pay. I knew there was no suggestion he could make which would surprise, let alone shock her.

I neither encouraged nor discouraged her, I simply gave her some of the facts and left her to make up her mind. And she did. She went to see Levi and what she saw convinced her that she could handle him.

'Obviously he's a bit of an old bastard,' she said, 'and it will be a challenge and I shall enjoy it.'

'It won't be a game,' I said. 'Levi doesn't play games.'

'A man is like a fish. Properly played, the biggest ones can be safely landed. But I shall need some money while I bait my hook.'

'You could get three years for blackmail. . . .'

She put her hand over mine. 'Yours would be a life sentence, my dear.'

Levi complained bitterly and violently about my professional treatment every time I saw him. There was little I could do except administer pain-killers. He knew that as well as I, but it amused him to pretend that I was grossly negligent; that an operation, which I was too lazy and inefficient to arrange, would have saved him; that a course of treatment newly available would have cured him but that I was so ignorant and behind the times that I had not heard of it; that it was my wrong diagnosis which had allowed his sickness to develop – he even claimed that my mishandling of his harmless lumbago had been carcinogenic.

'Stick your needle in!' he used to say, thrusting his stringy wrist at me. 'Keep me going, you must keep me going – I haven't finished yet!' and he would watch my ministrations with a hunger which would have been pitiful were it not so rapacious.

I did not look forward to my visits to the Abbey, Levi's semi-ecclesiastical house on the edge of the old deer forest, and when Mary had taken up residence you may imagine I was even less keen to go. I deferred my routine call for as long as I could, and when at last I drove through the gates I was prepared for a tirade.

Levi's housekeeper, Mrs Steen, opened the door. She was a massively proportioned woman whose silence was due not so much to taciturnity as to poor mental calibre. I estimated her to be but a degree or two removed from a vegetable.

'Good morning Mrs Steen,' I said briskly. 'How are things?'

She moved her heavy shoulders, which with her was the equivalent of the conventional reply to a conventional question.

I had another, less conventional one to ask. 'What happened to Nurse Croxley?'

It was a faint-hearted attempt, a gesture, no more. Mrs Steen turned away without a word and I followed her upstairs, dismissing the matter from my mind. Looking back, I marvel at my self-deception. But truth is relative, and even if I had found out what had happened I would have been no nearer to it. For me the truth would be only what I could take, and I know now that of this I can take very little.

There had been a noticeable deterioration in Levi's condition since my last visit. He was skin and bone, and what remained of his muscular system was frail and flaccid, like empty cobwebs. His eyes I never liked to look into: I shall be thought superstitious, which is not in my character or my calling to be, and a Catholic, which is not my faith, if I say that I felt the need to cross myself when I met his gaze.

I do not think I would have found reassurance in the act: there was a glare of such triumph in his dilated pupils – I have observed something of the kind at the end of a terminal illness. As death approaches and the body prepares to capitulate, the spirit experiences a last fierce resurgence. One might be encouraged, exalted even, at the sight. I hasten to add that the uprising of Thomas Levi's spirit boded no good, and certainly no elevation, for anyone else's.

For once, he spoke little, but watched me with a malignancy which I found more disturbing than open threat. I asked if he was in any pain. He made an impatient gesture.

'How long have I got?'

It was not a question he had asked before and he put it like a man incensed at a broken-down machine rather than enquiring about his own death.

When I hesitated, he said, 'Oh don't be a fool! I've got things to do.'

'It's not possible to be definite. A lot depends on you, on your reserves of strength, and will-power. Six months, perhaps.' In fact I did not anticipate he could last that long.

He nodded. 'I have to thank you for sending me Mary Tobias.'

'She is not a qualified nurse –'

'She is better than the others. That isn't saying much, but she will have to do.'

'Where is she now?'

'In the garden. I sent her out for a breath of air.' He made a painful rictus of the lips which with him passed for a smile. 'Can't have her overtaxing her strength.'

There was small chance of that, I thought wryly, and felt, in my abysmal innocence, a grudging admiration for Mary at having inspired the old tyrant to some human consideration.

I found her in the summerhouse. She was sitting smoking and looking out over the forest. I noticed several cigarette butts on the ground at her feet and surmised she had been there some while.

'You bastard,' she greeted me.

'I told you he wasn't a pleasant character. I tried to warn you.'

She looked tired and cold. She had lost something, a persona which one liked or hated, but which she had always had.

'What's that Shakespearean thing about being better to stick with what we know?'

'From Hamlet you mean? About death? It "makes us rather bear those ills we have, than fly to others that we know not of." Let Levi worry about what's coming to him.'

'My God, do you think I care if he roasts in hell – which he will if there is one.'

'I believe he'd outlast the fire.'

'If there's a God I mean,' she said grimly. 'But I don't think there is. Better the devil you know than the devil you don't, that about sums it up. I've been sitting here wondering how much I can take.'

She looked a different woman from the one who had come to my surgery barely a fortnight ago. I almost felt sorry for her. But then the woman she had been, and still was, reappeared. 'He's worth at least a million and there's no one to leave it to.'

She threw down her cigarette and ground it under her heel. 'I guess I can take all that.'

Soon afterwards I went as one of a group of doctors invited to observe new techniques in obstetrics at a medical centre in Berlin. As I had not had a holiday that year, I arranged to stay on for a while after the course ended. I did not inform Mary Tobias of my plans.

When the locum who had been looking after my practice reported to me on my return I waited, with some trepidation, to hear the news from the Abbey. But Levi's name was not mentioned and finally I was obliged to ask about him.

'He wouldn't see me,' was the reply. 'I was told by the nurse that he chose to wait till you came back. She was very particular to establish just when that would be. We had a bit of an argument, and she took me upstairs and showed me that he'd locked his door. He shouted at me to leave him alone. Well, there was nothing I could do, I couldn't even shoot him any pethidine, so I left. I was glad to, not the sort of place I'd care to hang about.'

He had scarcely finished speaking when there was a telephone call from Mary. Would I come to the Abbey at once, it was imperative she see me immediately.

'I haven't had time to unpack yet. Won't tomorrow do?'

'No, it will not. You have a patient waiting here for you!' and she slammed down the receiver.

The locum, a peripatetic type if ever there was one, laughed. 'Not only the patient! Never saw a woman so put out as she was when I turned up instead of you.'

My absence, I thought ruefully as I drove to the Abbey, had not made the situation any more tenable. I had tried not to think about it and had succeeded so well that finding this thing still going on was like finding a promise broken.

My story now becomes progressively less credible. I am bound to say that it will reach a point when it will be completely incredible. I am also bound to say that I do not care. For if truth is relative, I am *not* bound, thank God, by the relations which anyone else may or may not have with such facts as I shall relate.

Mary opened the door. There had always been a rapport between us which I would certainly prefer to be without, and I knew at once that something had happened.

'How is he?'

'I'm waiting for you to tell me,' she said.

She appeared calm, her face more drawn than when I saw her last, but with a compression of the nostrils which I recognised as excitement. There was something else which I did not recognise – or rather there was something missing. For the first time in her sentient life, I should think Mary Tobias was not in full possession of herself.

As I followed her upstairs, Mrs Steen came into the hall. She was fingering her heavy jaw and pretty plainly expressing mistrust, of whom or of what there was no knowing.

Levi slept, lying on his back, one hand uncurled on the pillow by his cheek. He breathed evenly through parted lips. I felt his pulse, finding it faint, but steady. His colour surprised me. His skin, which had been a yellowish brown, almost black, was suffused with pink. On his closed eyelids was a little soft moisture, and something which I had never noticed before. He had quite a fringe of brown eyelashes.

'Well,' I said, somewhat at a loss. 'Well, well.'

'Is that your professional opinion?'

'He's sleeping soundly. I shan't wake him.'

She seized my wrist and pulled me round to face her. 'He's getting better, isn't he?'

'That's impossible.'

'Will you swear it?'

Her eyes were wild and I perceived that she had been driven to the brink. The only reason she did not go over was because she was clinging desperately to one last hope. I neither knew nor cared about the extent of it, but I knew what it was *not*: no one in their right mind could honestly wish Thomas Levi to be restored to health and his malign power.

I indicated that she should follow me out of the room, and when I closed the door I said, 'There is no question of recovery. Do you want details of what the disease has done to his vital organs? Of the final stages? Of how, in all probability, the end will come?'

'Yes!'

Half-informed as I was, I found her callousness revolting. 'I'll sent you my notes on the case,' I said coldly, and walked out of the house.

Less than a week later I was called to the Abbey again. This time, at sight of Mary Tobias the thought struck me – without, I must add, any sympathy or concern – that she was heading for a serious breakdown. She did not speak: silence was, I surmise, her last attempt at self-control.

I stood on one side of Levi's bed, she on the other, and for a fraction of time when I first looked down at him my eyes saw only what my brain was prepared to see. I swear that Thomas Levi appeared to me as a knowledge of medicine and the ineluctable laws of Nature led me to expect him to appear at this stage of his disease.

I glanced up. She was watching my face with a desperation almost unhinged.

'Look! For God's sake – look!' she cried, pointing to the bed.

A phrase had sprung to my mind on the previous occasion when I saw Levi. I had thought no more of it than of the kind of commonplace it was – a useful encapsulation – albeit, like all such nutshells, often fallacious.

Physically, he had not been a big man and his illness had wasted him down to the ivory twigs of his bones. Now I saw that the shape under the bedclothes was even more reduced. It was scarcely half the size he had been.

Again, he lay on his back, head turned on the pillow, eyes closed, that tender dew on the lids, and in his cheeks, his gently rounded cheeks, a sweet pink and white.

'Sleeping like a baby,' I had thought, and now, as I looked down at him and my intelligence recoiled in disbelief, I seemed to hear the words, spoken with a mockery which caused the short hairs to stir along my spine.

I rounded on Mary Tobias, 'What the devil are you up to? This isn't Levi. . . .'

He turned his head, opened his eyes, and looked at me. I think my heart stopped with shock. Never, even from that terrible old man, had I received a glare of such malignancy and triumph. I do believe that it was quintessential evil, the source, the genesis, the immortal germ of it. If it was, there was no hope for the world. With that knowledge we had to live, Mary Tobias and I. She too had looked into those eyes, set, God help us, in the flower-soft face of a baby. She dared not look again, across the bed from me she was following my every expression, in the vain hope, poor wretch, that I with my expertise, my 'advantages', would somehow awaken her from the nightmare. But I, in my shock and dread, could only gaze at the infant mouth, parted on toothless gums. From one corner a milky bubble escaped and gently swelled.

I ran from the room.

Mary found me leaning against the wall of the passage. I was experiencing the nausea and chill which overtakes the depleted system after a severe shock.

'Oh my God!' was all I could say. There did not seem to be anything else.

She clutched at me, and for a moment we clung together, like two straws.

'What are you going to do?'

'Do?'

'You're a doctor – you've got to stop it!'

'How can I?'

'You know what he's doing, don't you?'

'He's dying – the man's dying!' I almost shouted. 'It's just a phase of his sickness – the last phase –'

'Oh certainly it's the last phase.' She smiled terribly, right into my face. 'But he's not dying. He's going out the same way he came in.'

'Don't be a fool!' I thrust her aside and blundered along the passage. Already I was starting to hope, to work towards the conviction that there had been some mistake, some aberration, a freak of vision, an impractical joke of the eyes and the brain, and that if I went away so would this monstrous humour, and when I looked again I should see only the necessary end – death.

My one thought was to get out of the house, but she ran before me and barred my way.

'I must talk to you!'

Out of the corner of my eye I glimpsed Mrs Steen standing in the shadows of the kitchen passage.

'Tomorrow,' I said, as briskly as I could, and jerked my head in the woman's direction.

Mary was obliged to let me go without further protest, even to stand and watch as I drove away, well knowing that my most fervent desire was never to set eyes on her or Levi again.

I know I shall not have to pass another such day and night as that which followed. I could not. Although I subdued my first horror, it recurred, like bouts of insanity, again and again, and settled into a fearful degradation of my own and mankind's general intelligence. I magnified the power of disease beyond all accepted and acceptable proportions. I had to, or acknowledge a power of another sort.

I ransacked the reputable and less reputable medical sources at my disposal. Of these last there were, I suppose, more available to me than to most general practitioners. My researches provided me with some slight comfort when I came across references to a thickening and rubescence of the skin at certain stages of arterial carcinoma. You may imagine, if you are so disposed, with what desperation I laboured that particular symptom. Partly from relief and partly to prevent myself from questioning more closely, I drank a great deal of whisky that night.

Next day I returned to the Abbey. By medical ethics, of course, I could not refuse to attend a patient. I had another reason for going back. I had convinced myself, to an obsessional, almost an insane degree, that the whole thing was a trauma of our two minds, Mary's and mine, affected by the turbulence naturally, or unnaturally, attending the passing of a strong and malefic spirit.

My mind was quite made up – screwed up, I could say – to stand no more nonsense from Mary.

'Well,' I said briskly, 'how is he today?'

Her gaze wavered over my face and hung beyond in the middle air.

'He is three months old. Last week he cut two teeth, today they are not yet through.'

Her speech was slurred, she had been drinking, although it was still early in the afternoon.

'How is his appetite?'

'He eats nothing and drinks nothing. Just lies there getting smaller and smaller and younger and younger.'

'I suggest you make yourself some strong black coffee,' I said sharply. 'I am going upstairs to examine my patient.'

Of course she was right. My heart did not so much sink as

plummet when I entered the sickroom and saw the figure in the very middle of the great bed.

It was sucking at one tiny doubled fist; the eyes, luckily, were half-closed, hooded by the lids as the old Levi's habit was while biding his time and concealing his real inclinations.

How can I convey the dread with which I approached the creature? The awful fascination as I drew back the bedclothes? The loathing as I put my hand under its neck? My flesh crept when it encountered silky new down on that soft skull. There could be no doubt that here, to all intent and purpose, was a three-month-old infant, perfectly formed, well-nourished and cared for. But to whose intent? To what purpose? Between the lowered lids was a glimmer of something which made my blood run cold.

I laid the creature down none too gently on the pillow, and came out of that room. In the bathroom I washed my hands, but could not cleanse them.

Mary stood in the doorway watching my face in the mirror. Desperately I soaped my fingers. 'I shall get a second opinion.'

'Fool! Who do you think will believe that is Tom Levi? They'll laugh at you!'

'I don't care. I must talk to someone!'

'If you do, if you breathe a word of this to anybody, I'll tell everything I know about you. It's enough – you realise that, don't you?' She was suddenly coldly, incisively sober. 'But in case it isn't, I'm prepared to add to it. And I can prove the essential facts up to the hilt. I promise you'll not only be a laughing-stock, you'll be a ruin!'

In the mirror I witnessed my own terror. The world about me was dissolving. Even the mundane fitments of that ugly Victorian bathroom swelled and shrank by turns into nightmare forms.

'What is it? What's happening in there? For God's sake, what's happening?'

'Don't fool yourself,' she said bitterly. 'Whatever it is, it's not for God's sake.'

'I can't stand any more!'

'In that case, go away and leave me to deal with it. I'm stronger than you are – women are stronger than men.'

Even in my extremity I wondered at her. She wasn't stupid, and the effect this thing was having on her was obvious, in magnitude, if not in depth. At that I could only guess.

Then she said, 'Besides, I have more to lose.'

'More?' I saw that her teeth were bared in wolfish grimace.

'Women always have more to lose.'

I took her at her word. I did not return to the Abbey the next day, or the next. Or the day after that. I tried not to think about what had happened, and was happening there.

Of course I thought about it incessantly, during surgery, during my round of visits, my lonely evenings and lonelier nights. I took whisky to help me though the daylight hours, and at bedtime progressively larger doses of nembutal. It caused me to lose consciousness until 2.00 or 3.00 a.m. I cannot convey, I shall not try, what I endured in those black morning hours, but I know now why they are called 'small'. I felt as if I was shut, prisoned, in a nutshell wherein was no reason and no law. Only one deadly fact remained: there was no natural order, there was no *order*, the first principle was anarchy.

If the women who brought their babies to me at that time knew with what dread I looked into the infants' faces and how unwillingly I met their innocent unfocused eyes, they would have transferred en masse to another doctor.

That fear, that reluctance, now entirely dominates me; I can no longer specialise in obstetrics, the area of medicine which used to interest me most.

But to return to the gravamen of my story.

A week passed without a word from Mary or any news from the Abbey. Finishing surgery one evening, I decided to go and see a patient of mine, an old man named Joe Tranter.

He lived by himself in a tin shack in the woods. He was a recluse, almost a vagrant, existing on what roots and berries he could find in the hedges and the few vegetables he bothered to grow and the small mammals and birds he snared and poached. He was harmless, but he had valvular disease of the heart. I had not seen him for a long time. I was, you must understand, simply trying to keep busy, and after Tranter I would have looked for another excuse to delay returning to my unremitting thoughts.

The necessity did not arise however, for when I pushed open the door of his shack I found that he was dead. He was sitting in his chair, and he was still warm.

I judged that he had been dead for about an hour, and by his peaceful, relaxed attitude that his heart had simply failed, perhaps as he slept.

There was nothing I could do for him, he was an old, frail man; it had been a solitary, tranquil end to his solitary days. Who could tell how tranquil, or how turbulent, they had been?

I gently closed his wide open eyes and came away, pulling the door of the shack to behind me. There was no means of locking it, and no need to. No one went to that sequestered place.

I returned to my surgery and prepared to take the necessary steps to notify a death. But even as I went to pick up the telephone, it rang. My nerves were frayed and I started violently. Mary's voice over the wire did nothing to reassure me.

'He's gone,' she said. 'Levi's gone.'

'Gone?'

'You must come at once. I need you.'

'You mean he's dead?'

'I can't talk – you must come!'

'I'll come as soon as I can.'

'At once! Or it will be the worse for you! There's not a moment to lose!'

The receiver was slammed down. Why should Tranter's face, almost beautiful in its serenity, rise before me at that moment? I think it was a sign of redemption – the only one I ever saw.

At the Abbey Mrs Steen opened the door. She remained standing massively in the doorway, barring my entry, and staring at me from under her brows.

'What's she up to?'

'I beg your pardon?'

She jerked her thumb at the staircase. 'Her up there.'

'I'm here to see my patient,' I said. 'Kindly let me pass.'

She stood aside with a grunt plainly intended to be offensive. It also obscurely alarmed me. I mounted the stairs with deliberation, conscious that she was watching.

Mary emerged from Levi's room, drew me inside and locked the door.

'That woman,' I said, 'Mrs Steen – she's suspicious.'

'Don't worry about her! I can handle a hundred Steens.'

Indeed she might have, at that moment. She was plainly in a state of extreme excitement, her eyes glittering, her cheeks drained of colour, her breathing shallow. She seized and held my arm with both hands.

'He's gone – vanished!'

'What?'

'Look. . . .' She pointed to the bed. It was empty; what is more, it was smooth, untouched. The little figure which had lain there – which I had dreaded seeing with a physical and mental sickness, a psychosomatic nausea – had gone, leaving no mark, no crease, not even a hollow in the pillow.

'Where is he?'

'I don't know. I don't care! He isn't here, he never will be again. We're finished with him!'

'Are we?'

'I'll tell you what happened, exactly what happened. I unlocked the door this morning – I always keep it locked, whether I'm in here or not – and there he was, about twelve inches long, lying on the pillow. He was covered in blood.'

'Blood? He was dead?'

'He'd just been born! He was just out of the womb, the umbilical cord had only just been cut! But he was watching me. . . .'

I felt myself starting to vomit and had to thrust my handkerchief into my mouth.

'Oh yes,' she said, smiling terribly, 'the eyes were still Levi's. And in case you think I got off lightly, let me tell you I can never forget the sight as long as I live.'

You won't believe me – why should you? – but I saw it too. God help me, God help us both, for there is no power on earth, not even death, I do believe, that can cleanse our minds' eyes of it.

'I fainted,' she said. 'I don't know for how long, but when I came to, he had gone. There wasn't a sign of him, the stains on the pillow had vanished, the sheets were clean and smooth, the bed had not been slept in – as you see it now.'

'Someone must have come in,' I said faintly. 'While you were unconscious Mrs Steen must have come in and taken him away –'

'The door was locked on the inside, no one could get in, or out.'

'But he must be somewhere! He couldn't just disappear –'

'He could. He has done. Do you think I haven't searched? I have – everywhere! I've spent the whole day searching, inside and outside the house. I've been over every inch, every drawer, every cupboard. I tell you, I've looked under every leaf, every blade of grass! He's gone, and there's an end of it.'

'I don't believe it. I can't!'

'Well I can.' Calmly she put one of her interminable cigarettes between her lips. I noticed that her hand shook as she held the match. 'You had better take my word that Levi's passed on or over, whatever direction he went, and he won't be back. The fact that he chose a damned funny way of doing it is beside the point. We have other things to think of.'

'What are we going to do? No one will believe he just disappeared.'

'Precisely. There has to be a body.'

I lifted the coverlets and looked into the bed. Scarce knowing what I did, I went about the room, peering under chairs, into closets, behind curtains. I plunged my arm into the depths of a great pitcher of water which had been used for Levi's ablutions and neither noticed nor heeded my soaked sleeve.

So extreme was my fear and misery, I had forgotten – or did I prefer not to remember? – what I was looking for, and I do believe those fruitless gestures were all the self-control I had left.

Mary watched with impatience. She was smoking hard, stubbing out one half-finished cigarette and immediately lighting another.

'You realise what this means? If there's no body, nothing can be settled.'

'Settled? You think this ever can be?'

'I'm talking about the business side of it, the legal side. I'm talking about the will.'

'I don't care about the will.'

'But I do.' She inhaled deeply, almost hungrily. 'I expect to benefit, so I care very much.'

'Benefit? You? You've only known Levi a few months!'

'Nevertheless, he promised to leave everything to me if I stayed with him until the end. He had no one else to leave it to, I made sure of that.'

'So that's why you stayed! I should have known. But I did not suppose you could be such a fool as to believe that Levi would honour a promise!'

'I believe he will. I believe he has,' she said calmly. 'You should know that I'm no fool where money is concerned.'

'You're right in one thing, the will cannot be proved unless there is evidence of death.'

'That is where you come in, my dear.'

'I?'

'As a doctor, it is relatively simply for you to provide a suitable corpse.'

Although I could scarcely credit what I heard, I felt a dreadful sinking of the heart. In that moment the monstrous thing – the whole of it, as I thought – was made plain to me.

'You may not be a fool about money, but you are certainly mad, and as far as I'm concerned there is very little difference. I shall have nothing more to do with this business!'

'Do not underestimate the difficulties I can make for you.'

'You may do what you like! I have not done, and I will not do, anything wrong.'

'Are you sure?' she said softly. Her voice hardened. 'How will you answer when they ask where your patient is? What will you say when they want to know what became of this sick old man in your care?'

'There is only one thing I can do, I shall tell the truth!'

'That is the only *other* thing you can do. Will they believe you? Aren't you afraid they'll simply laugh at you for a bad liar, and arrest you on suspicion of murder?'

'Murder!'

'Since I don't choose to be laughed at,' she said coldly and
incisively, 'I shall tell a more convincing story. It will totally
incriminate you – and don't forget there are things in your past which
will predispose people to believe the worst. I have thought about this
very carefully and I am not making idle threats. You may rest
assured I shall be neither casual nor idle about Levi's kind of money.'

'I will do nothing – nothing, do you hear – to help you to a penny of
it!'

She heard, as I did, the rising note of fear in my voice. For that
same revelation which had shown me what I could do, had also
shown me what *she* could do. I knew exactly the extent of my ruin and
discredit.

'Think now,' she said calmly, almost amusedly, 'there must be a
body somewhere that would serve our purpose. Some old man who
has just died, or can be expected to die very shortly, with no family or
friends to be curious, who could stand – or rather lie – in, for Levi?'

You may condemn me as a muddled fool, but it seemed like
blasphemy to think of old Tranter, serene, almost beautiful in his
normal passing, and Thomas Levi, bloody and grotesque in his.

'I can't do it! I won't do it!'

She nodded. 'There will be no problem. He promised me that
everything would be made easy.'

You have concluded that I am a liar or, at best, the teller of a tall
story. As I said, I do not care what you think; indeed it will be better
for you if you do not believe a word.

Why did I allow this woman to bend me to her will? At the time it
seemed the lesser of two evils. I did not know, I did not dream, that it
was immeasurably the greater. There was a force which predisposed
me to obey her. She was under the same compulsion. We were, both
of us, the means to an end.

When she threatened me I had no doubt that she would do what
she said. In any case, I know now that, even had I successfully
resisted, she would have achieved her purpose – which was but a
trifle compared to what was behind it all – and she would then, very
pleasurably, have taken her revenge on me.

I tried reason. Even were I able to procure a corpse, I said – I did
not tell her about Tranter and in fact she never questioned whose
body it was – how could we hope to pass it off as Levi's?

She replied, impatiently, that she had thought of all that and
everything could be arranged. Her greed was such that she could not
see that there had been another hand in it before hers.

Levi had no family and no friends, she said: if nobody came to see him alive, who would do so now that he was dead? The undertaker's men would not know him, people in the district had not set eyes on him for over a year, and he had directed that he was to be cremated. The period of risk was short, for once the body had been reduced to ashes, who could prove that they were not Levi's?

I did what she wanted. My part of the operation went so smoothly as to be unremarkable. Unremarkable, that is, if you discount the nature of it. I was not even conscious of being particularly apprehensive. Deep down, I was aware of what promised to be an abiding self-disgust, but I carried out my task with a dogged fatalism, being neither especially cautious, nor needlessly rash. I believed I was so sick at heart that I did not care if I was caught: but, remembering that night's dreadful work, I think I knew all the time that nothing would *be allowed* to go wrong.

There is therefore scant interest in detailing how I went back to Tranter's shack as soon as it was dark, and conveyed his corpse to the Abbey. There was but little time left before rigor mortis could be expected to begin, and his frail bones would become immovable.

Mary Tobias let me in by the cellar entrance and I carried my burden up a dismal staircase into an unoccupied wing of the house and from thence, without incident, to Levi's bedroom.

It was then my wish and intention to take no further part in the business, except to sign the death certificate. But in assuming that no one would want to gaze upon Levi in death, we had reckoned without Mrs Steen.

Mary had scarcely finished arraying the body in one of Levi's nightshirts when the handle of the locked door was sharply rattled. Someone dealt the door a blow from outside.

Mary stared at me, her face ashen. The side of a fist struck the door panel. Again the handle was seized and shaken.

I called out, 'Who's there?'

'Steen.'

'What do you want?'

'To see the master.'

'You can't!' cried Mary.

She was frightened, as well she might be. I put my finger to my lips and signed to her to keep silent. I unlocked the door.

Mrs Steen faced me across the threshold, stolid as ever.

'Your master is dead,' I told her.

'Dead?' Her eyes narrowed to slits with a wariness that was animal. 'What's going on?'

'You know he has been at the point of death for a long time.'

'I don't know anything. I want to see him.'

Mary darted forward, but I caught her arm. 'She has a right to see him if she wishes.'

'She has no right!'

I said softly, in her ear, 'You must let her, or she will think you have something to hide.'

'She can't see him –'

Ungently I held her back, she would have slammed the door in Mrs Steen's face.

'You can come in and look,' I said.

Foolhardy, yes. It was a last gesture, made without any real thought to the consequences to myself, that is. For Mary Tobias, for the intent behind her, which I divined but could not identify, I anticipated, and hoped, the worst.

Mary struggled in vain to free herself. She was obliged to watch, aghast, her arm in mine, while Mrs Steen approached the bed.

The woman stood looking down at the body. Her solid slab of a face did not change, evidenced no flicker of feeling. She could have been looking at one of her own unwholesome puddings.

'Well,' I said, 'have you never seen a dead man before?'

I glanced at the figure on the bed. And as God is my witness, the face on the pillow, in the sleep of death, was Thomas Levi's. Age, sickness, and the depredations of his barely departed spirit had left it like a battlefield.

Mrs Steen spoke. It was the longest utterance I had ever heard from her.

'I didn't think to see him look peaceful. The Old One himself was inside Mr Levi, and it's my belief he was out to get his revenge on the whole creation.'

Levi had left his instructions. 'Burn what you are pleased to call my body,' he wrote, 'and scatter the ash as you choose. The flesh is a faulty weapon, and when the sword breaks or the rifle jams, one takes up another.'

I thought the words ambiguous, which was typical of Levi. They made me uneasy. If what he said could be taken two ways, the unlooked-for way would certainly be unpleasant. How much more than unpleasant it proved to be!

His directions were carried out; a week later the body of Joseph Tranter was cremated, following a ceremony attended by the few, myself included, who had occasion to follow Thomas Levi to his official end. I daresay there would have been even fewer if the truth had been known, for Tranter was well-nigh penniless as well as

240

friendless. Being in the habit of wandering off and returning, without a word to anyone, to the isolated shack in the woods, it was some time before his absence was remarked upon.

The police made some desultory enquiries as to his whereabouts, but found no clues. The case of the missing hermit, though never officially closed, was soon forgotten.

It may be imagined what relief I felt when the service of committal was over. But none can guess at the complexity of my guilt and shame, nor the intimations of blasphemy I received while the pious words were being spoken and the reverent gestures made.

Of course I hoped – how fervently! – that I need never again set eyes on Mary Tobias. Equally predictably, that hope was not to be realised. I soon had another visit from her.

It is not in my nature or philosophy to forgive that woman. I feel pity for her only because no human creature should be afflicted with the burden she carries. No human creature could carry it, without the compulsion of superhuman greed.

I saw it in her face the day she came to me following the charade of Levi's funeral. I saw it in her body, when she burst into my surgery, paced ceaselessly to and fro, picked up and threw down objects on my desk as if they had offended her. In fact I have not seen evidence of any other emotion in her since. Except mortal fear.

She could not rest, and it occurred to me – with satisfaction, I admit – that she might never do so again.

'Well,' I said, 'have things turned out as you hoped?'

She stopped in mid-movement and stared at me without a word.

'Did he not keep his promise? Aren't you a wealthy woman?'

'Oh yes, he kept it. But there are certain conditions. You will know how certain.'

'I?'

'Haven't you a drink in this place?'

'As I told you before, this is a doctor's surgery, not a bar. And I tell you now – I intend to have nothing more to do with this business. I wish to God it had never happened. For all practical purposes, so far as I am concerned, it never has.'

'How very convenient! But I have something to tell you. The will has been read.' She laughed bitterly. 'It was more of a life-cycle than a will. I am to have the house and everything in it, the interest on all his investments for the next ten years, outright payments of five thousand pounds every three years, and a hundred thousand to come to me, without strings, at the end of the ten year period. Provided, that is, that I fulfil his conditions.'

'You will, won't you?' I shrugged. 'Whatever they are!'

'That depends on you.'

'I have told you – I wash my hands of it!'

'Do you think you can? Why, they're dirtier than mine!' She leaned across my desk, our faces were close and I saw with distaste the predatory dryness of her mouth. 'Do you remember the first time we met?'

'I prefer not to!'

'Do you remember why I came to you – and what you told me – about myself?'

'I told you you could never have a child.'

'Is it true?'

'It is a fact,' I said coldly. 'You are sterile.'

'You're lying!'

'Why should I be? Then, or now?'

'It was years ago!'

'Without surgery the condition is unlikely to have changed.'

She had been gripping the edges of my desk so desperately that her knuckles were white. Now she let go and sat down in the chair facing me.

'Surgery?'

I have never heard the word spoken like that, with what I might almost describe as appetite.

'Why do you ask?' I did not hide my disgust. 'Do you intend to start a family?'

She uttered a sound between a laugh and a groan.

'I've damned well got to. Under the terms of the will I don't get a penny unless I give birth within nine months of Levi's death.'

'What?'

'I get the three-yearly legacies only if I rear the child. And if it dies or comes to harm before it reaches the age of ten, I lose my hundred thousand.'

Incredulous, I felt my jaw drop. I could not have been more startled if she had aimed a gun at me.

'But what on earth –'

'Oh I shan't take your word for it! I don't trust you.' She stood up and began feverishly to beat around the room again. 'I shall go to another doctor.'

'You have – you had – scarring and obstruction of the fallopian tubes following a severe attack of salpingitis. Conception is impossible. Any specialist will tell you the same.'

She swung round. 'But I could have an operation!'

'The result could not be guaranteed. Even if it was completely successful, you could not immediately become pregnant.'

242

'You'd be surprised what I can do for a hundred thousand pounds.'

She did not smile, nor did I.

'You cannot command Nature. I am afraid it will be out of the question for you to meet Levi's –' I felt my lips tighten to a grimace, 'birthline. One would almost think he knew.'

'He did not know! How could he?'

'I warned you that he was a vicious, evil-minded man. He has made a fool of you.'

Whereupon she threw back her head and uttered an animal shriek. 'Damn him to hell!'

'He is that already,' I said, shuddering.

There, by the mercy of God, this story should have ended, with its questions unanswered. But by the iniquity of some power beyond my comprehension, an answer was forthcoming.

I would give anything not to have learned it. I would give the remaining years of my life not to believe it. God help that wretched woman. God help us all!

Some two months later, I was dining with a friend of mine, a gynaecologist eminent in his field. He had been pressing me for an explanation as to why I had elected not to go on with my plans to specialise.

'Surely you will not be content to remain in general practice?'

'Not content,' I said. 'Acquiescent.'

'But why?'

'I cannot explain.'

'Whatever the reason, it is nonsense,' he declared roundly.

I had an impulse to tell him about Levi's metamorphosis – God knows I needed to tell someone – but I knew him as a man of rigid principle and a zealously guarded reputation. I feared his contempt, still more I feared his probity.

'I dislike seeing capabilities wasted, there are not enough to go round. From the purely personal and practical aspect, can you afford not to specialise?'

'You must accept that I have had fairly exhaustive second thoughts.'

'If ever you care to tell me what they are, I should like to try to refute them.' He poured me some of his excellent brandy. 'By the way, I saw a patient of yours the other day. A Mrs Montalban.'

I could not restrain a gasp. Indeed, it was a purely physical reaction, for at the sound of that name I was remembering the hotel in Vienna, and what had taken place there.

He regarded me keenly. 'I see you recall her.'

That name was like an artery. Through it flowed my guilt, from the past to the present. I could not meet his eyes.

Sipping his brandy, he smiled. 'Rather an attractive creature. Has she been on the stage?'

'I believe so.' I spoke with difficulty. My heart, if not in my mouth, seemed to be battering at the wall of my chest. 'Did she – speak of me?'

'Only to say that she had seen you. I gather you have not examined her recently?'

'No. Why?'

'Had you done so, your diagnosis would have been the same as mine. She seemed to be under the impression that she could not conceive.'

'Impression?'

'I was able to reassure her on that point.' The sober lines of his face relaxed into a broad smile. 'Quite conclusively, I'm happy to say.'

I was already cold with dread. But now my fear was compounded with bewilderment. All I could trust myself to say was, 'Indeed?'

'The lady is well and truly pregnant.'

The shock was violent, my hand shook so that the brandy leaped out of the glass. Fortunately, he was refilling his own and did not observe my agitation.

'Pregnant!'

'Nearly three months so,' he said cheerfully. 'She is a strong healthy woman – perhaps not quite so young to bear a first child – but I foresee no problems. The birth should be normal.'

'Three months?' I said stupidly. 'It was three months ago that Levi –'

'I beg your pardon?'

'It is nothing. I was thinking of something else – quite irrelevant. . . .'

He eyed me shrewdly. 'The lady is married, I take it?'

I felt as if I was drowning, fighting to keep my head above black waters.

'I don't know much about her personal circumstances.'

He shrugged. 'We must hope she has not been foolish.' Then he frowned. 'She made a somewhat frivolous comment when I had occasion to mention her husband.'

'Frivolous?'

'She said, "I suppose you could call it an immaculate conception." '